USA TODAY bestselling author **Sarah Morgan** writes hot, happy contemporary romance, and her trademark humor and sensuality have gained her fans across the globe. Described as "a magician with words" by *RT Book Reviews*, she has been nominated three years in succession for a prestigious RITA® Award from the Romance Writers of America and won the award twice: in 2012 for her book *Doukakis's Apprentice* and 2013 for *A Night of No Return*. She also won the RT Reviewers' Choice Award in 2012 and has made numerous appearances in their Top Pick slot.

Sarah lives near London with her husband and children, and when she isn't reading or writing she loves being outdoors, preferably on vacation so she can forget the house needs tidying. You can visit Sarah online at sarahmorgan.com, on Facebook at facebook.com/authorsarahmorgan and on Twitter, @SarahMorgan_.

Look for Sarah's The O'Neill Brothers novels available from HQN Books.

USA TODAY Bestselling Authors

Sarah Morgan, Cara Lockwood and Heidi Rice

BEST MEN

HARLEQUIN® COSMOPOLITAN RED-HOT READS

ISBN-13: 978-0-373-60970-3

Best Men

Copyright © 2014 by Harlequin Books S.A.

The publisher acknowledges the copyright holders
of the individual works as follows:

Ripped
Copyright © 2013 by Sarah Morgan

Boys and Toys
Copyright © 2014 by Cara Lockwood

10 Ways to Handle the Best Man
Copyright © 2014 by Heidi Rice

Recycling programs
for this product may
not exist in your area.

This edition published by arrangement with Harlequin Books S.A.

For questions and comments about the quality of this book,
please contact us at CustomerService@Harlequin.com.

® and TM are trademarks of the publisher. Trademarks indicated with
® are registered in the United States Patent and Trademark Office, the
Canadian Intellectual Property Office and in other countries.

Printed in U.S.A.

www.Harlequin.com

CONTENTS

RIPPED
Sarah Morgan

To Katie, with love.
Have fun and be fearless.
Xxxx

CHAPTER ONE

'DEARLY BELOVED,' THE priest droned, 'we are gathered here today to witness—'

A mistake of massive proportions, I thought gloomily, holding my breath and sitting up straight in a bid to stop my bridesmaid dress splitting at the seams. Any moment now I was going to burst out of this pukey-yellow tube and the wedding would forever be remembered as the one where the bridesmaid exposed herself. Not that I was prudish. Far from it. I'd danced on plenty of tables in my time, but on an ideal day I'd prefer not to find myself revealing *all* Victoria's secrets to Great-Uncle Henry.

Some girls went through their lives dreaming of being a bridesmaid. You heard people talking about it as if it were a life goal. I had a list of life goals. I wanted to build a robot, visit Peru (I've always had a thing about llamas), work for NASA. *Bridesmaid?* That was nowhere on my list.

My parents married when they were both twenty-one. They stood at the front of a church much like this one wearing ridiculous clothes they wouldn't normally be seen dead in, made all the usual promises—have and hold, death us do part, blah, blah—and then divorced when I was eight. Which taught me one thing—that a wedding is just a party by another name.

Because my neck was the only part of me that could move without straining a seam, I turned my head and glanced sideways. Through a forest of fascinators and absurd hats that made me think of UFOs, I could see the door that led to a pretty private churchyard, now covered in a light dusting of snow. I was glad it was pretty because I was sure I was going to be there soon. *Here lies Hayley, who exploded out of her dress at the most inconvenient moment of her short, very unsatisfactory life and promptly died of shame.*

The tiny church was crammed with people and stuffed full of extravagant flower displays, the cloying scent of lilies thickening the air and mingling unpleasantly with the smell of perfume from the elderly aunts. My nose tickled and my head started to throb.

The priest was still droning on in a hypnotic voice that could have been recorded and sold for millions as a cure for insomnia. 'If anyone knows any reason why these two may not be joined, speak now….'

Any reason?

Was he kidding?

I could have given him at least ten reasons without even revving up a brain cell.

Number one—the groom was a total bastard.

Number two—he'd slept with the bride's sister and at least two of the bride's friends.

Number three—it was three days until Christmas and who the hell was dumb enough to get married when they should have been rushing round buying last-minute presents?

Number four—it was far too cold to be wearing a strapless dress and at this rate I was going to be eat-

ing my Christmas dinner in hospital with a nasty bout
of pneumonia.

Number five—

'Hayley, are you OK?' My sister Rosie nudged me
in the ribs, increasing the strain on my dress.

Of course I wasn't OK. We both knew I wasn't
fucking OK. That was why she'd agreed to come with
me, but this was hardly the moment for sisterly bond-
ing over margaritas. To be honest, if she'd passed me
a margarita I wouldn't have known whether to drink
it or drown myself in it.

I was good at statistics and I could tell you right
now there was a 99 percent chance this wedding was
going to end in tears. Probably mine.

'You should have said no when she asked you to be
her bridesmaid,' Rosie hissed. 'It was a mean thing to
do when everyone knows you used to date him.'

And there it was. Right there. Reason number five
why the bride and groom shouldn't get married. Because he'd once said he wanted to marry me.

I'd told him no. I didn't want to get married. Ever.
I'd never had ambitions to be a bridesmaid and I had
even fewer to be a bride. I assumed if he loved me,
it wouldn't make a difference. I mean, what was the
big deal about a wedding ceremony? It wasn't as if it
stopped people breaking up. All that mattered was
being together, wasn't it?

Apparently not.

Turned out Charles was very traditional. He was
climbing the ladder in an investment bank in the city
and needed a wife prepared to devote herself to the
advancement of his career. I've always been crap on
ladders. I tried explaining I was as excited about my

own career as he was about his and his response had been to dump me. In a very public way, I might add, just so that no one was under any illusions as to who had done the dumping.

Admittedly it hurt to be dumped, but nowhere near as much as it hurt to admit I'd wasted ten months on a guy who wasn't remotely interested in the real me.

I realized everyone in the church was looking at me accusingly, as if I'd come here on purpose to make things awkward. To somehow punish him for not choosing me.

Look again, I wanted to yell, *and see which one of us is being punished.*

What girl in her right mind would choose to turn up at her ex's wedding dressed in the fashion equivalent of a giant condom?

Was it my fault the bride wanted to make a public declaration about which one of us the groom was marrying? And I knew I wasn't exactly guilt-free in all this. I could have said no. But then everyone would have thought I was moping and broken-hearted and I had my pride.

That was the first thing Mum taught us—never let a man know you're broken-hearted. Which might be why our dad didn't stick around for long, but more on that later.

I could feel myself turn pink, which I knew had to look horrible against the pukey yellow. I think the fabric was officially described as 'misty dawn' but if I saw a dawn like that I wouldn't put a foot out of bed.

Worst of all? *He* was looking at me. No, not Charlie—he hadn't once glanced in my direction, the coward. The best man. Charlie's friend from school, although they'd grown apart in recent years and the friend was now a super successful lawyer. To be honest I was a bit surprised he'd agreed to be best man, but Charlie had lost a lot of friends since he'd taken a job in the city and started only hanging out with people who were 'useful' to him.

The best man's name was Niccolò Rossi and he was half Italian. And hot. Seriously hot. In the looks department this man had been gifted by the gods.

Unfortunately immediately after the gods had dished out super clever brain, dark good looks and an incredible body, they obviously decided too much of a good thing was a bad thing and withheld humour. Which was a shame because Nico had an amazing mouth. A perfect sensual curve that would probably look good in a smile. Only he never used it to smile. Never. And he wasn't using it now as he looked at me. He clearly wasn't amused to see me sitting there. I wasn't amused either. It was probably the first time we'd felt the same way about anything. He lived in London. We'd met the same night I met Charlie and although we were always bumping into each other on the social circuit, we'd barely spoken. I knew he wasn't my type. He disapproved of me and I was done with men who disapproved of me. Charlie hated the fact I was an engineer. He always wanted me to wear frilly dresses to compensate. No wonder we came unstuck.

Nico cast me an icy glance at the same moment I looked at him.

Bad timing.

Our eyes clashed. His were a dark, dangerous black and everything inside me turned to liquid.

I glared, taking my anger with myself out on him.

I hated that he made me feel this way. He didn't like me. I didn't like him. We were polar opposites. I was fun-loving, friendly and honest about my feelings. He was zipped up, ruthlessly contained and cold as the inside of my freezer. There had been moments over the past few years when I'd been tempted to leap on him with a blowtorch to see if I could thaw him out.

He'd given me a lift home in his car once when Charlie had been too drunk to walk, let alone drive. It was a night I'd tried to forget. We'd been celebrating my job, which for some reason had sent Charlie over the edge.

Nico drove a red Ferrari, just about the sexiest car on the planet, and he was ruthlessly tidy. There wasn't a single screwed-up piece of paper in sight. No mess (although by the time he dropped me off there may have been traces of saliva where I'd drooled all over his car). His suits were Tom Ford, his shoes polished and his shirts a crisp, pristine white. But underneath that carefully polished appearance there was something raw and elemental that no amount of sophisticated tailoring could conceal.

I'd been wearing my favourite black dress that night and I remember he didn't look at me once. Not even at my legs, which were definitely my best feature, especially when I dressed them up in four-inch stilettos (no pain no gain). He hadn't bothered to hide his disapproval then and he wasn't hiding it now.

His burning gaze lowered to my neckline and that sensual, unsmiling mouth tightened into a line of grim censure.

I wanted to stand up and point out that the dress wasn't my choice. That it was yet another trick on the part of the bride to make sure I looked hideous. Quite honestly my breasts were too big for this dress and breasts generally weren't on the guest list to a wedding. Mine were so big they could have qualified for separate invitations.

Nico Rossi obviously didn't think they should have been invited at all.

Truth? I found him intimidating and I hated that.

I was a modern, independent woman. I'd never worn pink and I'd never had the urge to coo over strange babies in prams. My best subjects at school were Math, Physics and Technology. I was the only girl in the class and I always had better marks than the boys, which usually pissed them off, but I figured that was their problem not mine. I had a degree in aeronautical engineering and was working on a supersecret project to do with satellites. I couldn't tell you more than that or I'd have to kill you and eat you and you didn't need a degree in engineering to know there was no room in this dress for two people. I loved my job. It excited me more than any man I'd ever met. But that could have been because I constantly messed up my love life.

Every. Single. Time.

Honestly, how could an intelligent woman get it so badly wrong? I'd tried to apply data analysis methods to my dating history but failed to extract anything meaningful from the results except that getting it wrong hurt. I always seemed to end up compromising who I was, but that's in the genes. Rosie and I watched our mum contort who she was for men who subsequently left her. As I said, we weren't good at relationships, which was probably why I was sitting here single, watching my ex get married.

I breathed in the smell of this musty old church and thought about all the promises that had been made here only to be broken a few years down the line. And right there and then, I made a decision.

No more feelings.

Feelings just led to misery and I was done with misery.

Not that I'd ever been the sort of girl to wait by the phone, willing it to ring. God, no. If a guy played those games with me, I deleted him from my contacts. But that didn't mean I couldn't be hurt. And frankly, what was the point?

'I've made a New Year's resolution.' I risked the dress and leaned closer to Rosie. 'And I'm starting right now.'

'You're never wearing pukey-yellow again?' She eyed my dress. 'Good decision.'

I ignored her. 'I'm sick of romantic relationships. Why bother? I can go to the movies with girlfriends. I can chat with girlfriends. I can laugh with girlfriends.'

'That's your New Year's resolution?'

'Everything I need in life I can get from girlfriends,' I hissed, 'apart from one thing—'

Rosie coughed. 'Well, you can—'

'No, I can't. I need a man for that part. But only that part. From now on I'm using men for sex. Nothing else.'

'Well, as resolutions go, I predict that one is going to be a lot more fun than giving up chocolate.'

I could always rely on my sister for support.

The more I thought about it, the more convinced I was it was a brilliant idea. 'I should have thought of it before.' I was talking out of the corner of my mouth, trying not to attract glares from the elderly aunts. 'Instead of trying to find a man who can make me laugh and is actually interested in me, instead of wondering what I can do for his career, I look for one thing. Sex appeal.'

'If all you're interested in is sex appeal, you could start with Nico Rossi,' Rosie whispered. 'He is scorching hot.'

Not just me then.

The problem was, I didn't want to find Nico sexy. I didn't want to think of him naked or wonder how it would feel to be kissed by him. He didn't like me. It disturbed my sense of order and fairness that I should find him attractive.

I looked away, but not for long.

I couldn't help myself. I sneaked another look. It was some consolation that every other woman under ninety was staring, too. If ever there was such a thing as raw sex appeal, Nico had it. He was the sort of guy that made you think about sin in a big way, which wasn't a good thing when you were sitting in church with your breasts half exposed.

I couldn't wait to get to the bathroom so that I could unzip my dress and give my ribs the freedom they deserved.

When was this wedding going to end?

Enough already.

Just say *I do* and go and live your lives until you realize what you should have said was *I don't*.

But now they were staring into each other's eyes and reciting handwritten personalized messages.

I promise to love you forever and cherish you.

I promise never to cancel your subscription to the sports channel.

(OK I made that one up but you get the point.)

I wriggled in my seat, wondering whether Nico Rossi spoke in Italian when he was having sex. He'd brought his younger sister to the wedding—a sleek, dark vision of slender perfection. She was poised and sophisticated, just like him. Every now and then she glanced at him adoringly, as if he were a god. It seemed unnatural to me. I mean, I loved my sister but there were plenty of days I wanted to poke her in the eye. But these were perfect people who would never show emotion in public. They probably never argued. They were the sort who believed marriage to be an exciting journey.

I was always sick on journeys.

Thanks to our parents' less than stellar example, my sister and I were both equally screwed-up about relationships. Not that there weren't men in our lives. Far from it. Men were always attracted by Rosie's sweet, heart-shaped face and her pretty smile. They thought she was fragile and needed protecting. Then they discovered my sister had a black belt in karate and could break a man's bones with one kick and they usually retreated nervously, licking their wounded machismo.

There *was* a guy once, but if I so much as thought his name she'd break my bones, too, so it was a subject I didn't touch.

Just when I thought this wedding was never going to end, the priest benevolently told the groom he could kiss the bride. He'd been kissing the bride and half her friends regularly for the past six months without permission from anyone, but no one seemed to care about that.

I couldn't help wondering if the kiss was for my benefit, to remind me what I'd turned down.

It was very Hollywood. No bumping noses or awkward moments. Scripted. The sort of kiss where you just knew they were thinking about how it looked on the outside, not how it felt on the inside.

There seemed to be an awful lot of tongue involved.

Rosie made sick choking noises next to me.

God, I loved my sister.

And then finally, *finally*, it was over.

I breathed a huge sigh of relief.

And my dress split.

CHAPTER TWO

Oh fuck, so now I was naked. Not just wearing a condom, but a split condom, and suddenly no one was looking at the bride and groom—they were staring at me and I couldn't exactly blame them because there was plenty to see. There were times when I was happy to be the centre of attention, but this wasn't one of them.

Why oh why hadn't I worn a bra?

I'd tried it, but it had shown through the cheap, shiny fabric, so I'd decided in the interests of vanity that if I *had* to wear this hideous dress at least my outline would be smooth and perfect.

Another bad decision. The dress had split down both side seams simultaneously, exposing me completely from the waist up. I felt like a half-peeled banana, but I probably looked like one of those women who turned up at stag parties and leapt out of cakes.

I was strip-o-gram bridesmaid.

Everyone was staring, transfixed by delicious horror, all deeply relieved it hadn't happened to them. But it could never have happened to them. Only to me. My life had a habit of unraveling, only usually not quite as literally as this.

The snow and the draughty, under-heated old church had conspired to make my nipples stand to attention.

I tried to cover them with my hands, but then I realized I was probably making it worse. Now I wasn't just naked—I was touching myself.

For the first time in quite a few years, I prayed.

Kill me now.

Mum had always drummed into Rosie and me that we should wear clean underwear in case of an accident, although to be fair I don't think this was the sort of accident she had in mind when she dished out that advice. I wished I'd listened, but I honestly hadn't thought my underwear, or lack of it, was going to be an issue. Every unattached girl hoped she would score at a wedding, but I was a realist. No man was going to hit on a woman wearing a giant body condom. Don't misunderstand me—I was all for safe sex. I insisted on condoms. It was just that I didn't usually try and squeeze my whole self into one.

The dress was a horribly tight tube, floor length, which basically meant my legs were locked together. I couldn't even run away. I was like a mermaid, but without an ocean to drown in. Escape would be a slow, shuffling, breast-bouncing affair.

Scarlet-faced, I tried to grab the misbehaving fabric and cover myself with that, but honestly it was like trying to cover Big Ben with a handkerchief.

Somewhere through the swirling clouds of embarrassment I heard Rosie snort. She was laughing so hard I knew she was going to be as much use to me as a non-alcoholic cocktail at a party. Rosie had a problem with laughter. She couldn't control it. Watching her laugh usually made me laugh, too, but any desire to laugh was squashed by the look in ruthless Nico Rossi's eyes.

While everyone else was gaping in horrified silence (and I can tell you they weren't looking at my face) he strode across the aisle towards me, all broad shouldered and powerful like a warrior preparing to repel an invading army.

I waited for Rosie to leap to her feet and execute one of her incredible scissor kicks that would flatten him, but my useless sister was doubled up with tears pouring down her face and Nico was still striding. I guessed it would take a lot to flatten a man like him.

Just for a moment I shivered because whatever he lacked in the emotional warmth department, physically he was truly spectacular—stomach-melting, willpower-destroying spectacular. The sort of man you couldn't look at without thinking about sex.

Dark, glittering eyes were focused on me like a laser-guided weapon programmed to destroy.

His role as best man was to support the groom and solve problems and right now I was the problem. Or at least, my breasts were. They were loose and free and I could tell from the look on his face he thought breasts like mine shouldn't be allowed out without a permit.

The elderly aunts had their eyes averted, but the elderly uncles were staring at me, their bulging eyes reminding me of sea creatures. I saw sweat on their brows and was just wondering whether I was going to be responsible for adding more bodies to that pretty churchyard when Nico reached me. He removed his jacket in a smooth movement that made me think he'd be good at undressing women, and wrapped it around my shoulders. Actually 'wrapped' was too gentle a word for what he did, but either way my bouncing breasts were now safely buried under Tom Ford. His jacket felt warm. It smelled delicious. It smelled of *him*.

'Move!' It was a command, not a request and I opened my mouth to point out my legs were tied together, but his hand was on my back and he was propelling me down the aisle. *Down the aisle*. That's right, I, Hayley Miller of 42 Cherry Tree Crescent, Notting Hill, was shuffling down the aisle with a man, something I always said I'd never do, except that I was doing it backwards and half-naked, so it probably didn't count.

I staggered past a sea of faces, all with their mouths hanging open. They reminded me of a nest of baby birds waiting to be fed and I wasn't just feeding them morsels of gossip—I'd given them a banquet. At least they wouldn't need to eat at the reception.

And behind the fascinated horror was the delight some people felt when they witnessed someone else's public humiliation. They'd be talking about this moment for weeks. Who was I kidding? Years. One thing I knew for sure—I was never trusting a condom again.

But I had more immediate problems to worry about.

I had no idea where we were going.

This was a small private church in the grounds of a stately home. England was full of that sort of thing and, since the credit crunch, even the very rich were looking for ways to supplement their income. Hiring out the dusty family chapel for weddings was a clever way of allowing less privileged folk to pretend for that one day of their lives that they actually lived like this. I didn't think it was any more fake than exchanging vows and promises about loving each other forever and then splitting up a few years later. In other words, none of it meant anything, so why not go over the top? If dressing like an over-whipped dessert made you happy, then go for it I say (but for God's sake get one that fits).

Everyone wanted to get married in this particular chapel, not for religious reasons but because the door was pretty and looked good in the photos.

'Oh, God, the photos! What about the photos?' I stopped dead, but he pushed me forward into a room and slammed the door.

It was just the two of us and the silence was really loud.

I looked around me and saw we were in a room with wood paneling and portraits of unsmiling dukes on unsmiling horses. In the corner was a perfectly decorated Christmas tree. No wonky home-made decorations like the ones Rosie and I used in our apartment, but designer perfection.

I was pretty sure we weren't supposed to be here, but I guessed Nico wasn't giving much thought to protecting the assets of our hosts. He was more interested in hiding *my* assets from the gawping guests.

What was I supposed to say?

What was the etiquette for a serious wardrobe malfunction?

I had a feeling 'oops' wasn't going to cut it and asking for a needle and thread would have been like asking for a teacup to bail out the Titanic.

'Er—nice jacket.' And because I was wearing his jacket, he was in his shirtsleeves and I could see the swell of hard male muscle pressing against the fabric. His shirt was pristine white and I noticed his skin was golden, not pale and pasty like Charlie's, and his jaw had the beginnings of a dark shadow. Thick, dark lashes framed eyes that were indecently sexy—the only thing that spoiled it was the dangerous glint of anger.

He dragged his fingers through hair that was usually smooth and sleek, exploded into Italian, and then switched language in midsentence as if realizing that if he wanted to insult me he'd better do it in a language I understood. '*Cristo*, what were you thinking choosing a dress that revealing?'

'I didn't choose it.'

'Then you should have refused to wear it.' His gaze was fixed on mine and didn't waver.

Clearly he'd had no desire to ogle my bare breasts. I told myself that didn't bother me.

What *did* bother me was the unconcealed look of disapproval on his handsome face.

I was sure he was a very successful lawyer. I didn't even know which bit of the law he dealt with, but whatever he did I was sure he was the best of the best. I knew that if I were on the witness stand and he fixed me with that penetrating gaze I would have confessed to pretty much anything.

Yes, Your Honour, it's true that on the twenty-second day of December I wore a giant condom to a wedding.... No, I had no idea I would be arrested for antisocial behavior—condoms are supposed to only have a 2 percent failure rate, but in my case it was 150 percent. Yes, I understand there were serious consequences. Wedding interruptus.

I wondered why he was so angry.

It wasn't as if the groom had ended up with me. This episode could have just been labeled 'narrow escape'.

Outrage started to simmer inside me. I was the victim of a cruel fashion crime, blameless in everything except my proportions and I wasn't about to apologize for my breasts.

And anyway, I felt a bit funny inside. Not queasy exactly, but a bit dizzy and swimmy-headed. I thought it was probably hearing him speaking Italian. The only Italian I knew I learned from a menu and there was nothing sexy about *Pizza Margherita* even if you tried saying it in a sultry voice.

This man, however, was spectacularly sexy and everything that came out of his mouth made me want to grab him and do very, *very* bad things which was definitely off limits because Nico was the sort who was always ruthlessly in control of himself and behaved impeccably in public. I assumed lawyers weren't allowed to misbehave.

'Why the fuck *are* you here, Hayley? You are the master of bad decisions.' He spoke through his teeth as if he were afraid that if he opened his mouth a tirade of insults would escape.

Frankly I was surprised to hear him say 'fuck'.

But now he'd said it, I started thinking about it. Not the word, but the act. I couldn't help it. Truthfully I'd been thinking about it long before he'd said that word. I doubted any woman could look at Nico and *not* think of it. Not love or romance, you understand. He wasn't the hearts and roses sort of man. I couldn't imagine him risking his suit by changing a nappy or rolling up his perfectly ironed sleeves to wash a greasy saucepan, but sex? God, yes. All it took was one look to know this man would know everything there was to know about hard, hot, sweaty sex.

For a wild moment I wanted to ask if he'd impart some of his knowledge, but then I remembered he'd just told me I made bad decisions. There was only so much abuse a girl could take in one day and I was right up to my limit. When you work in a male dominated profession as I do, you're used to being judged. Most of the time I let it wash over me. If I threatened their masculinity that was their problem, not mine. Occasionally I fought back. Sometimes I took sadistic pleasure in surprising people, but I was damned if I'd allow myself to be told I made bad decisions by a man who never let himself go.

I stood up straighter and pushed my chest out (good job I was wearing his jacket). 'Excuse *me*, but what gives you the right to judge my decisions?'

'We could start with the fact you're currently naked from the waist up under my jacket. Fix the dress. I'm the best man. I have duties to perform.'

And I was willing to bet he'd perform them well. *Oh, God, I had to stop thinking like that.*

'The dress is unfixable. And I couldn't refuse to wear it. This was what Cressida wanted.'

'Your half-naked body on display? I don't think so.' He threw me a look that would have terrified an entire army into immediate surrender. 'But you're just a girl who can't say no.'

'What's that supposed to mean?' I exploded, which considering I was half-naked wasn't a good idea. Because I was quite physical I tended to add emphasis to what I was saying by using my hands. Up until a moment ago my hands had been holding the front of his jacket together. Now they were waving around wildly, preparing to act in my defense. Unfortunately they were not the only part of me to be waving around wildly.

His eyes darkened and I realized that he had stopped looking at my face.

Suddenly there were four of us in the room.

Me, him and my breasts.

I saw a tiny muscle move in his jaw and then his gaze lifted to mine and that was the moment I discovered that looking at someone could make you burn inside.

'I can say no.' My voice came out croaky and I realized the timing of that sentence wasn't great because I knew, I just knew, that both of us were thinking about sex.

'What the hell are you doing here, Hayley? At this wedding? Have you no pride?'

'Pride is the reason I'm here. If I'd stayed away everyone would have thought I was broken-hearted.'

'And are you?' His question surprised me as much as the roughness of his voice.

We didn't exactly have the sort of relationship that included an exchange of confidences and that was a deeply personal question. I had no intention of answering it.

I hadn't even told Rosie how bad I felt, although she knew of course. That was why she was here. Solidarity even in the absence of confession. That was one of the unspoken rules of true sisterhood.

The second was that we were going to leave at the first possible moment, scoot back to our apartment in London and drown the memories of today in a large bottle of wine while we wrapped presents and finished decorating our apartment for Christmas.

Not that I was broken-hearted about Charlie—
I wasn't. It was more the misery of being forced to
confront yet more evidence of how utterly impossible
relationships were.

I was mourning the fairy tale, which was ridiculous
when I thought about it because I'd never believed in
the fairy tale.

'Hayley? *Cristo*, answer the question.' His voice
was raw and thickened by an emotion I didn't recognize. I assumed it was anger, since that was the only
emotion he ever seemed to feel around me. 'Are you
broken-hearted?'

The question hung between us in an atmosphere
that was heavy and sweaty. A moment ago I'd been
freezing. Someone needed to open a window. It was
stifling in here.

'Unless you're a cardiologist, the condition of my
heart is none of your business.' I might have been
hiding my feelings but I wasn't hiding anything else.
I lifted my hands to close my jacket but he was there
before me. Strong male fingers tangled with mine and
the backs of his fingers brushed against my breasts.
His hands were warm and chemistry shot through me.
It was like falling on an electric fence.

Both of us froze.

The only sound in the room was his breathing. Or
maybe it was my breathing.

He was standing really close to me, so close I had
a magnified view of hot masculinity. My eyes were
level with that darkened jaw, that unsmiling mouth and
those incredible *bed me if you're lucky* eyes.

Right at the moment I so, *so* wanted to get that
lucky.

I knew he wouldn't be good for me. He'd probably be a bit like junk food—something you could crave even while knowing it had no nutritional value and might make you feel sick later.

I didn't care about the wedding. I didn't care that I'd be gossiped about for the next two decades. All I wanted was to feel that mouth on mine and find out whether kissing him would be as good as I thought it would.

Oh, God, why not?

Today had been such a total disaster I might as well try and extract one decent memory to comfort me in the hours of cringing flashbacks that were bound to follow.

Telling myself I was doing us both a favor, I grabbed the front of his shirt and was about to pull him towards me when he muttered something in Italian and dragged me towards him by the lapels of his jacket.

We collided, locked together like wild animals in the mating season.

CHAPTER THREE

BODIES, MOUTHS, EVERY part of us that could touch were touching, and although I had no idea who made the first move I didn't care any more because his mouth was warm and skilled and his kiss confirmed what I'd already suspected—

That he was the hottest man on the face of the earth.

Whatever else it was, this wasn't a scripted kiss.

I doubted either of us would have known or cared if anyone else was watching. We were so wrapped up in each other, so absorbed in the moment, we wouldn't have noticed if a horse had leapt from one of the paintings and started galloping around the room.

I felt the erotic slide of his tongue in my mouth and moaned aloud because what he was doing connected a million tiny circuits inside me and set off a chain reaction until I was fairly sure my body was close to meltdown. I didn't care that he never smiled because I knew now his mouth was made for kissing and he proved it with every delicious, skilled stroke of his tongue. My arms were round his neck, my body pressed against his—and his was hard, muscular and just about perfect. Under that shockingly expensive suit, the man was ripped. Everything was ripped. My dress, his body and my reputation.

I couldn't help myself. I covered the front of his

trousers with the flat of my hand and felt him, hard and thick against my palm.

'*Cristo*—' he muttered against my lips and slammed me back against the wall, his mouth hot and demanding on mine. His hands had moved from the jacket to my breasts and I felt a thrill of delicious excitement as his thumbs grazed my nipples.

Usually I closed my eyes when I kissed, but not this time.

His eyes were fixed on mine, dark with heat and raw desire. It was the sexiest experience of my life and I didn't want to miss a single moment of it.

My mind wasn't capable of much coherent thought, but I knew I'd been wrong about one thing—

Nico Rossi wasn't a good boy. He was a bad boy dressed in a good suit.

Heat pulsed between us, the chemistry screaming, scorching and intense. His fingers drove into my hair, which tumbled out of its clip and slid over his hand. His mouth was pressing hot, sensual kisses against my neck and lower.

He murmured something in Italian and I was about to ask him to translate when I realized I didn't want him to. Knowing what he was saying might spoil everything. There was no way I was ever going to understand what was going on here anyway, so what was the point in trying?

I felt the thrust of his hard thigh between mine and there was another ripping sound as the seams tore a bit further. If the bridesmaid dress hadn't already been ruined it would have been now. I didn't think he even noticed. His mouth devoured mine and he yanked what was left of the stupid dress up and locked his hands on my shifting hips.

I strained against him, feeling the hard thrust of him against me and then I felt his hand move to my inner thigh. The anticipation almost killed me, and then he was stroking me with those long, knowing fingers, somehow programmed to touch me in exactly the right place even though I hadn't said a word or made a sound. My mouth was on his, we were breathing the same air, biting, licking and it was the most erotic thing I've ever experienced. I wasn't thinking about anything except how good it felt and then he slid his fingers inside me and good became incredible and I could feel myself pulse around him. I was gripping his shoulder because my knees were so weak I thought I might slide to the floor if I wasn't holding on, but that left me with one hand free and I wasn't going to waste it.

I wrapped my hand around him and felt him thicken in my grasp. As I stroked him I heard him growl deep in his throat and it was the sexiest sound I'd ever heard, even sexier because I knew I was the one who had done that to him. This man who was so big on control was *losing* control, and he was losing it because of me.

His fingers were skilled, finding that exact spot with unerring accuracy and I felt the first flutters of orgasm.

We'd barely exchanged a word before today, this man and I, and yet here we were locked in this unimaginable intimacy. His knee nudged my thighs further apart, giving him full access and he kept using his fingers, kept kissing me until I felt everything inside me tighten and pulse. I was close, *so close*, and he knew because he was right there with me, his fingers controlling everything I was feeling, his mouth breathing in my gasps.

'Come,' he ordered softly, and normally I was very bad at doing what I was told but this time our objectives were clearly aligned and I tightened my hand around the glorious thickness of him and then heard someone calling my name.

'Hayley?' It was my sister, using one of her frantic stage whispers, knocking on doors as she searched for me. Presumably she'd finally stopped laughing for long enough to work out I might be in trouble.

Shit.

Nico and I stared at each other, eyes and mouths still locked together. My body was suspended in a state of intense excitement.

For once in my life I wished Rosie had just carried on laughing and not tried to help me out.

Here I was, hovering on the edge of what I knew was going to be the best orgasm of my life with the hottest man I was ever going to meet and my sister was banging on the door.

I was going to kill her. Slowly. If I was going to die in agony then I was going to make sure she did, too.

'Hayley? Are you OK?'

It was a measure of how turned on I was that having my sister banging on the door hadn't made any difference to the way I felt.

Nico swore against my mouth (in both Italian and English, in case you were wondering), and I was just about to ask whether he'd locked the door when it burst open.

Fortunately Nico had his back to our audience,

shielding me. I had yet another reason to be thankful for those broad, muscular shoulders.

With admirable calm, he removed his fingers and his mouth from my body and somehow managed to pull my dress down and draw the lapels of his jacket together at the same time. He was impressive in a crisis—smooth and composed. Rosie had seen most of it before, of course. We'd lived together since we left home to go to college and we didn't lock doors very often, so at this point I was more exasperated than embarrassed.

But then I looked past his shoulders (and that took some willpower, I can tell you, because it was the best view I'd seen in a long time) and saw a shocked face that didn't belong to my sister.

Nico's sister was staring at him as if she'd never seen him before.

Oh crappity, crap, crap.

Her eyes were wide and shocked, her mouth slightly agape.

She obviously thought I'd corrupted her usually controlled brother. And maybe I had. I was certainly well on my way. From the moment he'd touched me, I'd thought about nothing but him. And before you judge me I can tell you without a flicker of doubt that if this man had kissed you, you wouldn't have been thinking of anything but him either.

He swore under his breath. 'Go back to the church, Kiara.' It was a command, and she colored and stepped back without question.

If he'd spoken to me like that I would have posted his Tom Ford suit to a worthy charity, but she didn't say a word. Just obeyed him like a puppy in an obedience class.

I decided it must be the shock that had stopped her from standing up for herself. And I was responsible for that shock.

So much for having a sexual relationship without emotional involvement. It seemed that no matter what rules you played by, *someone* always got hurt.

I wanted to tell her not to worry, that we hated each other really, but she'd already gone and I was left with more than a split dress to worry about.

I'd thought my embarrassment couldn't get any deeper.

Turned out I'd been wrong about that, too.

CHAPTER FOUR

'BEST WEDDING *EVER*.' It was Christmas Eve and Rosie was stretching on the living room floor, surrounded by half-wrapped Christmas presents. She spent a lot of time stretching. I'd learned to give her a wide berth because there had been more than one occasion when I'd moved too close and ended up with her foot in my face. She'd started karate at the age of six, then she'd added in Muay Thai when she was eighteen and met— But I wasn't allowed to mention him. Let's just say we call him He Who Shall Not Be Named (and he's not that Voldemort guy from *Harry Potter*, although from the smile on my sister's face at the time I think he might have had a magic wand hidden somewhere).

'Glad you were entertained.'

Snow drifted lazily past the windows. The streets of London were white and everyone was wrapped up against the cold in bright scarves and outrageous hats. That was one of the many things I loved about living in London. People weren't afraid to dress creatively, especially where we lived. In Notting Hill we were surrounded by artists, musicians and writers. And my angel-faced, karate-loving, kick-boxing sister.

I snuggled deeper into the sofa, my laptop balanced on my thighs because I couldn't be bothered to walk to the table and anyway, it saved on heating bills. 'Can we stop talking about the wedding?'

She'd been laughing non-stop for the past three days.

Sisterly love was wearing thin.

I pretended to be absorbed by my laptop, but if I was honest I'd barely done any work since we'd arrived home from the wedding. I couldn't concentrate. My brain was jammed up with the hottest memory of my life. I couldn't stop thinking about it. About *him*. Mostly about the way Mr Super Cool had gone from ignoring me to virtually having sex with me. The change in him had been shocking and, well, exciting. What wasn't so exciting was the fact it had been interrupted and there was no chance of a repeat performance, which basically meant I was doomed to die of sexual frustration. Not that I hadn't tried to do something about that, but no vibrator was ever going to come close to the unique bedroom talents of Nico Rossi. It was like watching a boxed set, ending an episode on a cliffhanger and then realizing you'd lost the final DVD. I desperately wanted to know what happened next.

But I was never going to because Nico hadn't liked me before the wedding, so he was going to like me even less since I ruined the day and walked off with his Tom Ford.

For a couple of days I'd nurtured a fantasy he might contact me, but of course he hadn't. Real life is a split dress and embarrassment, not a hot guy ringing you.

I answered another email, trying to block out the memory of the wedding. I'd scoured YouTube for days, checking that no one had uploaded a video of my dizzying descent into ignominy. So far all seemed well, but if I could have dug a hole and lived underground for a while, I would have done. 'Why the hell did you have to walk in when you did?'

'Why the hell didn't you lock the door if you were planning to have sex? I've wrapped a load of "spare" presents by the way. They're the ones without labels.' She spun and kicked, almost removing a lamp from the table. If the lamp had been a person, it would have been unconscious. And she wondered why men were intimidated by her. Sex with my sister could probably have been classified as a lethal sport.

And talking of sex…

'We weren't having sex!' I watched as Rosie paused to arrange the presents in a pile under the perfectly shaped fir tree we'd picked up from the garden centre. I would have had a fake one, but she said we had so much fake in our lives growing up, we deserved the real thing. Personally I didn't see anything romantic about picking dried green needles out of the bottom of your feet in March, but that was just me. 'Haven't you overdone the "spare" presents this year?'

My sister always bought extra Christmas presents. She said it was because it made the tree look festive, but I knew her idea of a terrible Christmas would be for someone to turn up and her not have a gift for them. She was very generous—it was all linked with her fairy-tale view of the world. Not that she was idealistic, but she believed you could make your own fairy tale if you worked hard enough at it. Who needed a prince when you had a credit card and online shopping? When we were little she was the one who danced around the room in pink tights with a tiara on her head,

pretending to be a princess. Then our parents split up
and she decided she'd rather be the Karate Kid.

My sister's most important self-created fairy tale
was Christmas. Because we'd never had a proper family Christmas, she overcompensated madly. Hence the
tree, the stockings and her determination that no one
we knew would spend the day alone.

'I'm going to pick up the turkey.' She spun and ex-
ecuted another kick and her blonde hair flew around
her face. There were times when I thought she should
have auditioned to play Bond (and I do mean Bond,
not the dopey girl planted in the film so he can have
sex). She trained for hours every day, but it had paid
off and she'd landed a great job coaching martial arts
at Fit and Physical in the City. She was also building
a list of clients for personal training. Her results were
startling, but I guessed that was because they were all
terrified of my sweet-faced sister. If you didn't put in
effort she kicked your butt. Literally.

Another ten emails pinged into my inbox. We were
in the middle of this huge project at work and it wasn't
going away just because most of London had shut
down for the holidays.

Half of me was hoping one of those emails was
from Nico. I didn't need to tell you which half but let's
put it this way—I was wondering if it was too late to
ask Santa for a new vibrator. Was there one called The
Niccolò? That was the one I wanted.

Idly I typed 'vibrator—the Niccolò' into the search
engine. 'I have to send the jacket back.'

'You can't do it today—he won't be in the office.
It's Christmas Eve and it's snowing.' Rosie grabbed
her coat. 'Come with me. Better than moping.'

'I'm not moping.'

'You're moping. And dreaming in Italian.'

I closed the lid of my laptop so she couldn't see what I'd just typed. I had *some* secrets. 'If it weren't for you I wouldn't have had to dream. I would have had reality. I would have put my New Year's resolution of emotionless sex into practice.'

'It would have been a waste to rush something so good with a man that hot.'

'So instead I didn't get to do it at all? How is that better?' I ducked as she threw me my coat. 'I'm not going out. I still haven't recovered from being naked in church. Someone might recognize me.'

'The advantage of being naked from the waist up is that no one was looking at your face.' Rosie threw my scarf. 'Unless what you're working on is an emergency, you're coming.'

I wished she hadn't used those exact words.

I wasn't coming. That was the point. And yes, it was close to an emergency. At this rate I'd need resuscitation. Mouth-to-mouth. And mouth to— Well, you get the point. All I could think of was sex, which wasn't good when there was no immediate hope for a satisfactory resolution.

Maybe freezing cold and snow would reduce the need for a vibrator.

It didn't, but I had to admit there was something uplifting about walking through Notting Hill on Christmas Eve. Shop windows sparkled with lights and decorations and everyone was smiling, which didn't make sense when you thought about the number of people who found this a miserable time of year or didn't celebrate, but maybe they'd all stayed indoors.

A family strolled past, dragging an enormous tree. They were all holding hands. A mother, father and two very excited children with pink cheeks and shiny expressions. Something twisted inside me. I didn't understand how I could envy that when it wasn't what I wanted.

I caught Rosie's eye and she shrugged, reading my mind.

That was one of the things I loved about my sister. Not only did she know what I was thinking without me saying it, but the past was the past. If something was messed up, then she was going to make sure she did it differently in the future. She was all about moving forward.

Snow was falling on her hair and I thought how pretty she was. Dancer-slim with amazing green eyes and blonde hair that licked around her face and fell to her shoulders. Long, slim limbs that could knock you out with one kick. It was her superpower.

Everyone else was thinking about Christmas, but I was thinking about the wedding. 'Do you think I ruined their big day?'

'No, but it would serve them right if you did. It was mean of them to insist you be a bridesmaid. Not that he was right for you, but they never should have put you in that position.'

She was my sister. It was her job to try and make me feel better, but I really wanted to believe her. It was Christmas Eve and no one wanted to feel bad about themselves on Christmas Eve.

'It's kind of ironic that I went because of my pride, and ended up half-naked in public and then kissing a man who hates me.'

Rosie made a snorting sound. 'He doesn't hate you. The two of you have chemistry. You always have. You two have always been much better suited than you and Charlie.'

I stopped dead and gaped at her. 'How can you say that?' I analyzed the evidence. 'Nico Rossi has barely ever spoken to me. Whenever we're in the same room, he ignores me. He doesn't like me.' Which made the whole thing all the more confusing. How could I possibly have had such a hot encounter with a man who didn't like me?

'He arranged for a car to drive us home from the wedding so you didn't have to face the guests. That must have cost him a fortune.'

And I'd already tucked the money into the pocket of his Tom Ford. I didn't want to be in debt to Nico. 'He did it because he wanted to get us out of there. I'd already ruined the wedding.'

'He rescued you when everyone else stood around gawping.' My sister had stopped, too. Snow settled on her blonde hair. 'He gave you his jacket. He didn't have to do that.'

I frowned. 'He didn't want me naked in a church.'

My sister bent gracefully and scooped up a handful of snow, forming it into a snowball. 'Who gave you a lift home the night you invited a load of us to celebrate your new job and Charlie proceeded to ignore you and get wasted?'

'Nico.' That evening had been the beginning of the end for Charlie and me. He'd proposed the day after, as an alternative to taking the job. I'd thought he was still drunk and kidding. Turned out he was sober and dead serious. He saw marriage to him as a preferable career option. 'Nico, but he was driving past my house anyway.'

I waited for her to say 'yes, you're right', but instead she watched me steadily and suddenly I wondered what explanation Nico had given his sister. Maybe he'd told her it hadn't been his fault, that he'd been assaulted by my bare breasts and had merely been defending himself. He was a lawyer. I was pretty sure he could plead self-defense better than anyone.

On the other hand he didn't strike me as the sort of man who made excuses.

Take him or leave him.

I'd tried to take him and look where that had got me.

I slid my arm through Rosie's and resolved to stop thinking about him. 'Let's talk about something else.' I'd never spent so long thinking about a man I wasn't even in a relationship with. 'So far my resolution to have emotionless sex isn't turning out so well. Maybe I should have just gone for something more traditional like losing weight and getting fit.'

'You're already fit, and you're not supposed to start your resolution until the New Year. Perhaps you'll meet someone cute tomorrow.' Something in the way she said it made me turn my head suspiciously.

'Who have you invited? Please don't tell me it's that journalist guy.'

'Just all our usual friends and a few others.' She was studying a gingerbread house in the window of our favorite bakery. 'Should we buy that?'

'If you buy any more food there won't be room for the guests. Rosie, who exactly is coming tomorrow?'

'I never know until they knock on the door. You know what it's like—not everyone confirms.' She didn't look at me. The year before she'd invited an entire class from her gym. They were all kicking in our living room.

We wandered on, staring in windows. I thought how much I loved London. We lived in a great area, with shops, markets and lively restaurants on our doorsteps. Our apartment was on the top floor of a beautiful red-brick Victorian house in the trendy part of Notting Hill. The streets were really pretty here and we were round the corner from Portobello market and an easy walk from Kensington Gardens. Loads of our friends lived nearby.

I wondered where Nico lived. Had he gone home to Italy for Christmas?

I hoped he didn't need his jacket.

'Hey, wake up. It's been snowing all night.'

I burrowed under the covers, resenting my sister's energy levels. 'It's too early.'

'It's Christmas. We have to open our stockings and there's loads to do.'

'Only because you insist on inviting half the world to lunch.' I emerged from under the covers and looked out of my attic window.

London was covered in another deep coating of sparkling snow. It almost *was* a fairy tale, except I had to get up and cook Christmas lunch for a bunch of people I'd probably never met before when all I wanted to do was lie in a heap, watch back-to-back TV and try to forget about the disastrous wedding.

Rosie sprang onto the bed and crossed her legs, her daisy pajamas a cheerful, springlike rebellion against

the winter weather. 'Do you mind? Would you rather
I didn't do this?'

I was about to confess that one year it might be
nice to just eat turkey sandwiches and flop in front of
the TV when I saw the look of excitement in her eyes
and knew I would never, ever, stop her doing this.
And anyway, I understood why she did it. We couldn't
have a proper 'family Christmas' so she had a 'friend
Christmas' instead.

Rosie was determined to create the life she wanted
to live and I admired that.

'I think it's great.' And I did. Because of my sister,
no one we knew spent Christmas on their own. Everyone with nowhere to go was invited, which meant that
some years our apartment was pretty crowded, but I
didn't really have a problem with that.

'Are you sure?' She dragged the stockings onto the
bed. 'I wondered whether you wouldn't rather just have
a quiet day.'

'Not in a million years.'

Don't get me wrong—my sister and I fought, but it
was always over the small things. When it was anything to do with our past, we were a united front.

We opened the 'stockings' we'd laid out the night
before (she filled mine and I filled hers. Last year we'd
bumped heads stuffing stockings at the same time).
Each was full of funny low-priced gifts. Thanks to
the stress of the wedding, I'd bought all mine on the
internet. I had no idea when Rosie had done her shopping. Soon my bed was covered in ripped paper and in
amongst chocolates, a notebook, an exceptionally cute
stuffed llama, and a festive bra and panty set in red

with white faux fur trim, there was a packet of condoms with 'not to be used until the New Year' on them.

I raised an eyebrow. 'I don't remember mentioning those when I wrote to Santa.'

'He knows you've been a good girl this year but he also knows you're going to be a bad girl very soon.' She winked at me. 'And he wants you to be prepared.'

Rosie was as subtle as a kick in the stomach from a reindeer.

I was pretty pleased with the presents I'd chosen for her, and as well as the small things I gave her my main gift—a leather handbag in a soft shade of cappuccino she'd admired in the market back in November.

'I love it.' She cooed over it and then threw me an enigmatic look. 'Your big present is coming later.'

I wondered how my present could be coming later when there were no deliveries on Christmas Day, but I had no time to dwell on it because we were expecting a load of people and we had to produce food.

Surrendering to the inevitable cooking marathon, I showered quickly and teamed my favorite skinny jeans with thigh-length boots and a cute shirt with shell buttons. Underneath I was wearing my new festive underwear (including the bra, in case you were wondering. Never let it be said I don't learn from my mistakes).

I reported for duty in the kitchen just as Rosie staggered through the door carrying the turkey. It had spent the night in our hallway, apparently reaching 'room temperature'.

'This needs a bit of attention. Can you do that while I make the stuffing?'

I looked at it doubtfully because I wasn't much of a cook. 'What sort of attention?'

'There are some stray feathers. Pluck them out.'

She wanted me to pluck the turkey?

'Poultry hair removal isn't exactly my specialty,' I began, but I was talking to myself. Rosie had already left the room, whirling through the flat singing Christmas carols. I wouldn't have minded, but my sister was a much better dancer than she was a singer.

I stared gloomily at the turkey. It had dark stubble on one leg. Clearly the person who had prepared this turkey for the oven had been anxious to leave work early. I looked at the stubby ends poking out of the plump pale skin and sympathized. It wasn't easy keeping yourself smooth. What the hell was I supposed to do?

I pulled my phone out of my pocket and checked my texts and emails but there was still nothing from Nico. Not that I was expecting 'Merry Christmas', but I thought he might at least have demanded his jacket back.

'Stop looking at your phone.' Rosie was back in the kitchen, squeezing orange juice into a bowl of cranberries. 'He isn't going to call you.'

'I have no idea what you mean. I was checking my work emails.'

'On Christmas Day?'

I wondered why she was so sure he wouldn't call me. I had his jacket. It was Tom Ford. If nothing else, he should want it back. A guy like him was bound to be going to lots of smart dinners over the holidays. 'This project is important. And you'll be busy once Christmas is over.' Rosie's phone never stopped ringing with people wanting her to help them get into shape. Usu-

ally I didn't see her until February when everyone
went back to being inactive slobs.

The doorbell rang. We were nowhere near ready for
guests and I looked at her in horror but Rosie smiled,
which I thought was a very odd reaction. Given the
hairy turkey and the state of our kitchen I would have
anticipated screaming.

She vanished to answer the door and I decided life
was too short to pluck a turkey. And anyway, I needed
rapid results.

I formulated a plan, congratulating myself on my in-
genuity. Behind me I could hear our apartment slowly
filling up with people and it was quite a few minutes
before Rosie came back into our pretty country-style
kitchen. 'Hayley, you need to—' She broke off and
stared at me in disbelief. 'You're *waxing* the turkey?'

'You told me to remove the stray feathers.' I ripped
the strip, removing feathers and most of the skin.
'Oops. That wasn't the way it was supposed to turn
out.'

'You were *supposed* to pluck it!'

'There was no time to pluck each feather individu-
ally.' We both stared at the skinless leg of the turkey,
me with morbid fascination and Rosie with horror.

'I can't believe you waxed our turkey! You've ruined it.'

I felt a stab of guilt. 'Just one leg. And leg meat is
often dry.'

'I'm never letting you near my kitchen again.' Rosie
shoved me aside and it was only then I remembered
she'd come in to tell me something.

'You were telling me I needed to do something.
What?' I turned my head and almost passed out be-

cause Nico was standing there, his broad shoulders
blocking my view of the living room and the other
guests.

I'd thought about nothing but him for the past few
days. Sometimes when you fantasized about a guy and
then you saw him again, you realized you'd built him
up in your head. Not Nico. He was truly spectacular.
And imposing. He filled the doorway of our kitchen
and he glanced from me to the turkey and lifted an
eyebrow.

Seriously unbalanced by his unexpected appearance, I gave what I hoped passed for a casual shrug.
'Not everyone likes leg.'

'True.' Those dark eyes met mine with sardonic humour. Not a smile, but definitely humour. 'I'm more
of a breast man myself.'

Oh, God, why did he have to say that?

Immediately I was back in that room at the wedding, with him showing me just how much of a breast
man he was. I wondered what the hell he was doing
here.

Presumably he needed his jacket for some Christmas gathering or other, but this seemed like an odd
time to show up on our doorstep.

I turned to look at Rosie, but she was in a panic
over the waxed turkey.

My sister had no sense of priorities.

I was about to fetch Nico's jacket and send him on
his way when I realised he wasn't alone.

Kiara stood in the doorway, groomed and polished
as ever. She gave me an awkward smile, which I returned. At a guess I'd say mine was more awkward
than hers. I felt more naked than the turkey (although

without being vain, I'd say my legs were looking a hell of a lot better).

Nico was leaning casually against the doorframe watching me from under those thick lashes, the way he had when we'd kissed. He might as well have been touching me because I could feel his gaze right through me. The sensation started as a tingling on the surface of my skin and then it was a warmth through my veins, and then the warmth turned to heat. The heat pooled low in my pelvis and I didn't think it had anything to do with my fur-trimmed panties. It exasperated me that I could feel like this. And what was even more exasperating was the fact he *knew* I was feeling like this. Not that he looked smug or anything. Oh, no. If I'd had to describe his expression I would have said 'watchful'.

He kept looking at me. Unflinching. Unembarrassed. As if he'd asked himself a question and was now looking at the answer.

Then he glanced from me to the woman standing quietly next to him.

'You haven't been formally introduced, have you?'

Oh, great. He was going to ram home the fact that his sister had only ever seen me half-naked. 'No.' I spoke between my teeth. 'We haven't.'

'This is Kiara. Kiara, this is Hayley. You saw her briefly at the wedding.'

All right, enough!

It might have been brief, but I had a feeling it had been fairly comprehensive.

What was the guy playing at? One more comment like that and I'd give him one of my own kicks, which might not have been as impressive or elegant as my sister's, but would still have threatened his ability to father children.

'Hi, Kiara. Lovely to meet you.'

I tried not to look at him even though I could feel him looking at me. He hadn't stopped looking at me since he'd walked into the kitchen. Being on the receiving end of that smoldering, intense gaze made my legs turn from a solid to a liquid. I was about to reach for the fire blanket Rosie kept in the kitchen and throw it over myself.

'It's lovely to meet *you*,' Kiara said earnestly. 'I know you're an engineer. I'm in awe. I'm hopeless at Math and Physics. Nico used to tear his hair out helping me with homework.'

He'd helped her with homework?

I blinked.

I tried to imagine this smooth, sophisticated guy sitting patiently by his sister, helping her with algebra.

'Well that's, er, lovely.' And honestly I *did* think it was lovely. Except that I was confused by the contradictions. 'You came here for your jacket, so I ought to get that for you—'

Nico was still watching me. I wondered if part of his job involved interrogation because his gaze was like a laser. If I'd had a mirror I would have checked there wasn't a red dot on my forehead.

There was a long, pulsing silence and he continued to look at me as if something I'd said had answered a question lingering in his head.

'I'm not here for the jacket. We're here because Rosie invited us to join you for Christmas.'

CHAPTER FIVE

SHE WHAT?

My sister had invited him without telling me.

I didn't know whether to kill her or kiss her.

Kiara was looking anxious. 'It was kind of you to invite us both. Are you sure it's all right?'

No, it wasn't all right.

Why hadn't she told me?

Coward.

I turned my head to look accusingly at Rosie. I felt like yelling 'chicken' but then realized it would confuse people as she currently had her head buried in a turkey.

I produced what I hoped was a smile, but felt closer to the face I pulled when I was on the receiving end of the wax. 'You're welcome.'

'The food is going to be a while,' Rosie said brightly, 'so why don't you just go into the living room and get to know each other better. Chill out and play some games.'

Chill? I was boiling hot. And as for games—there were already enough games going on in this kitchen. Unfortunately no one had told me the rules.

One look at Rosie's face told me she not only thought she'd already played the first game, she was the winner.

She wafted past me and murmured under her breath, 'Happy Christmas. Enjoy your present.'

Nico was my present?

That was what she'd meant when she'd said it would be arriving later?

I wondered if she'd told him he was my gift. I sincerely hoped not, but knowing my sister she probably had.

I followed her into the living room, avoiding his gaze. Not that I was particularly shy or anything, but I'd been thinking about nothing but sex with him for the past four days. I wasn't confident that my eyes wouldn't light up like slot machines.

Thank goodness he couldn't read my mind.

He sat down on the sofa, nudging my laptop to one side. He'd abandoned Tom Ford, presumably because I was now in possession of half of it, and was wearing a pair of black jeans. They molded themselves to his long, powerful legs as if there was nowhere they'd rather be than snuggled against those hard thighs. I didn't blame them. In fact I envied those jeans. Through the gap in the neck of his shirt I could see a hint of dark hair against bronzed flesh.

I was just pondering the etiquette of accepting a gift who didn't know he was your gift, when he reached idly for my laptop.

'I don't normally work on Christmas day, but do you mind if I just check something?'

I opened my mouth to tell him to help himself when I remembered that not only had I not shut my laptop down the night before, but that the last search had been 'vibrator—the Niccolò'.

I flung myself across the room but it was too late.

He'd already opened it and I stood, marinating slowly in embarrassment for the second time in less than four days. It seemed I was destined to humiliate myself around this man. First he'd seen the outer me stripped bare, and now he was seeing the inner me similarly naked.

I was doomed.

'Nico can't stop himself checking the court cases.' Kiara walked across the room balancing the bowls of nuts and crisps my sister had given her. 'Normally he does it on his phone, but I unplugged his charger last night, so I'm in trouble.'

Nowhere near as much trouble as I was in.

Shit, shit, *shit*.

I waited for him to skewer me with one of his severe, disapproving looks, but he didn't. Instead he tapped the keyboard with those strong, clever fingers that knew exactly how to drive a woman crazy and checked whatever it was he wanted to check.

His expression didn't flicker. He was the most inscrutable man I'd ever met. In fact he was so calm and controlled, I wondered if maybe my memory was failing me. Maybe I *had* closed that page down. I must have done, or he would have said something or at least given me one of his looks.

The doorbell rang again and other people started streaming into our apartment, leaving me no opportunity to dwell on it.

It was a good job Rosie had bought those extra presents because pretty soon we were up to twelve people. I knew about eight of them, but it didn't really make any difference because I wasn't looking at them anyway. They might as well have not been there for all the impact they made on me. For me there was only one man in the room.

We popped bottles of bubbly, opened presents, then helped Rosie carry the food to the table. And all the time I was aware of Nico. Kiara had suddenly become the life and soul of the party, but he'd barely opened his mouth. I knew that, because I kept looking at it. I loved the shape of his lips and kept remembering how they'd felt as they'd moved over mine.

'I should give you your jacket.' I blurted the words out, wishing I had a tenth of his control.

'No hurry.'

That was all he was going to say?

The atmosphere was so tense that by the time my sister placed the turkey in the centre of the table I was hotter than any of the food.

Because our table was designed to seat eight at the most, twelve was a squash. I sat down at the end, because at least then I'd be up close and personal with just one other person.

Nico sat down next to me.

My heart bumped. I tried to work out if this was accident or design and decided he wasn't a man who did anything by accident. He didn't look at me and as usual there was nothing in his expression that gave me any clues as to what he was thinking. His arm brushed against mine. We were jammed together like atoms in a molecule. Anyone looking at us would probably have assumed it was lack of space that necessitated the closeness, but I knew differently.

I'd like to say lunch was delicious, but honestly I couldn't have told you what I ate because Christmas lunch was all about the man seated next to me.

When he reached across and forked turkey onto my plate all I saw were lean, bronzed hands and a dusting of dark hair on his forearms. He'd rolled his sleeves to the elbow. I guessed that was as close to casual as this man got.

'Enough?'

I looked at him blankly.

'Turkey,' he said gently and I blinked.

'Yes. Thanks.' What was it about a man's forearms? Although, if I were honest, it wasn't just his forearms. It was all of him.

He leaned forward to pick up a dish of potatoes and I saw the muscle flex in his powerful shoulders. Then he sat down again and this time he was thigh to thigh with me. Our legs might as well have been glued together.

I experimented and eased my leg away slightly, but his followed.

My heart swooped upwards like a paraglider hitting a thermal, taking my mood with it.

Rosie glanced at me. 'Is it good?'

'Oh, yes.' I focused on my plate even though I knew she wasn't talking about the turkey. 'Brilliant. *You're* brilliant.'

People were swapping stories about their Christmas traditions, but I didn't hear a word because I had this noisy, happy sound ringing in my head.

Nico was here.

Sitting next to me.

And whatever our relationship had been in the past, right now it was hot and electric.

I decided one of us had to say something or we'd

draw attention to ourselves. 'So what sort of lawyer are you?'

He reached for his glass, although I'd noticed earlier that he was drinking water. Maybe he was afraid his control would slip if he drank alcohol. 'A good one.'

'That's not an answer.' I turned my head to look at him and of course that turned out to be a mistake because his wasn't a face you wanted to look away from. I could have stared at him until I'd died of hunger, thirst or frustration, whichever came first. I could tell you at this rate it was going to be frustration.

And of course, he knew. 'You really want to talk about law?'

There ought to be a law preventing a man driving a woman this crazy.

His voice was so soft I knew no one else would be able to hear him.

The blood was pumping through my veins and I could still feel his thigh pressed hard against mine.

I was just about to make a second attempt at polite conversation, when I felt his hand slide over my thigh. The warmth of his palm pressed through my jeans and I almost jumped out of my seat with shock.

I could no longer pretend any of this was an accident or that we were fused together because of a lack of space. He left his hand there, as if testing to see if I was going to jump, jog the table and knock all the glasses over.

When I didn't move, he slid his hand higher up my thigh and no matter what anyone said about some men, I could tell you there was nothing wrong with his sense of direction. He knew *exactly* where he was going.

My stomach clenched. The excitement was almost

painful. The chemistry was off the scale. I didn't understand it, and I was good with all the sciences. I could explain nuclear fission but I couldn't explain this. What I felt made no sense at all to me, but that didn't stop me feeling it and also the frustration that came from being in public.

There always seemed to be something between me and sexual satisfaction. In this case it was denim and a room full of my friends.

I wished I'd worn a dress with stockings instead of skinny jeans and thigh-length boots, but he was obviously a man who didn't let obstacles get in his way because his fingers moved higher and higher until he was pressing right *there*.

I knocked my wine glass over. Fortunately I'd already drunk half of it, so we had a puddle, not a lake.

'Oh, *crap.*'

My sister threw me a look and a napkin. Then she turned back to her neighbour and continued the conversation.

Nico didn't move his hand, nor did he relax the pressure. As I said, obviously not a man to let anything stand in his way. I felt shivery and weak. The atmosphere between us was heavy, thick and so scorching hot I was surprised we hadn't set off the smoke alarm.

I decided I might as well make the most of the thigh-length boots and ran my foot up his calf.

'More turkey, Hayley?' A guy I knew vaguely from Rosie's gym smiled at me from across the table and I smiled back, shook my head and murmured an acceptable response. It was a surprise to me I could still string a sentence together because I was gripped by raw desire and the delicious friction created by Nico's clever, persistent fingers. The frustration was almost unbearable. I decided pleasure this good shouldn't be one-way and slid my hand up his thigh and covered him. If I'd needed confirmation that he felt the same way, I had it now. His erection was a thick, hard ridge under my hand, pressing through the constraining fabric of his jeans. For a moment I was tempted to pull that zip down, but I decided I'd had enough public exposure for one year.

'Answer me a question—' His voice was soft and just for me.

Given where my hand was, I was worried about what the question might be.

'Only the one?' I had millions I wanted to ask him, and then I remembered my resolution to have a sex-only relationship. I'd never done it before, but I was fairly sure a sex-only relationship involved—well, sex only. Asking questions about other things, particularly family, was a fast way of turning it into something I didn't want. 'What's your question?'

At the far end of the table Kiara was laughing with the man from Rosie's gym. Either Nico hadn't noticed, or he didn't care. Obviously he wasn't his sister's keeper.

'Are you broken-hearted?'

He'd asked me the same question at the wedding. I hadn't answered it. Why would I offer up something so personal to someone who disapproved of me?

But now—?

'No,' I croaked. 'I'm not broken-hearted.'

He turned his head and gave me a look that told me nothing. 'What time does your "friend Christmas" usually end?'

'It's been known to continue until New Year. Once we had a guest who enjoyed himself so much he stayed until we kicked him out on January 1. We were about to start charging him rent.'

His gaze dropped to my mouth and lingered there.

God, he was serious. I mean *really* serious. Most of the time I was pretty silly. My instinct was to joke around a lot, although I'd worked hard to rein that side of me in, especially around Charlie's family, who had made no secret of the fact they found my sense of humour inappropriate (and that was *before* I'd burst out of my dress at the wedding).

Nico confused me. I'd thought he disapproved of me, but here he was with his hand…where it was.

I sensed something lurking behind those layers of ruthless control, something dark layered under the poker face he presented to the world.

I wondered what his secrets were.

Everyone had secrets, didn't they?

I wouldn't have minded discovering a few of his.

For once I wished our apartment were bigger. I loved it, but it wasn't big enough for me to vanish to the bedroom without all twelve people around the table noticing. It was a miracle they hadn't already noticed what was going on under the turkey. It was a good job Christmas was chaotic.

I really should have helped clear the table, but honestly I couldn't stand up, let alone walk. All that gentle under-table stroking had driven me crazy. I was so, *so* close and the building desperation was killing me and yet still he was relentless, stroking and teasing until I had to clamp my thighs together to stop him.

I could feel him throbbing under my hand. Turning

my head to look at him I met his gaze and saw that his
eyes were darker than usual. Almost black. I shivered,
wondering what it would take to make him drop his
guard the way he had at the wedding. I'd never seen
him laugh, but it occurred to me I'd never seen him
show any other emotion either. Except desire. There
was no missing that. It simmered in the depths of those
black eyes and pulsed between both of us. I looked at
his mouth and remembered how it had felt when we'd
kissed. I knew that jaw would feel rough against my
palms, because I'd had my hands on it only days earlier. I wanted to have my hands on it again.

I was so absorbed by him I was only dimly aware of
my sister bringing in the Christmas pudding, a perfect
dome of alcohol-infused dried fruit brought as a gift
by one of our guests. Rosie had put holly in the centre, doused it in more alcohol and set fire to it in traditional British style. What wasn't so traditional was
that as she put it down on the table, the flame licked
one the napkins. It caught fire.

Nico was on his feet instantly. Calmly, he doused
the flames with a jug of water and then grabbed a pile
of napkins and mopped up the water before it could do
more damage. And all without ruining the pudding.

'Hey, quick work.' My sister looked shaken but she
smiled at Nico and then at me, as if she was approv-
ing my choice.

I was starting to approve of my choice, too. The
man might be a little uncommunicative, but he was
good to have around in a crisis. First my dress, and
now this. He wasn't a man who hesitated. And I liked
the way he helped my sister with clearing the table
before sitting down again.

I was surprised our little fire hadn't set off the smoke alarm, but Nico and I were producing far more heat than the flames on that pudding, so the smoke alarm was probably unconscious by now.

I'd stopped eating and so had he. I wished there was a way to make Christmas lunch go on forever because I didn't want today to end. But of course in real life good things always ended.

'We have to leave now.' He spoke softly so that no one else could hear, not that they were paying any attention to us anyway. They were too wrapped up in Christmas pudding and conversation.

'Of course.' I hadn't expected him to leave quite this soon and the level of disappointment appalled me. The whole idea of a sex-based relationship was to avoid these emotional lows. Clearly I was doing something wrong. 'I'm sure you and Kiara have lots to do.'

'I'm not leaving with Kiara,' he said calmly. 'I'm leaving with you.'

'Me?' My mouth was drier than overcooked turkey breast. The same couldn't be said for the part of me that was under his fingers. 'I can't leave. I live here. It's Christmas.'

He glanced at our friends, most of whom were by now laughing uncontrollably. 'They're happy. And I need to give you my gift.'

'You bought me a gift? You didn't have to do that.' I felt a little embarrassed because obviously I didn't have anything for him. Presumably he'd considered it an obligation to his host. 'Why didn't you just give it to Rosie when you arrived?'

'It isn't for Rosie. It's for you. It's personal.'

'You could give it to me here.'

'I don't think so.' He reached for his glass and I noticed that he was still drinking water. I wondered again whether this was all part of his determination to hang onto control. It scared me how badly I wanted to push him and rip it all back until I exposed the real him, but maybe that was because I'd been nothing but exposed in the past week, so it was definitely his turn.

'Why not?'

'Because my gift is just for you. Not to be shared.'

'How do you know it's something I want?' I jumped as someone popped a cork on another bottle of champagne. The movement increased the friction against his hand and I almost moaned.

'I know it's something you want, Hayley.'

'How?'

'Because you'd already typed it into a search engine on your laptop.'

I was so distracted by the sensations exploding through my body, it took a moment for his words to sink in.

When they did, I turned my head again.

His eyes were velvet dark and locked on mine. There was a faint gleam of humour there, and something else—something that made my stomach twist and spin and then drop like a stone from a high cliff.

'My laptop?'

He leaned closer. His lips brushed my ear. 'Did you manage to locate "The Niccolò"?'

Heat poured over me and warmth pooled in my pelvis. If he was waiting for me to respond, he was going to be waiting a long time. I couldn't form a word let alone a sentence. I made an inarticulate sound that drew Rosie's attention.

She frowned slightly, satisfied herself I didn't need the Heimlich manoeuvre and drew everyone's attention to herself by telling a funny joke that required sound effects and hand gestures.

Did I mention I loved my sister?

Nico didn't seem to care what anybody else at the table thought. He was focused just on me and it was the sexiest, most intense experience of my life. Charlie had looked over my shoulder most of the time, as if conversing with me was an irritation he had to endure. The boyfriend I'd had before him used to just start talking about himself.

I'd never had a man look at me the way this man was looking at me.

As if everyone else in the room was inconsequential.

'I don't know what you're talking about.'

His eyes were two shimmering pools of dark promise. 'No? Because I happen to know where you can find what you were looking for.'

God, his voice was sexy. And the way his breath warmed my neck. I quivered and shivered. 'You do?'

'Yes.' I could hear the smile in his voice and feel the sure, confident slide of his hand between my shaking thighs. 'But you'll have to come with me.'

'You're suggesting I leave my own Christmas party?'

'You haven't talked to anyone else since we sat down.'

A burst of raucous laughter brought me back to the present and I glanced at Rosie, who winked at me and raised her glass.

A different person might have scowled at the

thought of being left with the washing up, but Rosie wasn't like that.

She'd set this up for me.

This was my Christmas present.

I owed it to her to make the most of it.

Deciding that this was one gift I was going to unwrap in private, I pushed my plate away and turned to Nico. 'Let's go.'

CHAPTER SIX

HIS CAR WAS still the same low red Ferrari. A growling gas-guzzling trophy of Italian engineering perfection.

I wondered if I was supposed to play it cool and pretend I travelled in cars like this all the time. Then I remembered he'd seen me half-exposed in a torn dress and found my computer search. Cool had flown the nest. I sank into expensive leather and sighed.

'Do you realize this has a 4.5 litre V8 engine? They reduced the piston compression height as they do in a racing engine. Oh, God, I love it. I want to crawl all over it and lick it.' I restricted myself to stroking the dashboard. 'I suppose being Italian, you have to have a car like this. You're not compensating for deficiencies in your masculinity, are you?'

His response was a slow smile because of course I already knew the answer to that question. I'd eaten Christmas lunch with one hand on his masculinity.

It was the first time I'd seen him smile and it was worth waiting for. It pulled his mouth into a sexy curve that hinted at more hidden layers. I stared for a moment, fascinated. There was so much more to this man and I couldn't wait to uncover those parts—all of them.

This promised to be the best Christmas Day I'd had in a long time.

Glancing in the mirror, he pulled smoothly away from the curb and down the empty streets.

It was still snowing. The Ferrari should have been a nightmare to drive in these conditions, but he didn't seem to have any problems.

Nico Rossi was a man who seemed to take everything in his stride, be it split dresses, table fires or a lethal road surface.

'So I guess the ability to drive fast cars is in Italian DNA.'

Risking life and limb, I put my hand between his thighs.

'*Cristo*—' He breathed in sharply but kept his eyes on the road and his hands on the wheel. Impressive. As I said, this man had iron control. 'You didn't know Kiara and I were coming today. I assumed Rosie had discussed it with you.'

'No. She sprung it on me.'

Cursing softly, he pulled in to the side of the road, the movement so sudden I was surprised the airbag didn't smack me in the face. 'Tell me the truth.' He spoke through his teeth and his eyes were a dark flash of molten passion.

I couldn't believe I'd ever thought him cold. 'About what?'

'About how you feel. I need you to be honest.'

I had no problem with honesty. I preferred it, even though honesty meant exposing yourself. Not the split dress type of exposing—the other type. 'I'm in your car. That should tell you how I feel.'

'I just want us both to be clear about what this is.'

I'd forgotten he was a lawyer. 'You want me to sign a contract or something?'

He shot me an exasperated look and I shrugged.

'Sorry, just checking. If you expect me to read your mind, you'll have to give me more clues. You don't reveal anything about yourself. Most of the time I can't even tell whether you're happy or sad.'

'What about turned on?' His voice vibrated, low and sexy. 'Can you tell when I'm turned on?'

I thought about how he felt under my hand. 'Those clues are easier to read.'

'They're the only clues you need.' His gaze held mine. 'I want you.'

It shouldn't have turned me on to hear that, but it did. In fact it was exactly what I wanted to hear. I didn't want anything else.

I wondered if the Ferrari came with a sprinkler system because I was fairly sure I was going to burst into flames at any moment.

'Fine by me. My New Year's resolution is to just have sex without the complicated, totally-messed-up relationship part.'

His eyes narrowed, as if he didn't believe me and his scepticism didn't surprise me. Why would it? We could put a man on the moon, but apparently we couldn't convince the majority of the male population that a woman could want sex without needing to hear the L word. I didn't have any reason to believe Nico Rossi was different to the average man.

There was a long, tense silence. Snow drifted onto the windscreen.

'Tell me how you felt at the wedding.'

'Honestly? I can't really explain it. Obviously you're an incredibly good kisser. And you're good at other things, too. I was excited. Turned on. Exasperated that both our sisters chose to knock when they did—' I stopped, thinking I'd pretty much summed it all up.

There was a long, pulsing pause and then he breathed deeply.

'I was asking how you felt about seeing Charlie marry another woman.'

'Oh…'

So now instead of a sprinkler system I had humiliation, washing over my skin like boiling oil, seeping into my pores and heating me up until I thought I might vaporize.

I'd been telling him how strongly I felt about him and all the time he'd been asking about Charlie.

I'd revealed so much. *Too much.*

Which was the story of my life if you thought about it.

Metaphorically and literally, my whole life was a ripped dress.

'Right. Well, this is embarrassing.'

'No, it isn't.'

'Not for you, maybe, but you're not the one who just put herself out there.'

'You weren't broken-hearted?'

'If we're going for honesty here, then I'd like to know why you kissed me when you don't even like me. I'm all for sex with no complications, but self-esteem demands it's at least with someone who likes who I am.'

His gaze was steady. 'Did you really think I would have had my hand up your dress if I didn't like you?'

'You're a man. Men do that sort of thing all the time.'

He flipped on the wipers, cleared the snow from

his windscreen and pulled back into the road. 'Some men make decisions based on something more than a surge of testosterone.'

He shifted gears smoothly and the engine purred, loving his skilled touch. I sympathized.

I shifted in my seat so that I could look at his face. It was past six o'clock and anywhere else in the country it would have been dark, but in London it was as if someone had forgotten to turn the lights off. The place blazed like the runway at Heathrow airport. 'Are you angry?'

It was a moment before he answered. 'Thinking about you with Charlie makes me angry. Why the hell were you with him, Hayley? He constantly tried to make you someone you weren't.'

'That isn't true.'

'When you got this job, did he help you celebrate? No, he got drunk.'

And Nico had driven me home.

As my sister had reminded me, it had been Nico who had dropped me safely at my door.

My heart hammered against my chest. It felt like a wake-up call because he was asking me the question I should have asked myself right from day one. 'I know you disapprove of me.'

As usual his expression revealed nothing. 'You don't know anything, Hayley.'

He pulled up at a junction.

The lights were on red and I found myself looking at the flex of thigh muscle as he stopped the car. And then he turned his head and I glanced from his leg to his face. I felt like a teenager unable to stop staring at the best-looking boy in the class. Right at that moment no one else existed for me. We could have been the only two people on an alien planet where lights blazed and the streets were empty.

'I don't want to talk about Charlie.' His voice had a rough quality that rubbed over my nerve endings and made me shiver.

'OK.' It wasn't exactly an eloquent response, but it was the best I could manage with him looking at me like that.

'And just for the record, I can't explain what happened at the wedding either.' There was an edge to his voice. 'It wasn't like me.'

One look at Kiara's face had told me that.

Now I couldn't speak at all. My insides were quivery. Warmth spread through me because right now I was the woman he was with and I didn't care what had happened before or what might come after.

The lights had changed, but he didn't move and neither did I.

We were locked together by a shocking chemistry and a total inability to look away.

Honestly, whenever this sort of thing happened in the movies I rolled my eyes. Although admittedly in the movies the heroine was staring at someone like Ryan Gosling, which maybe made the whole 'struck by lightning' thing slightly more believable.

But I hadn't ever imagined it could happen in real life to an everyday person like me.

The connection was so intense and powerful I wanted to bottle it. I wanted to feel that same revved-up level of excitement for the rest of my life. Or maybe I didn't. I wouldn't be able to eat or sleep feeling like this.

I thought about *Groundhog Day* and decided if I could stay in a moment forever it would be this one, suspended in the blissful, almost unbearable excitement of what was to come without any of the trauma afterwards.

Maybe with my New Year's resolution, all my relationships would feel like this. I'd live the excitement, then walk away before the collapse part.

A horn sounded behind us and I realized we weren't the only people on the roads.

Nico swore softly and turned his attention back to the car.

He was driving towards the river and I realized I hadn't even asked where he lived. I didn't know where he was taking me.

We drove along the embankment, past the Albert Bridge. It was my favorite bridge in London. Elegant and floodlit, it sent sparkles of light over the inky black surface of the water below. When I was little it used to make me think of a woman putting on diamonds for an exciting night out. Rosie called it the Bling Bridge. I didn't believe in fairy tales, but if I did, this bridge would definitely have featured in mine.

We were in Chelsea and I expected him to drive south because I didn't know anyone who could afford to live here, but he suddenly swooped into an underground car park.

It was spacious and well lit, but away from the bright lights of the city, the truth suddenly hit me. I was with a man I barely knew.

The blood pulsed in my ears and then he reached across and undid my seat belt. 'It's cold. We should go up.'

Cold? I wasn't cold. I was burning hot.

I was also having second thoughts, despite reminding myself that the fact we barely knew each other was supposed to be a good thing. That was the *point* of emotionless sex.

And it wasn't as if he was a stranger. We'd bumped into each other on and off for years, just never really spoken. But honestly, how well did any of us ever really know anyone? My mum was married to my dad for fifteen years before she found out he was having affairs. She'd trusted him. I'd been with Charlie for ten months and he'd behaved in ways that made it obvious to me I'd never known him. All we knew about another person was what they chose to show us. You could only know someone if they let you know them.

His apartment was on the top floor and my jaw was also on the floor because it was the penthouse, complete with balcony and views over the river towards my fairy-tale bridge.

'Wow.' As praise went, it wasn't that eloquent, but it was all I could manage. Honestly, I was dumbstruck. How the hell could he afford this? 'What sort of lawyer did you say you were again?' He'd told me he was a good one. It was obvious he was a very, *very* good one.

'Do you really want to talk about work?'

His voice came from right behind me and I turned and saw that he was holding a bottle of champagne.

I was surprised. 'You didn't drink anything at lunchtime.'

'I knew I'd be driving you home.'

I licked my lips. 'What if I'd said no?'

'I was in possession of evidence that suggested you wouldn't.' His response was sure and confident. The

corners of his mouth flickered and he eased the cork
out of the champagne like a pro. By now I was so
jumpy and on edge that when it popped, I flinched.

'I don't see how a few words typed into a search
engine could be used as evidence. Several people had
access to that laptop, including yourself.'

He raised an eyebrow and poured me the sparkling
liquid into a tall, thin-stemmed glass.

I didn't want to be impressed, but I was.

Rosie and I only drank champagne if someone else
bought it and we never drank out of glasses like these.
It made it feel special. He made *me* feel special. I wondered what he'd thought of our apartment with its non-
matching plates and table designed to seat half the
number of people we'd squashed around it.

His home was all polished wood and soft leather.

'What are we celebrating?' I watched as the bubbles
rose and wondered what it was about champagne that
lifted the mood. 'Christmas?'

'You. Naked in my apartment.'

My tummy tightened. 'I'm still dressed.'

His eyes met mine and he handed me a glass. 'Not
for long.'

My pulse was racing and I lifted my glass. 'Merry
Christmas.'

'*Buon Natale! Salute!*'

Oh, God, Italian was a hot language.

We drank and the champagne fizzed in my mouth
and spread through my veins. Or maybe it was the
chemistry that was fizzing, but whatever it was I could
feel it all the way through me. 'The only Italian I know
is *Pizza Margherita*. And you're the first Italian man
I've met.'

The corners of his mouth flickered. 'I'm Sicilian.'

'Like Al Pacino.'

'Al Pacino was born in New York.'

Shut up, Hayley. 'I'll stop talking.'

'Don't,' he breathed and he turned to put his champagne glass down on the low glass table. '*Don't* stop talking. I like it.'

'You like it when I talk crap?'

'You're not talking crap. You're just nervous.' He removed my glass from my hand and I should have objected, not just because I was enjoying the champagne but because after Charlie I didn't want any man telling me when I could or couldn't drink.

'Actually—'

'I like it when you don't censor what you say and do.'

Just when I was ready to punch him, he said something like that.

'You didn't look as if you liked it when my dress gave way.'

'I didn't want all those wedding guests having heart attacks. I didn't think the hospital could cope with a major incident that close to Christmas.'

I was laughing and blushing at the same time because it was impossible to remember it without also remembering the moments we'd shared. 'I still don't know what happened.'

'The inevitable happened.'

'Not true. I'm not saying it hadn't crossed my mind but not in a million years did I really think it would happen.'

He paused. 'I wasn't talking about the dress.'

'Neither was I.' I was eye level with his throat and

I could see the dark stubble shadowing his jaw. I'd seen the Grand Canyon and Niagara Falls, but I decided there weren't many better views than this one. 'I just didn't ever see us together. I didn't think you liked who I was.'

'I didn't like who you were when you were with Charlie, because that wasn't the real you. You were constantly trying to rein yourself in.' He stroked his finger over my jaw, studying me and I gulped, wondering how he knew so much.

'Maybe you're not going to like the real me.'

'Hayley, I saw who you were the first time I met you. I spotted you across the room and you were so full of energy, so excited about your topic that I moved closer because I had to hear what you were saying.'

'Probably something boring.' The truth was I'd noticed him, too. 'It was at Charlie's party. Two years ago.'

'Twenty months, two weeks, two days.'

I choked on the champagne. 'Is that a lawyer thing? Remembering the tiny details?'

He looked at me steadily. 'Some things stay in my head.'

'You didn't talk to me that night.'

He gave a funny smile. 'You were talking to Charlie. And after that, I never saw that same excitement again. You reined it in.'

'Charlie didn't get too excited about satellites. Except the sort that gave him the sports channel.'

'He molded you into a different person and you were so anxious to keep the relationship going, you went along with it.'

Ashamed though I was to admit it, it was all true. I

suppose I'd needed to know I could hold on to a man if I'd wanted to. Turned out I couldn't.

Little by little, I'd subdued my real self. I'd stopped talking about my work when we went out and smiled when Charlie had talked about his. It had happened a bit at a time, so I barely noticed I was doing it. I was like the Arctic fox who changed his coat from brown to white in the winter to blend into his surroundings. On the inside I was the same, but on the outside I blended with the crowd. I'd never been in a relationship that worked on any other level. Never been with anyone, apart from my sister, who only ever expected me to be *me*.

But I had no idea how Nico knew that.

'I thought you disapproved of me being with him.'

He lowered his head and leaned his forehead against mine. 'I did. It was like giving a Ferrari to someone who only ever drives to the supermarket. A tragic waste.'

'No man has ever compared me to a Ferrari before.' To me, it was a compliment. And so was the way he was looking at me, as if I was the best Christmas present any guy could be given.

'He was wrong for you in every way.'

I wasn't going to argue with that. Especially not right now when Nico was moments away from kissing me. I wished I had a tenth of his control. Given that I'd been waiting all day for this moment I thought I was showing great restraint. I discovered I actually quite liked the slow, desperate build of anticipation and maybe he did, too, because instead of bringing his mouth down on mine, he gave a half smile and slid his fingers through my hair. It didn't matter what he did

with his fingers, which part of me he was stroking—
it always had the same effect on me. I'd thought about
nothing but being kissed by him for the past four days
and the wait was killing me. It didn't help that we'd
driven each other mad all day.

I broke first.

One moment I had my hand locked in the front
of his shirt. The next I was undoing buttons. Finally.
The big reveal. 'You saw me naked from the waist up.
You owe me.'

His mouth hovered close to mine, but still he didn't
kiss me. He was either a skilled torturer or he knew
everything there was to know about delayed gratification. 'I always pay my debts.' His eyes were half shut
and the way he was looking at me made my stomach
flip.

I had his shirt undone to the waist and my fingers
went all fumbly, mostly because I saw sex in his eyes.
I lost patience and yanked the shirt. Buttons skittered
and bounced over the pale wooden floor, but I was too
busy looking at the smooth, powerful contours of his
chest through the shadowing of dark hair.

*Oh, Santa, Santa, what have you brought me this
year....*

His eyes darkened. 'You just ripped my shirt.'

'Sorry.' Never in the history of apologies had an
apology sounded less sincere. I wasn't sorry at all, and
just to prove it I slid my hands slowly up his chest. I
felt hard muscle and the steady beat of his heart. 'You
saw me in a ripped dress, so now we're even.'

'You seem to have a thing about ripping clothes.'
The gleam in his eyes made it hard to breathe.

'It's Christmas. You're allowed to rip open your

Christmas presents. And anyway, I figured if you can afford to live here, you can afford another shirt.' I pushed the shirt off those muscular shoulders and sucked in a breath because there, curling over the top of his biceps, was a symbol inked into his flesh.

I think my heart might have stopped. It definitely did something strange in my chest.

'OK, well, that's—' I breathed and stared at it for a moment. Then I lifted my hand and traced it with the tips of my fingers. 'Surprising.' Not in a million years would I have expected this man to have a tattoo. 'I thought you were this ruthlessly controlled, conservative, Eton-then-straight-to-Oxford type.'

'Did you?' His husky question slid against my knees and weakened them.

I thought about the wedding, when I'd spent a good ten minutes staring at him acknowledging the raw, elemental quality that lurked beneath the beautifully cut suit. About that car journey, when the tension had almost fried both of us. I'd always known what lay beneath the surface.

'I guess I made assumptions.'

'People do that. They look and they think they know. And sometimes they don't look because they don't want to know.'

'Charlie—'

'I don't want to talk about Charlie any more.'

Neither did I.

I wondered how a man who never showed emotion could be so perceptive. So in tune with my feelings. It unsettled me. I was used to people believing in the person I presented to the world. I chose how much of myself I revealed. Discounting the day of the wedding where I'd revealed far more than I'd wanted to, I didn't show much.

I thought about all the parts of myself I'd never shared with anyone. Thoughts that were all mine and not for sharing.

'Tell me about the tattoo.'

'A tattoo is just on the surface. You and I are going deeper than that.'

I swallowed. *We were?*

'A tattoo isn't who I am any more than a ripped dress is who you are.' His mouth was closer to mine. I could feel the warmth of his breath against my lips.

I'd got used to thinking relationships were mostly fake and superficial, but this didn't feel either of those things. There was nothing fake about the way his tongue traced the seam of my lips. Nothing fake about the way his hands eased my hips into his, and certainly nothing fake about the thickness of the erection I felt throbbing against me.

I leaned forward and pressed my mouth to his shoulder. The tattoo shocked me because it was so unexpected. I'd always known there was so much more to him. I ran my fingers down the swell of hard muscle, feeling the leashed power under the dark ink of his tattoo. I heard the slight change in his breathing and could feel him fighting for control.

'You hold yourself back.' I thought about how ruthlessly he held himself in check and wondered what had made him like that. 'Who are you really?'

'Does it matter?' He cupped my face in his hands and his voice had a raw edge to it that was impossibly exciting.

I remembered my resolution to have uncomplicated sex with a hot man. They didn't come any hotter than Nico.

'No.' I silenced the questions in my head, telling myself they weren't relevant to the moment. 'I want you.'

The corner of his mouth tilted into the sexiest smile I'd ever seen. He might not smile often, but when he did he did it *really* well. His mouth hovered wickedly close to mine until I was afraid I might knock him over and damage him in my haste and desperation to finish what we'd started at the wedding.

And then finally, after days of my waiting and thinking of nothing else, he lowered his head and kissed me.

CHAPTER SEVEN

As I'D BEEN thinking of nothing else for days I thought my mind had probably exaggerated his skill at kissing. It should have been a disappointment. It wasn't. It was as good as I remembered. Better, because this time he was half-naked, too, and I finally had full access to his ripped body. His hand was hard on my back and I could feel the warmth of his palm pressing through my shirt, flattening me against him. God, he was strong. He had the body of a fighter. I knew. I'd seen plenty when I'd been to Rosie's gym and I knew this man could have kept pace with all of them.

After the almost intolerable build-up of the past few days I was desperate, but he kept it slow, torturing both of us with pleasure.

I moaned as his mouth slid to my neck. 'I hate to rush something so good, but I think I might need you to—' The words died as my shirt slid to the floor. I hadn't even felt him undo the buttons and he must have done it with one hand. I remembered what else he could do with his fingers and shivered in anticipation. He was smooth, skilled and in control whereas I just wanted to crawl all over him like a desperate puppy and lick his face. OK, not just his face. All of him.

I slid my hands down his chest (oh, my *God*), lingered over his hard abs and then moved to the snap of his jeans just as his hands parted my shirt.

His eyes darkened, but there was a glimmer of amusement. 'You're wearing a bra.'

'Of course.' I stared up at him, deadpan. 'I would never be seen in public without a bra, Your Honour.'

He traced the line of fur with one finger. 'I'm not a judge.'

'Everyone's a judge, especially where I'm concerned.'

'In that case, I'm going to declare you guilty.' His voice was husky and I found myself looking at his mouth. That wicked, sinful line of sensual torture. I didn't care that he rarely used it to smile. I wanted him to use it for other things and I wanted him to do it right now. I was at the point of explosion.

'If I'm guilty, then I'll take whatever punishment I have coming, but just get on with it. I'm ready to pay the price for my sins.'

'I like your festive bra, but it's going to have to come off.'

I didn't even feel his hand move but the silky bra slithered to the floor after my shirt. For the second time in a week Nico had an uninterrupted view of my bare breasts. Just for a moment I felt shy, which was ridiculous when you thought about how we'd got to this point.

Maybe it was because up until now it hadn't mattered what he thought of me.

I was totally hopeless at this unemotional sex thing.

I tried to focus on the physical.

'*Cristo*, you have the most incredible breasts.'

His voice was raw and the look in his eyes removed shyness.

'There are plenty of people who wouldn't agree with you. Like most of the guests at the wedding.'

'They all agreed with me, *dolcezza*. That was the problem.' His mouth was on mine and he powered me back to the sofa. I fell backwards, off balance in every single way, but he caught me and lowered me carefully, like those couples you see doing a very sexy tango. God, he was strong. Then he came down on top of me like a conquering hero, his hand on my thigh.

'I love your thigh-length boots,' he breathed, 'but they're going to have to come off, too. I want you naked. In fact I want *you*. Now.'

His words turned me on almost as much as the look in his eyes. All I could think of was him.

Us.

Together.

His hands were on my boots and I was about to give him instructions because they were really awkward to remove, when he slid them off my legs. When *I* did it there was loads of tugging and swearing and falling over and yelling for Rosie. He managed to do it in one perfect movement. Same with my jeans. Not a man to let anything stand in his way.

I swallowed. 'So you're obviously good at undressing women—'

'Let's just say in this case I'm motivated.'

I was naked apart from the red thong trimmed with white fur and I decided it needed some explanation.

'Rosie gave it to me for Christmas.'

'You look like Santa's sexy little helper.' He slid a

lazy finger over the fur. 'It looks much too hot to be worn indoors.'

It suddenly occurred to me that I was all but naked and he was still clothed.

'It's your turn. Strip.'

One eyebrow lifted. 'Are you giving me orders?'

'You give people orders all the time.'

Eyes mocking, he rose to his feet and stood there for a moment just watching me, legs spread, powerful chest on display and his hands on his zip.

'What do you want me to do, Hayley? Tell me.'

His use of my name made the whole thing more intimate. No matter how much I kidded myself, we weren't strangers. Far from it. We'd circled round each other for years.

As he slid his zip down, my eyes saw what my hand already knew and my mouth dried. The same couldn't be said for other parts of me. I was desperate. I squirmed on his sofa. 'Hurry up. This is an emergency.'

He undressed swiftly and gracefully, but that didn't surprise me. Everything about him was controlled.

Actually, not everything.

There was one part of him he couldn't control and that part was thrusting hard against a pair of black boxer briefs. I felt sympathy for those briefs. Containing an erection of that size just wasn't in the job description. If I'd needed evidence he felt the same way I did, I had it now.

My gaze fixed on the line of dark hair that disappeared beneath the waistband. I needed to see where it ended. 'You're going to be hot in those.'

He slid them off and I stopped joking. Honestly,

there was nothing to joke about. The atmosphere had snapped tight. I knew he felt it, too.

A muscle worked in his lean jaw and I could almost feel the battle he was fighting. Tension throbbed from those sleek, powerful muscles. With a soft curse he came back down on top of me, removing the last barrier between us so I was as naked as him. '*Cristo*, I promised myself I was going to make this last—'

'We've made it last for days.' I slid my palms down his back, savouring the feel of sleek skin over hard muscle. He was heavy, but I loved the way it felt having him like this. 'Longest foreplay ever.' The roughness of his thigh grazed the softness of mine as he pushed my thighs apart.

Our eyes were locked together. I could have looked at him all day. He was the most spectacular man I'd ever seen and if I was honest, part of me couldn't quite believe I was doing this. With him. Not that I undersold myself or anything, but men like him didn't come along very often. I knew, because I'd been looking for long enough. I wanted to grab my iPhone and take a picture, just so I could prove it to myself later. I wanted to post his picture on Twitter (would have got me at least 40,000 new followers, I can tell you) to increase my street cred, but then I felt his hand move lower and he stroked that quivering, damp part of me with sure, skillful fingers and I stopped thinking about anything except the moment, and he was a man who knew exactly how to make the most of the moment.

I think I moaned, and that was probably uncool but there was no way to keep the sound inside while he was touching me the way he was touching me. His fingers were knowing and clever, sliding over me and into

me in exactly the right way and I knew from the way
he was looking at me, at the way he kissed me, that
this was just the beginning of what we were going to
do together. I was about to tell him I couldn't stand it
any longer when he eased away from me and worked
his way down my body. He started at my neck and then
moved lower and by the time he'd teased and toyed
with my nipples I was squirming with desperation. It
was almost too much to bear.

When he moved lower, I shifted restlessly but he
clamped his hands on my hips and pushed my legs
apart, giving himself full access. The first stroke of
his tongue made me gasp and I soon discovered he was
as talented with that part of himself as he was with his
fingers. Each skilled flick of his tongue, each slow,
delicious stroke was designed to drive me crazy and
it did. I tried to move my hips, tried desperately to relieve the almost intolerable ache, but the hard grip of
his hands were holding me still. Not that he was hurting me, but it was obvious there was no way I was
moving until he was ready to let me go. I was totally
at his mercy and I'd never known excitement this intense. I needed to come, but he wouldn't let me. Deprived of any other outlet, I dug my fingers into the
soft cushions of his sofa.

'Please, *please*—' I couldn't believe I was begging. I'd never begged a man for anything in my life
and I knew I was going to be horribly embarrassed
later, but I seemed to spend my whole life in a state
of embarrassment around this guy, so I figured at this
point it wasn't going to make much difference. 'Nico,
I really need—' My words were disjointed, mostly
because his tongue was inside me, licking me shame-

lessly, and now he was using his fingers, too, so that my body was a mass of delicious, shivering sensation hovering on the edge of the incredible. And I was on the edge. Right on the edge. If he hadn't been holding me firmly I could have moved my hips and finished it myself. But instead of letting me do that, he eased away from me slightly, leaving me hovering between ecstasy and insanity.

'Tell me what you need, *dolcezza*.'

As if I wasn't already desperate enough, now he had to speak to me in Italian, the bastard. His Italian accent and the way he lingered over the word *dolcezza* almost finished me off.

'You know what I need—' I couldn't believe he could be so cruel, but then he put his mouth on me again and I forgave him everything. Every provocative slide of his tongue was designed to torment me— only, this time he gave me what I wanted.

It was the most intense experience of my life. Everything inside me tightened and then orgasm crashed down on me, the rush of pleasure almost agonizing. And still he held my hips, controlling everything I was feeling until I lay limp and weak.

I thought I heard him murmur, 'Merry Christmas, Hayley', but I could have imagined it.

Then he reached down and pulled something from the pocket of his jeans. I'd thought I'd never want to see a condom again after the wedding, but it turned out I was wrong.

I lay dazed, watching as he sheathed himself and then came down over me. I was worried I'd be too sensitive, but just looking at him made me want him again and I wrapped my legs around him and felt his hand slide underneath my buttocks, lifting me. My breathing was shallow and my cheeks were burning, but I didn't think the heat had anything to do with the flames flickering in the fireplace. It was him.

I was glad our first time was going to be this way because I wanted to look at him.

And he obviously wanted to look at me, too, because he kissed me again, holding my gaze as he shifted his position. I felt him against me, felt him hard and smooth against the slippery wetness he'd created and I held my breath. Still, he took his time. His mouth seduced mine, his hand was hard on my bottom and his gaze was locked with mine and finally he was inside me, sliding deep in a series of slow, expert thrusts. Oh, *God*. It felt incredible. I didn't think I could feel like this again so soon. He was hard and thick and I could feel him pulse inside me, feel his own battle to hold back the primal, primitive desire that had sunk its teeth into both of us. He stopped for a moment, his breathing unsteady and I sort of understood because I wanted it to last, too, but I was also desperate. I dug my fingers into the smooth, solid bulk of his shoulders and rocked into him. I felt the tension and strain in his muscles increase.

'*Cristo*, Hayley—' His eyes were impossibly dark and then he gave a groan and surged into me, and I knew he was as out of control as I was. He was deep inside me, moving with a perfect rhythm and I cried out because I'd never felt anything like it. Never. Until a few days before we'd never touched each other, and yet somehow he knew my body. He knew just how to move, how to touch me, how to adjust the angle and the rhythm of his movements so that I felt every inch of him. With each expert thrust he drove me higher and higher and all the time I could feel him, all of him, strength, power, masculinity and I moved with him, my hands on his shoulders and then buried in his hair.

He'd dimmed the lights, but the room was lit by the dancing flames of the fire and the glow of the city at night. We were surrounded by glass and the London skyline. It was like having sex outdoors, only without the risk of frostbite. Afterwards I realized that anyone with a pair of binoculars might have been able to see us from the apartments on the other side of the river, but I didn't even think about it at the time and neither did he. We were just too into each other.

The whole of me was trembling and held in a state of heightened suspension. I shouldn't have been this desperate, but I was, and so was he. He said something to me in Italian, his lips dragging along my jaw and then lingering on my mouth. Presumably he didn't expect me to answer him, which was a good thing because I wasn't capable of speech. I didn't know whether it was all the foreplay under the Christmas lunch table, whether this whole thing had been building since the wedding or whether this was sex Italian style (if so, I was emigrating), but I couldn't hold anything back. Feelings and sensations spread through me. It started somewhere I couldn't identify, deep in my soul, and then filtered and rippled through my body until I came in a glorious rush of pulsing pleasure. I felt myself tighten around him and heard him groan in his throat as he tried to hold on to control, but the ripples of my orgasm sent him over the edge.

I heard him curse, but he was lost just as I was, and in a way I was relieved his grip on control was as use-

less as mine. If he could have detached himself from
pleasure this intense I would have been worried.

We didn't stop kissing. Not once. Not as he thrust
hard, or as my body gripped his—we just kept kissing and his tongue was in my mouth and mine in his
and we just shared all of it. Everything. Every pulse,
throb, flutter, moan and gasp.

One of my hands was jammed into his hair, the
other clutching his shoulder, now slick with sweat,
and I lay for a moment stunned and shaken, just staring up at him trying to make sense of it.

I didn't know what was going to happen next.
After all, this level of intimacy was new to both of
us. I suppose part of me, the part responsible for self-
protection, was braced for him to just roll away. And I
suppose if he'd done that I would have said something
like, 'Well, I think "The Niccolò" is a product with a
future,' or something really glib that wouldn't reveal
how deeply the whole experience had affected me.

I thought that was probably what someone would
say after emotionless sex.

But he didn't roll away. He didn't pull away. Instead
he slowly, gently lowered his mouth to mine and kissed
me again. But it was different now. This was a different type of intimacy. It was slow, sexy with a hint of
gentleness that made my heart squeeze. I hadn't expected tenderness. Even as I felt myself melt, I felt a
faint flicker of panic. My heart was the one organ that
wasn't invited to this party.

This was where he was supposed to do that classic
man thing and say and do the wrong thing so that I
could flounce back to Notting Hill and spend the rest
of the night curled up with Rosie agreeing that men

weren't just from Mars—most of them were from a galaxy far, far away. But he didn't. He lingered over the kiss, pushed my hair gently back from my face and studied me for a moment and then rolled onto his side and pulled me against him. If he'd done that in my apartment we would have both ended up on the floor, but fortunately his sofa was bigger than ours. His arms held me in a possessive grip and it surprised me. I'd thought him cold and distant and had wrongly taken that to mean he wasn't good at intimacy. On the other hand I hadn't anticipated the tattoo either, which just proved I was clueless about this man.

Because I had no choice in the matter I stayed where I was, locked in the circle of his arms, my head on his chest. The differences between us fascinated me and I lay there, absorbing the contrast. My blonde hair draped itself all over him and mingled with the dark hairs on his chest. My skin looked creamy pale against the warmer tones of his. The inner skin of my thigh was soft against the hardness of his.

He lifted his hand and twisted a strand of my hair around his fingers and I wondered if he was noticing the differences, too.

I'd never been the sort to lean on a man, probably because when I was growing up I'd learned first-hand that leaning was a lethal sport that inevitably ended in serious injury. My mum had leaned on my dad and he hadn't exactly proved himself to be a sturdy stake. I'd decided right from the start I was going to stand tall by myself, so I was surprised by how good it felt to be held like this. I had to confess it made me feel safe, which made no sense at all because why would I suddenly feel safe when I hadn't ever felt unsafe?

He pushed my tousled hair away from my face and
tilted my chin so that I was forced to look at him. What
I saw there made my heart bump hard. I'd got so used
to thinking of him as remote and cold that the warmth
in his eyes wrecked me.

'*Bellissima*,' he murmured softly and I didn't speak
any Italian, but I knew he was telling me I was beautiful.

Sexual intimacy had turned into something else and
nerves were jumping in my tummy when he lowered
his head, delivered a lingering kiss to my mouth and
then stood up. He picked up my discarded hair clip,
handed it to me and then scooped me into his arms. I
locked my arms round his neck because although he'd
more than demonstrated how strong he was, I didn't
trust him not to drop me. I wasn't used to being carried
anywhere, but nothing about this night was normal.

'Why are you giving me my hair clip? Where are
we going?'

'It's a surprise.'

'After that disastrous wedding I've gone off surprises. I prefer to know what's going to happen so I
can prepare for it.'

His mouth flickered at the corners. 'We're going to
the bedroom. I don't want you to get cold.'

Cold? Was he kidding? I was so hot that if he'd put
a slice of bread on me I could have turned it into toast.

But it was evidence he didn't intend to end the evening yet, so I wasn't about to argue with his reason-
ing. And anyway, if I was honest, I was enjoying the
cuddle.

I tore my greedy gaze away from the strong lines of

his jaw to take a glimpse of his apartment. 'It's amazing. The view is incredible.'

He lowered me to the floor and I saw that his bedroom was dominated by—well, the bed. It was slightly raised and positioned to take advantage of the incredible views. Not that I expected to be looking at anything except him.

I pressed my lips to his shoulder. His skin was salty with sweat and he cupped my face in his hands and took my mouth with his. He coaxed my lips apart and kissed me and I was instantly desperate again.

I'd expected him to pull me onto the bed, but instead he took my hand and walked with me towards the window. I resisted.

'You really are an exhibitionist,' I began, but then he opened the glass door and I saw that there, on the deck with a perfect view of the River Thames snaking towards the city, was a hot tub.

'Pin your hair back up.'

It was freezing outside, snow still floating down like confetti, but he pulled off the cover and we slid into the hot water and honestly, it was the most delicious thing ever.

The guy knew how to live, I had to give him that. The heat seeped into my limbs and soothed. The scent was blissful.

Now I understood why he'd told me to pin my hair up. 'I love this part of London. Have you always lived here?'

'No.' Something about the way he said it made me glance at him, but his gaze was on my mouth and suddenly I didn't care if he'd lived here for five minutes or five years. We were both on a little seat under the water, my thigh pressed against the hardness of his. Far beneath us London was carrying on as normal, oblivious to our presence, and I wondered how the city could be oblivious to the amazing thing that was happening between us.

'It's a fantastic apartment. Where does Kiara live?'

'She lived here with me until a year ago when she started college. Now she rents somewhere with two friends. She wanted her independence.'

I was surprised he'd lived with his sister. This place had 'bachelor' written all over it. Perhaps she'd only moved in briefly. 'How long did she live with you?'

'Since she was twelve.' His voice didn't change, but still I sensed something different. Something complicated. I'd grown up with complicated, so I probably had sensitive radar. And I was good enough with numbers to work out that he must have taken on that responsibility at a young age.

'No family?'

'Just the two of us. How long have you and Rosie lived together?' He was changing the subject, but I didn't mind. I wasn't usually mad keen on talking about family either, but for some reason right now, with him, it felt comfortable.

'Pretty much all our lives.' I leaned my head back and gazed up at the sky. Snow was still falling, light, feathery flakes that dusted my hair and his. I skimmed my hand over the surface of the water, watching as they melted. 'There's only ten months between us. We shared a room when we were growing up. They almost split us up, but we objected.'

'Split you up?'

'Dad walked out when we were eight. They fought

over who was going to have us. All a bit crap if I'm honest. They thought it would make sense if each parent had one of us, but that didn't make any sense at all to us.' Rosie had once said it was like being the rope in a tug of war, but I didn't tell him that. Nor did I tell him about the time Rosie had hung on to me like a barnacle while Dad had tried to pull her away from me and carry her to the car. In the end he'd given up. They'd never tried to split us up again, but Rosie had insisted on switching her ballet classes to karate just in case.

'Hence the "friend Christmas"?'

'Rosie likes to create her version of the fairy tale.'

'Your sister is very generous. She invited half of London for Christmas lunch.'

'Friends are our family.' I slid deeper under the water. 'What would you have done for Christmas if you hadn't come to us?'

'Worked.'

'So I distracted you. Sorry about that.' My voice was smoky soft and he gave a mocking smile.

'If that's your sorry look, it needs work.'

I lowered my eyelashes. 'Better?'

'No.'

'You want me to beg forgiveness?' I remembered I'd already begged and felt myself colour. His eyes dropped to my mouth and I knew he was remembering the same thing.

'You're so sexy. Keeping my hands off you has been the hardest thing I've ever done.'

It was so not what I'd expected him to say I almost sank under the water. 'Really?'

His eyes gleamed with incredulity. 'You have to know that, Hayley.'

'Er—no. Why would I know that? You've barely ever spoken to me.'

'Exactly.' There was a hint of exasperation in his voice, as if we were talking about something that should have been obvious.

I thought about what Rosie had said on Christmas Eve. 'So if you felt that way, why didn't you ever talk to me?'

'You were with Charlie.'

'And I don't even know why.' I slid deeper in the water, forcing myself to think about stuff I'd avoided. 'Rosie and I have never been very good at relationships. Charlie seemed like the stable, traditional type. I suppose part of me thought if I was going to make a relationship work with anyone, it would be with someone like him.'

'Someone who would ignore the person you really are and sleep with your friend?'

'Thanks for reminding me.' I didn't even think of Cressida as a friend any more. Friends didn't do that.

'Does it hurt?'

I skimmed my hand over the surface of the water. 'No. Not any more. And if I'm honest, it was only ever my pride that hurt. I should have been heartbroken, but I wasn't. I suppose that should tell me something. Honestly, I'm just rubbish at relationships. My New Year's resolution is to have emotionless sex. That's why I'm here.'

'Right.' The way he was looking at me made my cheeks burn.

'You haven't told me what happened after I left the wedding.'

'I had to arrange a fleet of ambulances to transport all the men who had heart attacks.'

'*Don't*.' I shrank at the thought. 'I honestly don't think I can ever show my face in daylight again.'

'No one was looking at your face, so you're fine.'

I laughed, surprised by how easy it was to talk to him. It was like removing a pile of rocks from a river. Conversation just flowed, held back for too long.

'I haven't thanked you for rescuing me. Everyone else just stood there gawping. Even Rosie was useless. If it hadn't been for you, I'd still be standing there like a *Playboy* centrefold. You were very quick on your feet. What happened during the speeches?'

'Having seen your impressive breasts, Cressida was in a foul mood for the rest of the wedding, but it served her right for stealing your man in the first place.'

'I'm glad she stole him. If she hadn't, I wouldn't be here now.'

'Yes, you would. It was always going to happen.'

My stomach flipped. 'It was? How do you know?'

'Because I was going to make it happen.' Droplets of water clung to his shoulders. 'I was just waiting for you to come to your senses and realize he wasn't going to make you happy.'

'You were?'

'I was hoping you'd make that decision, not him. When *he* made it I was worried you hadn't had time to come to that conclusion yourself and that he'd hurt you.'

I thought about my job promotion party when Charlie had got drunk and not even offered congratulations. 'I suppose I hate giving up on things. It feels like failure. Anyway, it won't happen again. No more relationships for me. Just crazy sex. More of this. I didn't know this was going to happen. I didn't know Rosie had invited you.'

'I know. That was obvious when I walked into the kitchen and saw your face.'

I turned my head and looked at him. 'I'm glad she did.'

'So am I.' He leaned towards me, his gaze on my mouth. His hand slid between my thighs. It wasn't that long since he'd been inside me, but I desperately wanted him there again.

I lifted myself out of the water briefly—very briefly because the blast of freezing air over my shoulders was enough to convince me that under the water was better than out of it—and straddled him. I slid down so that my shoulders were under the water and saw he was watching me with that sexy, hooded gaze that made me want to do wicked things to him.

'You are the best Christmas present I've ever had—' I murmured the words against his lips and felt him smile. His hands were locked on my hips, preventing me from moving. His eyes glittered and his jaw was clenched.

'Let's go back inside.'

'Now?'

'Yes, right now. I want to see you. All of you, and I can't do that without giving you frostbite.' With his arm around me, he lifted us both out of the water and steadied me while he grabbed a towel.

CHAPTER EIGHT

WE LEFT DAMP footprints on his bedroom floor. He closed the door on the cold, the snow and the rest of the world and urged me into the master bathroom.

His arm was still around my waist, his mouth on mine and he reached out an arm and thumped a button on the wall, sending needles of hot water over both of us.

Finally I understood the true appeal of a walk-in shower. We didn't have to stop kissing. Water streamed over my hair and down my back and I think he must have altered the flow or I probably would have drowned. He removed the clip from my hair again and it slithered down my back in a damp mass. His hands slid over my body, leaving no part of me untouched and I did the same to him until I thought I was going to explode. I wanted to open my eyes and look at him, so I groped for the wall and switched off the water. Steam swirled between us. I was standing toe to toe with him and I leaned forward and pressed my mouth to his skin. Droplets of water clung to his flesh and with hands and mouth I explored his chest, the flat planes of his abdomen, the power of his thighs. I took my time, licking him, tasting him and then dropped to my knees. There was only one part of him I didn't touch and I heard the breath hiss through his teeth as

I teased him as mercilessly as he'd teased me. I came close several times, sliding my tongue over his warm skin, tantalizingly close to the hard length of him. In fairness I was willing to bet I was as desperate as he was.

'*Cristo*, Hayley—'

I glanced up and saw his eyes, inky dark and focused on me. A muscle flickered in his lean jaw. He was right on the edge of control and I kept him there for a moment, just to show I could prolong gratification if I had to. That I could match everything he did to me.

Of course I didn't last as long as he had.

I slid my tongue over him and then took him in my mouth, inch by glorious smooth, pulsing inch and I heard him groan something in Italian and felt his fingers lock in my hair. I wondered how I could ever have thought him icy cold. He was raw Italian passion—it was just that he managed to conceal it in public and I loved that. I loved that I knew a part of him others didn't. That he was like this only with me. I saw the *real* Nico Rossi. I preferred that version. More human. Hotter in every way. I used my lips and tongue, sucked and licked until he hauled me to my feet and pressed me back against the smooth, damp wall of his wet room, his eyes fierce and his breathing uneven.

I was breathless, desperate, but nothing compared to him. His eyes were fierce and he slammed his arms either side of me, caging me. Not that I needed to be caged. I wasn't going anywhere. I could feel the cool, smooth tiles pressing against my back and the hard heat of his body. It was the best kind of trapped I'd ever felt.

Water clung to his forehead and turned his inky

dark lashes to spikes. He was the hottest man I'd ever laid eyes on and I hooked my leg behind his hips, pressing him closer, not wanting any space between us. He lifted me easily and I wrapped my legs around him and my arms around his neck. Heat throbbed between us and his first thrust into my body made me cry out.

'You feel incredible—' His voice was raw, but at least he could still speak.

I was incapable of making any sound that wasn't an animal moan and I simply clung to his wide shoulders, kissing him as he drove into me. We came together in a simultaneous rush of ecstasy.

He lowered me gently to the floor, but didn't let me go, which was a good thing because my legs were like jelly.

The room was steamy and warm, presumably from the heat of the shower, but to be honest it could have been from us.

Still with his arm around me, he reached for another towel—he seemed to have an endless supply—wrapped it around me, kissed me gently on the mouth and led me through to the bedroom. My hair hung in a damp mass past my shoulders and he dried it carefully and then dropped the towel on the floor without looking at it. He was looking at me.

One thing I knew for sure—if this was emotionless sex, I was going to do it every single day for the rest of my life.

I KNEW IT was late the moment I woke. The sun was blazing through the glass wall of his bedroom, bouncing off the river like a million tiny diamonds.

I rolled onto my side and saw the bed was empty.

Then I smelled bacon.

I sat up in bed and realised my clothes were probably still scattered across his living room. Feeling like a burglar, I walked into his closet and found a shirt. One of his perfect white ones. Smiling, I slipped it on and it fell past my bottom and over my hands. I rolled the sleeves back, raked my fingers through my hair and walked in the direction of the delicious smells.

He was standing with his back to me, but he turned the moment I entered the room. He'd pulled on his jeans but nothing else and I stared at his chest and wondered how I could possibly want to drag him straight back to bed after the night we'd spent.

I wasn't any good at morning-after conversations and I gestured towards the door, conscious that I was naked under his shirt. 'I should probably get going—'

'Why?'

I tucked my hair behind my ear. 'I thought you might have things to do today.'

'I have.' He flipped the bacon. 'And I plan to do them with you.'

'Oh.' My stomach curled. A night with him hadn't cured me of anything. I found myself staring at his shoulders and the lean, athletic lines of his body. He was the hottest guy on the face of the earth.

'Unless you think Rosie needs you?'

I watched the way his biceps flexed as he reached for a plate. 'She's working today. Christmas Day is the only day of the year she doesn't train. But I should text her.' Dragging my eyes away from sleek male muscle, I wandered through to the living room. Light poured through the windows, reflecting off glass and polished surfaces. Outside the sky was a perfect winter blue and the sun sparkled on the surface of the river.

I found my phone, sent my sister a text thanking her for my Christmas 'gift', which I had no intention of returning for a refund, and then stood for a moment, distracted by the view, thinking about the night we'd spent.

'Coffee?' He had the sexiest voice I'd ever heard and I turned and saw he'd put two plates on the table and was now holding out a mug to me.

'Thanks.' I took it and curled my hands around the warmth, even though his apartment was a perfect temperature. 'I love looking at the river.'

'Me, too.' He hadn't shaved and his jaw was darkened by stubble. 'That's why I chose this place. Are you hungry?'

'Starving.' I hadn't eaten since the turkey and we'd done some serious exercise. 'So you can cook.'

'I cooked for my sister for years. She's still alive.' He handed me a plate piled with fluffy scrambled eggs and rashers of crisp bacon and I carried it over to the glass table by the window.

My stomach growled. 'If I had a view like this I'd never go to work.'

'You're not working this week?'

'Officially my department is closed until January 2, but that doesn't stop the emails.'

'You're still loving your work?' He sprawled in the chair opposite me and suddenly the view had serious competition. I picked up my fork, cautious about answering. Thanks to Charlie I was programmed not to talk about my work.

'It's fine, thanks.'

'I remember how excited you were when you got the job.'

And I remembered he'd been the only one to ask questions. 'It's exciting and the people are—' I broke off, reminding myself he was probably just being polite, but then I realized he was still listening and looking at me, not at his watch or over my shoulder as Charlie had always done. And because of that I found myself telling him everything I was doing, and the more I talked the more enthusiastic I was until I realized I'd cleared my plate and must have bored him rigid. 'Sorry.'

'For what? That is the first time I've seen you that enthusiastic since that first night we met.' And he didn't look bored. He looked interested and he asked me a few questions that proved he was as bright as he was spectacular looking. 'I'm pleased it's working out. So NASA isn't going to get you yet.'

I blushed, thinking about that awful dinner when everyone had talked about their hopes for the future and I'd confessed I wanted to work for NASA. Charlie had mocked me (I think his exact words were 'Apollo Hayley—God help us all'). It wasn't ladylike to be interested in rockets and jet propulsion (although frankly, since that hot encounter with Nico at the wedding I'd though of nothing but thrust, and not the sort taught by physics teachers).

I changed the subject. 'Tell me the history of the tattoo.'

He drank his coffee and for a moment I thought he wasn't going to answer.

Then he put his mug down. 'We moved from Sicily to London when I was ten. My English was terrible and—' he dismissed it all with a shrug '—let's just say school was hell, so I stayed away.'

'Really? I imagined you being a straight-A student.'

'That part came later. Back then, I was out of control.'

I eyed the tattoo wrapped round hard bulge of his bicep. 'So that was that when—?'

'That and other things.' His tone was flat. 'I was sixteen when my father died and Kiara was taken into foster care. I argued that I was her only family and that we should be together. Of course no one listened.'

I put my fork down, knowing how I'd felt when my parents had tried to separate Rosie and me. 'What did you do?'

'I grew up. I worked out what sort of job would make sure I got Kiara back and decided I had to be a lawyer because they earned good money and knew how to argue.' His smile mocked himself. 'I went back to school and worked every hour of every day. I got a scholarship to a top school. I was a social experiment—kid with a brain but no income, let's give that a try.'

'That must have been tough.'

'Tough was seeing my sister in a foster home. But they were kind people and they helped both of us.'

'And you did it. You made a life for both of you.' I mentally compared him to my dad, who'd left us. 'You did a great job. She's confident and charming and thinks you're the best.' It explained the bond I saw and the respect she showed him.

'It was hard letting her move into an apartment with her friends.'

'Independence is a good thing. And I'm glad you did,' I said softly, 'or we wouldn't be on our own now.'

His eyes met mine and then he stood up and pulled me to my feet.

'Let's make the most of it.'

WE DIDN'T LEAVE the apartment for five days. Most of that time was spent in bed having amazing sex, but also talking and laughing as we swapped stories.

I told him about the time I'd built a rocket in the kitchen and made a hole in the ceiling. He told me how he'd blown up the toilets in school using sodium taken from an unlocked chemistry lab.

I still couldn't believe how much this cool, controlled guy had hidden in his past. I was thirsty to know more. Favourite band, favourite drink, best place he'd visited... 'Tell me your most embarrassing moment ever.'

He rolled onto his side and looked at me from under those thick, dark lashes. 'I once went to this wedding where the bridesmaid burst out of her dress—'

Laughing, I pushed him onto his back and straddled him. My hair slid forward, covering us both. 'If that hadn't happened we wouldn't be here.'

'Yes, we would.' His hands were in my hair. 'But I was planning to make my move *after* the wedding, not during. I was going to persuade you to cry on my shoulder.'

'I'm not much of a crier.' I lowered my head and kissed him, my mouth lingering on his. 'You're so sexy. Say something to me in Italian.'

'*Pizza Margherita.*'

I giggled, but the crazy thing was he even managed to make *that* sound sexy.

My phone beeped. I ignored it.

'Say something else.'

'*Il mio vestito è strappato.*'

'What does that mean?'

'My dress has torn.'

And I was laughing. Laughing in bed with a guy I wanted to know more about. I wanted to know everything, and finally I reached across to read my text from Rosie: *five days in bed with the same guy isn't emotionless sex.*

And I stopped laughing and realized with a flash of panic that I wasn't supposed to want to know more. Emotionless, unattached sex should be exactly that, but somehow over the past five days I'd managed to form an attachment.

I was in trouble.

CHAPTER NINE

'THIS IS YOUR FAULT.' I stopped eating Nutella out of the jar and poked the spoon towards my sister. 'You invited him here for Christmas.'

'Yes. Christmas! I didn't expect you to go home with him and stay until Easter. I was about to report you to the police as a missing person. What the hell did you do for five days?'

I grinned and she rolled her eyes.

'Really? So he's even hotter than he looks. Way to go.'

I abandoned the comfort eating and slumped back against the sofa. 'I promised myself I was done with misery.'

'Sex with him was miserable?'

'No, it was incredible! But now I can't stop thinking about him. Crap.'

And it wasn't just the sex I was thinking about. I kept picturing the way he looked asleep—those lashes shadowing his cheeks, strands of dark hair sliding across his forehead. I thought about the hours we'd spent talking. The things I'd told him. Things I hadn't told anyone else.

I'd discovered intimacy wasn't just about getting naked with someone.

Bathed in panic, I sprang to my feet. 'It was supposed to be just sex. Emotionless sex.'

'Right. Emotionless sex that lasted five days.'

I paced across the living room and then turned to her, desperate. 'What am I going to do? I need to forget him straight away and move on.'

'Is that really what you want?'

'Absolutely. Definitely. No emotional involvement.' I didn't tell her I was worried it was too late for that, but she probably knew because she stared at me for a moment and then sighed.

'OK, well, the good news is that it isn't New Year for another six hours, so you haven't blown your resolution. You can start fresh at one minute past midnight. I've got VIP tickets to The Skyline. Tonight we are going to party.'

'The Skyline?' It was my turn to stare. 'How did you manage that? Their New Year's Eve parties are legendary.'

'I meet a lot of people at the gym.' My sister looked smug. 'We will have a great time and you can forget all about him.'

I knew I wasn't going to forget all about him.

I wanted to ask if she'd really forgotten He Who Must Not Be Named, but I didn't dare. 'Will anyone we know be there?'

'Yes, a whole group of us and you are going to hold your head up high and wear your favorite black dress because it makes you look fabulous.'

'Great. Let's do it.' I ignored the part of me that just wanted to be back in Nico's apartment. 'It will be my first public appearance since I exposed myself (I didn't count Christmas). Might as well make it high profile.'

I did love my black dress. It had tiny crystals sewn into the fabric and shimmered when it caught the light.

I'd found it in a charity shop in Notting Hill, otherwise I never would have been able to afford the label. It was brand new. Still had the tags on it. The owner told me that the woman who had brought it in had fallen in love with it and bought it, intending to slim into it. Fortunately for me, she hadn't.

Rosie was right. It was the perfect dress for tonight.

I presumed my lack of excitement was caused by the prospect of meeting so many people who had seen me half-naked.

'We're going to get ready together like we always do, and while we're doing that you can tell me everything.'

And because she was my sister and this was what we did, I did tell her everything. How it had felt. How *I* had felt. And how I felt now, which was totally crap if I was honest.

Getting ready to go out together should have been fun. Rosie opened a bottle of champagne left over from Christmas, but it reminded me so much of being with Nico.

'Are you nearly ready?' My sister was wearing a velvet skater dress with mesh at the sides and no back that looked perfect on her toned body. Her blonde hair was loose around her shoulders, a little messy, but that made it all the sexier. She wore a pair of vertiginous heels on the ends of those incredible, kick-boxing legs.

I blinked. 'Wow.'

'Wow yourself.' She eyed me and smiled. 'I predict emotionless sex will begin at five seconds past midnight. Let's go. The cab is here.'

I wished I could have felt more excited about the night ahead. It might have been easier had the cab not taken the exact route along the river Nico had taken when he'd driven me to his apartment on Christmas Day.

'This is where he lives.'

'In Chelsea?' Rosie craned her neck. 'Colour me impressed.'

She would have been even more impressed if she'd known how hard he'd worked to get to this point and all the sacrifices he'd made for his sister, but I wasn't ready to talk about any of it. Nor was I supposed to be talking about Nico.

We arrived at The Skyline and took the glass elevator to the top floor.

The views of London were incredible and everyone was in party mood. Everyone except me.

Rosie handed our coats over and frowned at me. 'You OK?'

'Great!'

We saw a crowd of our friends and joined them. The ones who hadn't accepted invitations to the wedding (because Charlie had alienated most of them) wanted to know if the rumours were true. Naturally when they heard that they were, they all wished they'd been there to 'support' me. Yeah, right.

'Nice one, Hayley.' Grinning, Rob put his arm round my shoulders and suddenly I was grateful for my friends. Friends were like shock absorbers. They made the bumps hurt less.

I saw Rosie watching me and tried to look as if I was having a good time, but of course she knew I wasn't.

'You'll forget him in time,' she murmured, handing me another glass of champagne. 'You wake up every day and one day you'll find it's stopped hurting.'

'Is that what happened with you and Hunter?'

Oh, God, I'd said his name. I'd gone five years without slipping up and now it had tumbled out.

I was dead.

My sister was going to kill me, right here on the dance floor on New Year's Eve.

I stood rigid, not knowing where to begin with my apology, when Rosie leaned in and hugged me.

'If he walked back into my life right now this minute, I wouldn't even notice him.' She whispered the words in my ear and then tapped her glass against mine and drank. And drank. And then helped herself to another glass and drank that, too.

I was about to point out that if Hunter walked back into her life now there was no chance of her noticing him because she'd be unconscious, but she slammed down her empty glass and grabbed my hand.

'Sister time. Let's dance.'

We loved dancing together. Considering what she could do with those legs of hers, Rosie was quite restrained. Half the men in the room were looking at her. Quite a few of the others were looking at me, but I was glad to be dancing with my sister. To be honest, I wasn't interested.

Then I looked up and saw him standing in the doorway.

Nico Rossi.

He hadn't seen me, but he was looking round the room, searching for someone. He was wearing a suit. It looked like the Tom Ford, only this time his shirt was black. As always he looked smoking hot, even more so now I knew how it felt to be with him.

An explosion of excitement and joy was followed by blinding panic.

I didn't think I was up to seeing him spend New Year's Eve picking up another woman and already I could see heads turning because he was the sort of guy who eclipsed every other man in the room without even trying.

I was in such a sorry state I didn't even realize I'd stopped dancing until Rosie took my arm and hauled me off the dance floor and behind a pillar.

'I have to get out of here,' I babbled. 'I'm really sorry to ruin your evening, but I'm going home.'

The music was throbbing and pounding and I saw her lips move, but I couldn't hear her and she rolled her eyes and dragged me out onto the terrace where everyone would gather to watch fireworks over the Thames at midnight.

'Breathe.'

'I'm going to grab a cab.'

'You are not leaving.'

'I have to.'

'Why?'

'Because—' I breathed and sent clouds into the freezing air. 'Because I can't bear to watch him picking up another woman. I can't bear to think of him with someone else.'

'And doesn't that tell you something?'

'Yes! It tells me I totally fucked up my New Year's resolution before the first chime of the clock!'

'So maybe you should rethink your resolution.'

I thought of all the pain and agony that went with relationships. The hope and then the horrible let-down. 'No. I'm just not putting myself through that again.'

'Through what? You just spent five days in bed with the guy. *Five days.* You laughed. You talked. He listened to you, which is more than Charlie ever did. He *likes* you for God's sake—'

'He's come here because he's looking for a date.'

'He's looking for *you.*' She said it quietly. 'Hayley, this super-hot guy is walking across the room right now looking for you and you are *not* going to hide.'

'I'll mess it up. Look what happened with Charlie.'

'Charlie is a dickhead,' Rose said calmly. 'You picked him because— Well, frankly I don't know why you picked him. We both know that when it comes to relationships our psychology is a bit warped, but he was totally wrong for you and Nico isn't. You two have something. Don't throw that away.'

'He probably isn't looking for me. I'm leaving and if you love me you'll let me go.' I winced as her hand locked around my wrist. Honestly, if the police ever ran short on handcuffs they could use my sister.

'I love you,' she said sweetly, 'which is why I am not letting you go. I'm not going to let you blow this.'

'I'm scared.'

'Yeah. I get all that. But it's OK to be scared, as long as you do it anyway.'

I thought about pointing out she hadn't done it since Mr You Know Who had broken her heart in two, but I decided that mentioning his name twice in one evening after five years of silence on the subject was a risk I wasn't prepared to take. And anyway, this was my panic. I didn't want to share it. 'He'll mess me up.'

'Maybe he won't.'

I'd never heard my sister sound so serious. 'What's

happened to you? You were the one who thought my New Year's resolution was a good one.'

'That was before I saw you with him.' She took a deep breath and smiled. 'If you run away from Nico Rossi then you are batshit crazy.'

I made a sound that was halfway between a laugh and a sob and saw Nico standing in the doorway. Those dark eyes were fixed on my face and he didn't glance left or right at the women who were staring at him hopefully.

Rosie released my wrist and my blood had a silent party, relieved to finally be able to flow around un-interrupted. 'Excuse me. There's a good dance floor going to waste,' she murmured and slid past him with a smile.

Nico nodded to her, his gaze still fixed on me.

There was nowhere I could go. I was trapped on the terrace and now I was shivering. It had stopped snow-ing, but the air was freezing.

He strolled across to me, removed his jacket and draped it around my shoulders. 'I thought you might be in need of a jacket.'

It felt warm and familiar and smelt like him. My tummy tensed. I was terrified I was going to give away how I was feeling. It had just been sex. I'd bro-ken our rules. I felt like a snail without its protective shell, exposed and just waiting to be crushed under someone's heavy boot.

'What are you doing here?'

'I came to find you.' He sounded so sure and con-fident. 'There are things I need to say. Preferably be-fore the clock strikes midnight.'

'Why? Does your Ferrari turn into a pumpkin at midnight?'

He didn't smile. He was too focused on me. 'I was ready to ask you out when you started going out with Charlie.'

Sound and people washed past me. I was oblivious to all of them. 'You were?'

'I told you I was ready to cross the room and talk to you, but I wasn't fast enough and for that I had to suffer watching you with him for ten long months. And then I had to watch you afterwards, coping with the fact he'd screwed your friend.' A muscle flickered in his jaw. 'Seeing you with him was like watching a car crash in slow motion. I just wanted to push you out of the way before you were crushed by it.'

'Nico—'

'He undermined you at every possible opportunity. That night in the restaurant when he put you down in front of everyone—' His voice was thick with anger and I wondered how I could ever have thought him cool and controlled. With me he was anything but.

'He didn't like me talking about work,' I muttered. 'He found it boring, especially on a night out.'

'Hayley, you threatened him. He wanted to be with someone who made him feel bigger, not an equal. He put you down and instead of bouncing up you stayed down. He stopped you being you.'

It was true. 'But that was my fault. I was trying to make it work.'

'How can a relationship work if you don't like each other as you really are? How can that sort of relationship be anything but false?'

It was a fair question. 'I was surprised you agreed to be his best man.'

'Why do you think I did that, Hayley?' There was something in his voice I didn't understand. An urgency that made no sense. 'Charlie and I have barely spoken since that night he got drunk and I drove you home.'

'Then why—'

'I agreed because he told me you were a bridesmaid. At first I didn't believe him. I couldn't *believe* they'd asked you to do that and I couldn't believe you'd agreed.'

I shifted awkwardly. 'You were worried I'd screw it up for them?'

'No. I was worried you'd be very hurt.' His jaw was tight. 'I was worried you'd fall apart at the wedding and need someone to look out for you. I was there because of you.'

I felt a lump in my throat. 'Me?'

'You asked why I agreed to be best man. That's why. You were the reason.'

'You—' I gulped. 'You kept looking at me throughout the ceremony. I thought you disapproved.'

'*Cristo*—' He dragged his fingers through his hair, exasperated. 'I was watching you to make sure you were all right. How could you not have known that? I was afraid you would fall apart.'

'I fell apart in a big way.'

'I must admit I hadn't expected it to be quite that literal.' His eyes gleamed. 'You looked so horrified I just wanted to get you out of there.'

'I've been checking YouTube for the video,' I confessed. 'There has to be one.'

'There was. But no one is going to upload it, I made sure of that.'

'You did? How?'

He stroked his thumb slowly over my lower lip. 'Let's just say I used lawyerly intimidation.'

I felt weak with relief. 'I knew there had to be a reason why no one had posted it. I had no idea it was you. You—you said I made bad decisions.'

'Dating Charlie was a bad decision. Agreeing to be their bridesmaid was worse.'

And I'd had no idea that was how he felt. But suddenly I was seeing it all differently. The way Rosie had seen it. 'You were always there when I needed someone. You gave me your jacket, you drove me home when Charlie was drunk and acted like a dickhead, you gave me multiple orgasms when I thought I was going to die of frustration—'

'I want so much more than your thanks.' He cupped my face in his hands and my heart was pounding so hard I was surprised people couldn't hear it over the music.

'You do?'

'Yes. I want you. And I really do mean you—' His fingers bit into my head and his eyes were fierce on mine. 'Not a version of you I've made up to suit my own needs, but the real you. The you I saw that first night. The clever you. The you that knows about engines and wants a job with NASA. The you that can add up endless numbers in your head as a party gimmick. The you that loves llamas and would do anything for her sister. The you I've thought about every night for twenty months, three weeks and one day.'

I couldn't breathe. 'Nico—'

'The you that would turn up at your ex's wedding because you're too proud to tell him he's a bastard. The you that would wax a turkey and search for "The Niccolò" on your laptop—'

'All right, enough—' Blushing furiously, I glanced around, but everyone was too busy gearing up for midnight to take any notice of us. But I'd had enough public humiliation for one year, so I grabbed his hand and dragged him back inside into a quieter corner. 'My New Year's resolution was to have emotionless relationships. Just sex and hot men.'

'I know. But it's not New Year yet.' His mouth was close to mine. 'You still have about four minutes to make a different resolution. Do it, Hayley.'

I stared up at him and what I saw in his eyes made me dizzy. 'What do you suggest? And I won't give up chocolate and I'm not keen on ditching alcohol either.'

'How about giving up having relationships with men who want you to be someone you're not?' He spoke softly, his eyes gentle. 'How about starting the New Year deciding to be you and enjoy it? How about coming back to my place and starting the New Year as we mean to continue it—in bed, in the hot tub, together.'

It was as if someone had kicked my knees. I wanted to slide to the floor.

Everyone was gathered on the terrace waiting for the first chime from Big Ben.

Across the room I could see Rosie with the rest of our friends, all linked together, waiting for the countdown to New Year. We exchanged looks and she smiled. I knew she was thinking I'd be crazy to turn my back on something that felt this good.

I agreed with her.

I slid my arms round his neck.

'The last five days were the best time I've had. Ever.' I heard Big Ben chime and people started to count. My eyes were fixed on his. This felt like so much more than the start of a New Year.

'For me, too.' He spoke against my lips and I smiled.

'Do I get permanent access to your Tom Ford?'

'You seem to be wearing it most of the time anyway.'

The clock was still chiming. I'd lost count, but everyone was gathering on the terrace, bumping into us in their haste to get the best view.

A final chime, loud cheers and then an explosion of fireworks and the London skyline lit up.

Nico kissed me, slowly and thoroughly, oblivious to everyone around us and there were definitely more fireworks inside me than there were outside. Finally, he lifted his head. 'So what's your New Year's resolution?'

For the first time in a long while I felt like me. Really me. I realized that this was my life and I could live it the way I wanted to live it. I didn't have to be someone I didn't want to be. I was allowed to have dreams and feel excited about my future. And I wanted Nico to be part of that future.

I smiled up at him. 'Let's go back to your apartment and I'll show you.'

* * * * *

Cara Lockwood is a *USA TODAY* bestselling author of eleven novels, including *I Do (But I Don't)*, which was made into a Lifetime Original Movie. She's written the Bard Academy series for young adults, and has had her work translated into several languages. Born and raised in Dallas, Cara, now divorced, lives near Chicago with her two beautiful daughters. When she's not writing, she keeps busy running 5K races for charity, kayaking and scuba diving. Find out more about her at caralockwood.com or follow her on Twitter, @caralockwood.

BOYS AND TOYS
Cara Lockwood

For Michael Dean

CHAPTER ONE

LIV'S HEART BEAT madly as she stood in the living room of the upscale penthouse, dressed in her work uniform of a push-up leather corset paired with sky-high stilettos. Her almond-shaped eyes, lined with smoky gray liner, focused on the man in front of her, a thirtysomething day trader wearing a Lacoste polo and faded jeans. He looked down at her hands, eyes wide, as she clasped the shaft, running a finger sensually over the top, causing his mouth to drop open in a small *O*. She knew she had him right there, in the flick of her bloodred nail over the tip. He'd be all hers.

"How much again?" he asked her, sounding nervous.

"Sixty," Liv Tanaka said brightly, her pouty red lips curving up in a smile. They both stared at the enormous vibrating purple dildo she held in her hand.

"I'll take it," he said, nodding vigorously, and the whole room laughed. Some bachelor party guests hooted and sent wadded-up napkins Paul's way. Paul, the groom-to-be, flushed a deeper shade of red, helped along by the beers he'd already drunk in the confines of his luxury penthouse on Chicago's Gold Coast. Still, he happily handed over a bunch of twenties to Liv, who rolled them up neatly and put them down the front of her corset. She may have come dressed as part-Asian Elvira, but she definitely showed that 100 percent sex sells.

"That'll make Carrie happy!" one of the other guys shouted.

"Careful, Paul, she might want to marry that instead of you!" the best man said, and the room roared with laughter again.

"Why is it *so big?*" Paul lamented, as he held an oversize vibrator in his hand.

"You feeling intimidated, Paul?" the best man joked.

Conversation happily buzzed as Liv went about showing her wares: dildos, edible panties, flavored oils. She wore a short skirt, as per usual, and her legs were bare. She could feel the eyes of some guys on the ever-rising hem of her spandex skirt, but the partygoers, all in their early thirties, were mostly behaving themselves, and she was beginning to think her reservations about taking on a bachelor party were unfounded. Up until now, she'd said no to most of them—she preferred to be in a roomful of girls or a small number of couples. She didn't trust a room of all boys to behave themselves.

But the groom-to-be was a friend of her roommate's so she knew him and his fiancée, and Liv was glad she'd said yes. She'd made enough in the last hour to pay her rent this month. So far, the party was topping the bachelorette one last month, and the couples therapy party the month before that.

As she sold some warming lube to the best man she thought, as she had many times before, that if her Chinese mother or Japanese father ever caught wind of her "job," she'd be banned from Thanksgiving for the rest of her life.

But she'd tried to find work with her marketing degree, and so far had failed miserably.

HER DAD HAD offered her a job at the law firm, of course, right out of school, but the last thing Liv wanted to do was spend all her time in her father's shadow or tucked away in some file room. When her good friend Kat had retired from the sex toy business last year, deciding to ditch it and go to law school, Liv needed serious convincing to take it over. What did she know about sex toys? She'd never even owned one before.

Besides that, she'd only ever had sex with two guys, anyhow.

There'd been her clumsy college boyfriend of six months who'd left her for a girl who lived *down the hall* in the dorm, and her second—a random hook-up from a neighbor's party—had been quick and blah and ended with him asking her if she would do him the favor of *not* sleeping over.

But, as it turned out, hosting sex parties was easier than having sex. It was playing a role, just like during her college stage days when she flirted with majoring in drama. Nobody expected her to deliver, and she found she liked acting naughty. It was the first time she'd ever really gotten the chance, if she was honest with herself.

Plus, the hours were flexible, the pay was great, and she wouldn't have to move in with Mom and Dad. It also gave her plenty of time during the day to go in for interviews. If she dressed up in a leather corset and heels on weekends, who cared? What her parents didn't know wouldn't kill them. She'd been an angel throughout high school, never seriously rebelling. She was long overdue some naughtiness, she thought.

The bachelor party was starting to get rowdy as two of the guests began a mock sword fight with pink vibrators. A knock on the door signaled a late arrival, and Paul got up to let him in.

"Hey, Liv, what are these for?" One of the guests held up two metal balls on a black string; pleasure balls, à la *Fifty Shades of Grey.*

"Those were made famous by Christian Grey," she said, grinning. "Ladies wear them."

"How?" the best man asked.

"How do you think?" Liv smiled devilishly as she took the silver balls from his hand and held them vertically, giving them a little nudge upward.

"No way! *Inside?*" Paul's eyes grew larger than the silver balls Liv held. He had returned to the living room with the new arrival, a tall, broad-shouldered man in a baseball cap and jeans who stood next to Paul by the couch. There was something familiar about him, Liv thought, but his cap was pulled down over his face.

"She puts those *up there?* Seriously?" One of the guests shook his head.

"They find the G-spot, so *you* don't have to," Liv sang, and the boys laughed. The new guest eyed her from behind the couch. She felt her neck flush a little. He was moving closer, toward the table of toys.

"I'm getting some," the best man declared, jumping up from the couch.

"Now you'll finally have some balls, Preston!" one of the others teased.

The stranger was near her now, and she could see him out of the corner of her eye. He grabbed a massive purple rabbit vibrator from the table.

"Okay, fellas, next up we've got flavored lubes," Liv said as she picked up some neon-colored bottles. The men hooted and hollered. "I'm going to pass out a few sample bottles. Don't get too crazy on me now…" Liv handed Paul some samples to distribute.

The new guest moved to her side, eyeing the contents of her table.

"Whoa," the stranger said, holding the oversize vibrator in his hands. "What's this one called?"

"That's the rabbit…" Liv took the latex-covered vibrator from the man and looked up, and then the rest of the sentence dried up on her tongue. She stood frozen, clutching the thing, in front of Porter Benjamin: a junior partner at her father's law firm. He looked so different wearing the baseball cap and sweatshirt—she only ever saw him in expensive dark suits.

Liv's stomach tightened, and a cold sweat broke out instantly on the back of her neck. Porter knew her family. Porter knew her *dad.* And she was in a leather corset and stilettos holding a purple vibrator, in a roomful of sex toys.

Porter was still looking at the rabbit and hadn't yet made eye contact with her. Liv considered simply walking out the door, leaving her $1,000 in merchandise sitting in Paul's living room. But then she'd be out $1,000, *and* the other $250 Paul owed her at the end of the night, plus anything she managed to sell before then. She couldn't afford to walk away, and she knew it.

Then Porter glanced up at her, and a smile of rec-

ognition formed on his face. *Too late to run, anyway,*
she thought.

"Olivia! I thought that was you."

"Porter," Olivia said almost grimly, and nodded.

"So…uh…you're…selling…?" Porter's eyes glanced
around the room at the various sex toys, his eyes wid-
ening in surprise.

Oh, God. This was not good. Her first instinct was
to lie. She had amnesia. Her body had been taken over
by aliens. She was *not* somehow Liv Tanaka, sex toy
goddess. But staring at Porter's sharp brown eyes, his
defined chin, she knew he would not buy any of that.
He was friends with Paul, and Paul knew she did this
for a living. She couldn't even say she was filling in
for a friend.

"That's right," Olivia said, as brightly as she could
muster. No sense in acting ashamed now. She was
holding a giant vibrator.

"That sounds like fun." Porter looked down at her
outfit, his gaze roaming up her body appreciatively.
"Wow, Olivia, I have to say…you look…"

Liv felt her face burn. The last time Porter had seen
her, it was at a family picnic at her parents' house
the past summer. She'd worn her face bare, her jet-
black hair in a hasty ponytail, with jeans and Converse
sneakers. Her mom didn't even approve of lipstick,
so makeup was out of the question. Both parents had
started going to a new, more conservative Protestant
church in the last ten years, so premarital sex and
makeup were sinful, in her mom's opinion, as were
flirting with boys, French-kissing, dancing, and drinking. Anything constituting a life.

If Porter told her parents what she was wearing, and in a roomful of men, most of whom were single…

"You look…amazing," he finally finished, nodding. "I mean…wow." His glance moved to the table behind her, filled with every kind of X-rated toy you could imagine: anal beads, cock rings, lube in a rainbow of flavors, and, of course, giant dildos and vibrators ranging from mini-size to, well…supersize—all realistically molded, complete with thick, thrumming veins. Porter barely restrained a smile as his eyes roamed the table. Liv might not have been as religious as her mother, but right at that moment, she prayed she could drop through the floor.

"Is this lube latex-safe?" one guest asked, holding up a bright yellow neon bottle of banana-flavored oil.

"Uh…" Liv was still off balance as Porter grinned at her. She glanced down at his tightly fitted T-shirt and wondered why she never noticed Porter was so ripped. She felt instantly on guard. He reminded her of her only one-night stand: Kincaid. Handsome, fit and only interested in new notches in his bedpost. "Liv?" The guest's voice snapped her back to hostess mode.

"Yes, a hundred percent latex safe," Liv said, thankful to have somewhere else to focus her attention. Porter or no Porter, she had a show to do.

"What about condoms? Got any flavored condoms?" one guy asked.

"Like you need any condoms, dude. When was the last time you got any?" another teased.

With great reluctance, Liv brought out the boxes of condoms, which came in all shapes and sizes, some even ribbed for her pleasure, and others that glowed in the dark. Porter leaned against the arm of the couch, watching her intently.

As she explained the specialties of each, she debated skipping the next part, which involved her rolling out an extra-large condom complete with tickler on a banana for effect. She tried to ignore Porter's intent stare as she went to work on it. Her neck burned the entire time, even as the guys hooted and cheered.

Porter Benjamin took steady sips of his beer, his face impossible to read. Did he enjoy the show? Did he disapprove? Liv couldn't tell.

The timer on Liv's phone dinged, announcing the end of the show. Paul stood and stretched.

"Okay, fellas, Liv's time is up with us, so make your last purchases," he announced.

The guys at the party bought more merchandise, pushing her totals even higher. She was running someone's credit card through her iPhone swipe when she felt Porter wander closer to the table. He picked up some cherry-flavored warming lube and smelled the bottle.

She finished up her last sale, and then hurriedly began packing her things, her mind running a mile a minute: *Do I tell Porter not to tell my dad? Would that just make it worse?*

Porter hung around, slowly sipping a beer, watching her as she packed her things. She certainly wasn't going to press him for a sale. She could imagine the conversation now. *Hey, Mr. Tanaka, guess what I did this weekend? I bought a leopard-print gold glass dildo from your daughter!*

Liv's mind whirled with all the excuses she could make. To Porter. To her dad. To everyone.

Porter picked up a box of edible cherry thongs she was about to put in her bag. "How much?" he asked in his deep, gravelly voice, the voice she imagined made other lawyers in the conference room instantly pee their pants and want to settle. She glanced at his deep brown eyes, and then anxiously down at the edible underwear. "Uh…those? Uh…"

She suddenly had an image of Porter with a gorgeous blonde somewhere, nibbling off a red thong. The image made her abruptly lose her train of thought, as she stumbled about trying to remember how much they cost. She'd never had trouble remembering inventory before. "Uh…I think twenty-five. No, wait. Twenty-nine."

Porter let his lips curl up in a lazy smile. "I mean for a party."

"Are you getting married, too?" Liv blinked fast. Now she had an image of him with a gorgeous lingerie model type on their honeymoon, of him nibbling on a frilly white lace garter. Unexpectedly, she felt a surge of jealousy.

"Me?" Porter raised his eyebrows in surprise. "No. I'm single."

"Oh." Liv sounded a little too relieved. Mentally, she kicked herself. Porter's smile grew bigger. "I mean, uh, well…how many guests?"

"Just one."

Liv swallowed hard as she reached for the cherry thongs and zipped her bag. "One?" she squeaked. The look on Porter's face told her this was no joke, either. He was dead serious.

"Right." He nodded, eyes set on hers. "How much for a party just for me?"

CHAPTER TWO

LIV STARED INTO Porter's brown eyes, craning her neck to meet them, not failing to notice his broad, muscled shoulders nearly bursting the seams of his cotton T-shirt.

"You want a private party?" Liv's mouth went dry. She didn't do private parties. She'd never even seriously considered doing one—until this moment. Why wasn't she saying no? Where was her knee-jerk, *hell no, perv,* response? Because Porter was no creep, that's why. Because showing Porter her wares, *all of them,* might be exactly what she wanted to do next Friday night.

Then she had a flash of trying to explain to her dad how she decided to date his junior partner, and how she introduced him to the rabbit on their first date. "Isn't that a conflict of interest? Would that go over well at Peterson and Tanaka?"

Porter took a casual swig of his beer and half shrugged his shoulder. "I'm not afraid of your father. Are you?"

Liv shifted uncomfortably in her stilettos. Laughter bellowed from the kitchen, where the other party-goers had gathered for a round of shots. "You're not going to tell him…uh…about…" Her eyes darted to her black duffel bag.

"I take it he doesn't know?"

Liv blushed crimson. "No. He doesn't. And I'd rather...keep it that way."

Paul strode out of the kitchen then, holding a folded check and her dark gray raincoat, which he handed to Liv. "Thanks for doing this," he said. "And I called the doorman for a cab. He said five minutes."

"Thanks, Paul," she said as she shrugged into her belted coat. She cinched it tightly. Paul handed her a folded $100 bill—her tip. "Wow, Paul, thank you." Porter watched her as she took the bill and added it to the rest.

"You're more than welcome, Liv. Need help with your bag?"

"I got it, Paul. I'll walk Olivia down." Porter grabbed the bag before Liv could answer. She could roll it just fine on her own, but she had to admit she didn't mind watching Porter's muscles work. He lifted it as if it weighed nothing and strode confidently to the front door. Porter swung it wide.

"Olivia...after you."

She felt his eyes on her body as she walked through the door, and the sensation sent a warm tingle down her spine.

As they waited for the elevator, Porter leaned closer.

"You know, I could get into that cab with you right now," Porter said, his voice a low rumble. "We could have that party tonight."

"Could we?" Liv's voice came out throaty and low as she sucked in a breath. Porter took a step closer. It was right then that she realized it had been far too long since she'd been this close to a man.

"I promise it'd be fun."

"I bet it would be." Liv's lips parted as she felt herself moving toward him. She reached up and touched his chest, feeling a wall of muscle. She traced down until she felt the hard point of his nipple.

Before she knew it, she was up on her tiptoes, kissing him.

It wasn't what she'd planned at all, but there she was, nibbling on his lower lip. He growled and moved in, pressing his body into hers. For a second she forgot about her family and what they might think; all she could focus on was how perfectly they fit together. She groped at the back of Porter's strong neck, wrapping her fingers into his dark brown hair. His tongue parted her lips, lightly at first, and then when she met his, frantic energy took over. He tasted so good, all she wanted was to devour him whole. He leaned against her, insistent, and she felt him come to life. She was struck by a sudden, delicious thought: he had nothing to fear from being compared to the rabbit. Nothing at all, by the feel of things.

She should be worried about Paul coming out in the hall and finding them, or about anyone else for that matter, but she didn't care. The kiss was too good.

The elevator dinged and Liv sprang away from Porter, who was breathing heavily, his eyes looking glazed. She moved past him into the elevator, sensing him staring at her legs as she went. Porter followed her in, plunking her bag down on the floor.

"You're not getting off that easily," he murmured, pulling her close.

"We're getting off, are we?" Liv raised an eyebrow. Porter tugged her close, trailing kisses down her neck, to her coat and beyond. Then, nearly on his knees, he slipped his hands through the folds of her coat.

Liv watched as the numbers counted down from the penthouse at fifty-five.

"Oh, God," Liv moaned, her back pressed against the wall of the elevator as Porter put his hand on her calf and worked it slowly up her inner thigh. He followed his hand with his mouth, leading a trail of dizzying warmth up her leg. She shuddered as his lips touched the softest part of her leg. He breathed in and whispered, "You smell so good. I just want to…"

Liv felt his warm breath on her skin as he explored upward with his hands, his fingers almost to her lace thong, which was drenched and warm. She forgot she was on an elevator and that Porter was the last man she ought to be making out with. She didn't care about anything but the feeling of his hands on her skin. She clutched the metal railing of the elevator and groaned, arching her back a little. The last thing on earth she wanted was for him to stop. She'd never felt this way before: out of control with need. She felt like something deep inside her had been awakened, something she hadn't even known was there.

She felt a gentle caress right there, on the damp black satin, and she gasped a little. But she didn't fight him. She couldn't.

"My, my…what do we have here?" he murmured as he went for the edge of her underwear, his finger slipping past the elastic.

But then the elevator dinged, breaking the spell, and the doors abruptly slid open.

The cold air of the lobby hit Liv's skin and instantly, Porter withdrew. Liv's coat flapped closed and she was

struck with cold disappointment as Porter grabbed the
bag from the corner and stood up. Liv tried to catch
her breath, her chest heaving as Porter held open the
elevator door with a devilish grin. Liv pushed her coat
together again and pulled on the belt as she stalked out.

The doorman, wearing a suit, sat behind a console
desk near the glass doors of the building, and watched
her as she walked toward him. He had a half smirk
on his face, but she ignored him as she flew out of
the door.

Liv looked for her cab, but it was nowhere to be
seen. Cars rushed by down a busy Clark Street. It had
rained while she'd been at the party and the streetlights
beamed up at her from the wet sidewalks. Out in the
cool September air she came to her senses again. Porter might be enticing, but he wasn't worth the risk.
Not with her parents involved. She felt a stone in her
stomach when she thought about having to explain
her work.

"Olivia…"

"Call me Liv. Only my…only my parents call me
Olivia." Her lips still felt warm from his kiss. She
rubbed them with her finger, wishing she didn't feel
like kissing him right there on the street, again.

"Okay, Liv." Porter cocked his head as he held her
bag. She noticed he didn't shiver in the cold, even
though he'd left his sweatshirt upstairs. Clearly, his
hotness wasn't just cosmetic, but seemed to radiate
out from his muscles. "I won't tell him, you know."

Liv turned her attention from the cars on the street.
"You won't?" she asked, hopeful.

"I won't. Scout's honor." He held up three fingers.

"You were a Boy Scout?" Liv scoffed, not believing him.

"Nope. Sure wasn't." He shrugged. Liv couldn't help herself and laughed. "But I respect the institution. I won't tell."

"Good. He'd have a heart attack. And don't get me started on Mom. She'd probably force me to join a convent."

"They can't be that bad. You're...liberal." He grinned.

Liv laughed, her breath visible in the sudden chill of the night. "I'm the liberal black sheep of the family, trust me. Sometimes, I think I was switched at birth." Then again, given her very thin sexual history, she thought, she wasn't quite so sure she was the black sheep. She thought of her meager two lovers, wondering if maybe her parents had rubbed off on her more than she thought.

"I won't tell, but you have to do me a favor." He ran a finger down the side of her arm.

"What?"

"You know what." His eyes told her she was planning no games.

Liv's heart kicked up a few notches. "The party? You're serious."

"I'm always serious about sex." Porter's brown eyes flashed with mischief.

Something about the way he looked made all her words dry up and shrivel in her throat. He stared at her as if he could already see her naked, and liked what he saw.

"Why don't we have a party right now?"

"What? But Paul..."

"Paul has a lot of his other friends to keep him company." Porter reached out and ran a finger through the belt loop of her raincoat. He tugged her closer. "I know you want to, Liv," he whispered, his breath warm on her ear, and she felt her cheeks flush as she remembered him touching her in the elevator. Yes, he did know just how much she wanted to go.

"Porter…" Liv hesitated. Her body screamed *yes*, but her common sense said she'd be a fool to do it. She was in enough trouble without sleeping with him on top of it. And she was positive that if she let him into her cab right now and took him back to Wicker Park, she probably wouldn't even make it to her bedroom before her panties were off. She'd just be digging herself in deeper. She needed to focus on damage control, not on white-hot sex with her father's employee. "Won't that be bad for you at work?" Liv couldn't imagine it would be a very good career move.

"I know it's a bad idea," Porter said, stepping closer. "But, Liv…looking at you…" His eyes flicked downward. "I just can't seem to help myself."

"Looks like I'll have to save you from yourself then," Liv said, as a yellow cab pulled up by the curb. Porter leaned over, opening the door and putting her bag in. As she stood there, he pulled her close, so she could feel his warm hands through the raincoat on the small of her back.

"I promise I'll be a gentleman," he whispered, almost a growl.

"You mean, like how you were a Boy Scout?" Liv murmured, eyes on his full bottom lip. His brown eyes sparkled.

Porter laughed a little. "You're too smart for me, Liv."

"Used to seducing only the simpleminded, huh? Not much of a challenge, then." She sent him her patented *not this time* smile, which she'd perfected in bars across Wrigleyville.

A low grumble of a laugh escaped Porter's throat as Liv ducked into the cab.

"You could make me up my game," Porter said, dipping into the cab door. "Want to let me try?"

Liv laughed. "You call this game?" She gave him her best flirty half smile, unable to help herself. "You're going to have to work harder than that."

Porter laughed. "Fair enough," he said as he leaned in the open door. "Okay, then a party next Friday. Seven. My place. Be there or…"

Liv felt nerves tingle on the backs of her legs. "Or what?" She held her breath, imagining Porter going back on his word and marching into her father's office Monday morning with this little juicy bone of gossip. Fear squeezed her heart. Fear and something else… anticipation. As much as she didn't want to be found out, she did want to see Porter again. Her whole body screamed to finish what they'd started in the elevator.

Porter grinned, showing off his dimple. "Wouldn't you like to know?" He slammed the car door then and thumped the top of the cab, which hit the gas, sending her back into her seat. She turned around on the black leather in time to see Porter, hands in his pockets, watching her go.

I'm in trouble, she thought as she bit her lower lip. *I'm in big, big trouble.*

CHAPTER THREE

LIV WOKE MONDAY morning feeling a deep sense of dread. She'd managed to avoid thinking about Porter for most of Sunday, running from one errand to another, but now she had no distractions. Now all she could do was relive that kiss over and over again. She'd never felt one so…earth-shaking. Was that how it was supposed to be? Was it just because she'd had so few kisses? That single kiss was hotter than most of the sex she'd had in her life.

She felt herself tingle with the memory.

She sighed. If a single kiss was so amazing, what would a sex toy party for one be like? she wondered.

Not that she could allow that to happen.

If she did, he would probably find out—firsthand— just how inexperienced she was.

She knew what guys expected from a sex hostess. It was exactly what Kincaid had wanted when she'd let slip that was what she did for a living. When he'd convinced her to come back to his place, he'd been disappointed when she hadn't pulled all means of entertainment out of her tiny black clutch.

She still remembered how indifferent he looked as he showed her the door afterward, as if he'd been disappointed by her, by the whole experience. A week later, she'd seen him kissing another girl at a neighborhood bar. She shouldn't have been upset by it, but she was. Since then, she'd become an expert at keeping men at arm's length.

She worried Porter would be just like him. Hot and heavy until he found out she didn't know what she was doing. He'd find her out. Just like Kincaid had.

"He wants *what?*" Liv's roommate, Jordan, said after Liv had told her everything. Jordan had just finished the early-morning shift as a barista, and she smelled strongly of espresso as she brushed out her ponytail in the bathroom mirror. She checked out her new neck tattoo, a butterfly, before turning back to Liv. "You know he's just after sex. Why else would he ask for a private party?"

"Yeah, I know. But I have half a mind to give it to him," Liv said, scooting past her part-time punk roommate into the bathroom to grab her toothbrush. Together, they shared the small apartment not far from North Avenue and Damen, in the heart of Wicker Park. It was the first one they'd moved into after college graduation, back when Liv thought her dream marketing job would fall into her lap and Jordan was sure she'd land a record deal for her garage band. Three years later, both dreams were still on hold.

It was a miracle her parents even let her room with Jordan. Somehow, she'd managed to slip past their defenses, mostly because she was a good egg, despite the tattoos. It had been Jordan who'd skipped a final so she could take Liv to student health when she'd come down with a very late and very serious case of chicken pox junior year. Her parents loved Jordan for it and were able to overlook the fact she played drums in a rock band.

Jordan brushed out her short blond hair and barked a laugh. "I told you your dry spell was going on too long. This is what happens when girls don't get laid. They get blackmailed."

"He didn't blackmail me!" Liv exclaimed.

"Didn't he?" Jordan quirked an eyebrow. "He says he won't tell your dad and then he asks for a party. Like they're not connected?"

Liv's mind whirled. "They're not. He wouldn't do something like that...."

"You sure?" Jordan challenged. "You think if you tell him no, he'll take it nicely?"

Liv sighed, pushing a jet-black strand of hair out of her eyes. "No," she admitted. She jammed the toothbrush in her mouth and scrubbed.

"That doesn't mean you should do it," Jordan said.

Jordan threw the towel back on the silver rack and retreated to her room as Liv finished brushing her teeth and spat.

"It does, though!"

Jordan shook her head. "You should just call his bluff. He's got his job to lose, you know."

Jordan winked as she shrugged out of her barista T-shirt, exchanging it for one that didn't smell like stale coffee.

"The worst that can happen is you have to come clean with your dad. So what?" Jordan kicked off her Converse shoes and plopped down in the center of the couch, reaching for her Mac.

Liv moaned. "You know he'd put me out of business. And then you'd have to take over for me."

Jordan just cackled. "I couldn't sell dildos and you know it. I can barely sell coffee and that practically sells itself." It was true Jordan wasn't a people person. She tended to be a bit blunt and to the point.

Liv heard the sounds of music as Jordan started to mix a new track before she plugged in her headphones. Liv cinched the belt tighter on her terry cloth robe and retreated back to her room, where she plopped on her bed and opened her laptop. She'd need to start working on her dream, too, landing a job she could talk about at Sunday dinner. The problem was nobody was hiring marketing writers these days, and even when she *did* land a job interview, she had the sticky situation of what she'd been doing for the last year. She'd been more than vague about her current work. And truth be told, she wasn't even sure she wanted to do marketing. Her communications degree had been a fallback. She was still trying to figure out her dream job.

LIV'S PHONE DINGED with an incoming message. Porter's number flashed across her phone.

You playing with toys?

Liv felt her mouth go dry as she glanced at the clock. It was just before noon. Was he texting when her father was around? Or was he out to lunch? She thought about ignoring him, but her fingers whipped across the keys before she could stop them.

I'm not on the clock.

His response was lightning fast: You will be Friday. His words made her shiver just a little. You're serious about Friday? Really?

Better believe it. And I want the most thorough party possible. Full demonstrations on everything.

Liv couldn't help but grin. That'll cost you extra.

Liv had just hit Send when her phone lit up with an incoming call from her dad, which nearly gave her a heart attack. She fumbled with the phone, quickly grabbing her hands-free Bluetooth and answering it, as if somehow her dad could read her naughty texts from the other end of the line.

"H-hello?" she stammered, sounding guilty, just as she always did when she was caught red-handed.

"Everything all right, Olivia?"

"Uh…yeah…" Liv cinched the belt on her robe and pulled her legs up under her on her bed. She sat up straighter, even though he couldn't see her slouch through the phone.

"Sorry to bother you at work," her dad's voice rumbled through the receiver. *Work?* Liv thought, confused. Then it hit her: of course, her *fake* job, the one her parents thought she went to every weekday from eight 'til six, in the far-flung burbs in a small company no one's heard of.

"Oh, it's okay. I've got a minute. What's up?" Liv slapped her laptop shut, too, as if her dad could miraculously read her online job listings, too.

"Uncle Robert is in town this weekend. We're going to have a few people over at the house, maybe even grill some steaks or something. We want to make sure you can make it."

Liv's phone dinged again. She glanced at it.

I'll pay whatever it takes.

She swallowed, hard, feeling hot and cold all at once. *What* was she doing? She was flirting with Porter, while her dad was on the line, and probably only a few office walls separated them. Nothing a good shout couldn't get through.

"Olivia?" Her dad was still waiting for an answer.

"Sorry, it's…uh…a bit hectic here. But, yeah, I can come. Sure."

"Great. I'll let you get back to work."

"Ok." Liv was already trying to figure out what to text Porter next.

"Oh, and Liv…" Her dad cleared his throat on the other end. "Just wanted to tell you that we're proud of you. With this new job, and making that first big step with your marketing career. I know your mother prayed for this to happen every day, and we're both so happy that it came to pass. It just proves that God has big things in store for you."

Liv felt as if someone had doused her with a bucket of cold water from Lake Michigan. She was completely sure that God's plan for her did not involve battery-operated vibrators.

"Uh…thanks, Dad." Liv hated lying to her parents, but she also couldn't see how she could be honest with them, either. Aside from her secret college boyfriend, she'd never lied on this scale to her parents before. This was her first big rebellion, and she didn't know how to handle it.

Liv hung up and opened her laptop again. She'd never intended to lie to her parents this long, but she also had drastically underestimated how bad the job market was at the moment. Her phone dinged with another message from Porter.

Come to my place. 2622 N. Orchard. Come hungry.
I'm serving dinner.

Dinner? That threw her. This was sounding like
more of a date than a sex party. Was Porter interested
in more than a casual hook-up? Liv shook her head.

She thought about texting right then and there and
calling the whole thing off. Why was she even seriously considering going? Jordan was wrong. Porter
wouldn't tell her dad, not if he valued his place at the
firm. But what if that wasn't true? Even worse, what
if she went through with the party, but then Porter
found out just how *little* she knew about the sex that
went along with her toys?

She'd have to stall. Put him off. But could she do it?
She thought about how little her willpower had mattered in the elevator.

As her fingers hovered near her phone, she remembered what Jordan had said, about Porter getting mad
and telling her dad everything.

She couldn't risk even a remote chance that Porter
would do that.

She still remembered the look of pure anger on her
father's face when he'd found that *Cosmo* magazine
she'd hidden under her mattress in her room when she
was in eighth grade, the one that blatantly offered tips
on blow jobs right on the cover. It wasn't her fault, exactly. They'd never even dreamed of sitting her down
and explaining the birds and the bees. She had to get
what she could from fifth-grade sex ed and magazines.

No, she had to do it. She couldn't risk calling Porter's bluff. She'd have to go through with the party,

but she certainly didn't have to sleep with him. *Unless she wanted to,* a little annoying voice whispered in her head. She texted back before she lost her nerve:

I'll be there.

CHAPTER FOUR

"This is a bad idea," Liv told her reflection as she stared at her long, shiny hair, which hung past her shoulders, and her almond-shaped eyes lined with smoky eyeliner that accentuated the corners. She wore her most modest hostess outfit: a just-above-the-knee knit black dress, long-sleeved, with a scoop neckline. But she couldn't decide on shoes: sky-high silver strappy stilettos, sensible black pumps, or full-on dominatrix lace-up knee-high black stiletto boots?

"The boots!" cried Jordan, popping her blond head in, her neon-green headphones hanging around her neck.

"Are you trying to get me into trouble?" Liv demanded, hands on hips.

Jordan shrugged. "Maybe. Or maybe if you show him the whips 'n' chains first, he'll get all scared and cut the party short."

"Oh, great, and then he'll go back and tell my dad I'm not just into sex toys, but I'm into S and M? That's *all* I need." Liv reached down to the pile of shoes at the bottom of her open closet. "Sensible pumps it is."

"You look like you're going to a funeral." Jordan leaned against the door frame of Liv's room as she chomped gum.

"I *am*—my funeral if my parents find out what I'm doing."

Liv slipped into her second shoe and studied herself in the mirror. She hated the frumpy rounded-toe pumps. She kicked them off and went for the flashy silver strappy stilettos. *There,* she thought. Not quite dominatrix, but not Sunday school, either.

"I hate to be the one to bring this up," Jordan said. "But what happens if he wants a sex party *every* weekend?"

"It's a sex *toy* party."

"Right." Jordan rolled her eyes. "I'm pretty sure sex *party* is going to be more accurate."

A small smile tugged at the corners of Liv's mouth before she wrestled it under control. "It's going to be purely professional."

"Do you need my extra can of pepper spray?" Jordan offered it from the back pocket of her jeans. It was decorated with a pink skull and crossbones.

"No," Liv scoffed, and was surprised that she meant it. She trusted Porter. "He's a nice guy."

Jordan let out a disgusted snort. "Right, because all *blackmailers* are nice guys. It's just a cheap trick to get into your panties, Liv. Period."

"He's not like that. He's buying me dinner." Liv was surprised at how quickly she rose to his defense. She tried to put into words the pull between them, the surprisingly strong current in their first kiss.

"Dinner? Oh, *that* changes everything," Jordan said, skepticism clear in her face. "Well, when he answers the door in a fuzzy leopard-print man-thong holding a strap-on, don't come crying to me. I'll say I told you so."

LIV CAUGHT A cab to Porter's posh Lincoln Park neighborhood, the driver gliding quickly through the darkened streets of Chicago's North Side. The sidewalks
were crowded with people hurrying to dates and dinners, concerts and clubs. She swallowed down the ball
of nerves in her throat as the driver stopped in front
of Porter's building—a sleek, three-story luxury brick
townhome just south of Diversy. Butterflies zigzagged
dangerously in her stomach as she stepped out of the
cab, pulling her wheeled suitcase filled with every
naughty kind of adult fun imaginable. She tipped the
cabbie and then made her way up the walkway to the
front door, her stilettos clicking against the concrete.

When she got to the buzzer, she hesitated, wondering if she ought to turn around and flee. Was she doing
the right thing? If she went in there, would he find out
she was a fraud? She glanced behind her as the cabbie sped away from the curb, red brake lights flashing
at the end of the block. Porter must've been watching
her from the window, because the door swung open
before she even hit the buzzer.

Too late to run.

"Liv, right on time." Porter was wearing a long-
sleeved crew neck that showed off the taut muscles of
his chest. His brown eyes gleamed as they took in her
black dress, short leather jacket and stilettos. Under
his appreciative gaze, she wasn't sure if she felt glad
or regretful of her outfit choice. Glad, she admitted.
Deep down, she wanted to impress him.

"Please, come in." He held the door and helped her
with the heavy rolling bag, picking it up effortlessly.
She stepped into his expensive marble-floored foyer
and marveled at his taste: modern, but not too clinical.

His townhome was huge, at least three bedrooms, she guessed, which for Lincoln Park might as well have been a mansion. The first floor was clearly for entertaining, with a huge open living room and an attached kitchen equipped with sleek stainless-steel countertops and appliances, calling to mind a professional kitchen at an upscale restaurant.

She smelled the delicious aroma of tomatoes, onion and garlic in the air.

"Smells good," she said as Porter showed her the way to the kitchen. "Did you order Italian?"

"Did I *order*," Porter scoffed as he stopped and turned, so that she almost collided straight into him. The close proximity made her suddenly disoriented, as if he existed in a place where the air was just a little bit thinner than everywhere else. As she craned her neck to meet his sharp brown eyes, she felt a little light-headed and giddy. He moved closer to her and touched her arm.

"I *cooked*."

"You did?" His words were barely even registering, as he was so close she could smell his aftershave, something expensive and earthy. He had nicked himself shaving, and she focused on that small little cut—the only flaw in his otherwise perfectly chiseled chin.

"I made my mom's chicken Parmesan, which should give you the energy you need to *last the night*." Porter's voice dropped to a whisper as he moved even closer. Was he going to kiss her? Her heart beat madly. She certainly hoped so.

No. No, *no*, she told herself. No ripping off his clothes inside of five seconds. She was here for a rea-

son, and she needed to get to it. Sex *toy* party. Not
sex party. Jordan was not going to be right about this.

"My roommate bet me that you were going to answer the door in a furry leopard-print 'man-thong,'"
Liv said, trying to keep the moment light, deflect with
humor.

Porter laughed, a deep, affable rumble. "Who says
I'm not?"

Liv glanced down at Porter's crotch and laughed.

"You hungry?" he asked.

"Starved," she breathed, using the opportunity to
move away from him, out of his gravitational pull.
Maybe if she ate she wouldn't be so eager to jump
him. She'd forgotten to have lunch. She'd been anxious
about coming over, about what would happen when
she got here. She realized she really was running on
fumes. Porter had place settings at the breakfast bar
at the end of his stainless-steel counters. Sleek high-
backed chairs sat together at the end, expensive china
laid out in front of them with linen napkins. She tried
not to look surprised. She wasn't used to guys who
owned linen napkins, much less who cooked. The best
meal her college boyfriend had offered was takeout
from a Thai place, eaten straight from the cardboard
containers.

She took a seat and shrugged out of her jacket.

"I hope you like red," he said, showing her a bottle
he'd already opened. She liked red, but she would've
drank anything to calm her nerves. Her heart thumped
a little as she took the glass he offered. She took a
bigger gulp than she'd planned, and inwardly ordered
herself to slow down. Porter set a steaming hot plate

of food in front of her that smelled delicious. He slid into the seat next to hers.

"This looks amazing," she said, and it did: breaded chicken with a marinara sauce and melted mozzarella and baby asparagus tips drizzled with balsamic vinaigrette, with a generous helping of baby portobello risotto.

"You made risotto," she said, staring at the dish, knowing exactly how painstaking it was to make it since she'd tried—and failed—not to burn the slow-cooking dish at an Italian cooking class at Old Town last summer. "I'm impressed."

"That's the idea," Porter said and winked. "My mom's Italian, so I learned all the tricks from her."

Liv glanced at the care he'd put into the food on her plate and wondered why he'd tried so hard. He seemed to be doing his best to make this an *official* date. But the mouthwatering aroma of food soon drowned out her reservations, and Liv dug into the meal. The food literally melted on her tongue. She hadn't tasted anything this good since her mom's famous beef and snow peas Szechuan stir-fry. The amazing food and wine instantly relaxed her, and she found herself falling into easy conversation with Porter. She learned he liked being a lawyer, but that it wasn't his passion. He loved to sail, which he did every summer out on Lake Michigan. He was saving up to buy his own boat. Compared to the men she usually dated—a string of aimless musicians or fast-talking sales guys living in cramped one-bedroom apartments with two other roommates—he was light-years ahead. He had ambition, he could cook, and he had a great job. He was the first guy with real relationship potential since, well…ever.

But she knew he'd go running the very second he found out she wasn't who she appeared to be. A sex toy party hostess with barely any experience! He'd be expecting a porn star in the bedroom, but instead he'd get a complete newbie.

He'd be just like the other two guys she'd slept with. All eager at first, and then couldn't wait to toss her aside for the next person they met.

All too soon, the meal was over, and Porter poured the last of the wine into her glass. She realized she'd have to get down to business soon. She stared at her black suitcase sitting in the corner and took a big swig of wine to shore up her confidence. She'd never felt this nervous before. Even at her first sex toy party she'd been strangely at ease. She knew how to play a part. That was something she did at home with her parents every day. And with a roomful of people, she knew she didn't have to *do* anything real. She just had to pretend. She was good at pretending.

"So I've been going on far too long," Porter said as he set his knife and fork down on the plate. "Tell me about you. How did you start doing…what you're doing?"

Liv took another sip of wine. She told him the whole story, how she'd failed to find a marketing job out of college, how her friend had offered her the business.

"So this isn't what you want to do for life," Porter said, moving his plate away so he could rest his elbow on the counter.

"Disappointed?" Liv dabbed at her lips with the napkin.

"No, I wouldn't say that." Porter leaned forward, his knee grazing hers at the breakfast bar. She felt the instant zing of heat and felt very aware of his body close to hers.

"Tell me the truth. You were shocked when you first saw me at the party," Liv said, carefully folding her napkin back on her lap as she crossed her legs, very much aware that her ankle swung closer to his leg.

"Not shocked." Porter clasped his hands in front of him. "Surprised, that's all. I had thought you were… shy."

"Hardly," Liv scoffed.

Porter watched her closely. "At all the family parties, you never said much."

"I was bored," she said, toying with a corner of the linen napkin on her lap. "That's all. Mom and Dad, I love them, but they want me to be someone I'm really not."

"Lots of parents do. Mine wanted me to be an electrician, not a lawyer. Nobody in my family likes lawyers all that much."

Liv barked a laugh. "You've got a strange family if going to law school made you the black sheep."

"You have no idea." He laughed ruefully.

Liv reached for her wineglass and was shocked to find it half-empty already. She'd lost count of the number of glasses she'd had: Porter had been steadily refilling them. She tossed her napkin on the counter and hopped down from her chair and found herself a little tipsy, but not too much. The wine warmed her, sending a nice, light buzz through her temples.

Just the right amount of liquid courage, she thought.

"Well, shall we get down to business?" she asked, dusting off her hands as if readying to get down to serious manual labor.

"Don't make it sound so...*not fun,*" Porter teased.

"Pardon me," Liv apologized, making a little curtsy. "Are you ready for *dessert?*" she asked Porter in one of her most exaggerated sexy-girl voices. She put a hand on her hip and jutted it out.

Porter laughed. "I'm ready." He moved over to his expensive leather sofa and slumped down, stretching out his long legs on the top of his sleek steel-and-glass coffee table.

"Well, then, what would you like to see first?" she asked him, unable to stop flirting, the wine having made her bolder than she would've been sober. Porter's eyes grew serious as he gazed at the full length of her body, making a slow, deliberate sweep downward. She'd been partly joking about dessert, but the way he looked at her gave her the distinct impression she was on the menu.

"Why don't you open up your bag of tricks, and let's see what we have?" He took his legs off the coffee table and leaned forward. Liv obliged, gently laying the rolling suitcase on his glossy, bare wood floor. She knelt beside the bag and unzipped it expertly, showing off rows of dildos, vibrators and colorful boxes of all sorts. Even, in case, a box of extra-large condoms.

His eyes widened a little at the diversity. She'd added a few more toys for shock value that he hadn't seen at the bachelor party, including an oversize corkscrew-shaped jelly-green vibrator. She held it up in front of him and powered it on. It undulated at high speed, like a massive drill, flopping in disturbing circles. She laughed as his mouth dropped open.

"Is *that* supposed to be what women want?" he

asked, as the vibrator spun around in a wide circle. "Please tell me that's not your favorite toy."

"No, it isn't," she said and laughed, switching it off and tucking it back into the suitcase.

"Thank God," he said, wiping his forehead in an exaggerated show of relief. "Why don't you show me your favorite?"

Liv hesitated. She had tried some of the toys, it was true, but she'd found most of them too plastic, too vinyl, too *fake*. In her mind, a toy could never replace the warm, living body of a man. That's why she preferred the simpler ones, with fewer bells and whistles. Her favorite vibrator was actually surprisingly small, just the size of an egg. She felt the color on her cheeks rise as she reached in and fished it out, a golden egg that fit exactly in the palm of her hand.

She met Porter's gaze as she sat next to him on the couch and handed him the small vibrator. He said nothing as he weighed it in his hands. She leaned over, her leg pressing into his, as she showed him how to turn it on.

"Not too fast," she said, tapping one of her burgundy-colored nails on the switch. "Medium is the perfect setting."

"Is it now?" Porter's lips parted just slightly as he leaned closer to her, his brown eyes intent on hers. He held the egg in his hand, and gently placed the vibrating tip just to the inside of her knee. She shivered in surprise as he rolled the egg farther up her inner thigh. She froze, wondering if she should stop him, realizing that she didn't want to.

He moved even closer then, putting his lips on hers and kissing her ever so gently, a teasing kind of kiss, as he moved the egg in dizzying circles, closer and closer to where she willed him to go. His tongue teased hers, and she found herself opening up for him, her knees inching apart. She prayed he didn't stop.

CHAPTER FIVE

PORTER DIDN'T. He pressed the small egg-shaped vibrator upward to its intended target, sending delicious vibrations straight through Liv, in a wave of pleasure so naughty she couldn't help but enjoy it. Instantly, she became slick with desire, her skirt inching ever upward, his large hands warming the egg and her at the same time. If he kept it up, she would come right there, fully clothed on his couch, but she was too far gone to care. She deepened the kiss, even as the warm sensations below her waist made her groan into his mouth. She grabbed the front of his shirt recklessly, untucking it, sliding her hands across the smooth, taut muscles of his chest. He sucked in a breath of air as he withdrew the egg with an amused growl.

"I can see why you like it so much," he said. "What else do you like?" His voice was throaty and low, his brown eyes nearly black. She tried to even out her focus, even though her head felt muddled and her heart pounded in her ears. She knew she liked Porter, that's for damn sure. She itched to get him out of his clothes, to feel his warm naked skin again beneath her fingers.

Porter shut off the vibrating egg and laid it aside. "Show me something else," he commanded, and all she wanted to do was obey.

She reached over into the bag and pulled out a

small, tasteful canister of vanilla-flavored body powder. Liv shook it a little as she handed it to Porter, who read the label intently.

"What's this for?" he asked.

"It makes me—all of me—taste good." Liv blushed again. "I've never used it, though, so I don't know… I've only heard…"

"You've only heard," Porter repeated.

Liv's heart beat hard in her chest. "Porter. There's something I should tell you.…" She didn't know why she was doing this. But she felt he should know. She wasn't a sex goddess. She hardly knew anything! "I'm not… I mean… I have had sex, but…" It wasn't coming out right at all.

"You're saying just because you sell sex toys, it doesn't mean you have sex all the time?"

Liv blushed bright red and nodded. "I haven't had sex much," she murmured, almost at a whisper, feeling too embarrassed to look him in the eye.

Porter put his finger under her chin and lifted it. "I don't care about that," he said, brown eyes intent on hers. "In fact, I pretty much guessed that already."

"You did?" Liv felt alarmed. Had she kissed badly? Was it that obvious?

"Liv, you're a complicated woman. And I like complicated." He kissed her gently then, and she kissed him back. He pulled away, eyes intent on hers. "You don't have anything to be embarrassed about. You know that, right? You are an amazingly gorgeous woman."

She smiled at him, feeling relieved.

"And you know that with every partner, it's like starting over, right? Everyone is different," he murmured, kissing down her neck. Her breath quickened. "We're all novices when it comes to having sex with someone new for the first time. We all have a learning curve." He pulled away and held up the flavored powder. "So, this is supposed to make you taste good?"

Liv nodded.

"I bet you taste good all on your own," he whispered as he stood, pulling her in close. He was kissing her again, and seconds later, tugging up her dress. Somehow, it ended up on his floor, and she wore her best black lace bra and slinky panties. Liv tugged on his shirt in return, and it came off. His chest was muscled, his abs flat and ripped. He was as gorgeous as she thought, and wished she could spend hours just looking at him, tracing the muscles. He kissed her again, pushing her back on the sofa, and then slid downward, tugging expertly on her underwear as he went. Suddenly, she was naked from the waist down, and he was there, at her center, flicking his tongue.

"Mmm." He raised his head from between her legs. "You taste so good, you don't need any powder," he said as he licked with gentle, experienced strokes. The heat built inside her as she arched her back, moaning, wanting more. He followed her, lick for lick, stroke for stroke, seeming to read her mind as he lapped greedily. Minutes later, she found herself tumbling over the edge, seized by a climax so strong, she could feel a shout ripped from her throat. Instantly, her body turned to jelly as he moved away from her, licking his lips.

She groaned and her eyes fluttered closed.

"Oh, we're not done yet," he said, and reached over to her suitcase, grabbing an extra-large condom. Liv propped herself up, watching him as he slipped out of his pants. She'd been right: he had nothing to fear from oversize vibrators. She reached out and touched his thick member, and he shivered, even as he worked to put the extra-large condom on. Once finished, he kissed her, his thickness rubbing against her belly. Instantly, her body came alive again, her nipples straining against her bra. He slipped down her bra straps, freeing her breasts, cupping her reverently.

"I can't wait any longer," he growled in her ear, and they tumbled back down on his couch and he plunged deep inside her, taking her breath away as he filled her. She couldn't think about anything else but how well they fit together, how she was going to come again, even harder this time. She matched his rhythm as he worked deep inside her, relentless in his demand. Before long, she came again, hard and fast, squeezing him fiercely in hot spasms, pushing him over the edge. He came, too, with a guttural growl of heated pleasure, his face flushed and hot. He fell on top of her, and they collapsed into a satisfied silence.

He eventually broke it.

"That was *amazing,*" he exhaled.

"Mmm-hmm," Liv agreed. It was, by far, the best sex she'd had in her life. She felt...transformed. She'd never felt anything like this before. So this is what all the fuss was about, she thought. *This* was what *bells and whistles* really meant. Her whole body felt as if it had been rung like a bell. It still reverberated with pleasure.

Yet as the good feelings slowly ebbed away, the same old anxiety took its place.

She lay very still, wondering if this was the moment, like all the rest she'd been with, where he'd throw on clothes and set about the awkward business of rushing her out the door.

LIV DREADED IT, but knew she ought to steel herself for the inevitable. She lay content for a few more seconds and then decided she should be the first to act. Rip the Band-Aid off before he could. She fidgeted beneath him and he rolled off her reluctantly. When she rose from the bed, he grabbed her by the waist.

"Where are you going?" he growled playfully.

"Home?" Liv offered, trying not to sound disappointed as she tried to find her clothes.

"No way," he said, tightening his grip. "You are not ditching me that easily."

She was surprised by his forcefulness. Could it be he really wanted her to stay?

"Getting cabs at this hour is a nightmare."

"It's only midnight," she pointed out. It had been three in the morning when Kincaid had kicked her out, she remembered. Porter pulled her to him and gave her another kiss.

"Good," he said. "Because I still need to try this." He shook the flavored body powder he'd grabbed from the coffee table. He cupped her bare butt and guided her to his bedroom. Her knees, still weak from before, had no resistance left in them, and she tumbled into his bed. He unscrewed the powder lid, sprinkling it below her belly button. "Now then, let's see why you like this powder so much," he said, dipping his head down.

LIV CAME AWAKE to the sensation of a strong arm around her waist, Porter's warm body tucked closely to hers, as they spooned together in the middle of his sprawling king-size bed. For those first bleary minutes awake, Liv simply enjoyed the warmth, marveling at how well their bodies fit together. Still naked from the night before, she felt deliciously sore, decidedly satisfied. Porter had the kind of stamina Liv hadn't seen before: he kept her up most of the night, trying out a dozen toys and even more positions. Porter had been right about one thing: he took sex *very* seriously.

The night had ended in his shower, where he still hadn't stopped exploring. They'd collapsed, damp and exhausted, in his bed around four in the morning. She stretched and yawned, the morning light filtering through his gauzy white curtains.

"Good morning, *gorgeous,*" Porter murmured into the back of her hair. He stroked her arm, trailing his index finger down to her elbow and beyond, to her hip.

"Good morning," Liv replied, feeling suddenly shy in Porter's muscled arms. He rolled her over and kissed her full on the mouth.

"That was some party last night," he said, pulling her up on top of him.

"Sure was," Liv agreed. Liv felt stiffness against her leg. "Don't tell me that's you. How do you have anything left?"

"I *always* have something left," Porter growled, wrapping his arms around the small of Liv's back and flipping her again, so he was on top. He nibbled on her ear and trailed kisses down the delicate skin of her neck. She shivered, feeling her own body respond, melting into his. They rolled once more, and she was on top again, his hands wrapped up in her hair. She wouldn't think about what a bad idea this was, about how now, in the bright morning light, she was stone-cold sober. She wouldn't have wine to blame this on later, and neither would he. Yet she couldn't seem to stop herself. Now should've been the time she was slinking quietly out of his townhome, hoping not to wake him on the way out.

Everything so far had been perfect beyond her wildest dreams. She hated the idea of overstaying her welcome, of spoiling the best night of sex of her life. If this was all she was going to get, she didn't want it marred by an awkward parting.

She couldn't shake the feeling that at some point Porter would grow bored of her, just like the others. She couldn't bear the thought of that rejection and felt the only way to handle it was to do it first.

Besides, did she even want to date Porter? A lawyer—like her father? Would she marry him and settle down in Oak Park and have a house like the one she grew up in?

She thought she'd spent most of her adult life trying *not* to be her parents, and now she was going to choose to mimic them to a tee? It was ironic, to say the least.

Her phone dinged, an incoming message. She saw it was from her mother, and in the next instant, realized with horror that it was nearly noon. Her uncle! She was supposed to be over at her parents' house now. She was beyond late.

"I've got to g-go!" she stammered, throwing the covers off as she tried to make a quick escape. Porter grabbed her arm.

"What's the hurry?"

"I…I…" She didn't want to mention she was late for a backyard barbecue. What if he asked to come along?

Liv felt her blood run cold. That could *not* happen. "I'm late!" She wiggled out of his grasp and leaped out of bed, frantically searching for her clothes. Where *were* they? *Downstairs.* She scurried out his bedroom door naked and down the stairs. She saw her clothes discarded all around the living room: her black lacy bra on the arm of the couch, her black dress in a silky puddle on the carpet. His coffee table was filled with the toys from their party: empty condom wrappers, the small egg vibrator, and canisters of flavored body powder. *Oh, boy,* she thought. She had gone too far. She'd had too much to drink and gone…*too far.*

Granted, it was some of the…no, scratch that…*the* best sex of her life. She couldn't really regret it, could she? She hurriedly slipped her bra on and scoured the carpet and sofa for her lacy underwear. She couldn't find them.

"Going already?" came Porter's deep and sexy voice from the top of the stairs. She glanced up and saw him leaning against the rail, a sly smile on his face. His taut muscles looked better than any shirt.

"I've got to…I'm late."

"You can't be having another party so soon."

"What? No! Not a party." Liv hurriedly pulled up sofa cushions, looking for her underwear. *Where* were they? They couldn't have just walked off.

"You're not going to tell me then?" Porter's lip curled up in a smile, as if he already knew where she was headed.

"I just…I…"

"I need to pay you."

"Pay me? For what?" She gave up looking for her

underwear and started dumping unopened toys back in her suitcase.

"For the *toys*. I assume you don't want to package some of them up again. And then there's the hostess fee."

"No, no. Don't worry about it. You just don't tell my dad and we'll call it even."

"It's hardly even." Porter came down the stairs slowly.

Her hair was no doubt a mess, and she hadn't bothered glancing in a mirror yet. Had she washed off all her makeup? Would she be arriving at the family barbecue looking like a raccoon?

And then it hit her: she didn't have time to go home and change. All she had was her dress from last night and…the stilettos. She'd be making the march of shame straight to *her parents' house*. She dug around in her hostess suitcase. Surely she had a something in there. She looked in the interior pocket, and pulled out a lace-up corset and then some lacy garter belts. This was just getting worse.

Then she hit the back pocket, where she had a pair of black ballet flats she packed for emergency relief from uncomfortable heels. *Thank God.* She might be wearing the dress from the night before, but the ballet flats made it look decidedly less trampy. If she wore no makeup and her hair in a ponytail, even her mom might not comment on the plunging neckline. *Might not*, but probably would. She didn't have underwear, though. That could be a problem. She considered wearing a pair of edibles, but didn't want to sweat through the barbecue, her legs smelling like jellied strawberries. The fact was, edibles were meant to be *eaten*, not *worn*. She had no idea what they did if you wore them all day. Probably turned to a gooey, sticky mess. She'd just have to go without. *Commando it is*.

She zipped up her suitcase and wheeled it to the front door.

"Liv! Wait. Seriously. I can drive you."

A bolt of panic shot through her. She imagined rolling up on the family gathering in Porter's sleek BMW. "No! No, a cab is fine. Really."

"Liv, come on. I'll give you a ride. No need to shame-walk it."

"Porter. Really. I've got this, okay?" She gave him a look that told him she meant it. He held up his hands, surrendering.

"If you insist."

Liv had her hand on the front doorknob, when Porter grabbed her and pulled her close to his bare chest.

"When am I going to see you again?" he asked her, a growl in her ear. She felt a tingle all the way down to her toes. She hadn't thought there would *be* a next time.

"I don't know," she whispered, voice low.

"Come on, Liv. I *know* you want to see me as much as I want to see you. You can't fool me," he said and pulled her in for a long, delicious kiss. Feeling the warmth of his tongue, she nearly forgot that she was late. Eventually, she broke the kiss, a little breathless.

"Sure you want to go?" he asked her, a gleam in his brown eyes.

"I'm not sure at all," she said, with more honesty than she'd banked on. She panted a little, trying to get her heart rate under control. "I've got to, though."

"Okay." Porter ran his finger down the side of her face. "But I can't wait to see you again."

"I'm not doing another private party." She wanted to be firm on that.

"Really?" He cocked an eyebrow, doubtful. His confidence made her doubt, too. Would she be able to stay away from him? "My guess is, I'll see you sooner than you think."

CHAPTER SIX

LIV DIDN'T HAVE time to worry about what Porter meant
as she slid into the cab and gave him directions to Oak
Park, the western burb where her parents lived. She
frantically worked on her hair in the back of the cab
that was taking her to her parents' house. She'd gotten
three more *Where are you?* texts from her parents, and
even though she'd made excuses, she could tell they
weren't happy she was late. She smoothed down the
front of her slightly wrinkled dress and fretted over the
plunging neckline. Her mother wouldn't approve, but
she didn't have an alternative. Not if she didn't want
to be later. Stopping by her own apartment, in the opposite direction, would add another forty minutes to
her already dismally long cab ride.

Liv glanced in her small compact and saw her eyes
looked a little puffy: it's not as though she'd gotten
much sleep. This particular morning, she thought she
looked even more Chinese than Japanese, more like
her mother's relatives than her father's. It was a subtle difference, and most people probably wouldn't be
able to spot it, but she could. She patted her face with
powder, but no blush. Her mom would try to rub it off
her cheeks if she saw her. That's just the way she was
about makeup.

Suddenly, in the cab, she had a memory of Porter's muscled arms and his sure hands on her body. She shivered. Who needed sleep when she'd come a half dozen times?

I can't wait to see you again, and part of Liv, the naughty part, certainly hoped that was true. Could she believe he really did want to see her again?

The cab pulled down the main street of quaint Oak Park, and Liv glanced at the familiar old buildings, looking out for the turn that would take them down her parents' modest residential street lined with enormous, ancient oaks. They didn't live in the huge, fancy Frank Lloyd Wright mansions adorning the old city avenues near where Ernest Hemingway grew up. Her father had chosen a down-to-earth three-bedroom bungalow, where she'd spent a good chunk of her childhood. She liked Oak Park and the quaint downtown, dozens of brightly painted Victorian houses lining the avenues, one of dozens of leafy Chicago suburbs that were once bustling little country towns in their own right.

She saw her family's bungalow come into view, its warm buttery-colored trim paint greeting her like an old smile. She did love her parents' house. It was full of memories: right out in front, down the small pull-in drive, was where she'd skinned her knee learning to ride her bike without training wheels.

Liv handed the cabbie the fare, and then got out of the cab, nearly forgetting her black suitcase, which the driver wheeled after her.

The suitcase!

She glanced at it in horror. Nothing like walking into her parents' house with proof their daughter is a liar *and* a hopeless sexual deviant! It hadn't occurred to her what she'd do with the luggage once she got here. She had been just so concerned about *getting* here.

Okay, *think*.

If her mother saw it, she'd assume Liv was staying the night, which wouldn't be the end of the world, except that she absolutely could not stay the night. She had a million things to do. Not to mention, the last thing she wanted was this suitcase sitting in her parents' house, just waiting to be found out. She glanced hurriedly around the outside of the house for a safe place to tuck the massive thing. Shrubs? Too brambly. Potted plant by the front door?

What if a relative came by and found it? Or a neighbor? She couldn't risk just leaving it in the open. Cold sweat broke out on the back of her neck as the cab drove off, leaving her hesitating on the sidewalk. She saw her father's garage, where he parked his Acura, and ran to tuck it away in there, back behind some old boxes of paint Dad had stashed near his workbench. It wasn't obviously visible on quick glance, but she couldn't forget it, she told herself. No matter what.

Suitcase, suitcase, suitcase, she chanted to herself as she walked to the front door to ring the bell. She tucked her small cross-body bag back near her hip and held her breath.

Her mother, Lian Lin Tanaka, swung open the door instantly. She looked as pristinely put together as ever: her bobbed, shoulder-length black hair tinged with the hint of gray was curled meticulously under, her pearl earrings and necklace in place. She hardly ever went anywhere without them. She wore one of her favorite ensembles: a black sweater set and plaid wool skirt, with a silk scarf around her neck for color. Only her mother would dress up for a barbecue. She gave Liv a swift glance and frowned.

"Ai-yah." She clucked her tongue against the roof of her mouth in disapproval as she whipped her burgundy silk scarf from around her neck and tucked it around Liv's. "You can't be showing so much skin, Olivia, my goodness." Lian tied the scarf expertly as Liv stood still and didn't bother to protest. Resistance was futile. At least she was wearing flats and no makeup. Lian squeezed Liv's cheeks to inject some color.

"Ow, *Mom*."

"A little color—the way nature intended. There…" Lian frowned at Liv's head, sweeping an errant hair back into place. "*Now* you look presentable."

Liv wondered what her mom would do if she admitted she'd just lost a pair of underwear at a man's house. *She'd flip,* Liv thought.

Lian stepped backward into the entry hall, letting Liv pass. There was no hugging. Lian wasn't a hugger. Open affection was saved only for the most dire of occasions: high fever, near-fatal car accidents and the like. Otherwise, Lian thought it was a bit of a sign of weakness, like other "tiger moms" of her generation.

"Your father is barbecuing, and lunch is ready. Where *have* you been?"

Liv thought about waking up naked in Porter's bed and nearly blushed, giving herself away. She glanced away from her mother just in time. "Traffic was bad—I told you. I'm sorry I'm late."

"Well, go on and say hello to your uncle. He's been asking about you."

Liv scoured the room, full of cousins and some of

her aunts from the burbs. The side table was full of delicious eats, as much Asian fusion as her own family was. She saw a plate of homemade sushi, some freshly rolled pot stickers, egg rolls and a bowl of Japanese rice crackers, among other mouthwatering snacks. Her stomach growled in protest. She realized she was famished. She hadn't eaten since dinner the night before and she'd had a little bit of exercise since then. More than she was used to, if she was honest. She tried to make a sneak snack attack, but Uncle Robert saw her before she made it to the table.

"Olivia, Olivia!" he sang, as he folded her into a big hug. The Tanaka side of the family didn't mind bone-crushing, shirt-wrinkling hugs. Uncle Robert was a big bear of a man, with a great, cheerful face like the happy Buddha. He was always the uncle who'd tickled her mercilessly as a kid, who'd teased her with all kinds of endless, impossible dares like *bet you can't hold your breath for ten minutes.*

"Sorry I'm late…" she said into his shirtfront.

"No apologies necessary, my favorite niece." He released her and grinned. "Your dad tells me you're the big marketing maven, now?"

"Uh…that's right…I guess." Liv shrugged, tucking strands of hair behind her ear as she avoided eye contact. She didn't like lying to her parents, but she really hated lying to Uncle Robert. He'd never been as uptight as her dad, always playing the part of the cool, younger uncle. If she fessed up, she somehow thought he'd probably understand. But she couldn't risk it, not when he might feel obligated to tell her parents. So she had to keep up the pretense. "I'm just happy to have a job," she said, and that much was true.

"Your dad couldn't be prouder, you know. Bet you'll be CEO someday. You'll make more than all of us!"

Liv wriggled, uncomfortable with the praise, especially since she knew he *wouldn't* be so proud if he ever found out the truth. Just then, Liv's father bounced in through the sliding glass patio back doors, wearing a tomato-red apron and matching oven mitts, carrying a plate of grilled teriyaki beef kabobs on metal skewers.

"Liv! Come here and give your old man a hand." Her dad nodded to the side table, which was already full of edibles. He had no place to put the platter. Liv went to help, picking up bowls of snacks and moving them to the nearby coffee table. Dad plopped the tray down. "I've got more on the grill. Come outside with me."

It wasn't a request so much as a demand. Liv followed her dad to the back deck, complete with railing and stairs that led to a decent-size lawn. The cool autumn breeze felt good on her face. It wasn't too cold yet to be outside, but the turning leaves in the yard told her winter was coming soon. A couple of cousins were drinking Cokes and sitting on patio furniture not too far away. There was no beer or wine in the house. Neither of her parents drank and didn't see why anyone else should, either.

"So, how's the job?" Dad was all business at the moment, as he opened the grill and carefully turned over sizzling kabobs with metal tongs.

"Good." Liv's stomach rumbled. If she was going to get an interrogation, she really needed some food. She spotted a cooler with Cokes nearby and grabbed one. Corn syrup was better than nothing. A cool wind rustled the amber leaves in the trees nearby, even as a few fluttered to the grass below.

"You *sure* everything is all right there?" Dad stopped focusing on the meat and stared at Liv, his face unreadable as usual. Dad had the best poker face on the planet. She could never tell what he was thinking. He had the kind of unnerving stare that made her want to confess to things she didn't even *do*. His cool, unnerving calm was legendary: boys used to not want to come by her house for that very reason.

"Yeah, why wouldn't it be?" Liv felt her heart rate double, even as cold sweat popped up on her lower back. Did he *know?* Had Porter speed-dialed him after she left? Liv swallowed a swig of Coke, so she could keep her hands busy.

"Big firms often take advantage of young workers," her dad said, shrugging as he rolled over another kabob on the grill. Liv instantly felt relief: he hadn't been fishing for a confession after all. Of course Porter wouldn't tell. Surely he'd know that would put an abrupt end to their sleeping together.

He grabbed a bowl full of sticky brown teriyaki sauce and painted it on the meat with a big brush. Some of it dribbled on the white-hot coals, sending up a burst of sweet-smelling smoke. Liv inhaled and it only made her more ravenous.

"I'm fine, Dad, really."

"Are they compensating you for overtime? Have they given you credit for the work you've done so far?"

The last thing Liv wanted to do was get into specifics. "I'm fine, Dad. Really."

He slung some more barbecue on a platter. "Well,

you let me know if you're not. I'm not afraid to write
a letter."

Liv sighed. She appreciated the concern, but at the
same time it hadn't been easy having a dad who was
an expert at writing sternly worded legalese letters
on imposing law firm letterhead. It's how she got re-
instated into summer camp the one year they tried to
send her home for refusing to paddle in a canoe. Annoying Charlie Jenner had threatened to capsize the
boat, which was why she wasn't going to get in.

"It's not necessary, Dad." Liv tried to help with the
platter, even as she tried to fight the urge to grab a hot
skewer and dig in. Her stomach growled relentlessly.
Inside her small cross-body bag, her phone dinged,
announcing an incoming message. She dug it out of
her purse and saw a text from Porter:

Hey, sexy.

Liv's cheeks burned crimson. She was standing next
to her *dad*. She wanted to drop the phone straight back
into her purse, but while she was holding it, one more
message came in:

You are so incredibly gorgeous. The hottest, best sex
I've had, maybe ever. I have to see you again.

"Who's that?" her dad asked, glancing up. In a
panic, Liv folded the phone to her chest, a reflexive
act since high school.

"No one," she said, her voice sounding a bit stressed.
"Just…uh…Jordan."

"She should have come," her dad said, suddenly
being magnanimous. "Tell her to come if she wants to."

"Okay."

Her phone dinged again with another message from Porter:

Wish you were in my bed right now.

Liv felt her whole body flush, from her cheeks all the way down her spine. She could not believe he was all but sexting her and she was standing next to her *dad*. She took a cautionary step away from the grill, even as she felt a little rush of naughtiness. Quickly, she texted back: Who said our best sex was in the bed?

Porter's message zinged instantly to her screen: Ha! You're right. There were so many places. The couch... the stairs...the shower.

"Is Jordan coming?" her dad asked, nodding at the phone.

"Jordan?" Liv echoed, and then quickly remembered her lie. "Oh, uh, looks like she has to work and can't make it. And, anyway, I thought it was just supposed to be family?"

Liv sent Porter another message. I don't think there's a room we didn't use.

Her dad flipped the skewers on the grill and then wiped his brow with the sleeve of his shirt. "Mostly family, but we invited some neighbors, and a few people from work are going to stop by."

At his words, Liv's fingers froze and she nearly dropped her phone. She caught it just before it slipped out of her fingers.

"What people from work?" She glanced anxiously around, as if Porter might jump out of one of her dad's shrubs.

"Oh, John and Scott."

"The partners, then?" *As in, hopefully only the partners.*

"And a few others," her dad said, being infuriatingly vague. She couldn't very well ask about Porter, because that would scream suspicion. She pulled up her phone again and asked Porter what he planned to do for the afternoon. Maybe he'd fess up if he was on his way. Then she remembered what he'd said.

Oh, God. Had he meant…at her dad's house?

No, she told herself firmly. She was being crazy and paranoid. Surely he had enough good sense not to show up at her parents' house mere hours after their little carnal sex toy party. It was just her guilt talking, she told herself, nothing more. Still, she couldn't help feel uneasy when he didn't text her back, when he didn't tell her his afternoon plans.

A burst of laughter from her cousins drew Liv's attention for a moment, and then she saw bustling in her mother's living room as the crowd gathered around the front door. A new guest had arrived. Probably one of her mother's sisters from the far-flung western burbs, all strip malls and acres of new construction. Still, she stretched, trying to see who it was.

Her dad slathered on more teriyaki and the grill sizzled. He shut it and then handed Liv a plate full of more skewers.

"Would you take those inside? I've got to watch these for just a few seconds more." Liv nodded as she put down her can of Coke on the deck railing and took them, heading back toward the sliding glass door. She nudged it open with one hand, her eyes on the mouthwatering kabobs even as she stepped inside. She saw one of her dad's law partners near the door, and saw her uncle clasping hands with him, introducing himself.

Liv's heart thumped, thinking for a split second she saw Porter's thick dark brown hair in the crowd. But she looked again, and couldn't see with more cousins in the way.

The crowd inside naturally parted, and Liv tried her best to move through the guests to the side table, but it was precarious and she was distracted by the commotion by the door. She had one close call with a small cherry tomato that threatened to roll off the end of one skewer. Liv only just caught it with the tip of her finger, when she crashed straight into *Porter Benjamin*.

CHAPTER SEVEN

THE TRAY OF teriyaki kabobs went flying and spinning, almost in slow motion. Liv watched them in paralyzed horror as they toppled onto Porter's pristine V-neck sweater, smudging brown sauce down the front, while the others landed gooiest side down on her mother's expensive Oriental rug.

"Ai-yee!" cried her mother in horror. *"Olivia!"*

All eyes in the room turned to her, and for a second, she felt as if she were an awkward thirteen-year-old again wearing braces and blunt-cut bangs. She wished, as she had then, that her life was a DVR, complete with pause and rewind buttons.

"Oh...*no,*" Liv said, as she dove to the floor to retrieve the ruined kabobs. Porter went, too, and they smacked heads, hard.

"Ow!" they cried in unison, even as her mother bustled over and pulled Liv up.

"Get Mr. Benjamin cleaned up this instant," her mother ordered, pointing Liv in the direction of the bungalow's kitchen. "I'll clean this up. Ai-yee." She looked at the ground and made a disappointed tsking sound.

The last thing she wanted to do was be alone with Porter Benjamin, but then again, maybe it was the only way to convince him he had to leave *immediately.*

"Wh-what are you doing here?" she managed to hiss, as she hurried him off to the kitchen. She kept her voice low, eyes darting about the room, as if her guilt were a neon sign hanging above her head for all to see.

"I was invited." His smile grew bigger, showing off his dimple. He was enjoying this, she thought—watching her squirm. "Besides, I wanted to give you these." He held up her sexy black lace underwear.

Liv grabbed them out of the air, eyeing the kitchen door with fear. What if her mom came in and found him giving her underwear? *How* would she explain that?

"Where did you find them?" Liv whispered, looking for a place to stash the pair. She had no pockets. And it's not as if she could just slip them in the tea towel drawer! She wadded them up in her palm.

"Underneath the couch." Porter's lip curled into a sly smile. "Remember what we did on the couch?"

"Porter…" The wheels in Liv's mind whirled. He was *invited?* Which meant, even this morning, he *knew* exactly where she was headed. "You knew you were coming here and you didn't bother to *mention it to me?*"

Porter shrugged, his dark eyes sparkling with glee. "You were in such a hurry."

They'd walked through the swinging doors of the kitchen, and Liv gave Porter a hard punch to the arm. He deserved it, and yet his hard biceps absorbed the blow as though it was nothing. He chuckled, deep in his throat. "Hey, you ruin my favorite sweater *and* assault me? That's not fair."

"It's not ruined." Liv swung open the stainless-steel fridge door and grabbed a bottle of soda water. She dumped some unceremoniously on a white dish towel and started patting him down. It was an expensive sweater, a nice one, and as she patted the stain, she could feel his perfectly hard abs beneath the fabric. She had the sudden urge to rip off the sweater right there, but in the very next second she realized how truly ridiculous that thought was: Porter was at her *parents'* house.... And that meant... Trouble.

She kept her eyes focused on the stain, even as she felt him staring.

"What?" she demanded. "Why are you staring?"

"You look beautiful, *that's* what." Liv glanced up, surprised. Porter's expression was all seriousness, not a bit of teasing in it. "I mean it.... You...look good enough to eat."

At his words, Liv had a flashback to his living room, and his very flexible, very talented tongue. She blushed bright pink, even as she felt her belly grow warm from the memory. Porter drew Liv closer, and she could feel his body pressed to hers. Her mother's kitchen faded to the background almost instantly as she focused on his lips. All she wanted to do was kiss him. Her brain went on autopilot; all rational thought fled. Porter drew closer to her, their noses nearly touching, when all of a sudden, the kitchen door swung open with a bang.

"Honestly, Liv. I just don't see how you are so clumsy." Her mother came bustling in carrying the tray of ruined kabobs and Liv sprang away from Porter, madly swiping at his shirt as if she'd been doing that all along. Liv kept her underwear tightly wrapped in her fist, hoping her mother didn't see them.

"Sorry, Mom, I..."

"Mr. Benjamin, I'm so very sorry," her mom continued. "Liv, don't *rub* the stain in and make it permanent! Blot it. Like this."

Her mom bustled over, grabbing the tea towel from Liv's hand, seemingly unaware her daughter had been thinking about committing a few dozen cardinal sins in the kitchen. Porter watched Liv with an amused expression as her mother went about clearing off what she could of the stain. "I've got stain-lifting wipes. Let me get one," she said, rushing off out of the kitchen.

As soon as she was gone, Porter grabbed Liv's wrist and pulled her in close. "Now…where were we?"

"Porter… No!" Liv put her hands against Porter's chest and pushed, but it was like trying to move a wall. "We can't, not…" Porter loosened his grip and Liv pulled away.

"You need to go," Liv said.

"Go? But I just got here." Porter leaned against the counter, refusing to get the hint.

"You can't be here."

"Well, I *was* invited." Porter grinned as his dark hair fell across his forehead. "And your dad's barbecue smells delicious…even if it is all over the front of my sweater."

"I—" Liv wasn't sure if she was going to apologize or smack him. She needed him to leave, but the stubborn look on his face told her that wasn't happening.

"Come on, Liv, you *know* you don't really want me to leave." Porter took a step closer and every nerve ending in her body lit up, anticipating his touch. Without even meaning to, she leaned closer into him.

Then the kitchen door swung open and her father burst in.

"There you are, Porter. Glad you came!" Her father held his hand out, and Porter took it for a hefty shake. "See you met my daughter?"

"We've met before," Porter said, with a knowing grin flashed over her father's shoulder.

"At the last barbecue," Liv quickly added, lest her father get the wrong idea. She sent Porter a stern warning look. *You promised,* she mouthed behind her father's back.

"What happened to you?" her father added, looking at his sweater.

"Just a little party foul, no big deal. I ran into Liv—er, Olivia. It was my fault." Porter gamely took the blame, but Liv still felt uneasy. He couldn't—shouldn't—call her *Liv* in front of her dad! Her parents weren't dumb; they knew it was the nickname all her close friends called her—even if they refused to use it.

"I've told you about Olivia and Denote? She's our rising marketing star." Her dad grabbed Liv by the shoulder and squeezed. She hated that he'd repeated the lie *right in front of Porter.* Usually, her dad never bragged to strangers. She wondered why he chose *this* moment to go all proud papa on her. She stared guiltily at Porter, praying he didn't take this moment to disabuse Dad of his notions.

"Yes, I hear she has *quite* a career." Porter's eyes sparkled. Liv really wished her life had that pause button. Pause, fast-forward, anything to get out of this moment.

"Uh, I should go see what's taking Mom so long with those wipes." Liv tried to wiggle away from her dad's grip. He held fast.

"Did you know she used to sing in the church choir?

Such a pretty voice." Dad squeezed Liv's shoulders. She tried not to flinch. Great, he was talking about the church now! Pretty soon, he'd talk about how she was an angel several years running in the Christmas pageant, from third through fifth grade.

"That was a long time ago, Dad."

"I've found the wipes," her mom said, trotting into the kitchen, and thankfully offering up a distraction. Liv moved away from her dad. She let her mom lather the stain fighter all over Porter's shirt. She wanted to leave the kitchen, but she feared if she did, Porter would take the opportunity to spill the beans. Mom backed away from him and admired her handiwork.

"You must be hungry," she said. "Why don't you get a plate to eat?"

Liv's stomach growled loudly. Porter quirked an eyebrow. "Only if Li—" Liv sent him a warning glare and he quickly corrected course. "Only if Olivia gets one, too."

That's how Liv ended up with a paper plate full of barbecue, hugging the corner of her dad's deck, clutching her plate and trying not to stare at Porter's gorgeous dark brown eyes. They really were big and deep and warm.

Her lacy black underwear was safely back where it should be, thanks to a quick trip to the bathroom before she piled her plate high with food.

Her stomach felt better with food, but she still felt a hard knot of anxiety there. For the moment, they had the deck to themselves. The wind had kicked up, making it cooler, and her cousins had headed inside to eat.

"Where did you put the toys?" he asked, his voice a low whisper.

"Hidden," she said. "And don't you even *think* about bringing that up."

"A promise is a promise," he said.

"Don't you dare say 'Scout's honor' again," she warned.

He laughed, a low, sexy rumble that she felt in her own stomach. Why did he have to be so damn gorgeous? Even with the fading teriyaki stain, he looked ready to star in his own commercial: the sexy young lawyer at play. "You know, your dad is a reasonable man. You should just tell him the truth."

Liv cackled out loud, nearly snorting. "You can't be serious."

"I mean it. You should try just being honest."

"Uh-huh. That doesn't work so well in this house. They're both so into church." Liv sighed.

"Nothing wrong with having faith. I come from a pretty serious Catholic family."

"Right, but you never tried to sell dildos and tell your folks about it, did you?"

Porter shook his head. "No, but it's not like I've been a choirboy all my life, either." Porter licked a bit of teriyaki sauce off his fingers.

"Really? But you're all Mr. Button-Up Lawyer Guy. Smart and handsome and…"

"You think I'm handsome?" Porter quirked an eyebrow as Liv squirmed.

"You know what I mean." Liv cleared her throat.

"Uh-huh." Porter nodded, clearly enjoying watching the blush creep up Liv's neck. "Anyway, I wasn't always the golden boy, if that's what you mean. I had a rebel phase. I worked as a bouncer to help me pay my way through law school."

"You did not." Liv looked at Porter—he certainly had enough muscles to be an intimidating bouncer. But she couldn't imagine him tossing out drunk patrons, or getting into a shoving match with disorderly ones. "Where? At, like, some upscale bar downtown?"

Porter laughed. "Nope. I worked the door at the Admiral."

"The *strip* club?" Liv's mouth dropped open. "*You?* A bouncer at a *strip club?*" Liv wasn't easily shocked, but this really floored her. Porter? Working at a *strip club?* The Admiral was legendary in the city.

"I know. Hard to imagine. But they paid really well, better than other bars, and it's really why I was able to get through law school."

"Was it dangerous?" Liv still couldn't imagine him working the door.

"Sometimes. Believe me, the guys could get out of hand. I've got stories you wouldn't believe, and I had more than a few fights, but usually I won. Fights aren't like what you see in the movies. They don't go on forever. One or two hits, usually, is enough to put someone down. And I was always the sober one."

Liv tried to imagine Porter in a fistfight. She just couldn't. And then there were the strippers. All those naked women… She felt a flame of jealousy rise up in her chest. She had a million more questions pop into her head. Did he date any of them? Did he watch them dance?

"Did you date any of the…uh…"

"Dancers? No. My job was to make sure they were safe. I didn't believe in fraternizing. A few of them *might* have hit on me once or twice."

Liv snorted her disbelief. "*Only* once or twice?"

Porter shrugged. "But I said no. I wasn't interested."

"Really?"

"Uh-huh." Porter nodded solemnly. "Scout's..."

"Don't you dare say 'honor.'" Liv gave him a playful punch in the arm. He only pretended it actually hurt. Hitting him was like bouncing off a wall of muscle. "And your parents were fine with you...working there."

"Not at first," Porter admitted. "They wanted me to quit. They didn't think it right for me to be there. They told me I should be an electrician, like my brother and my father. Fixing wires was the family business, and they didn't approve of me going a different way. All parents have plans for their kids, and I didn't fit into their plans."

"Wow, that must've been hard, telling your family," Liv muttered, thinking about all those naked women swinging on poles, probably lathered in some cheap body glitter. Not to mention the rows of drunk men watching them, throwing dollar bills on the stage, some probably even thinking it would be a good idea to get up on stage, too.

"It was hard, but I had to be honest with them," he said. "And it was better coming from me than them finding out through the grapevine."

"I guess." Liv considered this. "But after you told them, did you quit?"

"Nope. I worked there two years. Paid for most of my tuition. I just had to explain to my parents that I was an adult. I had to make my own choices. I had no interest in being an electrician *and* I was bad at it. I wanted to be a lawyer, but I didn't want to graduate with a quarter of a million dollars in student loans."

"And they were fine with that." Liv couldn't keep the skepticism out of her voice. She imagined sitting down with her mom and dad and just *explaining* she was an adult. Somehow, she didn't think that conversation would go over so well.

"They grew to be fine with it," Porter said. "They had to let go, eventually. I just helped them see that it was time."

Liv took a sip of her Coke as she noticed her father walking out the side door of the house, on the path to the detached garage. She temporarily froze, until she realized he was too far away to hear anything they were saying. Thank goodness.

He was probably looking for one of his lost barbecue tools, she thought. She saw a flash of her sex toy suitcase tucked in the corner. Surely he wouldn't see it. Porter was talking again and she focused on what he was saying.

"What I was doing wasn't reckless," Porter said. "It was practical. Just like what you're doing. The sex toy business is temporary. You're using it to pay bills until you land a job you really want. It's no different than what I did."

"Maybe." Liv wondered if Porter was right. Could she just come clean with her parents? She couldn't even imagine starting that conversation. She'd always been the golden child: straight A's, dozens of ribbons from ice skating and ballet, the whole nine yards.

"Secrets aren't good for anybody," Porter said. "Trust me that it'll be better for you *and them* if you're honest."

"I'm not ready to go there." Liv took a swig of the Coke in her hand. That much was true: she wasn't ready to face the truth. Her lie felt bad, but she didn't believe Porter. Somehow, she was certain the truth would feel far, far worse. Suddenly, she was struck with panic. Would Porter feel the need to come clean *for* her? Would he feel obligated to be all Mr. Honesty with her parents? "You're not going to tell, are you? You promised."

"It's not my secret to tell," Porter said.

Liv nodded, feeling relieved. He wasn't going to tell—for now. She took another sip of her Coke and then glanced over to the back of the detached garage. She looked over just in time to see her father wheeling her suitcase out of the door.

The suitcase filled with purple dildos and bright neon-orange cock rings.

"Oh, *no*," Liv breathed. "Oh, *no, no*."

CHAPTER EIGHT

LIV HAD A sudden flash of her father wheeling in the sex toy suitcase, opening it up in the living room, and then having all the penis-shaped toys fall out onto the rug in front of all her cousins, aunts and uncles. That could *not* happen.

"Dad! What are you doing? Dad!"

Her father looked up at Liv. "Getting your uncle's suitcase. He's headed to the airport soon."

That rolling black bag had a neon-pink leopard-print ribbon around the handle. Liv knew it was hers, not her uncle's. Liv saw that one of the side zippers wasn't completely zipped on the front pocket. A tiny sliver of a condom package stuck out from the little opening, a bright little flash of neon yellow. It was the banana-flavored ones! Liv felt light-headed suddenly as her heart rushed blood to her head.

Her dad took a bump on the knobby stone-covered path from the garage. The condom all but popped out, its label now nearly in full view.

"No, that's…" Liv trailed off. Was she going to fess up to owning it? Now—when there was a condom sticking out of it? Liv's throat went dry.

"It's mine," Porter said, gallantly stepping up toward her dad.

"Yours?" Her father showed skepticism in his voice.

"I was headed out of town tonight," Porter said, smoothly. "A trip to see my parents in Milwaukee. My niece tied a pink ribbon on so I wouldn't forget that I promised her I'd play Barbie tea party next time I visited." He nodded at the handle, as he easily took it from Mr. Tanaka, and positioned the bag, condom wrapper hidden from her dad's view. Her dad looked down at the handle and frowned.

"Oh, I didn't see that there." He frowned again. "Why was it in the garage?" he asked.

"Uh…" Porter looked at Liv.

"He took it out to show me the toy he got for his niece. See if a girl would like it," Liv explained quickly. "We just hadn't had a chance to put it back into his car, yet."

"Oh." Her father seemed to absorb that explanation.

Porter just smiled, holding the handle in his hand. Her dad shrugged and then went back to the garage in search of her uncle's bag.

"You saved me," Liv breathed when her father was out of earshot. She nimbly tucked the condom wrapper back into the zippered front.

"You're my favorite kind of damsel," Porter said, his mouth curving into a teasing smile. "The kind who owns a suitcase full of sex toys."

Liv barked a laugh.

"Come on," he said, putting his hand at the small of her back. "I'll drive you and your bag of naughty tricks home."

DESPITE LIV'S MANY protests that she was fine taking a cab, Porter insisted, which is how she ended up riding in his BMW all the way back to her condo in Wicker

Park. When they got there, he parked and insisted on carrying her suitcase up to her second-floor walk-up.

"Thanks again," Liv said, lingering by the door, keys in hand. She glanced up at Porter's intense brown eyes and his broad shoulders, and all she wanted to do was put her hands on him. She'd been on G-rated mode all through the family barbecue, but now she felt that pull again. Porter leaned closer, magnifying her desire.

"That's no way to thank me," he said as he slyly ran his hand behind her and pulled her closer to him. She arched her back a little, anticipating the kiss, as he lowered his head and covered her lips with his. She felt a surge of pure excitement as a current traveled the length of her body. She wrapped her arms around his neck and pressed her body further into his, cursing the fabric that kept them apart, wishing she could yank off his sweater right there and feel his smooth, hard muscles. She'd spent the whole night naked with him, and now all she wanted to do was go back for more.

His tongue flicked hers, and she welcomed the taste of him and the hint of the cinnamon gum he'd chewed in the car. He tightened his grip, pulling her in closer, deepening the kiss. A groan escaped her lips, straight into his mouth. He moved her so her back was against the wall, and lifted her easily, as if she weighed nothing. Her legs naturally went around his waist, as he held her there, trailing kisses down her neck as she threw back her head against the hallway wall and moaned a little. Her body felt as though it was on fire, an exposed wire of heat. Pretty soon, she'd have to invite him inside. She prayed Jordan had found something else to do this Saturday.

She only barely heard the lock being thrown at her

front door. Suddenly, Jordan was standing in the doorway, grinning, headphones around her neck.

"I thought it was the neighbor's dog out here causing all this noise," she said, hand on hip. "And here it's just you."

Porter set Liv down gently and then backed away, grinning himself, as he ran a hand through his dark hair. Liv already felt her face burn red as she sent her roommate a look that said *be nice*.

"You must be Porter," Jordan said, holding out her hand. "I'm glad to see you aren't some kind of sex offender slash serial killer and that you brought her home in one piece."

"Jordan!" Liv cried.

Porter just laughed. "Would you like to run a criminal background check on me, just to be sure?"

"I might." Jordan cocked her head to one side, assessing.

"No, she won't," Liv said, pushing Jordan back inside their apartment. "She was just going back inside."

"I was?" Jordan feigned ignorance.

"You are," Liv said, as she determinedly stuffed her roommate back into their shared living room. Porter handed Liv her suitcase and dipped down for one last quick kiss.

"I've got to travel this week, but I'll call you," he said, and Liv knew he was serious. He ducked out of their door and reluctantly Liv closed it, her body thrumming with disappointment. She had been so ready for another round.

"You didn't tell me he was *that* hot," Jordan said as she slipped back down on the couch. "No *wonder* you agreed to a private party."

"That's not the only reason," Liv reminded her.

Jordan snorted, showing her skepticism clear as day on her face. "Uh-huh, whatever you say."

A WEEK LATER, Liv sat in the bride-to-be's living room in a cozy town house in the West Loop and waited for the giggling fit to subside. Sarah, the petite, slim bride, was holding a giant rotating vibrator. Most of the time, it was bought for gag-gift value only, although Liv didn't judge people who wanted it for themselves. She'd learned a long time ago that what people did in their bedrooms was nobody's business but theirs.

She always started with the most outrageous to get the giggling fits out of the way, before she settled into serious, hard-sell mode. She picked up her favorite egg, a new one in the package, and held it up for all to see. She took it out and passed it around to the party, to let them feel the weight of it and the subtle vibrations.

"This is *much* better," Jill said as she held the pink egg in her hand. "Does it come in other colors?"

Liv didn't hear the question. She was too busy thinking about what Porter had done with the gold one. She shuddered, remembering his hands on her, trailing the egg down the middle of her stomach, across her belly button, and ever farther down. Porter had the best instincts. Some guys felt the needed to jam everything a little too hard against her, but he'd been teasing, subtle, barely touching her, making her arch her back in want of more.

"Hello?" Jill asked again, waving the egg in front of Liv. "Does this come in other colors?"

"Oh? What? Yes, I'm sorry. Yes, it does. Silver, white, pink and...blue." Liv tried to refocus on the party. She needed to stop daydreaming about Porter and get back to business. He'd been out of town this week, but he'd called nearly every day. Liv had gotten used to hearing from him, the sound of his laugh on the phone. His flight had been scheduled to get in this afternoon, but bad weather in the Northeast had led to extensive delays. He'd forgotten to charge his phone the night before in the hotel, so the last message she'd gotten from him was hours ago, warning her his phone was dying.

She itched to see him, but she'd scheduled this party weeks ago, and he'd promised they'd get together Sunday. She found herself nearly tingling with excitement in all the right places. She'd missed his touch, was eager to get with him again, to find out if their explosive connection could be repeated.

Not that she ought to be thinking about Porter and repeats. This wasn't even a relationship. It was a *nonrelationship*. Nothing about her and Porter would ever be long term, she told herself sternly. It would only be a matter of time before he got bored, like the others.

Still, her thoughts kept creeping back to the night they'd shared. Porter had shown her quite a few refined talents in his bedroom. She wondered if she'd seen all his tricks, or not.... Her phone rang. She jumped, instantly thinking it might be Porter calling. Normally, she put her phone on silent during parties, but this time she'd forgotten.

"I'm sorry. Let me just turn that off," she said as she grabbed the phone from her bag. Her mother was calling. At ten-thirty on a Saturday night? She felt a sudden gnawing worry: Was everything okay? What if her dad—not exactly young anymore—had had a heart attack? "Oh, I... Let me get this. I'll be right back."

"Hello?" Liv answered as she made a beeline for the kitchen, the phone pressed tightly to her ear. "Pour Some Sugar on Me" played obnoxiously in the background. She prayed her mother couldn't hear.

"Where are you?" Her mother sounded annoyed.

"Uh...nowhere...uh...a party. Is everything okay?"

"A *party?* Where?" Liv couldn't even believe her mother. She was an adult. It's not as though she was in high school, or even college anymore. But this was her tiger mom, never off the clock.

"It's a bachelorette party, Mom. Now, what's wrong? Is Dad okay?"

"What? Your dad is fine! He's here with me. We just finished dinner in your neighborhood. We were going to stop by and say hello."

More like check up on me, Liv thought. It wouldn't have been the first time her parents "dropped by" on a Saturday night, just to see what she was up to. The visits always seemed to happen when Liv had a crush on someone, too. There'd been more than one close call at her own apartment. It's like her mother had a sixth sense about when Liv was having sex.

"Mom, I'm at a party. I just saw you yesterday."

"A mother can't want to see her daughter *every* day? *Ai-yee,* Olivia. Leave the party. You've been there long enough. It's too late for you to be out."

"Really? It's *ten-thirty.*"

Liv felt her temper rising: this was her mother to a tee, always thinking she knew best for Liv, no matter the case.

"How much was this one again?" Sarah was standing near the kitchen door, holding up the egg vibrator.

Liv cupped the receiver, but wasn't sure her mother had heard or not. She held up a finger. *One second,* she mouthed, followed by *sorry.*

"Who was that?" Her mother was on high-alert mode now.

"No one you know," Liv said. *And it's not any of your business, anyway,* Liv thought, but didn't say.

"Was that Jordan?" Liv heard sounds of her mother getting into a car and her dad starting the engine.

"No, Mom. I need to go. You and Dad go home. I'll try to drop by tomorrow."

"Where is the party? We could drop by and pick you up—give you a ride home."

Not a chance, Liv thought. "No, Mom. You and Dad go home. I'll call you tomorrow."

"We are *right* here," her mother said. "And you left your jacket at our house. Won't take a minute to drop it off. And I can say hello to Jordan."

"Mom! She's probably not even home." Although technically she had been there when Liv left, wearing flannel pajamas and declaring it a "hibernation" Saturday, which usually meant she ordered pizza and watched Wes Anderson movies. Jordan had been playing gigs for the past six weekends in a row and vowed she needed a stay-in. Although that rarely materialized with Jordan—some of her bandmates or other friends would no doubt have her out and clubbing sometime in the night.

"Then I'll leave the jacket on the stairs," her mom said and hung up.

Liv blew out a frustrated breath. Her mother never

took *no* for an answer for anything. Oh, well. Let her
go ring the buzzer of an empty apartment. What did
Liv care?

Liv went back to the party and sold several more
toys. The bride-to-be had turned up the music, and
several guests had broken out in dance. She would
have to wrap up soon, before it became a full-fledged
bachelorette party. Besides, she'd already made quite
a lot on the evening. Enough to cover the rest of her
bills for the month, and maybe even a little left over
for a treat such as new shoes.

Her phone dinged with an incoming message. She
grabbed it and saw it was from Jordan. Great, Liv
thought, her parents were torturing her roommate.
She'd have to buy Jordan groceries for the rest of the
month to make up for it. So long, shopping spree.

She clicked on Jordan's message:

Porter's here with his handsome on. Says he's going
to wait for you.

Liv's stomach nearly jumped out of her body. Porter was there? He'd made it home! And she couldn't
wait to see him…. But her parents were probably on
the way! Jordan would let them in and…chaos, total
chaos would ensue.

My parents are coming! You have to tell him to go!

Liv waited, nearly holding her breath, for Jordan's
response.

Oops—too late. They're here.

Liv felt hot and cold all at once. Porter *and* her parents in her apartment at the same time? How in the world would she even begin to explain that? Would Porter feel the need to tell them everything? He'd been so all about honesty, there was no telling. He certainly wasn't afraid of her father finding out, either, and without her there to mitigate, it could be disastrous.

"Sarah?" she called to the bride. "Sarah, I hate to do this to you, but I've got to wrap up early. I've got a…" She struggled to find the right excuse. "A family emergency."

CHAPTER NINE

LIV JUMPED OUT of the cab almost before it had stopped moving. She'd nearly tossed cash at the driver, hardly caring about change, as she ran to her front door. She wheeled her awkward bag up the stairs to her walk-up, pushing through the front door out of breath. She'd left her suitcase on the landing, and she stood panting in her own foyer.

Her parents, holding coffee mugs, glanced up in surprise. Jordan, still in her flannel PJs, put up both hands as if to say, *calm down.*

"I got your parents some tea. They just returned your jacket." Jordan held up Liv's trench coat. "You might want to go *put it in your closet.*" She held out the jacket and gave Liv a meaningful arch of her eyebrow.

"Right, uh…I'll be just a second." Liv skidded across the living room and ducked into her bedroom, closing the door shut behind her. No sign of Porter anywhere. The room was empty. She opened the closet, door, however, and found out just exactly what Jordan had been talking about. There, squeezed among her dresses and her shirts, stood Porter, his hair askew, but everything else looking good: his crisp blue oxford tucked neatly into his dark khakis, his expensive loafers shiny and new. Jordan must've shoved him in here before opening the door to her parents.

Before she could say a word, he grabbed her and pulled her into the closet, laying an enormous kiss on her. It instantly went deeper as he pushed her mouth open, exploring her tongue with his. She felt her body respond as if he'd flipped a switch. She pressed herself into him fully, feeling his taut, flat abs. She wanted to yank his shirt straight off, popping buttons if she had to. A second later, she realized it was impossible: her parents were standing in the living room. She pulled herself away.

"Can't..." she whispered. When he tried to speak, she put a finger over his mouth. "Stay here," she said in a voice so low, she was certain it didn't carry. Even as he tried to protest, she shut the door on him.

She hurried back in the living room, not even thinking about what she was wearing: her standard sex toy party fare. This time, a black jumpsuit cinched at the waist and her knee-high stiletto boots. She had her shirt unbuttoned down to almost her bra.

Her mother, seeing her neckline, frowned and put her cup down. She walked over and started buttoning Liv's buttons.

"Mom, *please*." Liv pulled away from her.

"Did you really go out *like that?*" Her mom frowned, giving her the same disapproving look she'd gotten as a teenager almost every weekend. Liv's father sat on the couch, quietly sipping tea and trying to stay out of it. He'd seen enough mother-daughter fights to last him a lifetime. Still, Liv found it a bit annoying. He always was silent when her mother dug into her for no good reason. There were times when Liv thought her father was just as scared of her mother as she'd been as kid.

"Mom, I'm an adult."

"You're still *my daughter*," her mother said, frowning. "You know what dressing like this says to boys? And you have too much makeup on. Ai-yee." Her mother pulled out a tissue from her purse and licked an edge, as if she planned to wipe her face like she was a toddler with apple sauce crayon on her.

"Mom—stop!" Liv deflected the tissue.

Jordan hid a smile, turning her back on the scene and heading back into the kitchen.

Her mother just made a tsking sound and gave her cheek a pinch, showing what she thought of that little burst of independence. Liv only hoped that Porter couldn't hear any of this. She'd die of embarrassment.

Her dad stretched and yawned. "Come on, Lian. It's time for us to get home. It's late."

Liv sent a grateful smile to her father, who was already putting on his jacket.

"Yes, Olivia should get her beauty rest. Now, Olivia, make sure you wash your face before you go to sleep," her mother cautioned, as she, too, slipped into her jacket. "You know how you break out if you don't."

Liv just sighed. Would it always be this way? Her parents babying her? Her mother refusing to believe she could take care of herself?

As soon as her parents were out the door, Jordan shoved Liv. "You owe me at least a week's worth of groceries, maybe more."

All Liv could do was nod as she hurried back into her room to check on Porter. When she opened the closet door, he was standing there, arms crossed, looking none too happy.

"Why did you shut me in here? I thought you were going to let me out!"

Liv hesitated. How could he think that? She couldn't just let him roam free. Her *parents* had been in the next room! If he'd come out, she'd have to tell them what he was doing there. They would've guessed the worst, and it would've been a disaster.

"But, my parents…" Liv struggled to explain.

"The closet? Really? Is *this* where you hid all your boyfriends when you were fourteen?" Porter wasn't entirely kidding. Liv could tell by the strained look on his face, and the fact that he didn't pounce on her the second she opened the door.

"I'm sorry, Porter… My parents…"

"It's not your parents that I'm worried about," Porter said, implying that she was the problem.

"Did you hear any of what they said?" In Liv's mind, it was proof enough of what she was dealing with: parents who refuse to see their daughter as an authentic adult, someone who could take care of herself.

"I heard some," Porter said. He stalked past Liv, out of the closet, and sat on her bed, where he leaned over to tie a shoelace. "You should've just come clean. I would've come out and talked to your dad."

"You couldn't."

"Why not? We're adults, and it's not like we were naked or anything. Having me over—fully clothed, with your roommate with us—what would they do to you? Really?" Porter yanked hard on his shoelace, completing the knot.

"Mom would have a fit—me having boys in my place. You heard how she was."

"So what if she did?"

"Well…" Liv tried to put into words the headache it would cause her: the endless rounds of phone calls, the fights, the relentless dogged determination of her mother to make sure she knew just *how* wrong she was. Mom didn't believe in cold shoulders. She believed in letting you have it with all she had.

"Liv, if you want to be treated like a grown woman, you have to act like one." Porter sat up, clasping his hands in his lap.

"I do act like one." Liv was beginning to take offense now. Was he calling her immature?

"If your parents won't see you as an adult, it's up to you to *make* them. Unless you're ashamed of me." Porter spread his hands, to show he really didn't know the answer to that.

"No, of course not…"

"You did hide me in the closet. Maybe you're the one who doesn't want *this* to go anywhere."

Liv felt dizzy. They'd had one amazing night, and he was bringing them dangerously close to a relationship talk. Was he serious? Did he want this to be… something? She felt as if she was losing her balance. She hadn't honestly considered it *would* be anything, and yet a part of her felt excited about the prospect. Could they really be a couple?

If she were honest, she'd never brought a boy around to meet her parents, not since high school, anyway. Her mother and father had picked them apart, making her feel that they'd never approve of any guy. In college, she was too busy trying to keep the fact that she was having sex a secret to bring around her then-boyfriend, so she didn't really know how they'd react. She just assumed they'd go negative.

Porter watched the emotions play out on her face, but when she didn't answer him, he stood up and brushed off his pants. "Okay, then, I guess I have my answer. I'll go then." He moved toward her door, and Liv was struck with a sudden panic. He couldn't leave. Not yet. Not like this.

"Wait," she said, moving in front of him, putting her hands on his fit chest. "Don't go."

"Do you want to shove me back in your closet again?"

"No, I don't." Liv shook her head. She rubbed her hand across his chest, almost unable to help herself. The muscles there rippled beneath her touch and he took in a sharp breath. "I want you to stay."

"You do?" Porter searched Liv's eyes as her hands wandered beneath his sweater, feeling his smooth, taut skin beneath.

"I do."

Porter leaned down and kissed Liv, slowly at first. She arched up on her tiptoes, meeting his tongue with hers. She felt a zing through her, straight to her toes, as Porter pulled her near, his hands gripping the small of her back. He walked her backward and they bounced together down on her bed. She straddled him, feeling him grow through his pants, relishing the effect she had on him. The bulge made her feel all warm and needy as she moved against it, her desire growing with every flick of her hips. She wanted to feel him inside her again, feel that delicious fullness. He rolled her over and suddenly he was on top, his weight against her chest. He pulled back then, panting, his eyes searching hers. Liv felt need wash over her: she wanted him, and she wanted him now. She couldn't wait a second longer.

"You're going to tell them about us, right?" Porter said, eyes on hers. "I don't mean tonight or tomorrow, but soon."

Liv nodded, murmuring "yes" as she grabbed his shirt and pulled him closer. He dipped his head down as her fingers went to his fly. She wanted to stop talking about her family. In fact, she wanted to stop talking altogether. She wanted him naked, *now*. Porter obliged, wiggling out of his pants. Then his hands roamed up the side of her bare legs, pushing up her skirt. With a hard yank, her underwear was gone, down by her ankles, and she kicked the lacy black pair to the floor. She reached for a glow-in-the-dark condom, one of many she kept in the drawer by her bed. She had it open in seconds, and was carefully rolling it on him as he trailed kisses down her neck. Liv felt as though she was losing track of what she was doing, wasn't even sure if she could finish the task before Porter had thrust hard, pushing into her. She felt as if she would come right then, and shivered at the pleasure of his thickness. He drove deeper, and Liv felt herself unwinding as the first orgasm hit, her muscles clenching as powerful waves of pleasure rolled through her.

"That's number one," he murmured into her ear. "Just two or three more to go." He chuckled as he moved her into a different position.

Liv's breath came raggedly, as her heart beat hard in her chest. "Just three?" she teased.

"Okay, you asked for it," Porter threatened. "No less than five!"

It was the kind of torture Liv didn't mind as she focused on enjoying Porter in every way possible.

CHAPTER TEN

THE NEXT MONTH passed in much the same way, with Liv seeing Porter multiple times a week. Even Jordan took note, teasing her relentlessly about her "sex toy boyfriend." Everything was great with Porter, except when he hinted that it was time she came clean with her family. She knew she'd have to eventually, but she hoped she could put it off long enough so she wouldn't have to: either the relationship would fizzle or Porter would get tired of asking to come to dinner at her family's house, though he sure seemed set on it. He said he didn't like sneaking around, didn't like lying to her father.

Not that Liv blamed him. She didn't like lying to her father, either, but it had become par for the course lately. One more lie…what did it matter?

Thankfully, she had plenty of other distractions. Business was also booming, as she booked parties nearly every weekend up until Thanksgiving—her usual slow season. She went to place more orders for her favorite vibrator and was surprised to get a phone call from the president of the company, asking for a meet-up in Chicago, since he was in town for a manufacturers' conference. He told her it was strictly professional; he had a business opportunity.

They met in a bustling bar in the Loop around five.

The president, Harvey Jacobs, wore a button-down shirt and khakis, and was probably in his forties. She was relieved when he didn't flirt, but instead shook her hand genially and got right down to business.

"You've been selling our products for two years, and I have to say, your numbers are better than any that we've seen in this area," he said as he flagged down the bartender. "I'll have a Tanqueray and tonic, and the lady will have…"

"Glass of chardonnay. Thank you."

The bartender nodded and went to get their drinks.

"Anyway, as I was saying, your numbers are amazing. I'm sure you like what you do, Ms. Tanaka, but I wanted to meet to ask you if you'd consider working for us." The bartender placed their drinks in front of them at the bar. Liv took a tentative sip of her wine. "We need a director of marketing, and we think you'd be perfect for the job."

"Me?" Liv almost spit out the wine she'd been drinking. She wasn't sure she'd heard correctly: Had he just offered her a job?

"We want to expand the sex toy hostess parties, and we want to make them more systematic, like Tupperware parties used to be. We want our own representatives. We want to build a web of contacts. We think you can help us do that."

Liv's mind whirled. This was just the kind of job she'd been looking for: a public relations and marketing maven's dream. She'd be a director, probably the youngest ever. It wouldn't just be another starter position where she'd be a glorified intern—she'd have loads of responsibility and could really see herself doing something innovative. This was a field she *knew*.

Instantly, she had a hundred ideas about how she could make networking sex toy parties a success. She knew instinctively she could do this job and do it well.

"How much were you thinking about paying?"

Mr. Jacobs grabbed a pen from his shirt pocket and scribbled a number on the paper napkin in front of her. She nearly gasped as what she saw: double what she was making now. On that salary, she could afford her own place, probably a car, too, and much, much more than that.

"Would I have to relocate?" Surely there was a catch to this job. It sounded just too good to be true.

"Our offices are located in California, but we think it would be a good idea for you to be stationed here. Work out of your home. Fly to California quarterly for meetings, but basically you'd make your own hours."

She was getting more excited by the minute. This was her dream job in every way imaginable, except for one little problem: If she took it, would she have to tell her parents what company she was working for? She pushed the thought out of her mind. Her parents didn't need to know. Yet taking the job seemed like one more step toward working in the sex toy industry more…permanently. Hosting parties was one thing. Working for a sex toy company…didn't that seem more serious somehow? Would she be pigeonholed for her career as the sex toy lady?

And wasn't she just *pretending* to be a sex goddess anyhow?

She thought about her night with Porter, and felt a shiver of pleasure run through her. Maybe she wasn't pretending anymore.

She had a lot to think about, she realized as the waitress arrived with their drinks.

"How soon would you need my answer?" she asked, staring at the wine in her glass as she held the slim stem.

"I'll give you two weeks to decide," he said, taking a swig of his gin and tonic, the ice plinking together. "Then I'll have to open the job up to all applicants and see what happens."

Liv agreed to think about it, and she would.

THAT EVENING, SHE went for an early dinner at her parents' house. She intended to drop in and leave early. She had a late-scheduled party at nine, which gave her just enough time for dinner and quick goodbyes. She wore a pencil skirt and blouse, and planned to change later for her party.

When she arrived, however, she realized there'd be no easy getaway. Inside the living room sat one of those quirky nerds her parents were so fond of trying to set her up with: a nephew of a neighbor's, a geeky, glasses-wearing sci-fi type. Someone who spent a lot of time lusting after the female characters on *World of Warcraft*. He was pale from complete lack of sunlight.

"This is *Steve* Moore," her mother said, complete with obvious inflection on his name. If he didn't know why he was here before, her mother just made it perfectly obvious now. "He sells computers."

"Mom…" Liv turned to address her mother. "I need to talk to you. In the kitchen."

Her mom quirked an eyebrow but followed her anyway.

"Mom, I don't want a setup!" Liv furiously whispered as the two stood toe-to-toe in front of her mother's range.

"Liv, it's about time you settled down."

"I can find my own dates." An image of Porter flickered in her mind.

"Liv, come on, your father wants grandchildren. You never date, and it's time to look *seriously*. After all we've done for you…"

Liv braced herself for the guilt trip that was inevitably coming. This was what made it so hard for her to stand up to her parents. Whenever she tried, she felt overwhelmed by the facts: her parents had given her so much—a stable upbringing in a great neighborhood, a college education, and the list went on and on. Liv knew her own mother hadn't been so lucky. Her parents had been poor, living in harder, tougher neighborhoods, barely affording rent. And her mother's parents had been worse off: immigrants from China, hardly speaking a word of English. Liv was the heir to all their sacrifices, and her mother made sure she knew it.

"One dinner—is it so hard to ask?" her mother prodded.

"Mom, you can't keep doing this," Liv said.

"He's already here. One dinner, Olivia. *One*. It's not like you have to work in a sweatshop." Her mother ushered her out of the kitchen.

Liv returned to the dining room reluctantly, glancing to all corners of the room, looking for a speedy getaway. There would be none. It appeared dinner was going to be just them, plus Steve's aunt Dorothy, their neighbor. Her mom hadn't told her of the setup, probably because she knew she'd make excuses and not come. They all sat down at the dinner table, even as

Steve stared straight at Liv's bare calf. He looked as though he'd never seen one before.

Steve sniffed loudly, a runny nose breaking him from his trance as he wiped it with his napkin, which didn't make him any more attractive. Neither did his caved-in posture, his complete lack of upper-body strength or the fact that he was a mouth-breather: keeping his mouth open and slack. He kept staring at her, as if he'd never seen a real, live Asian girl close-up before. If she had to guess, he'd be one of those geeky white guys with an obsession with Asian girls. She called them AOs, Asian-Obsessed.

Liv coughed, wondering if she could feign sudden illness, when the doorbell rang. Her father put his napkin on his clean plate in front of him and went to answer the door. Liv glanced over, hoping for any distraction, when she heard the familiar voice of Porter in the hall.

Oh, God, she thought. *Do not let him come in here.*

She wasn't sure about what was more awful: that Porter would find her in one of her parents' surprise setups, or that he'd probably want to tell the entire room that she wasn't so available, after all, since she'd been warming his bed for the last six weeks. This was why she should've never gotten involved with one of her father's employees, she thought. That had been her mistake from the start.

She glanced nervously at Steve, but he was oblivious, picking some lint off his lap. *Please, do not let Porter come in here.... No...no...no!*

The voices got louder, and she heard her dad laugh. Porter had made him laugh. Then she heard her dad say, "I insist."

Next thing she knew, Porter was standing in the dining room, his eyes sweeping the scene. And her. His gaze lingered on her just a moment, his eyes sparkling with mischief.

"Porter here had some papers for me to sign, but I've invited him to join us," her dad said as he entered the room. "Do we have room, Lian?"

"Of course." Liv's mother stood and bustled around the dining room, pulling a chair from the wall so Porter could sit—opposite Liv. He sent her a smug smile. *Don't,* she silently warned him. *Whatever you've got planned—just don't!*

"Porter, this is Dorothy, our neighbor, and her nephew, Steve. We were just saying how much Steve and Liv have in common," her mother said.

Liv nearly spit out her water. "Really?" Porter asked, as he studied the slim, pale frame of Steve, sitting slouched in his chair, mouth slightly open.

Liv wanted to die of embarrassment. This is the caliber of man her parents thought worthy of her. Steve—the man-child, the one she could completely take in an arm-wrestling contest.

"No, we don't," Liv added quickly.

"But you both like iPhones," her mother said.

"I've got the latest version," he said, holding up his slick new brick of a phone.

"Mom, *everyone* likes iPhones." Liv felt like rolling her eyes, but only just refrained.

"And you both like Chinese food." Her mother bustled around the table, putting out her piping-hot lasagna for the table to eat. "In fact, there's a new restaurant in your neighborhood. Maybe you and Steve would want to go?"

This was bold, even for her mother. Liv glanced at Porter, who let out a little cough of surprise. She couldn't believe her mother was trying to set her up so obviously! Beside her, Steve sat frozen, like a lump.

"No, Mom. I'm busy."

"You can't be that busy," her mother said. "What do you say, Steve? Would you like to go?"

This was not happening. She glanced at her father, who mutely reached for some lasagna. Again, not intervening. Dorothy stared at Liv with a half smile of excitement on her face, probably because she was desperate to get her nephew out of her basement.

"Uh, yeah, I mean…I like Chinese…food." He paused just long enough to make it clear that wasn't the only thing he liked that was Chinese. Proof positive he was AO. She bet if she looked under his bed, she'd find a stash of Asian-only porn. Porter watched Liv carefully. She could not let this go on, not with him in the room.

"Sorry, Steve. Not going to happen." Liv helped herself to some lasagna.

"Olivia! Where are your manners?" her mother exclaimed, disapproving.

"I'm just being honest, Mom. Remember the importance of honesty?"

"Not at the dinner table," she muttered. "And, besides, Liv, you're not getting any younger. Steve is a nice young boy."

Steve wiggled his bushy eyebrows. It was all Liv could do not to openly gag. He was literally the last man on earth she'd ever consider dating.

"Mom…stop."

"Olivia, this is serious now. Steve has been nice

enough to come, and I don't see why you're being so rude." Her mother reached for the giant salad bowl in the middle of the table and heaped greens on her plate. "You'll need to start thinking about marriage and finding the right man before you start aging too much." She pointed the salad tongs in her direction for emphasis.

"Mom!" Liv's temper began to flare. *Aging?* She wasn't even twenty-five yet, and her mother was talking about her as if she were forty. She had a long time before she had to worry about getting old!

"Honestly, Olivia, we try to introduce you to eligible bachelors and you just don't seem grateful at all…"

Porter cleared his throat. He lifted any eyebrow as if to say *how many bachelors?* He took a bite of lasagna and chewed, thoughtfully. Liv felt the frustration rise. Dating was only okay for her if she did it on her mother's terms. That had always been true.

But her mother wasn't finished. "I don't understand why you insist on not dating. Is it that you're gay? Is that it? Is that what you're not telling us?"

Porter nearly choked on his bite of lasagna, which quickly spiraled into a coughing fit.

"Mom! No, I'm not…. Not that there's anything wrong with that, but it's not the point!"

"Then why are you single? Why are you always single?" Her mother's voice had reached an uncomfortable pitch.

"Mom…"

Porter was still coughing, still trying to get the lasagna out of his throat, and she was almost sure he planned to say something. He'd been sitting silently long enough. He nodded at her as if to *go on*.

"I'm not single!" Liv all but shouted, throwing down her fork, having had enough.

The entire room went silent enough you could hear a pin drop. Even Porter looked shocked, his mouth half covered by a napkin. Her dad had frozen, fork halfway to his mouth, and Dorothy frowned.

"Do not tell fibs," her mother said finally. "What have I told you about telling fibs?" Lying was a grounding offense in their house when she was growing up. Always had been.

"I'm not lying," she insisted. She looked at Porter, who still seemed surprised as he wiped his mouth. "I'm dating Porter Benjamin."

CHAPTER ELEVEN

FOR ONCE, LIV'S mother was shocked speechless. Dorothy and her nephew, Steve, shifted uncomfortably in their seats. Porter, who had been so gung ho about honesty, now looked a little pale. Her father turned an angry shade of red, and then a furious white, as he slowly put down his fork.

"Mr. Tanaka, I'm sorry you had to find out this way, I…" Porter began.

Her father shook his head angrily, holding up a hand. "Don't speak," he growled angrily, in a tone that let Liv know just how upset he really was. Liv's mother looked uneasy as she watched her husband's fury grow.

"Dad, if you'll just listen."

"No," her father said, standing up and slamming his palm down on the table, making the china rattle and the glasses shake. "I will *not* listen. You…you…" He glanced at Porter, and then at Liv again, unsure where to send his anger first. *"Out of my house."* He pointed a steely finger at Porter's chest. "Out…"

"Dad!"

"Out!"

Porter nodded slowly and stood, carefully and calmly folding his napkin and putting it in his chair. "The lasagna was delicious, Mrs. Tanaka," he said as he pushed back his chair. He was completely calm and composed as he stood and made his way to the door.

Liv threw back her chair with a screech and went after him.

"Porter! I'm sorry. I thought…I thought you were going to say something, and I thought it would be better if I did."

Porter shrugged. "I wasn't going to say a word. It was your secret to tell."

Liv felt hot and cold all at once. She'd blurted out the truth for no good reason?

Porter took Liv's hands. "But I'm not sorry you did."

"You don't have to go." She squeezed his fingers.

"Yes, I do," he said, covering her hand with his. "You have to talk to your father."

Liv swallowed, feeling butterflies dance in her stomach at the prospect. "But what can I say?"

"The truth. All of it."

"*Now?* When he's furious?"

Porter buttoned up his jacket and swung open the front door. "Take my advice, Liv. Rip the Band-Aid off all at once. It'll be better this way."

"I don't know if I can."

Mr. Tanaka appeared in the foyer, looking livid. Porter nodded at Liv and then went out through the front door. Liv watched him go, feeling the dread rise in her stomach. She wished he could've stayed, at least for moral support. But even she knew that he'd only be a lightning rod for her father's temper.

"I want to speak to you, Olivia. Study. Now." Her father barely got the words out through his clenched teeth.

Liv followed, shoulders slumped, feeling as though

she was in high school again. Once in his study, her
father paced in front of his bookshelf, hands clasped
firmly behind his back.

"How long has this been going on?" he demanded.

"A couple of months."

"Has he been…a gentleman?" Her father kneaded
his hands in worry.

"Dad, I'm not a kid anymore." Liv was tired of
being treated like one, too. "I'm nearly twenty-five,
not fifteen. It's time for you and Mom to let go."

"Olivia, you didn't answer my question. Porter is
a good man, a good worker, but he's much older than
you. Men his age…they want more things. He's…"

Liv crossed her arms angrily across her chest. "Dad,
he's only a few years older. We're both adults."

Her father slumped in his desk chair and sighed.
Suddenly, he looked much older than he had just five
minutes ago. Liv noticed more gray in his hair and
more worry lines on his face. "I'm sorry, but I can't
condone this relationship. He's too old for you. He'll
want…things you shouldn't be thinking about at your
age."

"At *my* age? Dad, do you even hear yourself? Mom
had already *had* me by my age. You two were already
married!" Liv swung her arms wide to emphasize her
point. She was tired of them thinking she was a kid,
when they'd started their adult lives at a much younger
age.

Her father's forehead wrinkled as if he was trying
to keep up with math that made no sense to him at all.
"We were married. That's different."

Liv let out a long sigh. "Dad, I respect you. I'm
asking that you respect me, and the choices I make."

A soft knock on the door sounded and her mother peeked in. "Can I come in?" she asked, voice low.

"Why not? Go ahead, Mom. You're always trying to set me up with someone. Don't tell me now you're against this, too."

"I wouldn't say that exactly," her mother began, looking torn.

"Mom's on my side," Liv said, triumphant.

"I wouldn't say that, either." Her mom shook her head slowly. "He's older, and more experienced, and…" Her parents exchanged a knowing look. Now, Liv saw clearly: they only really wanted her to date virgins. That was the entire plan! That's why she'd seen a stream of lonely nerds who spent Saturday nights chained to their PlayStations.

"Mom, you can't be serious. I'm an adult now. *I* have experience."

Her mother just shook her head in disbelief. "Not *this* kind of experience." Her mother sounded so sure. As if the very idea that she'd been naked with a man was completely preposterous.

"No!" Her father shook his head angrily. "I'm sorry, Olivia. But I can't allow this relationship."

"Allow?" Liv was stumped. "I'm not a teenager. I don't live here anymore. You can't tell me what to do anymore."

"I can, and I *will!*" her dad bellowed. "I'm your father."

Liv laughed bitterly, throwing her head back and shaking her long dark hair in disbelief. No matter what she did, her father would always see her as a little girl. Her mother sat mute, watching the drama unfold, silently agreeing with her father. She suddenly felt trapped, as if it was hard to breathe, tired of pretending to be someone she wasn't. Liv simply couldn't swallow the irony anymore. Here her father was worried about her virtue when she probably knew more about sex, and certainly sex toys, than Porter did. It was beyond ridiculous. Only *her* parents would be worried about her virginity when she'd lost it years ago.

"And if you don't stop this, I'll ask Porter to stop it."

"Dad…you can't." Liv was struck with a sudden fear: Porter losing his job because of her. "You can't do that."

"I'll do it if you don't."

Somewhere deep inside, this felt like the last straw, the very final absurdity she just couldn't swallow. Her heart thudded hard in her chest, pumping anger and adrenaline through her veins.

"Dad…" She was tempted to tell him everything. She wasn't a marketing maven at all; she was a sex toy expert. She was no innocent little girl who didn't know anything about the world. He was worried about a thirty-year-old man corrupting her, when she was the one who knew enough to corrupt him! "I'm dating him. It's my decision. If you threaten Porter, then you'll lose me. For good. I mean it."

Liv stalked out of her father's study, grabbed her bag and her jacket, and left, her mother calling her name as she went.

LIV ONLY WENT through the motions at her sex toy party that night—though the couples there didn't seem to notice. They were too busy digging through her *Kama Sutra* books and testing out oils to much care that she was a million miles away and not her usual bubbly self.

"Look at this pose!" one of the ladies squealed as she showed her husband. "Could we even *do* that?"

Her husband cocked his head to one side, tilting the book from side to side to get a better look. "I am *not* that limber," he declared, and the other three couples laughed.

Liv watched the husbands flirting with their wives and felt a flicker of goodwill inside. After all, she *did* help people. It wasn't all just dirty jokes. She saw the middle-aged couples here connecting again with each other, in ways maybe they hadn't in a long time. Intimacy was a good thing, and a party like hers could help bring it back. If only she could make her parents see this, then they'd understand. But first she'd have to tell them. She pushed the thought away. Later, she thought. *Always later.*

Seeing the loving couples around her, her mind went to Porter. She'd called him before the party started, warning him her dad was on the warpath. He'd told her not to worry. He wasn't afraid of what her father could do to him, and if it came down to having to leave the firm and look for a new job, he would. Her insides felt twisted. But it was long past time they saw her as an adult. She was tired of them trying to impose the same rules on her that they had when she was twelve. It wasn't healthy. She was a grown woman, and it was time they let her be one.

The couples at the party bought various toys and oils, some promising to try them out on weekend getaways, and others leaving the party shyly holding hands. Liv felt good about it, helping the couples find themselves again, and she refused to feel guilty as she packed up her wares. As she rode back to her own apartment in the back of cab, her head felt heavy with regret. She should've just told them about what she really did for a living. Then they'd have no choice but to accept the fact that she was an adult. What was wrong with her that she couldn't just *tell* them? What was she afraid of? Being grounded?

Liv snorted to herself, shaking her head. Porter was right. If she wanted to be treated like an adult, it was about time she acted like one. She needed to stop being afraid of her parents. They couldn't ground her or take away her favorite toys anymore. They had no real hold over her. The cab pulled up in front of her Wicker Park apartment and she paid the driver and lugged her suitcase to the door, her mind whirling. She looked up and noticed a light on in her apartment, which she found strange. She knew Jordan was out tonight, her band landing a gig as an opening act at the Vic. Jordan, an environment nut, hardly ever left the lights on.

Liv pulled her suitcase up the stairs and opened her front door.

Inside, she saw her parents: her mother paced the living room rug, and her father sat with his arms crossed, face looking stern.

"What are you doing here?" Liv couldn't contain her shock. Her parents had a spare key, but they'd never used it before. They'd never invaded her privacy in such a bald-faced way.

"We need to talk to you, young lady." Her mother sounded stern. "We called and you ignored us."

Liv had turned off her phone for the party. She'd forgotten to turn it back on. Her mother glanced at the high hem of her skirt, frowning. Liv wore one of her favorite hostess outfits: a tight black minidress and her knee-high boots, her hair up in a high, glossy black ponytail, her lips painted in killer red lipstick.

"Is that what you're wearing? Olivia! My goodness!"

"Mom, don't start," Liv warned.

Liv's mother moved closer, tissue out, ready to smear off her expensive lipstick. "Mom, I mean it." Liv held up one hand, ready to grab the tissue if necessary. She was in no mood to deal with lectures about her fashion choices. Sensing she had gone too far, her mother stopped, tissue in midair, and glanced at her father for support.

"Olivia," her father warned.

"No, Dad. You two need to go. You don't have a right to be here."

"We're your *parents!* We have every right." Her father was still angry. His voice shook.

"You've come in uninvited. You *do not* have a right." Liv stood, fuming. Her anger growing with every second. How dare they bully her like this? They were going too far.

"You have to stop seeing Porter Benjamin." Her dad just wouldn't let it go.

"No," Liv said. "I already told you, I won't."

Her dad let out a frustrated groan. Even he knew he couldn't really do anything.

"I'm going to ask you one more time to go."

"Why do you have a suitcase?" her mother said, pointing to the rolling bag near the door. "Did you come from his house? Have you been staying there?"

Liv glanced at her bag, the anger in her rising. They just wouldn't leave her alone. They just wouldn't let go. She simply couldn't take it anymore.

"I didn't want to have to tell you both this, *like* this, but you leave me no choice." Liv reached into her pocket and grabbed one of her hostess business cards. The pink curlicue letters read clearly:

> *Adult Play Time Parties!*
> *Buy and Try Adult Toys!*

Her name and contact email were written clearly underneath.

Her father blinked at it, not making sense of the card. He handed it to Liv's mother.

"I don't understand," Liv's mother said. "What is this? Why is your name on this?"

"I don't have that marketing job. *This* is what I do. I host parties with adult toys. I *sell* adult toys. I'm not some little girl. I *know* how the world works."

"Adult…toys?" Her mother looked completely baffled. "What are adult…toys?"

Her father, too, seemed confused.

"You wanted to see what was in the bag, Mom? Well, I'll show you." Liv swiped at the bag, and unzipped it angrily. All manner of toys fell out: pink vibrators, purple dildos, dozens of wrapped condoms.

"What in the world…" Her mom's eyes grew wide like saucers. "What *are* those?"

Her father knew. His face turned red and then white, and he looked like he might faint. "They're…uh…" He cleared his throat.

"Vibrators, Mom," Liv said, uncharitably. "Condoms. Flavored oils. Edible underwear." Liv was too angry to be embarrassed or shy. She was tired of them not understanding. Not seeing her as an adult. Shocking them was the only way. "I *sell* these."

"What?" Her mother grabbed her chest as if her heart might pop out of it. "You sell… Filth?"

"Not filth, Mom. Things that adults enjoy. That's all."

"Do you sell…more than toys?" Her mother could barely get the question out as she pressed her fist against her mouth, bracing herself for the answer.

"I'm not a prostitute! Jeez, Mom! This is all legal, and there's *nothing wrong with it*."

"Nothing wrong…!" Her mom put her hands to her temples as if her brain simply couldn't absorb the shock of the news. "You're going to have to quit. *Tomorrow*. And then you're going to church. To ask the Lord for forgiveness."

"Mom, I didn't do anything *wrong!* I sell toys to married couples, mostly, or couples *about* to be married. It's about giving them something to help them *keep* their marriages together."

"What about Denote? Was that all a lie?" Her father didn't want to believe, either.

"I tried looking for a job everywhere, but no one was hiring. I fell into this, and guess what? I'm *good* at it. The president of one of the toy companies asked me to be his marketing director. I'm probably going to take the job." After the words were out of her mouth, she realized with surprise that they were true. She did want that job.

Her mother turned her gaze skyward in silent prayer.

"You can't work for a pornography company!" shouted her father. "I will *not* tolerate this! Not at all!"

"It's not a pornography company, Dad! They make all kinds of things. And I make *my own decisions!*"

She glared at her dad, and he stared right back, both of them flushed with fury, both with fists clenched at their sides. Her mother looked as if she might faint at any moment. Liv glanced over at her mother and realized it was just as bad as she thought: neither one of them understood. She knew they wouldn't. They'd just always see her as a little girl, helpless and naive.

"This is who I am," Liv said. "Take me or leave me."

Her father just shook his head sadly from side to side. He rose silently and grabbed his overcoat from the ottoman. "Come on, Lian. We're going."

"But…" Her mom still looked as if she were reeling from shock.

"Now," her father said, grabbing his wife's arm. Numbly, she walked with him to the door. They left without another word.

CHAPTER TWELVE

LIV FELT STRANGELY relieved to have the secret finally out. She didn't have to lie anymore, and she'd faced the worst of it, her parents leaving her apartment stunned and dejected. Liv hadn't realized how much the secret had weighed on her, how much she worried about her parents' finding out. Well, now they knew. There wasn't anything she could do about it, and now they had to figure out a way to deal with it. Or not.

Jordan had cackled out loud when Liv told her the story the next day. Jordan had come home late from her band's gig. Midafternoon daylight streamed in the windows as Jordan poured herself a cup of instant coffee.

Liv put her head in her hands, feeling a sudden surge of regret. "Did I do the right thing, Jordan? I mean, maybe I shouldn't have told them. Maybe…"

"You had to tell them," Jordan reasoned. "They'd been babying you for too long. And just coming into your place? *Our* place? So not cool."

"You're right, it's just…I don't know. The look on their faces. I don't know if they'll get over it." Liv bit her bottom lip. The relief at having her secret out was fading.

"If they love you, they will get over it," Jordan said, giving her roommate a pat on the shoulder.

HER PARENTS' SILENT treatment went on for nearly a

month. It had been the longest Liv had gone without speaking to them. Their silence hurt her in surprising ways. She'd always known they'd be angry when they found out, but somewhere, deep down, she'd held out hope that maybe they'd understand. That they'd come around. That they'd finally see her for who she was: a smart, resourceful young woman who could make her own decisions. Thanksgiving was right around the corner, and they still weren't returning her phone calls. She might never spend another holiday with them again.

"They'll come around," Porter said, as she lay in his arms in his townhome, stroking her hair. They both lay naked beneath his sheets, the full moon outside shining in through his bedroom window, casting a silver glow on his furniture. It was late, but Liv wasn't tired.

"No, they won't," Liv said, feeling sure. Complete radio silence told Liv that her parents had given up on her, saw her as a lost cause. "Dad isn't even talking to you at work, is he?"

"Monosyllables, mostly," Porter said, as he tucked a strand of Liv's long black hair behind one ear. "But I think he's thawing a little."

"By grunting at you, huh? Dad holds grudges. You might have to look for a new job." Liv turned around, rolling up on Porter's bare chest, as she lay her chin on her folded hands.

"If I get you, a new job is a small price to pay," Porter said, kissing her nose.

Liv felt a twinge of guilt. This was all her fault. If only she'd been more up-front with her parents before Porter, he wouldn't be having such trouble at work now.

"Maybe we really shouldn't be together," Liv said, doubt gnawing away at her. "I'm causing you headaches at work and..."

"Hey...wait." Porter lifted her chin. "Are you not happy with me...with us?"

Liv laughed, the question was so absurd. They'd just finished another marathon sex session and he had the nerve to ask if she was happy? She couldn't get enough of him, and that was the truth.

"I'm *more* than happy," Liv said, snuggling against him. "You know that."

"Then *stop* talking about breaking up with me. I mean it. My delicate ego can't handle it." Porter flashed a grin and Liv giggled. Porter's ego was anything but delicate.

"You sure you don't mind me working for a porn company? I mean, am I doing the right thing?" In the darkness, she started to second-guess all her decisions. With her parents so angry, she felt adrift.

"You love your new job," Porter said, putting his muscled arms around her. She felt his warmth and support. "And you said so yourself, it's not a porn company. They make lots of things."

It was true. Beyond just adult toys, they made high-end lotions and bath gels, among other mainstream items found at most local drugstores.

Liv lay her cheek against Porter, feeling thankful to have him. Still, as her own anger against her parents faded, she felt a pang of loss. "I just wish I could make them understand," she said.

"Why not try to talk to them again?"

"They don't answer my calls." Liv sighed.

Porter thought about this, his dark eyes somber as

he thought through the problem. "Why not try to talk to them in person? Thanksgiving is next week. You're welcome to spend it with my family, but I know you'd really rather spend it with yours."

LIV KNEW PORTER was right. Jordan had said the same thing—that she ought to go talk to them. So she borrowed Jordan's car one weekend and drove out to her parents' house. She rang the bell, but found the house empty. That's when she remembered that the weekend before Thanksgiving was always the soup kitchen at the church. Her parents volunteered there, helping the less fortunate.

She drove down the main avenue of Oak Park, lined with giant oaks and maples, their leaves bright orange and red. Colored leaves fell to the ground, and stacks of them stood in yards as neighbors raked. She saw children jumping into leaf piles and remembered doing the same thing when she was little. Sometimes she wished she could be a kid again, be as her parents saw her. Things were much simpler then.

But she couldn't go back in time, and she wouldn't, really, if given a choice. She drove to the huge stone church with the tall steeple and impressive stained-glass windows at the end of the street. She'd been coming here her whole life. Her parents had always been somewhat religious, but their fervor had increased in recent years when they switched to a more conservative church. The big red doors of the church were unlocked, and Liv walked into the main sanctuary, not quite sure she remembered where the soup kitchen was. Walking by the pews, she stared down the long altar, and then eventually sat down, bowing her head in prayer for her parents' forgiveness.

"OLIVIA?" IT WAS her mother's voice, from somewhere behind her. Liv turned to see her mother wearing a black-and-white checkered apron, her white oxford rolled up at the elbows, looking as if she'd just come from the soup kitchen.

"Mom! I wanted to talk to you."

Her mother hesitated, glancing back over her shoulder. Then she wiped her hands on her apron and came over, sitting down in the empty pew next to Liv. "I've got a minute," she said. "How are you? Did you… take the job?"

"Yeah, I did."

"I see." Her mother seemed to absorb the information and consider it. "Your dad will be angry."

"I know. But how about you, Mom? Are you still mad?"

Her mom let out a long sigh. "You know, I was for a while. But the interesting thing is, I talked to Pastor Jake. And he seemed to think that maybe this is one way He helps couples stay together. Like you said."

"What do you think?"

Her mother patted her hand. "I think that all I wanted was to raise a strong daughter who was tough and knew her own mind. That's why I was so hard on you, you know."

Liv thought about all the times her mother had made her do her homework over again, or made her practice her ballet recital steps, or insisted she do things a different way.

"You once made me *redo* a Valentine," Liv exclaimed, remembering her tiger mom's stern face, demanding she start all over with a new piece of red construction paper.

"You misspelled the word *Valentine!*"

"I was *five!*" Liv said, remembering her mother shaking her finger, demanding better.

"How else would you learn to spell 'Valentine'? You know what I always said."

"'Do it 'til you get it right.'" Liv quoted her mother easily, since she'd heard the motto nearly every day growing up.

"My mother was worse, you know," Lian said, remembering her own childhood. "She was born in China, and she didn't even let me play on playgrounds! Said it was a waste of time when I could be learning something useful. She grew up very poor. She wanted us to be survivors."

"Why didn't you tell me this before?" Liv knew her own mother had an even stricter upbringing, but she didn't know it had been quite *so* strict. Her mother hardly ever talked about it. Never wanted to talk about it.

"Complaining is for the weak," she said and shrugged. "That's what my mom taught me. So I never wanted to burden you with my memories."

"Mom…that is tough."

"At least I let you play on playgrounds."

"Thanks for that." Liv smiled. She felt as though she understood her mother better than she had in years.

Her mother looked thoughtful as she patted Liv's knee. "I'm glad you know your own mind. I'm glad you're strong and independent and make your own money. Do you know how many of my friends have kids living on their couches? Eating everything in the fridge? So many have failed to launch. But not mine. You're a survivor, a hard worker, and I'm proud of you, Olivia."

"You are?"

"I am."

Liv turned to her mother, whose arms were open wide, uncharacteristically open for a rare hug. Liv wrapped her arms around her mother and felt her embrace.

"Why don't you come for Thanksgiving?" her mother asked. "Bring Porter, too. I like him. He's clean-cut and respectful."

"I thought you didn't want me to date him." Liv couldn't believe her ears.

"I've come around to the idea," her mother said, shrugging. "He's a lawyer with a steady job. He has good manners. You could do worse."

"What about Dad? Will he want me there?" Liv asked.

"You leave him to me," her mother said, squeezing her tight.

"DON'T BE NERVOUS," Porter told her, as they stood on the porch of her parents' house. Liv carried a pumpkin pie she'd bought at a local bakery on the way. She wore her most conservative black sweater set, her hair up in a prim bun, but makeup firmly on. Subtle and neutral, but there all the same. She'd decided she wouldn't be two different people anymore, pretending to be what her parents wanted. She was who she was.

"I am, though. What if Dad kicks you out?" Liv's stomach was a knot of butterflies. Her mother had said she would take care of her father, but could she really? Could she convince him?

"He won't." Porter put his hand at the small of Liv's back. She took strength from his touch. Whatever happened, she felt she could handle it with Porter by her side.

The door swung open and her mother stood there, smiling.

"There you are. Come in." She opened the door wide. Her father stood in the living room, sipping a Coke. When he saw her, he gave her a stern nod. He eyed Porter a minute, the hint of a frown crossing his face, before he settled into a neutral expression. Liv felt her stomach tighten. Was this going to be a disaster? Would it be a Thanksgiving that ended in a screaming match and tears?

She held her breath as her father approached, stiffly at first.

"Olivia," he said. "Porter." He nodded his head at both of them, his face still stern and expressionless. Liv wished she knew what he was thinking. It was impossible to know. Another butterfly lurched in her stomach, even as she held her chin high. Porter squeezed her hand for support. Liv squeezed his fingers back. She wasn't going to back down, whatever happened.

"Thanks for coming," her father said at last, his expression softening somewhat. "I'm sorry, Porter, about the way things ended the last time you were here."

Surprised by the apology, Porter raised his eyebrows. "No hard feelings at all," he said. "I completely understand."

Her father nodded and then looked at Liv. "And your

mother feels I owe you an apology, too." Liv froze, waiting to hear what came next.

"Do you feel that you do?" she asked her father.

He paused, staring at the liquid in his glass, waiting so long, Liv felt that she would die from suspense.

"Yes," he said, slowly. "I do. You were right that I had no business telling you what to do. You're a grown woman now, and I have to accept that." He met her eyes, and Liv saw they were wet with tears. Surprised by the sudden show of emotion, she felt her heart swell with relief and also with a little guilt.

"I never meant to disappoint you," Liv said. "I never meant to do that to you or Mom."

"You haven't disappointed us at all," her father said. "I'm proud of you, Olivia. I always have been. You're strong and you're smart and you could teach your old man a thing or two about business, I'm sure."

Liv laughed anxiously. She didn't know if she wanted to teach her father about selling dildos. That was taking things a bit too far.

"Whatever you do, we'll support you," her father said. "I'll try to let you have more freedom. But you know, to me, you'll always be my little girl. I'll work on it, though."

Her father opened his arms and Liv went to him, hugging her dad, feeling tears sting her eyes.

"Thanks, Dad," she said, feeling such relief that her father wasn't mad at her anymore. That he was letting her be who she had to be.

He pulled away first, swiping at his eyes, trying to hide his tears. He looked at Porter. "Now, you'd better take good care of her, young man," her dad warned. "Or I *will* fire you."

"Yes, sir," Porter said, giving her dad a mock salute. "I promise that it will be *my pleasure* taking care of Liv."

Liv glanced up at Porter, his handsome brown eyes on her, and felt her whole body grow warm. She knew he meant take care of her in *every* possible way. She blushed, even as he pulled her close and gently kissed the top of her head. "And she'll take care of me, too," he murmured into her hair.

That was when she realized being with Porter wasn't about living her parents' lives at all. That no matter what she did—even if she married a lawyer and settled into the suburbs—she'd still be herself. Being an adult meant making her own decisions, and she chose Porter. He offered the perfect blend of naughty and nice. He was right for her, and she knew it.

"There, that wasn't so hard, was it?" her mother said, joining the group. Her father rolled his eyes.

"Easy for you to say," he grumbled.

"Come on now, dear, I need help in the kitchen." Her mother pulled her dad away.

Liv watched them go and then craned her neck to look at Porter. He flashed her a white smile.

"See? I was right. Being honest was the way to go. Just like the Boy Scouts. Always tell the truth."

Liv gave Porter a playful punch. "You were *never* a Boy Scout! So how do you know?"

"You got me there," Porter said, pulling her close. He sneaked a look at the closed door of the kitchen and then dipped down to kiss her. She rose up to meet him, her feet light and her heart swelling with love.

Porter pulled away just as her mother bustled out of the kitchen.

"Well, what are you doing just standing around? Let's eat," she declared.

"After you," Porter said, bowing to Liv. She grinned and took his hand, feeling a strong premonition that this would be one of many shared Thanksgivings to come.

* * * * *

USA TODAY bestselling author **Heidi Rice** lives in London, England. She is married with two teenage sons (which gives her rather too much of an insight into the male psyche) and also works as a film journalist. She adores her job, which involves getting swept up in a world of high emotions, sensual excitement, funny feisty women, sexy tortured men and glamourous locations where laundry doesn't exist. Once she turns off her computer, she often does chores (usually involving laundry!). Visit her online at heidi-rice.com.

10 WAYS TO HANDLE THE BEST MAN

Heidi Rice

To Miss Abby Green for being a fabulous cheerleader and an invaluable arbitrator of "How kinky is too kinky?" while I wrote this book

1) Schmooze Him, Don't Lose Him: Start your charm offensive early, and don't give your best man too much wiggle room.

'I DIDN'T SAY I can't dance—I said I *won't* dance.'

Sabrina Millard resisted the urge to roll her eyeballs at the man sitting opposite her in the crowded Soho pub, while silently cursing her BFF, Libby, and Libby's fiancé, Jamie.

Wow, Libs, thanks so much for saddling me with the best man from hell to handle.

As a maid of honour with enough experience to write a book about the pitfalls of the role, Sabrina knew handling the best man vied for the top spot in 'Wedding Crap the Maid of Honour Has to Deal With' right alongside:

1. Wearing an exceptionally unflattering dress (puffball sleeves optional)—so as not to upstage the bride.

2. Making sure the bride doesn't have a nervous breakdown or develop an eating disorder before her big day.

3. Getting hit on by tipsy groomsmen—who assume that if you are single and a member of the bridal

party, you'll put up with getting shagged sense-
less against a wall by any eligible bachelor within
a ten-mile radius.

Luckily, as the company manager at The Phoenix,
a non-profit theatre on London's South Bank, Sabrina happened to be exceptionally talented at planning events while coping with colossal egos, making
her confident she could even whip Jamie's half-brother
Connor McCoy—the Creature from the Testosterone
Lagoon—into shape.

But even with her excellent man-handling strate-
gies, Sabrina was struggling to suppress a scowl after
only fifteen minutes in McCoy's company. That he
kept challenging every single thing she said with that
surly, I-couldn't-give-a-shit look in his pale blue eyes
was not helping with her scowl control.

'Yes, well, I'm afraid as the best man you're going
to have to dance,' she said, subtly alerting him to the
fact he wasn't the most knowledgeable person on the
subject of wedding etiquette.

If Libby hadn't already clued her in about the com-
mitment-phobic dating habits of her beloved's older
brother, Sabrina could have guessed from the way his
smouldering gaze had checked out every woman in
the place in the ten minutes since he'd arrived. Every
woman that was, except her.

Not that she cared about his lack of interest *per se*.
All right, so Connor McCoy was undeniably hot, she'd
give him that. The combination of cool azure eyes,
dark brows, jet-black hair long enough to curl around
his ears and sharp angular cheekbones made him ar-
resting—not to mention the cloud of testosterone that

hovered in the air around him and had been a siren call to every other woman in The Pillars of Hercules pub on Greek Street. But luckily, she'd never been susceptible to alpha-jerk types who spent a small fortune on their gym membership—if the overdeveloped biceps stretching the sleeves of his black T-shirt were anything to go by.

Not that she'd noticed those hard, round orbs of muscle much—that flexed and bulged every time he raised his beer bottle to his lips. But when a girl hadn't had a meaningful relationship with anything other than her vibrator since last July, well, upper body strength like that was kind of hard to ignore entirely.

She drew her gaze away from his distracting biceps and concentrated on getting her point across—firmly and succinctly—again.

'Libby wants us to join the floor together after her and Jamie finish their first dance. So really, whether you *want* to dance or not is a moot point.'

He shrugged. 'I'll talk to Jamie, tell him to scratch that part.'

'No, you will not,' she replied, somewhat less subtly. 'This is Libby's big day, and the first dance is an important tradition at weddings in the UK—'

'Hey, they have the same dumb deal in the US,' he interrupted, the cynical edge to his voice making his thoughts on marriage abundantly clear. 'So what? If my brother wants to make a jackass of himself, he can—he's the one getting married. I'm just the best man, which makes me a jackass-free zone.'

'That's where you're wrong,' Sabrina replied, making her thoughts on his crappy attitude abundantly clear. 'Because in this instance, the first dance tradition also includes the maid of honour and the best man introducing the other couples to the dance floor.' He swore under his breath, but she soldiered on. 'Libby and Jamie are practicing a whole routine for "Ooh Baby Baby".' She swallowed to stop her gag reflex from engaging, the way she had when Libby had informed her of the music choice with a breathless huff of pleasure the week before. Far be it from her—or Mr Testosterone—to rain on Libby's schmaltz-fest. 'All they require us to do is join them for the slow-dance when the DJ fades into the next song.'

'A slow-dance?' he spluttered, his eyes going a little squinty around the edges. 'Right, no fucking way am I doing that.'

'What is your problem?' Sabrina felt her forehead tighten as the scowl won out. Forget subtle, the guy was obviously far too closely related to Cro-Magnon man to even process subtlety. 'This isn't actually about you. It's about Libby and Jamie. All you have to do is sway in time to the music for one song. If you're so worried about making a tit of yourself, I can lead,' she added, knowing the suggestion was liable to trip his I'm-the-one-with-a-dick-here switch, but unable to stop herself in the face of so much provocation.

'I know how to slow-dance, sweetheart' came the predictably testosterone-laced response. He rested a muscled forearm on the pub's tiny table, perilously close to her own arm, invading her personal space and making her far too aware of the dimple in his chin and the flecks of silver in the piercing blue of his irises. 'My point is I'm not slow-dancing with *you*.'

Sabrina set her margarita on the table, sucked in a calming breath to stop herself from hyperventilating—

which unfortunately filled her lungs with the enticing scent of his sandlewood soap—and struggled to get a stranglehold on her patience.

'Okay, I'm starting to sense a certain amount of hostility towards me personally.' She forced her voice out of the shrill register. 'And I'm not sure where it's coming from?' she continued. 'As I've never met you before,' she lied, hoping he didn't notice the small quiver in her voice.

Unfortunately, she had met Connor McCoy once before, but she was fairly confident he'd forgotten about it.

She'd always been smart, focused, ambitious and goal-orientated, and she wasn't afraid to show it. Slightly more regular sex would be nice, but she didn't need a man to complete her life—which she knew made her completely invisible to men like Connor McCoy, who thrived on female attention.

For once, she was grateful for her invisibility, when he sent her a blank look and didn't call her on the lie.

CONNOR MCCOY STARED at the woman opposite him and knew exactly where his hostility was coming from. But he'd rather shoot himself in the nuts than admit it, especially to her.

Why the hell wouldn't she let this drop? He'd agreed to wear a monkey suit. He'd agreed to stand at the front of the church like a prize douchebag and witness something he'd always thought was overrated. And he'd agreed to give a speech even though he didn't know what the hell to say…. But there was no way he was taking this uptight British chick in his arms, on or off a dance floor.

He'd met Libby's best friend, Sabrina Millard, before. For approximately ten minutes, five years ago.
But the memory remained burned into his brain like
battery acid.

It had been the end of the spring semester, and he'd
been in the UK on business. He'd agreed to pick up
Jamie and his stuff from the coed dorm in Manchester University that his brother had been sharing with
his pretty English girlfriend, Libby, and Sabrina, because he hadn't seen the kid in years. While Jamie and
Libby had been saying a lengthy goodbye involving
a lot of tongue on the sidewalk, Sabrina had insisted
on directing him on how to pack Jamie's stuff into the
admittedly space-challenged muscle car he'd rented
at Manchester Airport. She'd issued instructions as
if she were the Queen of England and he one of her
lowly footmen, while wearing a shorty red dress over
combat boots that should have made her look like a
lesbian stormtrooper. But hadn't.

He'd been avoiding meeting up with her again, ever
since Jamie had told him she was the maid of honour.
For the simple reason that the woman's outspoken,
pushy personality grated on his last nerve—and turned
him on to the point of madness.

Sabrina had a definite touch of the dominatrix about
her—that made him want to dominate her right back.
The way that Mary Poppins accent went from clipped
to throaty and her magnificent cleavage swelled to
mind-boggling proportions when she went into full
Mein Führer mode had called to his inner caveman—
and kicked off a hot, sweet ache in his crotch that had
his palm itching to spank her generous butt.

The male libido was a strange and beautiful thing,

so he wasn't much surprised about being aroused by a woman he couldn't stand. He'd never wanted to have a conversation with Pamela Anderson, but it hadn't stopped him jerking off over her poster as a kid. But as he didn't much care for vanilla sex—and he'd bet his left nut Sabrina had never had a single sex-for-the-hell-of-it experience in her whole, well-ordered life—nailing Sabrina was definitely out.

Which would make slow-dancing with the woman at his brother's wedding yet more aggravation he didn't need. If he got that close to her, there was a real risk of him sporting wood. She'd notice and she'd say something—because women like Sabrina weren't the type to let sleeping hard-ons lie—and if that happened, he wasn't sure he'd be able to resist the urge to show her who was boss.

There'd be a scene at Jamie's wedding—a scene that Jamie's mom, Elizabeth, and their father, Daniel, would feed off like zombies feasting on a rotting corpse. Not that he gave a shit what either of them thought of him anymore. But it would remind him way too forcefully of being that scared, screwed-up fourteen-year-old runaway who had arrived on their doorstep with a birth certificate in his hand and some dumb notion in his head about hunting up the father he had never met.

Connor clenched his fingers into a fist to quell the persistent itch in his palm.

'Unnecessary hostility…?' he scoffed, because letting Sabrina get away with busting his balls went against his natural instincts. 'So now this is all about you? Maybe I just don't want to make a jackass of myself—for my brother's benefit.'

'Fine, well, I'm glad it's not me.' She let out a lengthy sigh—the long-suffering kind that his step-mother had become a master of. 'But I really don't see why you assume that your brother is doing this to humiliate you. Honestly, it's not like that. The first dance is all Libby's idea. And believe me, when it comes to being part of the wedding party you just have to park your ego at the door and do what has to be done for the people you love.'

Her voice had softened and her mossy-green eyes had gone a little glassy—making it obvious her speech was heartfelt. He felt an odd flutter in his chest. Love was way too strong a word for what he and Jamie shared. To be honest, he still wasn't sure why Jamie had asked him to be his best man—or why he'd agreed to do it. But even so, her comment intrigued him.

'You sound like you've done this before?' he said, wondering how many times she'd gotten stuck with being the bride's go-to girl. And whether she resented it. Maybe that explained the snotty attitude.

'You have no idea.' She rolled her eyes and sent him the first unguarded smile he'd ever seen on her face. The hot, sweet ache in his crotch pulsed, and it struck him she ought to let those smiles loose more often.

'That bad, huh?' He smiled back, the loud buzz of conversation in the bar dimming as he got fixated on the curve of her full bottom lip.

'Put it this way—when I get married I'd rather opt for Vegas and an Elvis impersonator than having to organise all this crap.'

'That's weird. I had you pegged as the white wedding type.'

She shuddered. 'Oh pur-lease. It's the marriage that's important. Not the trimmings.'

Yeah, right, he thought, but didn't argue, intrigued by the flash of passion in the mossy green.

'And do I look like the sort of person who would throw away thousands of pounds on an event that I'd be far too stressed to enjoy?' she continued. 'Did you know that five percent of marriages end after the honeymoon simply because of the stress of the big day?'

'Can't argue with the stats.' Or the fact that all the blood was draining out of his head when she quoted figures with that furrow of consternation on her brow.

'So look, are we good with the first dance thing?' she asked. 'Seriously, apart from remembering the rings, giving a crude speech detailing all the most embarrassing things Jamie has ever done in his entire life and making sure he doesn't puke before Libby gets to the altar, that's your job over and done with.'

'That's *all*? No one told me about the barfing clause—does that entitle me to hazard pay?'

She laughed, the throaty rumble echoing in his crotch. 'Just be glad you don't have to wear five-inch heels and a dress which dips at the back right down to the curve of your bum cheeks!'

Shit.

Why did she have to go and mention her ass? He rubbed his palms on the rough fabric of his jeans to stop the renewed twitching. But he couldn't resist leaning to one side so that he could direct his gaze under the table. 'Your bum cheeks, huh? Suddenly, this gig is looking more appealing.'

It was a pick-up line and not one of his best, but she'd given him the opening, so it surprised him when

her pale face flushed a bright, glowing red—right up
to her hairline. Exactly like it had five years ago in
Manchester when he'd told her where he was going
to shove his brother's baseball bat if she didn't stop
directing him like a member of the damn Gestapo.

He'd never seen a woman blush like that before,
even then—and he'd found it strangely compelling. As
if he was getting a glimpse into her soul she couldn't
prevent. What was uncomfortable and just plain weird,
though, was that he found those hot red cheeks a heck
of a lot more compelling now.

*WHY THE BLOODY hell did you mention the stripper
dress?*

Sabrina blinked, trapped in the tractor beam of
Connor McCoy's seductive stare, and hoped that the
blood throbbing in her cheeks—and not just the ones
on her face—wouldn't be visible in the low lighting.

'Yes, well...' She stroked the stem of her margarita
glass, then took a steadying sip, trying to regain some
of her usual cool and focus on the task in hand instead
of the fact that all the oxygen had been sucked out of
her lungs with a single crummy chat-up line.

Libby had warned her about her soon-to-be brother-
in-law's phenomenal success with women, but until
this moment she really hadn't thought she'd be susceptible. It was somewhat lowering to realise that despite
her phenomenal intellect and feminist sensibilities, she
wasn't completely immune to the moves of a practised
player. Taking the softly-softly approach and trying to
find some common ground had obviously been a mistake when you were dealing with a tiger who would
pounce on any passing prey.

She raised her head to find him watching her in that focused, silent way that made the skin on her spine tingle as if it were being stroked with a vibrator. 'So you'll do the second dance with me?' she asked, struggling for businesslike.

Instead of giving her an answer, he lifted the bottle of beer to his lips and took a leisurely swallow, his gaze riveted on her burning cheeks.

The blush went radioactive as she pictured herself as the gazelle in this scenario—and it occurred to her that slow-dancing with this guy would be fraught with dangers she hadn't prepared herself for. Like the fact that the large square hand holding the beer bottle would have free range of her naked back thanks to the ridiculously revealing dress Libby had chosen.

The imaginary vibrator caressing her spine hit maximum pulse and stroked down to her bottom.

He lowered his bottle and the soft smack of glass on wood made her jump. 'Okay, I guess you can count me in.' His wide mouth curled up on one side in a crooked smile that looked almost boyish. 'How bad can it be?'

'Fabulous. I appreciate your cooperation,' she said, thinking no such thing.

From the dark, challenging look in those lake-blue eyes she had the definite impression that being cooperative was the very last thing on Connor McCoy's agenda.

2) Knowledge Is Power: Quiz family and friends to gather relevant information about your best man's skill set.

'I'M JUST SAYING, I don't understand why Jamie didn't pick DJ or Vikram to be his best man.' Sabrina took a sip of her iced coffee.

'Hmm?' Libby murmured, not listening as she placed yet another minuscule piece of French lace masquerading as a negligee onto the bed of her cramped apartment overlooking Islington Green—to add to the display of 'garments to inspire the maximum amount of wedding night sex' being laid out for consideration.

'They're his best friends,' Sabrina continued, trying to sound nonchalant instead of whiny. 'And I thought you said Jamie doesn't know his brother that well.'

Libby lifted her gaze from her contemplation of the options and quirked a perfectly plucked eyebrow. 'What's the problem with Connor? I thought you guys met up last night to talk about your—' she did air quotes with her fingers while sending Sabrina a saucy smile '—mutual roles in the wedding.'

'We did.' The anxiety tugging at Sabrina's stomach—ever since her drink with Connor the night before—became a definite yank. 'This isn't about him, specifically.'

'I thought you'd be pleased to have a chance to slow-dance with him,' Libby bulldozed over her attempt at misdirection. 'Not only is he one of the hottest guys on the planet, I happen to know you fancy him.'

'Says who?' Sabrina blurted out, nonchalant losing ground fast.

'Says me.' Libby's smile became smug. 'I distinctly recall you ordering him about like a member of the luggage police the first time we met him. And you only get arsy with guys when you want to shag them.'

Sabrina cursed the flush of colour working its way up her neck. *Bugger.* Trust Lib to remember that, even though her best friend had had a good portion of her tongue down Jamie's throat at the time.

'Fine. I'm not trying to dispute the fact that he's hot.' Because she simply wasn't a good enough liar to make that one stick. 'But he's also extremely stroppy, a loose cannon and I got the definite impression yesterday night that he's far from ecstatic about being Jamie's best man.' She tried to smooth out her forehead, fairly sure the scowl was back with a vengeance. 'I want to relax at the wedding reception, instead of having to worry about whether the best man's going to go AWOL before the first dance.'

'Stop panicking! Connor's not the type of guy to pass up a slow-dance with a woman who'll look like a sex goddess thanks to the deliciously revealing gown and push-up bra I'm forcing her to wear.' Libby's smug smile turned into a cheeky grin—the same cheeky grin that had made Sabrina adore her, when they'd both been ten and Libby had told the class bully Petra Genero to eat snot and die for calling Sabrina a swot. 'If I were you, I'd be more worried about drowning in your own drool when you get your hands on that much man candy after your year-long drought.'

'It hasn't been a year—it's only been eleven months.' Sabrina scowled. Nothing like having your best friend think you were a charity case.

'Only eleven months, eh?' Libby's grin only got cheekier. 'Not that you've been counting or anything.'

'As your best friend, I feel honour-bound to tell you that smug really isn't a good look for you,' Sabrina replied—even as her own grin got the better of her. Libby's teasing never failed to lift her out of the deepest funk—even one this never-ending. 'Did you know, you've become completely insufferable since Jamie located your G spot?'

Libby laughed. 'And as *your* best friend I feel honour-bound to point out that you might actually have an opportunity to try on smug for size.' Libby fluttered her eyelashes over the wicked glint in her eye. 'If you had the balls to bite into the fabulous feast of studmuffin I'm providing for you at my reception—instead of bitching about him.'

'Wait a minute...' Sabrina got off the bed as the niggling suspicion that had been lurking at the back of her mind blasted into her frontal lobe. 'Oh. My. God. You've set me up.' Suddenly, it all became blindingly obvious. 'That's why Jamie asked Connor to be his best man. Because you told him to.'

Libby flicked a turquoise teddy onto the pile of lingerie on the bed, apparently unfazed by Sabrina's accusation. 'Stop giving me your responsible look. I did it for your own good. You need to get laid, and I happen to know Connor McCoy is a master in the art of fornication. He's a thank-you gift. For all the time and trouble you've put into making this wedding fabulous.'

'I do not believe this.' Sabrina sunk back onto the bed. Her stomach rolled into her throat and warred with the heat crawling across her scalp.

'I really don't see what the big problem is?' Libby added.

'Didn't it occur to you that Jamie should have picked his own best man instead of being browbeaten by you into picking Connor? The wedding's not just some flashy, overblown party. It's supposed to be symbolic of your life together going forward.' *Or it should be— if the marriage is going to last.*

Wasn't that how her parents had screwed up their own marriage? By viewing it as a disposable excuse for never-ending parties, high-stakes drama and an endless merry-go-round of flings and counter-flings? Even after she had come along, her parents had resolutely refused to grow up. It had been frightening to live with as a child, and pathetic to watch as an adult.

Libby frowned, looking completely nonplussed. 'No browbeating went on. Jamie's completely in awe of Connor. And what's wrong with having fun at your own wedding? Seriously, Bree, just because you're not a party animal… Getting married is the ultimate excuse for one of the best parties of your life.'

Sabrina sighed. Fine, scratch the mature and responsible approach. She didn't want to sound like a killjoy—and while Libby might be immature, she wasn't reckless or selfish, like her parents. Plus, Libby didn't do deep—it was one of her charms.

'But what about Connor in all this?' Sabrina began again. 'He's not a thank-you gift. He's a person. Maybe he doesn't want to be objectified.' She trailed off, knowing she was probably reaching. The male ego was generally a lot more robust where sex was involved. And when it came to Connor McCoy—and his sexy grin, and distracting biceps—his ego was clearly indestructible.

'Oh, come on, Bree. The guy practically oozes sex appeal. If he minded being objectified he wouldn't have perfected a look that can trigger spontaneous ovulation at thirty paces,' Libby said, not buying that argument either.

'Okay, fine,' Sabrina conceded, not wanting to dwell on spontaneous ovulation and Connor McCoy all in one conversation or the yank in her belly was liable to hit meltdown. 'But how about the fact that he's not that thrilled about being Jamie's best man and he's not that keen on me either. And now we know why.' Mortification engulfed her as the reason for Connor's hostility the night before became blindingly obvious. 'He must have found out about your little plan to get him to sleep with me. So thanks a bunch for that.' As if it wasn't bad enough that Libby thought she was a charity case. Now Connor did, too.

That's me totally screwed, then. And not in a good way.

'Bollox,' Libby scoffed. 'Connor's hang-ups about being the best man have nothing to do with you.'

'Oh, yeah?' Sabrina asked. 'Well, what do they have to do with, then?'

Libby huffed and propped her hands on her hips, looking harassed. 'Probably the simple fact that he hasn't spoken to his dad or Elizabeth since they kicked him out of their home when he was sixteen.'

'What?' Sabrina gaped. 'I never knew he lived with them?' she continued, not even attempting to hide her curiosity. Or her dismay. She'd known the McCoy family set-up was a complicated one. That Connor was Jamie's illegitimate half-brother—the product of a fling Jamie's father had had while at Yale, years before his marriage to Jamie's mother, Elizabeth. But she'd just assumed that Connor had grown up with his mother. 'What happened to his mum?'

'Jamie says she died when he was fourteen—he ran away and ended up in Newport, looking for the man who was listed on his birth certificate.'

'But if Daniel and Elizabeth took him in, why did they kick him out again?'

Libby plopped down on the bed beside Sabrina. 'Jamie says Connor never talks about it, but apparently the years he lived with his birth mum were really tough. When he turned up in Newport, he wasn't the kind of kid Elizabeth would trust to do her yard work, let alone want in the house—and I'm sure she let him know it.'

'But it's not like Connor's that rough kid anymore,' Sabrina added, the wave of sympathy surprising her. She knew what it was like to be the odd one out. The outsider, the misfit, the person who resolutely refused to fit in—because that's exactly what she'd been to her own parents. 'Isn't he super successful, now?'

Libby nodded. 'Jamie says his nightclub business is worth millions. But that's not going to cut any ice with a woman like Elizabeth—you know what a snob she is.'

The wave of sympathy crested.

What must it have been like for Connor? The illegitimate runaway son of a barmaid being thrust into a world where appearances were everything? And into the home of a woman who despised him? That must have been hard.

'No wonder he feels uncomfortable being the best man, then….'

So that was why he'd been so hostile about being involved in the wedding? She sent an accusatory glance at Libby—ignoring the foolish little lift in her heart at the thought that his hostility had nothing to do with her. 'You shouldn't have put him in that position.'

Sabrina's agitation returned. If there was anything she hated more than unnecessary drama it was thoughtlessness.

'Oh, bugger off!' Libby said jauntily. 'I'm sure Connor will survive—does he strike you as the type to fold under a little social pressure?'

Sabrina's glare faltered at the memory of the sexual confidence in his blue gaze as it dropped to her bum. *Okay, there was that.*

'And anyway, there's no point in stressing about it now, because we can't un-make him the best man.' Libby's lips firmed in a determined expression that Sabrina recognised only too well. 'And now that I've gone to all that trouble, and Connor's going to be forced to withstand the killer glare of his evil stepmother, you could at least make it worth all our whiles.'

Sabrina stared at her best friend—not sure how to handle the empathy she felt for Connor the boy and the way it was making her feel about Connor the man. And resenting Libby big time for putting her in this position.

Like this situation needed to get any more complicated.

'You're unbelievable. You are not seriously trying to guilt me into shagging him? Why is my getting laid so bloody important to you?'

'Because I want you to have fun,' Libby replied, the sudden passion in her voice unsettling. 'Because Carl did a number on you that you didn't deserve.' She grasped Sabrina's hands and let out a slow breath, the cheeky grin fluttering back to life. 'And because you need to get back in the game before your ovaries dry up and you become one of those dotty old dears who has a hundred cats.'

'I'm only twenty-eight! And I'm allergic to cats.' This had to be Libby's love-dazed mind talking. She wasn't *that* unhappy. Yes, Carl had been an arsehole, but she'd dumped him.

She tugged her hands out of Libby's. 'And how exactly would getting hooked up with a guy who's got less staying power than a rabbit when it comes to relationships be a good idea?'

'Because given his track record, we're not talking about more than one night…. And Connor's got exceptional staying power—where it counts,' Libby continued, her cheeky grin now rife with innuendo.

'How on earth would you know that?' Sabrina demanded. 'Just because he's Jamie's brother and he…'

'Because I have irrefutable proof,' Libby interrupted.

Sabrina stared. 'What proof?'

Libby's bright chestnut eyes danced with excitement—making Sabrina feel like a trout who had bitten into a juicy worm, only to discover there was a hook embedded in the middle of it.

'Remember the skiing holiday me and Jamie had in Colorado last November?'

Sabrina nodded as Libby reeled her in.

'Remember I told you Connor was snowboarding in the next valley. And he turned up for dinner one night with a date, an actress from LA who didn't eat, but drank like a fish. And that they had to stay the night in the chalet's spare bedroom because a snowstorm hit.'

'Yes,' Sabrina said cautiously, remembering far too well the sting of envy when Libby had described in glowing detail the anorexic beauty of Connor's date. 'So?'

'*So* the walls in that chalet were paper thin—' Libby paused for effect and Sabrina leaned in—like a moth gravitating towards the flame. '*So* we could hear every single thing Connor and his date got up to that night.' Libby paused again, the silence unbroken as Sabrina stopped breathing. 'And I do mean *all* night.'

'You listened?' Sabrina hissed, trying for appalled but getting enthralled instead—thanks to the lack of oxygen now reaching her brain.

'Well, it was kind of hard to avoid because they were so loud. And it was funny at first, but then it got extremely bloody hot.' Libby's voice dropped to a conspiratorial whisper. 'He spanked her.'

'He... *What?*' A fireball detonated in Sabrina's arse and radiated up her spine. 'That's disgusting.' Or at least it would be, if she could just get her arse to stop sizzling and her brain to start functioning. 'Why didn't you do something, if he was abusing her?'

'Don't be daft, Bree. It wasn't abuse.' Libby laughed,

the husky sound not helping with the sizzling—or the lack of functioning brain cells. 'Believe me, this was entirely consensual—emphasis on the sensual.'

'How do you know?'

'Because we could hear her moaning and panting during her spanking and then screaming her head off—when he was rogering her with his—' Libby paused to do air quotes again. 'Awesome cock. Her words, not mine.' Libby propped a considering finger under her chin. 'I wonder, what do you think "awesome" translates as in feet and inches? Because Jamie's extremely well hung and they are half-brothers.'

Feet? What the...?

'Shut up.' Sabrina squeezed her thighs together, disturbed by the picture that appeared in her mind of Connor McCoy and his 'awesome cock' pounding into her.

Bloody hell, was she actually getting moist imagining it?

'I don't believe it.' The erotic vision dissolved as her common sense intervened. 'I've never screamed when I come. Have you? No guy's that good in bed, no matter how big his dick is.' Or no guy she'd ever slept with. 'I bet she was faking it. She *was* an actress.'

'Jamie's made me scream a number of times.' Libby's eyes clouded with pity. 'You've just been doing it with the wrong guys.' Then the cheeky grin returned with a vengeance. 'Plus I saw one of Marlena's movies. Believe me, she's not that good an actress.'

3) Be Aware, Size Matters: Especially when it comes to your best man's ego. Tread carefully if he has a big one.

I don't believe it! She rearranged our carefully considered seating plan to sit me next to Connor and his foot-long cock.

Sabrina stared in disbelief at the board displayed outside the elegant private dining salon in Rules, the historic Covent Garden restaurant Jamie's parents had booked for the rehearsal dinner. Her scalp burned, while a disturbing heat smouldered much lower down.

I'm going to throttle my best friend less than a week before her wedding.

She tried to catch Libby's eye as their party of sixteen filed into the room—but the bride-to-be was busy ignoring her, all her attention focused on her fiancé. Jamie looked suitably debonair in his dark grey single-breasted suit—until his hand strayed to Libby's backside and squeezed in a very public display of affection for the centuries-old establishment. Sabrina spotted Elizabeth watching her son and future daughter-in-law, the lift of a perfectly arched eyebrow telegraphing her disgust.

Sabrina glared at the back of Elizabeth's perfect chignon as the exquisitely dressed woman swept ahead of her into the salon, her resentment spurred on by what

Libby had told her the day before about the woman's treatment of Connor.

Lighten up, you snooty cow. Libby and Jamie are in love with each other. Why shouldn't they show it?

Some of the tension in her shoulders released. She needed to lighten up, too. Sitting next to Connor didn't have to be bad. Libby's hidden agenda wasn't a problem as long as Connor never found out about it. And there was no reason why he should, as long as Sabrina remembered to breathe and remained focused on their collaboration at the wedding—instead of his awesome cock.

'You better watch it—Elizabeth can strike you cross-eyed if you look at her the wrong way.'

Sabrina swung round at the intimate whisper over her left shoulder. To find Connor smiling at her, his deep blue eyes hooded.

She swallowed down the foolish pang of sympathy at the thought of him as a teenage tearaway, subjected to Elizabeth's constant disapproval.

He certainly wasn't a teenage tearaway anymore.

A crisp white shirt and expertly tailored dark blue suit did nothing to disguise the exceptionally well-developed body beneath. Sabrina's assessing gaze roamed down his torso entirely of its own accord—only coming to an abrupt halt when it landed on the pleated crotch of his trousers.

Stop staring at his lunch box. Are you bonkers?

Her gaze shot back to his face. 'I beg your pardon?'

She didn't just want to throttle Libby now, she wanted to eviscerate her—for putting speculative thoughts about Connor McCoy's size into her head.

Strong white teeth flashed in his tanned face. 'You

can beg if you want to, Sabrina.' His voice came out in a husky rumble. 'But I'm not sure I'm going to pardon *that*. Were you just checking out my junk?' The smouldering blue of his irises sparkled with amusement.

A guilty flush blasted up to incinerate the tips of Sabrina's ears.

'Of course not.' She stepped away, planning to march into the salon and hopefully stop her radioactive cheeks from giving her away.

But he gripped her elbow, bringing her getaway to an indignant halt. 'Hold up.'

The rest of the bridal party walked past them as he held her anchored to the spot.

'We got off to a rocky start a couple of days ago,' he murmured. 'Which was mostly my fault.'

She faced him, prepared to accept his apology graciously, so they could move on—preferably into the crowded salon and away from the secluded alcove.

But the apology didn't come. Instead his thumb caressed the inside of her elbow, making tingles radiate up her arm.

'It's okay…' She tugged her arm, but his grip held firm. 'After speaking to Libby about your history with Jamie's family, I totally understand now where your hostility was coming from. So your snit is forgiven.'

'My snit, huh?' Anger flickered in his eyes, but he masked it quickly.

Hmm, so conversation about his family was off limits. The telltale dart of sympathy resurfaced.

'You've got a hell of an attitude on you.' Cynicism edged the word and a muscle twitched in his jaw. 'But then, I like attitude in a lady.' The tingles in her arm sunk beneath her belly button at the heat in his voice. 'Especially in bed. It gives me that much more to tame.'

She jerked her elbow free this time, her sympathy evaporating—unlike the bloody tingles.

Tame, my arse.

'I'd strongly suggest you don't try to tame me. Or you're liable to get more than you bargained for.'

He laughed. 'Is that a promise, Sabrina?'

'Hardly,' she mumbled, the pithy slap-down she wanted eluding her while his gaze, bold and deliberately insolent, drifted down to her cleavage.

She'd chosen the electric-blue silk jersey dress because it was the perfect combination of chic and sexy, and yet sophisticated enough for London's oldest eating establishment, where everyone from Dickens to Betjeman had dined over the past two hundred years. But as her nipples swelled into hard peaks—poking out through her bra and the clingy silk—she felt about as sophisticated as Lady Godiva.

'I guess we better get this shit out the way first.' He glanced towards the salon—where everyone was now seated, and waiting for them. 'We can discuss your attitude problem later.'

He took her arm again in the same firm, proprietary grip—which she couldn't get out of without causing a scene.

'*I* don't have an attitude problem,' she hissed, as he escorted her into the salon.

Holding out her chair, Connor leaned over, crowding her while she took her seat. 'Behave,' he murmured ominously, before tucking the chair under her butt.

She caught Libby's cheeky grin from the head of the

table as Connor sat in the chair beside her, his muscular thigh touching hers.

Libby demonstrated a length of at least a foot between her two index fingers—like a fisherman exaggerating his catch—her grin going from cheeky to naughty. Then she mimed the word *Awesome*.

Sabrina mimed the words *Piss off* back.

And decided evisceration was far too good for her best friend.

'DIDN'T YOUR MOM ever tell you not to play with your food?' The husky comment shivered down Sabrina's spine.

She put down her fork as her gaze connected with the mischievous blue twinkle in the eyes of the man beside her—who had been tormenting her with a series of similarly whispered criticisms through five never-ending courses of Cordon Bleu cuisine.

'Didn't your mum ever tell you not to harass women while they're eating?' she countered through the lump of something hot and unyielding in her throat—which had stopped her from swallowing more than a few bites of her meal.

The sensual line of his lips curled and his gaze sharpened. 'My mom wasn't real big on rules.'

'Why does that not surprise me?'

He lifted his arm in slow motion, moved it beneath the table and a warm palm landed on her knee.

Sabrina jolted, shocked not just by the contact but the answering spike in her pulse rate.

'Surprised yet?' he asked.

'Not at all,' she said, but her knee trembled as he squeezed.

'Liar.'

She shivered, sure she could feel the calluses on the ridge of his palm as it moved up her leg.

'You seem kind of jumpy, Sabrina.' His palm slid under the silky material of her dress. 'Why is that?'

'I think you know why, Connor.' Delicious tingles radiated up the inside of her thigh under his trailing fingers.

Fine, if he wanted to play, she'd play. They were in a restaurant, surrounded by his family and her friends—how far could he go?

A lot further than you'd anticipated came the indisputable reply as his palm rose higher in devastatingly slow increments, undaunted. The flickering candlelight seemed to cloak them in a strange sort of anonymity in the crowded room—plus nobody was paying them any attention.

Even Libby, who had been checking up on her and Connor with alarming regularity throughout the evening—and sending not-remotely-subtle encouragement via her hyperactive eyebrows—was busy ignoring them while she fed Jamie spoonfuls of white-chocolate brownie.

'Don't worry, your secret's safe with me,' he taunted as the rough palm climbed perilously close to the juncture of her thighs.

Sabrina shuddered—and clamped her knees together, trapping his wandering fingers before the hot, unyielding lump in her stomach plummeted any further south.

One dark brow lifted fractionally, his thumb stroking in slow circles as he made no move to remove his hand. But then she had to admit she wasn't entirely sure she wanted him to. The slow curl of his lips as he watched her reaction was an impossibly tempting invitation to sin.

'I don't remember giving you permission to touch me.' She squeezed his trapped fingers to emphasise the point. Given all the spin classes she did religiously he ought to be feeling quite contrite by now, but he didn't even flinch.

'And I don't remember asking for it.' His fingers flexed as his thumb slid perilously close to the sensitive seam of flesh at the top of the thigh where the edge of her knickers lay.

Her lungs clogged, electricity shimmering towards her already throbbing clitoris.

'Surely your mother must have mentioned the rule about not groping women in public?' she demanded, disguising her breathlessness. She hoped.

The glint in his eye took on a feral gleam. 'Open your legs, Sabrina.'

Her thigh muscles quaked at the command, but she shook her head. 'I think that would be dangerous.'

'What are you so scared of? That you'll like it?'

The challenging taunt struck right at the heart of all her insecurities. Carl had always accused her of being too safe, too boring. And her parents had told her on numerous occasions she lacked fire, lacked courage.

Her muscles loosened and she spread her knees to make a point. But before she had a chance to rethink the sudden burst of recklessness, his hand cupped the damp gusset of her panties. And all thinking stopped.

Her hands tightened into fists on either side of her dinner plate as she held back the gasp of shock—blood throbbed as the heel of his palm pressed against the bundle of nerves—and she completely forgot what point it was she was supposed to be making.

'Good girl,' he mocked, his fingers locating her clitoris at last.

God, she'd been far too long without the touch of a man's hand, because she could feel the moisture gushing through the thin satin. It would have been mortifying. Should have been. Because it was him, and he was only doing it to tease her. But somehow the press of those stroking fingers, so arrogant, so deliberate, wasn't mortifying—it was glorious.

'I think now would be a good time to discuss your attitude problem, Sabrina.'

She ignored him and the insistent desire to reach down and direct those knowing fingers beneath the barrier of silk, only to spot Libby gaping at them from the end of the table. Libby's gaze dropped, acknowledging the position of Connor's arm, and then shot back to Sabrina's face, her jaw going slack.

Fire rocketed up Sabrina's neck—and not the good kind—and her knees snapped shut with an audible slap, trapping Connor's hand again and making him grunt.

'Take your hand away,' she whispered furiously. 'Libby can see what you're doing.'

'Then you'll have to open your legs. You've got me caught fast.'

She did so immediately, the synapses in her brain finally linking up with her muscle fibres, but instead of removing his hand, his fingers dipped beneath the elastic of her panties and plunged into the slick folds of her sex. She stiffened in shock—pleasure radiating out as he glided over the swollen nub.

'Ugh…' She grasped the tablecloth, dragged air into burning lungs, and struggled to stay still under Libby's watchful stare as he fondled her already painfully engorged clitoris.

'Bingo,' he whispered.

Sabrina kept her eyes riveted on Libby's shocked face. She couldn't look at him, already far too aware of those sharp eyes boring into the back of her head as his thumb toyed with her.

Then her friend mouthed the letters O. M. G.

'Please…' she hissed, not sure quite what she was begging for, the touch of his fingers both exquisite and excruciating.

'How about I make you come,' Connor murmured next to her ear. 'With everyone watching?'

'Please don't. I don't want you to,' she begged, the breathless plea not even convincing herself as her knees fell open farther to give him better access.

'You're lying. I can feel how wet you are.' His thumb circled again, and the heat ebbed and flowed, making her knees tremble, the muscles in her thighs go slack and her breathing burn. 'And I can smell it, too.'

Oh God, I'm going to climax in full view of the whole wedding party.

She dug her fingernails into the linen cloth—her whole being concentrated on that delving, devious caress, driving her ever closer to the edge of something wonderful.

'Don't you want to come?' he coaxed, his voice so low it seemed to ripple over her skin. 'Why deny yourself when you're so damn close?'

'I can't,' she whimpered, having to force the word out. 'Please stop,' she begged, her voice breaking as his thumb flicked at the burning nub. 'I don't want to make a scene.'

His hand suddenly pulled out of her knickers and she sagged in her seat, close to tears—although she wasn't sure if the urge to weep came from relief or mind-numbing frustration.

She'd had orgasms before that hadn't been as spontaneous, as seductive, as breathtaking as the feel of his fingers stroking her so expertly. She'd been on the brink of something awe-inspiring. She was sure of it, because her body felt bereft now—and her mind couldn't quite engage with why it would have been so wrong. To let Connor McCoy treat her to a shouting, sobbing, table-thumping climax of Meg Ryan proportions.

Except you wouldn't be faking anything, you muppet! And the whole wedding party would have been treated to your Orgasma-geddon, too.

'You need to learn to unwind, sweetheart. And I'm just the guy for the job.'

Sabrina's head whipped round at the mocking words, still dazed by the aching heat in her clitoris—and the blood thundering in her ears.

'Are you completely fucking insane?' she whispered, grateful to discover after a frantic glance round the table that no one but Libby seemed to have spotted their indiscretion.

'I'm insane to fuck you. Does that count?'

'You're…? What…?'

For Chrissake, breathe.

She hauled air into her lungs, trying to still her galloping heartbeat before she had a heart attack.

'You're a ball-buster, Sabrina.' He shrugged. 'I find that one hell of a turn-on.'

The gruff admission sounded like an endearment. Which was probably why her heart did a foolish little flip-flop. But the rush of pleasure didn't last long.

He'd insulted her. She wasn't a ball-buster—not by any stretch of the imagination. Connor McCoy only thought she was, because he was probably accustomed to instant surrender from every woman he touched—with those mind-altering magic fingers of his.

'I know just how to unleash all the passion you've got on lockdown,' he added.

She stared at his mesmerising face, buffeted by the giddy rush of heat. And the thought that the passion wasn't locked up nearly as tight as she'd like.

'We're not talking about this,' she said, struggling to find solid ground again. 'What just happened was a mistake. It isn't going to happen again.'

'You sure about that?'

She crossed her legs, hoping to relieve the pulsing ache for release still throbbing in her clitoris. 'Yes.'

He lifted his elbows onto the table, steepled his fingers and pressed his thumbs against his lips. 'Really? Despite all the evidence to the contrary?'

Her lungs seized, the throbbing ache increasing tenfold. Were those her juices she could see on his thumb, glistening in the candlelight? And mocking her.

He licked at his thumb. And she squirmed, sure she could feel the rough swipe of his tongue drawing across her labia. She drew in a sharp breath and caught the musky hint of her own arousal above the aroma of chocolate and brandy and coffee.

He winked—a sinfully sexy grin lifting his lips.

'I can make you come so hard and so long,' he said, the playful tone belied by the intensity of that pure azure gaze. 'You'll be begging me to stop for real.'

Sabrina gave her head a little shake, having fixated on the growled words *hard* and *long*. 'I'm begging you to stop now. I'm not interested in having a relationship with you.'

'Well hell, that's sure kicked my ego into touch.' The sexy smile took on an arrogant tilt. 'FYI, Sabrina, I *never* use the R word, not even as a joke.'

'Great. Then we clearly have nothing left to discuss,' she said, struggling not to acknowledge the tiny spurt of disappointment.

'We've got tons of stuff to discuss.'

'Such as?'

'Such as, what your safeword's gonna be.'

Whoa! What the fuck?

His lips twitched at her reaction, so she tried to haul her jaw off the floor. But her eyebrows refused point-blank to return from her hairline.

'You mean you're…?' She hesitated.

Spit it out, for God's sake, before he figures out how vanilla you actually are.

'You're into BDSM?'

His lips tilted into the crooked smile she'd once found boyishly appealing. It didn't look remotely boyish now.

'I'm not a sadist. But I like to dominate.' His lips quirked some more, making it clear he did not consider this a weird or even remotely kinky conversation. 'And you've got a really exceptional ass that I've been itching to spank for a while now. Which means a safeword is gonna be kind of essential.'

Her exceptional ass twitched.

Bloody hell.

He wanted to spank her. Like the actress in Libby and Jamie's ski cabin. The image of which had been really hot—in her imagination. But only in her imagination. So where was that nuclear-powered tingling sensation in her bum coming from?

'Why would I need a safeword? Aren't women allowed to say no to you?'

'Sure. But when things get hot…' He paused, and she thought of how hot they'd already gotten. 'A safeword's better. Then we're clear.'

'Exactly what would you want to do?' she asked, the flutter of anticipation under her breastbone getting harder and harder to ignore. 'Because I'm pretty sure I'm not into pain.'

Good lord, was she actually considering getting sweet-talked into having demeaning, kinky sex with Connor McCoy on the basis of one almost-orgasm?

Well, okay, one really spectacular almost-orgasm. In fact, her best almost-orgasm ever. There was that.

'Only pretty sure? That sounds like something to explore.' He chuckled. 'Don't worry—the safeword will guarantee we don't go over your pain limits.'

Pain limits? Holy shit.

This was starting to go way beyond what she would be comfortable discussing with Libby after a truckload of tequila slammers—let alone with Connor McCoy in a crowded restaurant, stone-cold sober.…

So why were all her nerve endings getting high on the illicit tingling? And why couldn't she seem to forget the glorious feeling moments before, when her body had been about to fly off into the cosmos—under the command of his magic fingers?

CONNOR ADJUSTED HIS raging cock, grateful for the loose-fitting suit pants, as he observed tiny frown lines furrow Sabrina's brow while she considered his proposal.

Her bottom lip curled up under her teeth and a groan of frustration rumbled up his chest. He gulped it down, drawing air into his lungs—to kick-start his brain.

Back off. Don't push too hard tonight.

He shouldn't have baited Sabrina when they'd gotten here, and he certainly shouldn't have touched her. But once he'd caught Elizabeth giving him her 'you're trash' look from across the table, the contempt rolling off his stepmother in waves had brought all the old anger and resentment and powerlessness surging back.

And the urge to prod and poke and push at someone had been inevitable. The woman sitting beside him had just been an easy target. But then everything had gone straight to hell in a handbasket—and Elizabeth and her evil eye had been the least of his troubles.

Because instead of being stuck-up or uptight or full of herself, his dinner companion had been sharp and witty and responsive.

Way too damn responsive.

Her pupils had dilated, her breathing had accelerated and those full lips had trembled—while he slid his fingertips up her smooth skin, and absorbed the quiver of reaction in the toned muscles of her thigh.

He breathed in the aroma of coffee and that sultry perfume she wore, recalling the scent of her arousal as his fingers plunged into her damp sex. And concentrated on getting an iron-hard grip on the painful swelling in his pants.

He wanted Sabrina Millard, but on his terms—and without that shit from his past shadowing a single second. She was a gift he hadn't expected. Smart and ballsy and sexy as hell. A gift that could help keep him sane during the family reunion from hell. A gift he would have more than enough time to unwrap in the luxury suite he'd booked for the night at Grantley Manor—where Jamie's wedding was taking place in five days' time.

It had been years since any woman had excited him and challenged him and intrigued him the way this woman did. And he intended to savour the experience—but only in a purely physical sense.

His swollen cock jerked in protest as Sabrina's tongue flicked out to moisten her bottom lip, and he noted the flicker of fascination and excitement in the mossy green of her eyes. He finally had Sabrina where he'd wanted her for five years. Alert and eager and open to the possibilities, that shield of aloof superiority shattering.

He wasn't about to blow the chance to smash the damn thing to smithereens by pushing too soon.

'Do you think…' she began, her voice a smoky purr of hesitation—which was all the more arousing, because he knew it wasn't deliberate. 'I could consider it?'

4) The Devil Is in the Detail: Be sure to coordinate all aspects of your mutual roles to avoid confusion, or unwelcome surprises.

What's your safeword?

SABRINA STARED AT the text message that had popped up on her smart phone from an unknown recipient. Except the recipient wasn't unknown. Not to her throbbing clitoris anyway. Especially as she'd been anticipating this contact for two days now—and had all but given up hope.

She glanced up the aisle of the pretty little country church in Grantley Meadows, and spotted the vicar still deep in conversation with Jamie and Libby about their preferred wording for the ceremony.

Sabrina hesitated as she gazed at Connor's message again. So he was actually serious about finishing what they'd started. She tapped out an answer, her fingers shaking as if she were preparing to bungee jump into a ravine.

Can u please show some respect? I happen to be busy at the church rehearsal you refused to go to. Fulfilling my duties as the MOH, unlike a best man I could mention. Who is anything but!

There, that ought to show him that she wasn't a push-over. And that she hadn't been climbing the walls wait-ing for him to contact her for two solid days ever since they'd gone their separate ways after the rehearsal din-ner, when he'd informed her that he wouldn't be at-tending the church rehearsal, and she, in a moment of insanity, had agreed to consider his offer of hot sex for one night only. Her foot tapped in nervous antici-pation as she awaited a reply.

The speech bubble on the other side of the screen appeared two seconds later.

Safe WORD. Not WORDS. That's way too many. Your gorgeous ass would be red hot by the time you got all that out.

A staggered laugh popped out—and proceeded to echo round the church's stone walls like a mission bell. She peeked down the aisle to find Libby and Jamie and the vicar, not to mention both groomsmen and the three bridesmaids, all staring her way.

She waved, blushing furiously, but was surprised to discover she didn't feel as guilty as she probably should. 'I definitely think the vows work better with-out obey,' she shouted down the aisle. 'Stop being such a Neanderthal, Jamie. It doesn't suit you.'

The groomsmen laughed—and she breathed out—turning her attention back to the cheeky bugger who was harassing her by instant messaging.

She clicked on the iPhone's keypad function to re-spond. Clearly, polite and superior wasn't going to work with Connor. Luckily she knew how to play dirty. When she had to.

Bugger. Off. Are those enough WORDS for you?

She pressed Send, exhilarated by her provocative response. She didn't usually swear and text. But when
you were dealing with a guy like Connor who had no
respect for social niceties…
    Then his reply appeared.

Still one word 2 many. Who the hell taught u 2 count?
& Bugger can B misinterpreted. BTW, any objections
to anal play I should know about?

Anal play? Her breathing seized to a halt. But before
she had time to reply, another dialogue box showed on
his side of the screen.

Consider yourself PUNKED, sweetheart. So how hot r
your cheeks right now? On a scale of 1 to 10?

Punked? Did that mean he'd been joking about the
'anal play'?
    'You complete sod,' she murmured, relief reinflat-
ing her lungs before she passed out. She typed furiously, somehow managing to spell and reoxygenate
her brain all at the same time.

Very funny. Unfortunately, I'm not laughing, because
I've gone into cardiac arrest.

His response took less than ten seconds to appear.

All the way to 11, huh? OK, we'll shelve anal for this
booty call.

She sucked in a breath, not entirely sure if he was joking again. Then let it out. No need to debate Connor's sense of humour—or his affinity for anal play. There wasn't going to be an opportunity for any more booty calls after the night of the wedding because he was flying back to New York the next day. She'd checked Connor's flight schedule with Jamie, just to be sure.

If she was going to risk having a wild, inappropriate fling with Connor McCoy, she wanted to make sure there was no chance of her getting in too deep.

Thnx, that's big of u, but I haven't made a decision about whether I want to go ahead with THIS booty call yet.

Time to slow him down a little. She needed to make an informed, sensible decision and sexting wasn't helping. Because Connor's playful side only made him more irresistible.

Give me a break. U made your decision when I had my fingers on that stiff little clit. Now pick a safeword, or I'll pick one 4 u.

She glared at the reply. So much for his bloody playful side. Then another dialogue box popped up on his side of the screen and she glared at her phone hard enough to melt the damn SIM card.

How about PantsOnFire? That fits on a number of levels.

She texted back, indignation staining her cheeks.

STOP bullying me!

Then STOP kidding yourself. You're primed and ready & you know it. MORE than ready. But the safeword comes B4 u do. That's the deal. Take it or leave it.

Her fingers stilled on the phone. He'd given her the opt-out clause she'd been looking for. She could end this right here, right now. After a quick grope in a restaurant and some playful sexting. No harm done.

But as soon as the thought entered her head, she knew she wasn't going to do it. She wanted what he was offering. The chance to be a purely sexual being, to fly out of her comfort zone and experience the wild, heady thrill she'd been on the verge of at the rehearsal dinner. For one night only. She owed it to herself— and her stiff little clit.

Yes, Connor McCoy was an unknown entity—a man with dark passions that he had no qualms about pursuing. But wasn't that all part of his attraction? And so far, he hadn't done anything that she hadn't enjoyed. A lot.

Plus there was no danger of her falling for him, however much she might enjoy flirting and sexting— and eventually even shagging him. They weren't friends—which meant they could never be lovers. Not in the true sense of the word.

OK, I want 2 take it. But I have some questions first.

Three question marks popped up in reply. Simple, honest and direct. Just like Connor. Her heartbeat ticked into her throat, the anticipation, the thrill of the forbidden making her giddy.

Do all the women u sleep with need to have a safeword?

It was a personal question, one she wasn't sure she had a right to ask.

No. But U do.

She frowned, vaguely insulted by the instant response. How much of a coward did he think she was? Did he think she wasn't sexually adventurous enough to handle him? Like his legion of other women? And exactly how many other women were there? Surely she had a right to know?

I wasn't talking about me. I want 2 know about the other women you've slept with. EG: 1) How many of them r there? (ballpark figure will do) 2) Do u always dominate? 3) Y?

1. No comment 2. Yes 3. It's HOT

Frustration tightened her throat. He hadn't answered a single one of her damn questions. Time to play hardball.

Y No Comment? R there so many u can't remember the number?

The ten-second delay for a response had her holding her breath.

I remember just fine…But I want 2 have sex with u, not hire u 2 write my biography. & FYI you're the only woman I'm sleeping with ATM. If u EVER pick a damn safeword, that is!!!!!

From the number of exclamation marks, she got the definite impression she was frustrating him. *Well, same goes, buster.* Her exhilaration increased until it was all but cutting off her air supply.

How about DICKHEAD?? That seems appropriate ATM!!!

She relished the rich spurt of adrenaline as she hit Send—and the accelerated tingling in her bottom at the thought that she'd provoked him deliberately. And she was actually looking forward not just to his response, but to the tantalising retribution he might devise.
Jeez, was she secretly as kinky as he was?

DICKHEAD it is. But I'm gonna make u eat that particular safeword @ sum point 2 keep that potty mouth of yours busy. U have been WARNED.

A wave of heat crested at the thought of sucking off his awesome cock—while on her knees, in her maid of honour gown—promptly followed by a wave of mortification.
Bloody hell, if she wasn't as kinky as him, she soon would be if she wasn't very careful.
Another message flashed up on his side.

Gotta go. Hard-ons R bad 4 business meetings. C u @ the church on Sat. & remember. No panties allowed under that ass-kissing gown…. Or u will B punished.

Trembling fingers stabbed out a reply.

Punished? How?

That's 4 me to know & u to wet your panties wondering about. Later. C.

Moist heat flooded into her knickers on cue.

'For God's sake, Bree, stop texting the bloody caterers again and come here. We need your input.'

Sabrina buried the iPhone back in her bag at Libby's pained shout—disguising the evidence before her best friend found out the canapé order was the least of her worries ATM.

5) Flexibility Is a Many-Splendoured Thing: Especially if your best man is the type who likes to wing it.

'Breathe into the bag—it'll help.' Sabrina scrunched up the paper and held it to Libby's lips, while patting her friend's back in what she hoped was a soothing manner.

Libby sucked in a few shallow breaths and handed the bag back. 'How much longer?'

'I told the organist to start the wedding march in ten minutes. Everyone's ready, even Connor deigned to turn up on time...' She pushed past the silly catch in her breathing at the mention of his name—and the thought of him stepping out of the low-slung convertible and striding up the church steps beside Jamie half an hour ago. Both men had looked tall and impossibly debonair in their matching dress suits, but Connor had the edge when it came to sex appeal—the dark intent in his expression as their gazes connected firing straight to her stomach and plunging low.

'I know. Connor popped in ten minutes ago actually, while you were drilling Huey, Dewey and Louie,' Libby said, referring to the bridesmaids with a deceptive nonchalance.

'Oh really?' Sabrina doubted her nonchalance was fooling anyone either.

'Mmm-hmm. To wish me luck.' Libby watched her intently. 'If I wasn't about to be shackled to his brother in unholy matrimony, I'd be sorely tempted to jump that man myself.' Libby pressed her hands to her heart in an exaggerated swoon. 'There's just something irresistible about a dangerous man in a tux. Especially one as dangerous as Connor.'

'Libs, has anyone ever told you subtlety is not your strong point?'

Libby drilled a finger at her. 'I knew it. Something is *so* going on between you two. And he was totally touching you up at the rehearsal dinner. No way did I buy all that bollox about a misplaced napkin.' Libby's grin took on a triumphant tilt. 'As my maid of honour you should fess up. It's your duty to distract me for the next ten minutes, before I pass out from nerves.'

Sabrina smiled, the sudden urge to confide irresistible. When had she ever had a sexual encounter worth boasting about? 'If you must know, he *was* touching me up under the table.'

'Holy shit!' Libby's eyes popped to saucer-size. 'Be still my beating clit.' Her hands flapped furiously in front of her face as it turned a delightful shade of pink. 'Oh crap, now I really can't breathe.'

Sabrina laughed, Libby's shock intoxicating. She'd spent so long being smart and sensible and boringly safe, it felt astonishingly good to be naughty for a change. 'Brace yourself.'

'What? There's more?'

'He ordered me not to wear knickers today. And we've arranged a safeword for tonight.'

'You dirty little slapper,' Libby said, her pride unmistakable. 'I love it. One handjob turns Sabrina the Sensible into Sabrina the Slut. He must be The Man with the Golden Touch?'

'That's putting it mildly.' Sabrina's chest swelled, alongside her clitoris at the memory of that golden touch.

The opening bars of the wedding march soared into the small vestry. And Libby's dad appeared at the door, resembling a penguin in his morning suit.

'Baby, you look wonderful.' A very proud penguin. 'Now stop nattering, you two, and get a move on.' He made a shooing motion towards the door. 'Or we're going to miss our cue.' A very proud, somewhat impatient penguin.

Sabrina lifted the lavish bridal bouquet of lilies, peonies and trailing ivy from its perch and handed it to Libby. 'It's show time, Libs,' she said, her throat closing at the enormity of what her friend was about to do. 'Are you ready?' she asked, happy for Libby and yet also a little sad that nothing would ever be quite the same again. Because Libby was moving forward, while she was staying in exactly the same place she'd always been.

'As I'll ever be.' Libby nodded.

But as Sabrina scooped up Libby's train, her friend hissed in her ear. 'Except that I'm now going to be picturing you and Con doing it doggy style during the most important moment of my life.'

Sabrina choked down a giggle as they stepped into the cool, incense-scented antechamber at the back of the church, her melancholy forgotten in a rush of love for her friend.

Libby's father folded his younger daughter's arm

into the crook of his elbow and kissed her cheek as Libby's three nieces—aka Huey, Dewey and Louie—were being corralled into position by their mother, Libby's older sister Ellie.

The strains of the wedding march echoed through the large oak doors that stood open onto the nave. The warm June sunlight filtered through the stained-glass transept, casting a shimmering rainbow onto Libby's ivory Indian satin wedding dress. Sabrina sniffed back the errant tears. She didn't want to be feeling wussy when she saw Connor next—it might confuse things.

As Libby's bridemaids began their march down the aisle like a parade of ducklings in frilly tutus, Sabrina took her place behind them.

Libby grasped her shoulder and whispered. 'So did you obey Con's order and go commando?'

Sabrina cupped her hand over her mouth to whisper back. 'Don't be daft! I'm wearing a thong.'

Libby sent her a quick grin. 'Let's hope he punishes you for that infraction later.'

Libby's naughty laugh punctured the strains of the wedding march as Sabrina took careful measured steps on the beat of the music, her thong riding up her now-sizzling bum cheeks and her heartbeat hammering her neck like a woodpecker on speed.

Her stomach rose up to press against her larynx as she located Connor, standing next to his brother at the front of the church. The swooping sensation in her tummy got worse as they approached the altar, re-minding her of a time when she'd been backpacking round New Zealand with Libby during her gap year, and her friend had tricked her into bungee jumping off a bridge.

'THANKS AGAIN FOR coming, Con, and for being my best man.'

Connor dragged his gaze away from Sabrina Millard, who was on the other side of the palatial reception hall at Grantley Manor chatting to the bride's parents as if her life depended on it.

'Not a problem.' He took a slug of his beer and smiled at his kid brother. 'I was happy to do it.'

'And for keeping your speech G-rated.' Jamie's cheeky grin reminded Connor of the gap-toothed ten-year-old who'd followed him around like a puppy a lifetime ago. 'Mostly.'

'Sure.' Connor smiled back, glad to be distracted from the ticking time bomb in his pants, which had been tormenting him ever since Sabrina had sashayed down the aisle towards him in that gravity-defying dress.

She'd been avoiding him ever since, flitting about like a butterfly among the guests at the sit-down dinner and now at the after-party—organising, instructing and always staying just out of his reach.

And all those stolen looks, those darting licks of her tongue across her top lip, the swing of her hips in that damn gown had been driving him nuts all evening. Inventing all sorts of hot ways to punish her when he finally got his hands on her was not making the ache in his crotch any less insistent.

But her number was nearly up. Because in less than ten minutes, according to Sabrina's own neatly typed schedule, the string quartet playing some fancy classical stuff in the corner of the salon were scheduled to be replaced by the DJ in the huge ballroom beyond, and Jamie and Libby's first dance would kick off.

Once that happened, Sabrina would be all out of places to run.

He slung his hand into his pocket to touch the remote-controlled bullet he'd purchased especially for later in the evening.

They hadn't okay'd the use of toys during their sexting marathon the other day, but given her smart, funny quick-fire response to him so far, he was confident he could finesse her into losing a few more of her inhibitions.

The thrill of being the first guy to push her outside the vanilla box—and see that stunned pleasure again when she discovered her wild side—was taking his anticipation to a whole new level.

Lifting his hand out of his pocket, he rubbed his palm on his pants, struggling to refocus his attention away from the vision of Sabrina naked and quivering with need for about the fiftieth time that day. He didn't usually have a problem with deferred gratification, but instructing her not to wear panties had definitely been a tactical error, because imagining her succulent pussy completely naked beneath her dress was crucifying him.

'Just give me the word if you ever want me to return the favour, man,' Jamie continued.

'I'll keep that in mind,' Connor said easily, secure in the knowledge marriage would never be on his radar.

'Sabrina's pretty cute, isn't she?'

Connor glanced at his brother, who was watching him—way too closely. 'I guess.'

Jamie looked down at his toes, then shoved both his hands into his pockets. It was an uncomfortable stance Connor recognised from way back, when Ja-

mie's mother had been giving Connor a hard time, and
Jamie had defended him. But Connor got the feeling
it wasn't him Jamie wanted to rescue now.

'Don't hurt her, man,' Jamie murmured, never rais-
ing his head.

Connor felt his brows knot. 'Hurt her? Why would
I hurt her? I hardly even know her.'

*What the hell? When had his kid brother started
believing the worst of him, too?*

Jamie's eyes met his at last. 'I saw you guys at the
rehearsal dinner. And you've been watching her like
a hawk all afternoon. I know you're planning to nail
her tonight.' He lifted his hands out of his pockets, his
expression pained. 'All I'm saying is be careful with
her. You're a player, Con. And she's not.'

Connor's stomach tightened. 'That sounds like your
mother talking.' He'd forgotten about that toxic time in
his life and he didn't much like the reminder.

Jamie's eyebrows rose up his forehead. 'That's
bullshit. I've always thought you were great, man.'

He felt a little of the tension releasing, and hated
himself for even caring what his brother thought. His
half-brother. His family's low opinion had lost the
ability to screw him up a long time ago. 'Then why
should you care what I do with Sabrina? She's a con-
senting adult.'

'I care because she's Libby's best friend. She's a
great person. And she's had a rough time.'

The skin on the back of Connor's neck prickled—
a sure sign that he wasn't going to like what he was
about to hear. 'Rough, how?'

'Her boyfriend, a douche called Carl, cheated on
her last summer. She's been down in the dumps ever

since. Libby wanted to hook you guys up, so you could cheer Sabrina up again.' He hitched his shoulders. 'But I guess I just wanted you to know she's not…'

'She's not what…?' Connor said, his tone as measured as he could make it with his temper kicking in.

If there was one thing he hated, one thing he couldn't stand, it was being led around by his damn cock. And yet that's exactly what had happened. He'd been panting after Sabrina like a damn dog—and bypassing his usual caution when it came to picking his sexual partners. He didn't sleep with women who were looking for anything other than a casual hook-up—so why hadn't he checked Sabrina out more carefully? And why was the thought of her douchebag ex making him so mad?

'You know…' Jamie shrugged again. 'Your usual type.'

'What do you mean by my usual type?' But he had a pretty good idea and it wasn't helping with his temper—or that grinding feeling of inadequacy in his gut that he remembered from when he was sixteen and he'd been standing in his father's study as his stepmother had slapped him across the face, and told him to get out of their home.

'Look, man, forget it. It's cool. Libby wants you two to get it on,' Jamie said. 'And I'm sure she's told Bree all about your rep with women. So I doubt she's expecting anything more.'

Connor swallowed past the renewed bolt of temper. That Libby had warned Sabrina about his rep was good—not annoying. 'Why the hell *is* Libby so keen for us to get it on, then?'

'Libby wants Bree to lighten up. And after the night

you spent at our cabin in Telluride, she got way too much information about how good you are in the sack.' His brother sent him a furtive look that at any other time he would have found funny. 'That actress sure could scream.'

'Libby heard that?' Shit, he could actually feel his cheeks getting warm. What was that about?

'Are you kidding me?' Jamie laughed. 'We're lucky you guys didn't start an avalanche.'

A drum roll from the other room drowned out their conversation. Then an announcement came over the PA system in a crisp, clear, efficient voice that had the short hairs on the back of Connor's neck bristling—and heat swelling in his groin.

'Ladies and gentlemen, you are now invited to the main ballroom where Jamie and Libby will be doing their first dance in precisely five minutes.'

So what the hell did he do—now he knew that Sabrina might not be such a sure bet for a no-strings booty call?

The smart option would be to walk away. To dance that damn waltz with her and then leave her hanging. He didn't like complications when it came to sex, and this little liaison was starting to feel a lot more complicated than he was used to.

One of Jamie's groomsmen emerged from the crowd now herding towards the ballroom. 'Bree told me to tell you the first dance is about to start.'

'Sure, Vik, I'll be right there.' Jamie turned to Connor. 'Come on, man. Forget I said anything. Bree's great. I'm sure whatever happens between you guys, she'll know not to make too much of it.'

'Right,' Connor said drily, the renewed spurt of temper only confusing him more.

Jamie chuckled, obviously immune to the subtext. 'Hey, just do us both a favour and don't start spanking her until you're out of earshot of my mother.'

The mention of the woman who had always despised him wasn't helping the futile feeling of resentment twisting his guts into knots.

Fuck that. Why should he walk away from Sabrina? If all she was looking for was a prize stud, that was something he could deliver. No problem.

The bullet in his pocket and the small remote control that went with it knocked against his hip as he followed his brother into the ballroom. The two-hundred-plus wedding guests stood waiting, leaving a vacant space in the middle of the dance floor for the happy couple.

Spotting them both from her place beside the DJ's station, Libby picked up the skirts of her bridal gown and raced towards them. She threw her arms around Jamie, who swung her round in a circle to the cheers of the crowd. Something weird gripped Connor at the sight of the two of them, their faces beaming with pleasure. He'd always thought marriage was for suckers—no smart man would choose to get led around by his balls for the rest of his life. But as his brother and Libby made puppy-dog eyes at each other, the cynicism tasted sour on his tongue.

The lights dimmed as the DJ cranked up the pounding intro of the old disco track and Jamie led Libby into the centre of the dance floor.

Connor's gaze scanned the crowd until it located

Sabrina. And every thought in his head was blown away by a surge of lust.

She stood stiff as a popsicle on the other side of the room, her teeth worrying her bottom lip. He made his way towards her, pushing past the swaying couples enjoying the show. His hand slipped into his pocket to locate the bullet.

Starting now, he was going to give Sabrina Millard the longest, hardest ride of her life. And once he'd proved to her that he was the best fuck she'd ever get—that's when he would walk away. Because that's what he always did.

And everyone knew it.

INCOMING STUDMUFFIN AT twelve o'clock.

Sabrina sucked in a breath, all the zaps and tingles that had been driving her insane since her walk down the aisle going into overdrive. Connor McCoy was headed her way, apparently oblivious to the crowd surging around him as Libby and Jamie took the floor.

The thumping disco track reverberated through her torso and she licked her lips, unable to take her eyes off him. The dark tux emphasised his broad shoulders and narrow hips while his long legs ate up the distance between them. He'd lost his tie, the first few buttons of his shirt undone as if he were prepared for action. Her stomach swooped into her throat and every ounce of moisture dried up in her mouth—and flooded between her thighs.

Time to take that leap, Bree. Do not look down.

He drew near, towering over her even in her heels. She opened her mouth to say something coherent and encouraging about their upcoming dance, but before she could utter a single syllable, he gripped her upper arm and whisked her round, not even breaking stride as he marched past her.

'Follow me.' The command came out on a growl, as she found herself propelled through the crowd towards the back of the ballroom.

'Where are we going? We have to do our slow-dance in a few minutes.' She stumbled on her heels, struggling to keep up with his long strides as he dragged her through the emergency exit at the far end of the room and into the intimate shadows of a utility corridor.

The door slammed shut behind them, and he trapped her against the wall.

'Connor, we haven't got time…' She ducked to get under the solid forearm, but he simply grasped her waist and dragged her back.

'We've got enough.'

Panic assailed her. And not just because her carefully planned schedule was about to go tits-up.

His hand dropped from her waist and slid over the satin covering her bottom.

'But we have to…'

'Shh…' He pressed a finger to her lips. She shuddered as his palm found the slit in her gown. All thoughts of her intricately planned schedule dissolved in the rush of heat as his fingers touched bare flesh, then grasped her hip.

He spun her round. 'Put your hands against the wall and spread your legs.' The command was barked out.

She obeyed, her body already mindless with lust, as her mind struggled to engage.

Holy shit, was he going to fuck her here? Now? Her sex swelled in anticipation, the need drenching her thighs, the pulsing yearning harsh and unbearable as he lifted her gown, thrust it to one side, exposing the bare cheeks of her arse.

He cradled them in callused palms.

'What's this?' he murmured against her hair, his thumb sliding under the string of her thong. 'I thought I made myself clear. No panties allowed.'

'It's not panties—it's a thong,' she said over her shoulder.

He gave the string a sharp twist, the tearing sound loud over the dim beat of the music as he ripped the delicate lace free.

'Not anymore.'

She gasped, her vulva throbbing as cool air brushed over her naked sex.

'I want that slick little pussy bare and available tonight.'

Shock and desire combined as his breath feathered against her lobe. Wrapping one arm round her waist, he delved beneath her gown with the other and found the slick folds of her sex.

'I intend to punish you for that infringement.'

Her answering moan sounded almost animalistic as his fingers delved.

'You're soaking wet for me again, aren't you, Sabrina?'

She nodded, her tongue numb, as his thumb found the stiff nub of her clitoris, circled and then flicked. She jerked, the exquisite zap of pleasure so intense her knees buckled.

The arm around her waist tightened, keeping her upright.

'I've got a gift that you're going to wear while we

dance.' He nipped at her lobe, the sharp bite sending shock waves through her system.

'A gift?' She struggled to process the comment. Why would he have bought her a gift? But then his seeking fingers stopped their play and he gripped her thigh, forcing her bottom further out, until her bare butt was thrust towards him.

'Don't stop,' she cried, hearing the desperation in her voice.

His laugh was harsh, strained. 'No orgasm for you yet, Sabrina. We haven't got time in your busy schedule.'

Her dazed mind was trying to grasp the mocking words, when something cold and smooth touched the wet lips of her sex. She yelped, tensing at the thick intrusion and tried to tuck in her bottom, but he held her in place.

'Relax,' he crooned, as if gentling a startled horse. 'It'll go in easier.'

She squirmed, moaned, shocked by the fullness as the lips of her sex stretched. Holding her steady, he thrust the object deep. Then gave her bare buttock a pat. 'Good girl.' He gathered her gown and smoothed it over her bum.

She shuddered, aware of the object lodged deep in her pussy. 'What is that thing inside me?' She turned to face him, unsteady on her feet, her sex tightening uncontrollably around the alien invasion.

She went to lift her gown, but he snagged her wrist, yanking her into his arms. 'The egg stays there, until I take it out.' He cupped her cheek with one hand, slipped his other hand into his pocket.

She heard a slight click and suddenly the *thing* came

alive. She grasped his forearms to stop from falling over, gave a shocked cry, her thighs trembling as if a major earthquake had just struck—in the middle of Surrey. The hum of sensation rippled through her sex and up her torso. Her nipples tightened, her vulva throbbed, her clitoris pulsed hard, forcing her to the knife-edge of pleasure, then holding her there, suspended. 'What did you do? It's vibrating.'

'Correct,' he murmured, his voice rich with amusement. 'It's going to keep you focused while we dance.'

Her breathing became ragged, the sensations staggering and overwhelming. Intensely pleasurable yes, but yet so alien, so uncontrollable, she wasn't sure she could endure them and stay upright.

'I can't dance with this inside me. Are you mad?' She wasn't even sure she could walk, her legs were shaking so badly. 'I have to take it out.'

He grasped her wrist again to prevent her from retrieving it. 'Leave it, Sabrina. All you have to do is focus. But don't you dare come.' His lips lifted in a wicked grin. 'Until I say so.' Tightening his grip on her wrist, he marched her along beside him, heading for the emergency door back into the ballroom.

She tried to dig in her heels, but he simply kept on walking.

Was he actually planning to make her dance with a vibrating sex toy inside her? Each step made her more aware of the decadent humming inside her. She widened her stance, to decrease the sensations, but he only laughed as he held open the door into the ballroom.

'Walk normally—you look like a Western gunslinger.'

Jamie and Libby's first dance had finished, the

cheers and whoops of applause pounding her ear-drums.

'I *can't* walk normally,' she hissed as he propelled her towards the crowd. 'It increases the sensation.'

'That's the idea. Just relax and enjoy it.'

Seriously? He was really going to make her do this? In front of everyone? Her juices leaked, drenching her thighs, as she tensed around the egg, her desperate effort to disguise its presence only increasing the effect.

The seductive opening tenor riff of the love ballad that signalled the start of their slow-dance purred over the applause.

Connor led her past the onlookers, escorting her into the middle of the dance floor in full view of everyone. In her knickerless state she could have sworn she felt a breeze drifting right over her naked sex.

The song built to a crescendo, the joyous lyrics permeating her panic, and the buzz humming through her sex-starved body heating her blood. The deep blue of Connor's irises had turned black as his gaze connected with hers, fierce with an arousal that matched her own. And suddenly all she could see was him.

Sabrina's heartbeat thrummed in time with the pulsing heat in her sex, the pounding beat of the music. Had she ever felt so desirable? So desired?

Connor swung her in a circle and back into his arms, the grand gesture making her feel like the star of a Hollywood movie as the crowd whistled and cheered from the sidelines. He drew her close, the white linen of his shirt crisp against her cheek, and that clean seductive laundry-soap scent wrapping around her like a caress. One large hand clasped hers, the other settled on the small of her back, the rough calluses on his palm rasping against the sensitive skin where her gown plunged low. He applied pressure, trapping her melting abdomen against his hips.

'Do as you're told,' he whispered against her ear through the song's jazzy trombone solo. 'Or I'll increase the vibrations.'

Her steps faltered. He could make the vibrations stronger than this? That would kill her.

His arm tightened, making her suddenly aware of the stiff length prodding her belly through his pants as he moved easily with the music.

Her thigh muscles tensed and released, her breathing accelerated as the song rose to another crescendo, and the singer crooned the chorus about a new life, a new dawn, a new day.

Confidence soared through her on the wings of the lyrics.

She draped her arm round Connor's shoulder, felt his muscles bunch with tension and swivelled her hips, the slow, sensuous movement rubbing that glorious erection. Could she feel it pounding? Lengthening? Leaping?

His groan gave her the only answer she needed.

Yes. Why not make this as torturous for him as it is for me?

His hand stroked down her spine, and he ground the pounding length into her belly, matching the song's raunchy bassline.

'Behave yourself,' he rasped. 'Or you'll suffer. I have my finger on the trigger, remember.'

She gyrated against the huge shaft, the grin spreading across her face. She was slow-dancing with the most dangerous guy in the room. She felt bold and brave and beautiful for the first time ever.

There were no expectations with Connor, no past and absolutely no future—and the thought was liberating. She had a tiger in her arms for one night only. Why be scared of tugging its tail?

Her fingers threaded into the hair at his nape and she rolled her hips again. 'Be careful, Connor, because I plan to make you suffer more.'

His eyes flashed with challenge, a muscle in his jaw twitching as his hand strayed to his pocket.

She stretched into the heavy palm caressing her spine, absorbing the riot of sensation as the vibrations flared, and desire coiled tighter inside her. She moaned, her whole body humming, and rode the wave of pleasure as it rose to an impossible peak.

Then took that final wild leap as the coil released in a magnificent rush and she gave herself up to the love song's glorious exhilaration.

Jesus Christ, she'd climaxed—in his arms, on the damn dance floor. And looked magnificent while doing it. Untamed, uninhibited and courageous. So magnificent, his raging cock was about to explode in his pants.

Connor cradled her head against his chest as her body shivered through the final waves of her orgasm and she softened against him. Her lush cleavage plumped up, threatening to spill out. He ground his teeth together, fighting the urge to scoop the ripe flesh out of her gown and suck the nipples poking at the shimmering satin like bullets.

He was going to hunt the crooner of this song down

and punch the guy's lights out if the damn thing didn't finish soon.

'Please turn it down,' she whispered against his neck in between her ragged breathing. 'I can't come again—I'll collapse.'

Tucking his hand into his pocket, he flipped the switch onto the lowest setting. He raised her chin with a knuckle. The dazed heavy-lidded eyes and the bright flush of embarrassment—and desire—staining those pale cheeks made his cock pound.

'You weren't supposed to come the first time.' He kept his voice firm, despite the tickle of humour at the thought of them trapped on a dance floor with her barely able to stay upright and him sporting an erection the size of the Statue of Liberty. 'What the hell happened to focus and concentration?'

Her bright green eyes narrowed, her lips thinning in a belligerent expression, and something clutched hard in his chest. Damn, he hated to be a cliché, but she was even more magnificent when she was pissed.

'I'd like to see you try focus and concentration with a huge power tool shoved up your arse.'

The rough chuckle spilled out. 'You're mighty grumpy considering you're the one who just had the orgasm.' The vivid pink went a dark red at the reminder—and his cock twitched. He moved his hips, backwards and forwards, brushing the swollen head against her to relieve the pulsing ache. 'And that power tool is tiny, compared to the one I'm going to be drilling your sweet little pussy with very soon.'

'I can tell.' She tried to ease back, but he simply spread his fingers across her spine and anchored her in place. Apart from the exquisite feel of her soft belly wedged against his hard-on, he needed to keep himself hidden until he could get his cock to behave itself.

She squirmed, obviously keen to escape. 'We need to separate. This isn't a slow-dance anymore and it looks inappropriate you holding me this close.'

The crooner had finally stopped warbling, and the music had switched to a recent R & B hit. Making them the only ones on the floor still dancing cheek to cheek.

He raised an eyebrow. As if she didn't know why he had to keep her close. 'If you don't stop wiggling, this slow-dance may never end. Watching you come has made my power tool hard enough to drill a hole to China.'

She stilled against him, relieving the ache a little, then ducked her head, her face now a cute shade of scarlet. The muscles of his sternum squeezed.

And for the first time in, well, forever, he wondered what it would be like to have more than just mind-blowing sex on the agenda.

He shook the thought off. He didn't do emotional depth, or empathy, or companionship, or any of that other bullshit that lasted beyond the first night, which was why he never bothered with a second. Sex was the only thing he was any good at when it came to relationships. So why the hell would he want more?

It was just that Sabrina was more vanilla than the women he usually dated. And what Jamie had told him about the jerk ex had made him feel protective towards her.

The pulsing pain in his gut finally began to die down. But he continued to stroke her back, drawing a slow circle on the smooth skin with his forefinger, liking the way her body quivered from the soft ripples of sensation still coming from the egg.

He pulled back. The bright mottled colour in her cheeks, and the feel of her body soft and trusting in his arms, was doing weird stuff to his equilibrium. Weird stuff he had no experience with, so he needed to be careful—for his own protection as much as hers.

She blinked up at him, as if she'd been a million miles away, too, then she rose up to place her lips next to his ear. 'You need to turn the egg off now,' she said, her breathing still a little fast, a little thready. 'As soon as you're decent I've got to go and organise the bridal car.'

He considered the request—for about a second—the surge of possessiveness surprising him. He didn't want her to organise the damn car. In fact, he didn't want her out of his sight again.

Placing his hands on her waist, he bent to whisper back. 'The egg stays on, until I take it out. It's on the lowest setting to help you work on your focus.' Something he needed to work on, too, if he was going to get through tonight without giving in to any more dumb notions about turning a one-night stand into something it was never meant to be. 'Plus I want you to remember who you belong to tonight.'

'But that's ridiculous—we've got ages yet until we can be alone. It's distracting enough having it inside me, let alone buzzing away for hours.'

He glanced at his watch. 'According to your schedule, Jamie and Libby are heading off at ten.' He touched his thumb to her cheek, brushed back the lock of hair that curled down. 'You've only got to deal with it for an hour before I come to get you.'

'But what if there's some kind of cock-up?' she said, sounding a little desperate.

'Tough.' He pressed his face into her hair, inhaling the summery scent, and taking a wicked joy in the tension vibrating through her body. The egg was gonna make it next to impossible for her to concentrate on her damn schedule for the next sixty minutes—instead she'd be focused on him and what he was going to do to her.

'But I might not be ready in an hour?'

'You're gonna have to be. Because come ten o'clock, we're out of here.' His erection finally having softened to a manageable level, he stepped away. 'No excuses, Sabrina.' Lifting her fingers to his lips, he kissed the knuckles, pleased to see her eyes widen. The gallant gesture had obviously stunned her. It had stunned him a little, too—he never sugar-coated his sexual encounters with romance. But keeping her off balance was becoming an addiction. 'You'll just have to use those epic organisational skills to make damn sure the only cock-up tonight is mine.'

6) Keep Your Eyes on the Prize: Stay focused and make sure your best man does, too.

I MAY HAVE to murder Connor McCoy before this night is over.

Sabrina flattened a hand against her abdomen, the egg pulsing like a metronome, making her clitoris yearn to be touched. After sixty long, tortuous minutes, the low-level sensations felt like a Chinese water torture, keeping her tense and on edge and totally distracted.

While she still couldn't believe she'd actually had an orgasm on the dance floor, more annoying now was the fact that it hadn't been a particularly impressive one. Certainly not satisfying enough to keep her raging hormones in check after an hour of torture by a love egg.

In fact, she was actually starting to get quite cranky. And very sexually frustrated. Which had never happened to her before ever. And especially not less than an hour after an orgasm. For God's sake, she'd managed to go nearly a year without having sex and now suddenly Connor McCoy and his little toy had turned her into some sort of insatiable nymphomaniac.

She'd already been sharp with Libby and Jamie, overwhelmed by all the duties she still had to complete before zero hour struck in ten minutes.

She paused at the top of the stairs and scanned the crowd in the entrance hall of the Georgian mansion house hotel, where everyone was gathering to see the happy couple off. Disappointment struck when she didn't spot the dark head she'd been looking for, swiftly followed by aggravation when the mere thought of him made the torturous vibrations increase in intensity.

Glancing out the window, she spotted DJ and Malik and a couple of Jamie's other friends putting the finishing flourishes to their Just Hitched design on the brand-new BMW Jamie's dad had bought his son and Libby as a wedding gift. The flicker of concern at seeing the gleaming vehicle covered in foam didn't last long.

Sod the car.

So what if she'd spent an hour on Wednesday researching all the different brands of shaving cream— spending sixty minutes with your clitoris swollen to twice its normal size was a great way to make you stop stressing about protecting the paintwork of your best friend's new Beemer.

A large hand settled on her hip and she jumped.

'Easy, sweetheart. Not long now.' The familiar scent of soap and man enveloped her as she turned to find Connor standing beside her, the mocking smile on his lips comprehensively contradicted by the heavy-lidded gaze.

By rights she should give him a jolly good slap for the torment he'd put her through, but the relief at seeing him was so intense, she felt a little woozy.

'You're still here.' The sense of longing wrapped

around her chest and squeezed. 'I thought you might have left.'

His eyebrow rose and she instantly wished she could take the words back. She sounded needy and pathetic, not at all like the confident sexual virago she had planned to be.

'Not a chance.' His hand strayed to her backside. 'I've got a date with this cute little butt tonight. You're not getting away from me that easily.'

The cute little butt in question hummed beneath the bold caress, the sensation a giddy mix of arousal and trepidation at the reminder of what he planned to do to it. She'd read up on erotic spanking and had convinced herself it wouldn't hurt. But the thought of being at Connor's mercy both terrified and excited her—and she wasn't sure she could stand to spin out the suspense much longer.

'I'm not trying to get away from you,' she declared, struggling to sound blasé.

The sudden chorus of cheers from the foyer focused her attention back where it belonged. But as she watched Libby and Jamie progress through the guests to the entrance, and stepped forward to descend the stairs, Connor's hand gripped her wrist.

She tried to tug it free. 'I need to bid Libby and Jamie farewell.' And a few more minutes to prepare herself wouldn't go amiss.

'Time's up. You're all mine now.'

He nodded to the ornate grandfather clock a few feet away. The deep sonorous chime as the big hand of the clock jolted into place was barely audible above the commotion below as Libby tossed her bouquet over her shoulder.

But despite the noise from the gaggle of single women clambering to catch the spray of flowers, Sabrina felt the chime reverberate in her abdomen—and match the pulsing hum of the egg.

'But don't you want to say goodbye to Jamie? You won't see him again before you leave tomorrow.' The words bubbled out, as the little blip of panic compressed her chest.

Was she fully prepared for this? Yes, she was ready physically, far too ready frankly. But why did this suddenly feel like so much more than just casual sex? Connor called to some dark, primal need inside her. But did she really want to unleash it? When she wasn't sure she could control it?

'I'll call him tomorrow.' Those mocking lips twisted. 'What's the problem, Sabrina? Running scared?'

'Don't be ridiculous. I'm not scared of you.' Or not in the way he thought.

His fingers tightened on her wrist. 'Then we don't have a problem, do we.'

Without another word, he turned and drew her down the darkened corridors of the mansion, to the wing containing the guest suites. The arousal pounded harder between her legs. But much more disturbing was her heartbeat fluttering in her chest, like the wings of a caged bird as the bars fell away.

And the cage that had felt so stifling, so restrictive, suddenly seemed remarkably safe and secure compared to the prospect of freedom.

'LOSE THE GOWN.'

Sabrina blinked at the curt command and the sight

of Connor, shrugging out of his tux jacket and fling-
ing it over a chair. He had clearly booked the biggest
suite in the place. It covered one corner of the mansion's east wing and had two sitting rooms.

*All the better to accommodate those enormous
shoulders.*

Hysteria bubbled as she studied Connor's tall frame
relaxing into one of the armchairs.

'That's a bit rude.'

Wrapping her arms around her waist, she swallowed
heavily, but it didn't do a thing for the parched sensations scraping her throat raw. Or the heady pulsing in
her sex, which had gained momentum as he led her
into his suite.

Leaning back, he pulled the string for the standing
lamp. The wide pool of diffused light illuminated his
harsh features. She watched mesmerised as he undid
the cuffs on his shirt and rolled the sleeves up forearms roped with muscle.

'Lose the gown,' he said, in exactly the same demanding tone as before. 'Please.'

Crossing his ankle over his knee, his gaze dipped
to her toes and then took its own sweet time rising up
her body.

'Do you need me to undo it?' he asked.

She shook her head. The weight in her abdomen
had heated under that penetrating gaze, as if he and
not the egg were caressing her insides with that steady,
focused stroke.

'Could you turn off the egg?' she murmured, positive there was no way she could stay upright if she had
to strip under that all-seeing gaze with the egg driving
her to the edge, too.

He chuckled, the sound deep and husky. Pulling the remote out of his pocket, he held it up, then slipped the button down. The humming subsided, but that low, insistent throbbing in her clitoris continued as if it were so swollen now it would never stop vibrating.

'Now lose the gown. No more delaying tactics.'

Busted. Bugger.

The gown felt tight and confining as he waited. One eyebrow quirked.

She wanted to be naked in front of him, she realised. She wanted to feel those rough hands on her bare flesh. But she'd never performed a striptease before—and she was suffering from an unfortunate dose of performance anxiety.

His blue eyes sharpened watching her like a hawk tracking a mouse—but then her gaze snagged on the impressive bulge in his lap.

Courage, Bree. He's in no condition to grade you.

Unhooking the straps, her heavy breasts swayed, no longer held in place by the gown's internal bra. Gripping the tab of the zip under her arm, she drew it down, the rasp of the teeth releasing loud enough to be heard above her own breathing. Her nipples hardened into tight buds, the silky fabric scraping over them like sandpaper as the bodice fell to her waist.

Those intense blue eyes fixed on her breasts. Her nipples pinched tighter, hard and pouting, his gaze like a physical caress.

'You have beautiful breasts, Sabrina. Have you ever had your nipples clamped?'

'What?'

'I'll take that as a no.' His lips quirked. Was he playing with her again? 'That's a shame. Clamps would look amazing on those nipples.'

Just the thought of the clamps sent a renewed shaft of heat to her sex. 'I don't think that's a good idea.' Had he brought some with him, like the egg? And did she have the will to object? 'My nipples are very sensitive—clamps might hurt.'

'The pain is supposed to enhance the pleasure. It's just a question of knowing how to use them correctly. Luckily, I've had a lot of practice.'

'Oh,' she said, feeling stupidly gauche again. So he hadn't been messing with her? Why had she thought he would be? He was obviously way, way more adventurous about this stuff than she was. And why did the thought of all his practice make her feel a little inadequate? This was in no way a romantic liaison, so why should she care how many women had benefitted from his nipple clamp expertise?

'But your nipples are safe. I wasn't expecting to get laid while I was here, so I don't have any other toys with me.'

Her breath scythed out, her heart pummelling harder at the blunt, impersonal reference to 'getting laid'.

Holding a finger up, he flicked it down in indication. 'Lose the rest. Before I die of suspense.'

She wanted to tell him no. That she wanted to see him, too, but after the near miss with the clamps, she wasn't sure she could talk.

She hooked her thumbs into the fabric bunched at her waist, and heard the hum of approval in his throat. The desire to provoke him returned in a rush.

She wiggled her bottom to ease the gown over her

hips. His eyes flared and his jaw tightened, intoxicating her.

He rubbed his hand absently against his trouser leg as the gown stretched over her bottom and then dropped, to pool at her ankles.

He exhaled sharply, and she stepped out of the garment and kicked it away.

'Happy now?' she asked, mesmerised by the growing tent in his pants. Moisture gathered in her sex. Could he see her juices glistening in the spotlight?

'Ecstatic. The suspender belt is a nice touch,' he murmured, his voice so low and raspy it scraped across her nerve endings.

She reached to unclip the belt.

'Leave it,' he ordered, and her fingers stilled. 'It's like your pussy is framed in lace, especially for me.'

Moisture gushed as he stood and came towards her. 'I bet that clitoris is desperate to be touched, isn't it?'

'What do you think?' She lifted her chin, determined not to show an ounce of vulnerability.

Teasing was all well and good, but she wanted to tease him now, too.

She'd enjoyed stripping for him, enjoyed the force of his reaction, but there was only so much torture she could take in one night without getting even.

'That's a bit rude, Sabrina,' he said, the amusement thick in his voice as he threw her own words back at her.

But when she lifted her hand to touch his cheek, intending to pull him down for a kiss, he grabbed her wrist, and swung her round.

'Let go of me.' She tried to wriggle free, but only became more aware of the muscular forearm banded

under her breasts—and the iron bar in his pants that
nudged her bottom. 'I wanted to kiss you.'

'No kissing allowed. Not on the lips.'

'Why not?' she asked, as it occurred to her they'd
never shared that small intimacy.

He didn't answer. Bracing his foot on the chair, he
bent her over his raised knee.

'What are you doing?' she gasped, struggling in
earnest now, abruptly aware of her naked backside
thrust up in the air.

'Something that's long overdue.'

The loud smacking sound shocked her almost as
much as the sharp, stinging heat on her left buttock.

'Ouch!'

The air expelled from her lungs in an astonished
yelp, and she squirmed, but he held her firm, as two
more slaps landed. Evenly spaced on her buttocks. Not
too hard, but hard enough to have the heat spreading
across her vulnerable bottom like wildfire. She opened
her mouth, finding her voice at last, but the protest dissolved in a moan, as his blunt fingers stroked down
the crease of her bum, and found her yearning clitoris,
instantly zeroing in on the perfect spot.

Sensation exploded, mixing with the stinging heat,
to create a warm wave of pure pleasure.

She shuddered, moaned, mindlessly moving into
his touch, desperate to increase the friction, desperate for him to take her all the way.

But just as the wave surged and gathered, inten-
sifying around his stroking fingers, he stopped and
spanked her again.

'Not yet, Sabrina, not until I say so.'

The stinging jolt stopped her right on the edge,

suspended between intense pleasure and hot, sting-ing pain.

'You bastard.' She moaned, desperate, needy, mind-less with lust. 'Please, just touch me again.'

His fingers delved, as if answering her plea, spread-ing her folds, circling exactly the right spot, guiding her back to that perfect oblivion.

'Hold on to your orgasm. If you go over without permission again I may keep you on the edge for the rest of the night.'

She clamped down hard, focusing on the tantalis-ing touch, as she struggled to control the torturous roll of pleasure.

'How's your arse?' he mocked. 'Nice and hot yet?'

'Maybe.' She squirmed and he laughed, spanking her again.

Forget hot, it was bloody burning, but each sharp slap intensified the magnificent wave which built every time his fingers caressed, tormenting the burn-ing nub.

'That's it,' he coaxed. 'The orgasm will be stronger if you learn to control it.'

The steady strokes drove her into a frenzy. She bucked, trying to escape his touch now. Sweat beaded on her lip, her breasts swinging, painfully tender. His fingertip teased the aching bud, flicked and circled and fondled.

'I can't hold off. It's too much.'

'Yes, you can, just a little longer.'

Tingles turned to sizzles, and then flared into an inferno as the vicious wave hurtled closer. Then he found the plump, hard nub of her clitoris and pinched.

'Come for me now, Sabrina,' he whispered, the

sound deafening as she let go, allowed at last to fly headfirst through that final barrier.

The wave of bliss slammed into her, gushing through all the places she ached. The fireball blazed right behind—pumping, burning—like a wildfire torching everything it touched.

The primal scream wrenched past dry lips—a high, keening sound she didn't even recognise as her own voice—as she gave herself up to the inferno.

7) Accentuate the Positive: If the best man is doing a good job, tell him so.

SABRINA FLOATED, WEIGHTLESS, boneless, disorientated. Her sex still throbbing, her mind drifting back to consciousness on a golden tide of sensations.

Had she ever had an orgasm that strong? That intense? That prolonged? She'd thought the handjob he'd treated her to in Rules had been the nirvana of sexual experiences. Boy, had she underestimated him.

But then she landed on something cool and her lids popped open, the heady buzz of afterglow dispersed by the scalding heat in her bottom. Connor was poised above her as she lay on the satin quilt in the suite's master bedroom. Her chest tightened. Had he carried her in here? While she was floating in afterglow?

'Oww,' she muttered, placing her hand on her smarting bum, brutally aware of the liberties he'd taken with her—and how much she'd enjoyed it.

'That's more like it.' He captured her chin between his thumb and forefinger and placed a kiss on her forehead, the affectionate gesture disconcerting. 'No sleeping allowed before Round Two.'

She frowned at the arrogant amusement in his tone.

'I'm hardly likely to fall asleep.' She rubbed her backside. 'Seeing as my bottom feels as if it's been branded.'

The rusty laugh didn't do much for her temper. 'Branded? Huh?' He placed a large calloused hand on her bum cheek. The cool caress on the heated flesh sent pleasant ripples of sensation through her nerve endings. 'Poor baby, you want me to kiss it better?'

'That would be a start.'

The cool caress lifted to her hip and he rolled her over onto her stomach.

'Hey, let me up.' She tried to roll back, but he held her in place. Her buttocks tensed. Was he going to spank her again? As mind-blowing as it had been the first time, she wasn't sure she wanted another round yet.

But then his lips buzzed her burning bottom—while his fingers plunged into her soaking sex. The glistening egg landed on the pillow in front of her. The sharp pat on her bottom made her yelp, not because it hurt but because it had all those delicious ripples zapping to full attention.

'Consider yourself branded, baby.'

Humiliation burned her neck, adding to the tingles of awareness, but by the time she'd twisted onto her back to protest, he was on his feet by the bed, unbuttoning his shirt.

Her indignation dried up alongside all the moisture in her mouth as the hard planes of muscle and sinew were revealed one teasing inch at a time. He tugged the tails of the shirt out of his waistband, and shrugged it off.

Wow.

Triceps and biceps and a ton of other muscle groups she didn't know by name bulged and flexed. Her nipples tightened as she followed the happy trail of dark

hair down the ridged muscles of his abdomen. He un-
hooked the waistband of his suit trousers and she swallowed past the obstruction in her throat.

The enormous tent in his trousers had gotten bigger.
Clearly awesome was a euphemism for colossal.

The flutter of anticipation warred with the hot,
heavy weight in her sex. And the burn of emotion
still lodged in her throat.

But as he gripped the tab on his zipper, her hand
shot out. 'No, wait.'

She scrambled across the bed on all fours, not caring how inelegant she looked. 'Can I?'

He lifted his hands in silent acknowledgement, the
twist of amusement on his lips both cocky and ridiculously sexy.

She swung her legs over the edge of the bed, clipped
off the suspender belt and rolled down the stockings.

'Did I say you could take those off?'

She looked through her lashes as she peeled the
gossamer silk the rest of the way down, then perched
on the edge of the bed, her bottom tingling, her face
at eye level with that awe-inspiring package.

'I want to be able to feel you. Everywhere.'

Blood flooded into her cheeks as his nostrils flared.
'Point taken,' he murmured, his voice rusty.

She dropped her chin, stared at the length in his
pants. And swallowed, her mouth actually watering
at the thought of seeing him at last.

Her manicured nails flashed pink against the dark
fabric of his tux pants. She located the tab, eased the
zip down over the straining bulge.

The thick outline became visible, only contained by
his boxers now. She ran her palms down his thighs, felt

the muscles tense beneath velvet skin as she pushed
his pants past narrow hips and watched him step out
of them.

Hooking the waistband of his boxers down, the
mammoth erection leapt free. The broad head, plump
and thick, surged towards her. She gasped, with a tinge
of dismay she couldn't disguise.

She'd seen several erect penises in her life, but she'd
never seen anything quite this overwhelming.

Forget awesome. He was spectacular. So long and
thick, the tip pointing skyward. Her pelvic muscles
tensed at the prospect of taking all of that inside her.
And she'd thought the egg was a tight fit.

A bead of moisture formed on the tip, fascinating
her. She circled the broad base in trembling fingers,
felt the thick pulse of blood, then lifted on her knees
and licked along the slit, savouring the salty taste on
her tongue.

'Damn it.' His agonised whisper spurred her on.

She swirled her tongue around the crown, feasting
on the tangy taste of musk and man, then traced the
thick vein that pulsed down his length. She cupped
the heavy testicles that had drawn up at the base in
her palm, and opened her lips, eager to take him into
her mouth, but his hands cradled her cheeks, jerking
her back.

'Don't.'

Her eyes met his, the piercing blue now black, the
lids drifting to half mast. The harsh rasp of his breathing matching her own tortured breaths.

'Why not?' She heard the yearning, knowing she
had never wanted anything more.

She'd never been into giving head, had always considered it a chore, but there was something about this bad, beautiful man. His strength, his solitude, the dangerous shadow that lurked just beneath the cynical charm, the constant control—it made her want to bring him to his knees and make that cast-iron control crack.

But he hooked his hands under her arms, drawing her onto her feet. 'Because if I don't get inside you in the next sixty seconds I'm liable to explode.'

Lifting her in his arms, he placed her on the bed.

'But wait a min…'

The rest of her protest got muffled by a mouthful of the quilt as he flipped her over, then lifted her hips, forcing her face into the bed.

The sudden shock of vulnerability arched through her as he positioned her on all fours—and the thick head of his penis touched her inner thigh. She shook, her pussy clamping down hard, her lungs seizing, as her body braced for the heavy thrust that would drive him deep.

But instead of the brutal invasion she had expected, he slid his length along the cleft, angling his erection to slip through the folds of her sex. And reached round to cup her swaying breasts.

'You're drenched.'

The swollen head of his erection prodded at the nub of her clitoris. And he squeezed her distended nipples between his fingers.

She groaned, the feel of his erection toying with her, the pinch of sensation darting down from her breasts to her core—both exquisitely arousing and yet exquisitely frustrating. Her pussy clenched on the emptiness, her overstimulated clitoris and her swollen nipples too sensitive for attention. She wanted him inside her. Buried deep. Why didn't he just do it?

He swore viciously and suddenly let her go. She heard the rustle of clothing, the rip of foil and realised he'd almost forgotten to suit up.

'What the hell do you do to me,' he muttered. But she wasn't sure the statement was meant for her to hear.

Then hard hands grasped her hips and the blunt head pressed into her, spreading the lips of her sex so much more than before. A whimper escaped as he entered her in one smooth, solid stroke, thrusting so deep she could have sworn she could feel him in her throat.

'You're so fucking tight.'

She pulled forward, struggling to ease the immense fullness, but he dragged her back, impaling her fully on the hard length.

Her breaths came out in ragged pants. He felt impossibly deep. Filling her, stretching her unbearably, pushing her through the pleasure barrier towards pain. His hand covered her hot bottom, caressed the flushed skin. Her thighs trembled as her pelvic muscles tightened and released in a desperate bid to accommodate his size.

He withdrew an inch, maybe two, then thrust back, solidly, firmly, and she realised she still hadn't taken the full measure of him. Because there was more, driving deeper.

'It's too much. You're too big,' she moaned, the sound feral in its desperation.

'Shh, baby,' he crooned, then he reached under her, pulling back the hood of her sex.

'No, don't,' she wailed, unable to bear any more sensation.

But her cry was already too late, as he located the pounding nub, and glided over it.

White-hot lightning streaked through her, coiling and releasing, triggering the long, slow roll of orgasm as he started to move—timing each stroke with the slick glide of his finger, fondling the burning nub.

Pulling out, pounding back, the heavy erection stroked a place deep inside, and another orgasm built, hard and fast on top of the first. Rolling through, breaking free.

She sobbed, her knees giving out, her body already battered, in the grip of the never-ending waves of orgasm. He yanked her up, pounding into her in a furious, merciless rhythm now. Blinding, unstoppable pleasure fired across her skin, stole her breath, smashing through every pulse point, and exploding in her veins.

His thrusts became jerky, jolting, animalistic, the massive erection driving into her the only thing she could feel, could fathom, her dazed mind reeling as the endless wave gathered again, washing through her like a tsunami.

She cried out, her voice hoarse now, and felt him swell, becoming even bigger inside her, as his shout of fulfilment joined her helpless sobs.

CONNOR ROARED AS his mind blanked, his hands clutching her hips as he pistoned, driving towards that final oblivion.

She squeezed around him one last time, milking him, and the devastating pleasure crested and surged at last, the climax bursting up from his balls and pumping into her tight, wet heat. The thick, barbaric release crashed through him—shattering him, draining him.

'Goddamn it,' he managed to whisper as the last of his semen pumped into the condom.

He struggled to brace his elbows, his mind numb, his limbs limp and uncoordinated, as he clung on to the last of his strength to stop from collapsing on top of her and crushing her into the mattress.

Her body shuddered beneath him and she whimpered, the small sound piercing his consciousness. He struggled to be careful as he eased the still thick erection from the clasp of her body. Tenderness closed his throat as he let go of her hips and she fell forward onto the bed.

Shit, he'd fucked her like a goddamn express train.

Somewhere around the moment she'd licked the tip of his cock, and he heard the deep purr of pleasure as she savoured his taste, his control had shattered. Everything else had been a blur.

She curled into a ball on the bed, her lush curves flushed, the brand he'd left on her butt rosy on her pale skin.

His softening cock twitched and he dragged in a breath. Dropping his chin to his chest, he tried to regulate his breathing—and the renewed pulse of desire.

Get a grip, McCoy.

He shouldn't have pushed her so far, so fast. So what if she had a safeword? He'd hardly given her a chance to use it.

'You okay, honey?' He stroked the slope of her spine, brushed his thumb over her arse—and swallowed down the shame when she flinched.

'I think so.' The tremor in her voice reminded him a little too forcefully of a time in his life when he'd been unable to control his actions. Unable to stop himself taking whatever he wanted, unable to give a shit about the consequences.

He dropped down next to her on the bed, pulled the coverlet over them both. 'You don't sound too sure.'

She remained on her stomach, curled into the mattress, her face turned away from him. He placed his hand on her back and rubbed, desperate to reassure himself that he hadn't hurt her. 'Look at me, sweetheart.'

She let out a soft sob of breath, and he had the terrible thought that she might be crying. But then she shifted round, and the grip on his heart loosened at the sight of her eyes—dry and wary. 'I'm okay,' she said. 'It was a bit intense, that's all.'

He tucked the shiny curls of her hair behind her ear, framed her face with his hand, stupidly comforted by the matter-of-fact response. To think he'd once thought her no-nonsense approach was annoying? Pretty dumb, given that it was one of the things he found so damn irresistible about her now.

'Only a *bit* intense?' he teased, keen to lighten the mood.

Colour blossomed in her cheeks and a frown line appeared on her brow. Damn, seeing that instant blush light up her face would never get old.

'All right, a lot intense.' She sent him a tremulous smile. 'What do you want? A testimonial?'

He chuckled, the tightness in his chest releasing at last. 'You offering?'

The blush brightened. 'Certainly not. Your ego's big enough already.'

'And whose fault is that?' He traced his thumb across her bottom lip, giving in to the urge to touch her again. 'For a vanilla girl, you're pretty fucking hot.'

She blinked, then sat up abruptly. His groin stirred anew at the sight of her full breasts, swaying inches from his face, those pert, rosy nipples begging for his attention. She'd said her nipples were sensitive—he couldn't wait to find out how sensitive.

She grasped the sheet, covering herself, and he forced his gaze back to her flushed face.

Slow the hell down.

He shouted the words in his head as he spotted the glassy sheen in her eyes. 'Is everything okay?'

She looked away, her teeth digging into her bottom lip.

'I'm not a vanilla girl.' He barely heard the words through the buzz of arousal making him stir back to life. 'Not anymore.'

'What?'

She lifted her head and the anguish on her face was one hell of a buzzkill.

A single tear trailed down her cheek and he bolted upright.

'What's the matter? Why are you crying?'

She swiped away the tear. 'I'm not crying.'

'The hell you aren't.' Panic squeezed his heart. 'What's wrong?'

She didn't answer, abandoning the sheet to scramble off the bed. 'I have to go to the bathroom.'

'Sabrina, come back here, damn it,' he shouted as she darted across the room, nude.

She slipped into the bathroom, the click of the lock echoing into silence.

To hell with that.

He threw back the sheet, charged off the bed, but his paces slowed as he got halfway across the room.

Where was he going? Wouldn't it be less messy to let her lock herself in the bathroom for a while and get over it? Whatever *it* was?

But then he thought of the genuine distress on her face moments before, and her honest, untutored responses to him throughout the evening—and the knowledge that her freak-out was most likely his fault made the shame bloom in his chest and panic tighten his throat.

He dragged a hand through his hair.

Calm down. Don't overreact.

Women could get emotional after great sex. Plus who said this had anything to do with him? With them? Maybe it was just the emotion of the day. Women could get real emotional about weddings, too.

He tugged a tissue out of the box on the vanity, pulled off the condom and checked it—relieved to see he hadn't burst the damn thing with that turbo-powered ejaculation.

Her best friend's wedding could have screwed with Sabrina's usual equilibrium. For all her pragmatism and practicality, she was still female.

He scooped his boxers off the floor and put them on. His groin stirred at the memory of her kneeling at his feet, the unguarded joy in her eyes when she'd pulled his boxers down to stare at his cock.

Make that very female.

He adjusted his junk to ease the growing ache.

Plus she'd organised the whole damn wedding to within an inch of her life. That had to be stressful. Hell, maybe the emotion and the stress had combined with the spectacular sex, and caused a triple whammy.

But despite all his careful justifications, he couldn't stop himself from knocking on the bathroom door. 'Sabrina, what's going on in there?'

The gush of water switched on, as if in response.

'I just needed to f-freshen up.' He would have bought her murmured reply, but for the stutter half-way through. 'I'll be out in a m-minute.'

Damn, there it was again.

He pressed his ear to the wood, strained to listen, until he made out the muffled sobs over the sound of running water.

The shame and panic combined to become a pile-driver thumping his solar plexus.

Shit, no way was he going to be able to ignore that.

So MULTIPLE ORGASM could cause hysteria. Who knew?

Sabrina tried to smile at the ridiculousness of her discovery, but the salty tears refused to stop streaming down her face.

Wrapping the bathrobe round her midriff, she burrowed into the fabric's comforting warmth, but couldn't stop trembling. Choking down another sob, she stuffed the sleeve into her mouth to silence the sound.

Stop crying, you stupid cow—he'll hear you.

The next hiccup made her throat hurt, but at least her shoulders had stopped shuddering.

She dropped her head back, and blinked sore lids at the ceiling.

'Sabrina, open the damn door.' The harsh demand, accompanied by the sharp knock on the door made her jolt, nearly falling off the toilet seat.

She shook her head, then realised he couldn't see her.

'I won't be l-long.' She bit down on her lip to stop the little hiccup giving her away.

'*How* long?'

How about till the next millennium?

'Not long, really. Why don't you go to bed?' She almost winced at the maudlin plea in her voice.

What on earth had happened to the woman who could organise a six-month tour of provincial theatres? Who could talk Hollywood stars earning seven-figure salaries into performing for peanuts on the London stage?

She shook off the thought. She knew what had happened to that woman. She'd allowed herself to be spanked—and loved it. That's what had happened to her.

'I'll be out in a minute,' she added, but heard the pathetic whimper in her—and wanted to cry some more.

Please, please let him fall asleep. Then I can sneak out of the suite and never ever have to see him again.

Maybe it was just another symptom of her new-found cowardice, but she didn't think she could face him again tonight.

'I need to use the john.'

'What?' She stared at the door in disbelief, her temples starting to pound. She couldn't let him in, she just couldn't. She didn't want him to see her like this.

He'd probably laugh at her meltdown. And who could blame him. She'd as good as thrown herself at him. She'd had the best sex of her life with a man she barely knew. A man she wasn't even sure she liked and who she was fairly sure didn't like her. He hadn't even wanted her to kiss him on the lips for heaven's sake.

She'd exposed herself, given up every ounce of her dignity, and he'd remained as closed off and controlled as ever. But far, far worse had been that sharp, aching need that had hit her in the chest and knocked the air out of her lungs after the sex. She'd been lying there, her mind dazed with afterglow, staring into those crystal-clear blue eyes and that's when it had struck with the force of a sledgehammer. The idiotic urge to have him hold her, to have him care about her, to have him want more from her than just sex. As if there could be more? As if she wanted there to be more?

Completely and utterly certifiable. And yet undeniable. Or she wouldn't be bawling her eyes out in a hotel bathroom for no apparent reason.

She twisted her fingers in her lap. How had this happened?

She'd been so certain she could keep her emotions out of the mix. But somehow that potent combination of endorphins and pheromones had messed with her head, and propelled her into this ridiculous alternative reality—where she had this ludicrous idea that she wanted to know Connor, to understand him, to reach past the sex god and discover the fascinating man beneath.

'Sabrina, I'm not kidding. I need to use the john.' The doorknob rattled ominously. 'If you don't unlock this damn door I'm going to kick it in.'

She hitched in a breath and glared at the door. The fascinating and infuriating man beneath.

'Okay, okay. Just one second.'

She climbed off the loo seat and grabbed a tissue. Ignoring the shock of her reflection—fabulous, she looked like a demented panda—she repaired as much of the damage as she could.

Taking a deep breath in, she held it for a few seconds. Swallowed past the jolt of emotion.

Pulling the lapels of the robe tight across her breasts, unbearably aware of her nakedness beneath, she slipped the bolt and stood back. He walked into the room, unaware of her hiding behind the door. But before she could slip out behind him, his head whipped round, and strong fingers locked on her wrist.

'Oh, no, you don't.'

Her gaze jerked to his face. 'But you need to use the loo.'

'I lied.'

'Oh.' Her mind scrambled to process the information, her face flaming now.

He tilted his head to one side, the considering look scraping at the ache in her chest. He cupped her chin, ran his thumb over the reddened skin of her cheek. 'What's with all the tears?'

He sounded more curious than concerned—but with her emotions so close to the surface that was bad enough.

'It's nothing. It's been an emotional day, that's all. I guess it got to me in the end.'

He held her chin, raised her face. 'That's not it. You're not the flaky type.'

'How would you know? You hardly know me.' His eyebrow rose at the stupid spurt of hurt in her voice. And she realised, too late, that she'd given herself away.

'I know you better than you think.' His lips curled, but she heard the hint of regret. 'And contrary to popular opinion I don't set out to hurt people. So if it was something I did that made you cry, you need to tell me.'

She could hear the regret clearly now. And wondered whose popular opinion he was referring to.

Was it the father who had rejected him? Or the stepmother who had judged him and always found him wanting?

Oh, shut up, Sabrina, you don't know the first thing about this guy or his past—and you don't want to.

'You didn't do anything. Really, it's just me being silly.' She lifted her chin and his fingers dropped away. 'I should go back to my own room.'

But as she turned to make a dignified exit—or as dignified as it could be while she was sporting panda eyes and a runny nose—he scooped her into his arms.

She yelped, stunned as he strolled back into the bedroom. 'Connor, put me down.'

'Nothing doing.'

He settled into a large armchair, with her still in his arms. She tried to stand, or at least get off his lap, but he simply banded his arms around her waist, holding her in place.

'Let me up, this is ridiculous.' As was the renewed jolt of emotion making her throat hurt. If he made her burst into tears again, she'd have to kill him— and herself.

'Not as ridiculous as you being too embarrassed to tell me what freaked you out.' He nuzzled her ear and nipped at the lobe. 'When I've been so deep inside you I could swear I felt your heart beating.'

Heat pulsed in her abdomen and sunk lower as his hand swept beneath the folds of terry cloth, skimmed across her belly and settled on her ribs.

'I told you it's nothing. I'm just tired. It's been a long day.'

'Try again,' he replied, his wandering thumb stroking the underside of her breast.

She sent him a glare, but it wasn't one of her best.

'Was it the spanking?' he asked, sounding oddly unsure of himself. 'You should have used your safe-word. I would have stopped.'

She shivered as his thumb brushed her nipple, lazily seducing her all over again. She sighed, stupidly touched by the casual caress, the moment of uncertainty. 'The spanking did not freak me out.'

'Sure it did—you're a vanilla girl.' The lazy stroke of his thumb made her nipple pucker, but the ache to be touched was languid, seductive—unlike the too sharp ache in her chest when he said, 'I should have been more careful with you.'

'I had a multiple orgasm while you were spanking me. So I'm obviously not *that* vanilla.'

His grin was quick and knowing, and unbearably sensual. 'But afterwards it made you feel ashamed. I know how that goes.'

'How do you know?' The question came out before she could stop it.

His thumb stilled on her breast and he gave a heavy sigh as his brow touched her shoulder. She waited, convinced he wasn't going to give her an answer, when his head lifted and he murmured, 'Because I spent most of my childhood being ashamed of stuff. And I know how shitty it makes you feel.'

He shifted her on his lap.

The thick ridge in his boxers pressed into her bottom through the robe. And she felt suddenly bold. She'd gotten a tiny glimpse behind the mask. Why shouldn't she probe?

He'd spanked her, for goodness' sake. They'd had mind-blowing sex. He'd given her her first and then her second multiple orgasm—or did that count as one mega-multiple orgasm? Whatever.

The point was, while this might not be a big deal for him, it was an enormous deal for her. Why shouldn't she want to know more about him?

'What stuff were you ashamed of?'

Instead of answering her question, he lifted the flap of her robe, exposing her breasts to his gaze. She stretched as his finger toyed with her aching nipple, sending darts of sensation arrowing down to her sex. He leaned forward to lathe the tender peak and capture it between his lips.

She gasped, her nipple drawing tight under the exquisite torture as he sucked it to the roof of his mouth. 'Are you trying to distract me?'

He breathed a laugh, letting her go. 'Is it working?'

She threaded her fingers into his hair, to tug his head back. 'You didn't answer me. What stuff did you do that was so terrible?'

A small line appeared on his brow. 'Why do you want to know?'

'Because I'm curious.'

He hitched a shoulder, but the movement was stiff,

defensive. 'It's no biggie. I was wild as a kid. I did loads of dumb stuff.'

She smoothed her fingers over the hair she'd pulled, the hollow weight in her abdomen making her want to soothe. 'Libby told me you had a tough childhood. I'm sure whatever you did, it wasn't really your fault.'

The rumble of laughter wasn't what she had expected. Nor the crooked smile. 'God, you're cute when you're earnest.'

'I hardly think it's funny.'

'Sure it is. I can see you making up all sorts of sob stories about me and my deprived childhood.' His hand sunk to her bottom, and curved over the flesh he'd made sting. 'My mom and me lived in a trailer park. It wasn't great, especially in the wintertime, because the insulation on those things is for shit. And she worked nights and slept most of the day, which meant I could do what the hell I liked without any parental supervision. But none of that gives me a free pass for being a troublemaking little shit—which is exactly what I was.'

She stiffened in his arms, the hollow weight growing heavy in her stomach at the bitterness in his voice. 'Maybe it doesn't excuse it, but it does explain it,' she said, keen to defend the boy he'd been, even if he refused to.

'Does it?' His hands tightened on her waist and his lips twisted, the smile unbearably cynical.

'Of course it does. And it certainly didn't give your stepmother the right to treat you with so little compassion after your mother died.'

His lips quirked, not the reaction she'd expected from her impassioned speech in his defence. 'So Libby told you a load of bullshit about that, too.'

'How is it bullshit?'

'For a start, my mom didn't die. Her...' He hesitated, but only for a moment. 'One of her boyfriends took exception to my smart mouth and kicked the shit out of me. So I hitched the five hundred miles to Newport, figuring I could fool the rich stiff named on my birth certificate into taking me in. And it worked. For a while.' He shrugged, calmly dismissing whatever had happened in his father's home. 'By sixteen I was on my own—and it forced me to get my shit together. End of story.'

'But that's dreadful. You were only a child.'

He shook his head, sending her a pitying look. 'Honey, I was fourteen going on thirty with a piss-poor attitude when I got to Newport. My old man made Elizabeth take me in because he felt guilty. She didn't want some little trailer-trash bastard messing up her perfect life and who can blame her?'

'I can. You needed help and understanding, not criticism. Can't you see that?' she added, distressed at the thought of what he must have gone through when his father and stepmother had rejected him, too. 'Surely they owed you that much? To at least try?'

'Are you for real?' He huffed out a laugh. 'No one owes anyone anything. You're on your own. All I needed was to figure that out.'

She pressed her palms to the soft hair on his chest, determined not to be distracted by the mocking light in his eyes, or the way his fingers were toying with her nipple again.

'All you needed was someone to care about you,' she said softly.

She touched his cheek, felt the rasp of his stubble,

her throat full and aching. Did his childhood explain the dominance that seemed so much a part of his personality? Did his rigid control come not just from the healthy pursuit of great sex, but also from the need to control his feelings? From the desire to keep people at a distance, so no one could reject him again?

He grasped her fingers, gave an incredulous laugh. 'Damn, who knew there was a bleeding heart hiding behind the ball-busting front?'

She wanted to protest, to tell him she knew what it was like to be rejected. That she understood. But how could she tell him that without exposing her own need?

His lips brushed her earlobe, making the shiver of sensation arrow down to her core. His warm palm snuck under the robe again, to stroke the sensitive skin of her belly. 'I want to fuck you again, Sabrina.'

The coarse word sent colour flushing into her cheeks, but the press of his erection through the layers of towelling made the statement seem earthy and enticing rather than crude.

'I want to suck that sweet pussy until you pass out, torture those tender nipples with my teeth.' His fingers rose to pluck at the sensitive tips, and sensation shimmered down to her sex. 'And fuck you so hard and so long, you'll still feel me in your pussy in a week's time.'

'I see,' she said, trying for nonchalance, but getting breathless instead as excitement and trepidation rippled across her skin.

His thumb brushed over her mound, gentle but possessive, and she lurched in his lap. 'Easy, sweetheart,' he murmured against her hair, nipping her earlobe as his large hand cupped her sex. 'But I don't want to hurt you. So now you need to tell me why you freaked out so we can fix it.'

She shook her head, her mind already dazed by the endorphin rush, at the promise of what was to come. She couldn't tell him about the emotional connection she felt with him. He'd think she was bonkers, or worse delusional. Especially as now that emotional connection felt so much stronger. And yet that much more hopeless—because now she knew his past made it impossible for him to trust in emotional intimacy.

And what would be the point of telling him about her parents? About how she'd denied her sex drive, all her darkest, deepest fantasies for so long, because of some stupid belief that being a sexual being would make her like them? Because that boat had already sailed over the horizon and far, far away. And it wasn't coming back, even if she wanted it to, and she was pretty sure she didn't.

But if their relationship could be only about sex, why not enjoy it, at least for the rest of the night?

She threaded her fingers through his hair, separated the silky strands, her pulse leaping in her throat. And she plunged in where she suspected no woman had ever dared to tread. 'Honestly?'

He nodded, giving her the permission she hadn't expected.

'I think what freaked me out was knowing you had all the power. Don't get me wrong—I enjoyed it, but afterwards it made me feel exposed. Like I wasn't myself anymore.' She drew in a breath and held it. 'I want to have some of the power, too.'

She watched his face carefully, prepared for resistance, or even irritation—especially now she knew where his desire for control came from—but instead his lips curved up on one side. And she could have sworn she saw a spark of admiration in those pale blue eyes. 'What are you getting at? You want to spank me?'

She could hear the amusement in his voice, but refused to rise to the bait. 'No, I'm not quite as kinky as you are.' She smiled back, enjoying the frankness of the discussion. When had she ever been able to do exactly what she wanted during sex? To demand whatever fantasy came into her head without feeling guilty about it? 'But maybe some light bondage wouldn't go amiss.'

He hadn't even let her kiss him. What she wouldn't do to have that big body, that magnificent cock completely at her mercy. Power surged through her. She could explore his body the way he'd explored hers. It was like having a tiger by the tail, and then getting the chance to pet him.

She'd always thought of herself as a confident woman, but she'd never been confident enough to take the initiative during sex—because she'd always been so bloody terrified of being as much of a sybarite as her parents. Of being controlled by her sexual desires. And the end result had been a sex life so bland, so boring, it wasn't even vanilla. Vanilla was a subtle but smooth and seductive taste. Her sex life had no taste at all.

Connor McCoy could never be Mr Right, but he was certainly Mr Right Out There. She'd broken down barriers she hadn't intended to tonight, but why not embrace her new freedom now? He'd opened up to her, told her about himself, and because of that she trusted him. Her breath hitched as she waited for his response.

'You want to tie me up, huh?' He huffed out an incredulous laugh. Still confident, still in total command.

'I can give you a safeword if you'd prefer,' she offered.

'You little...' His eyebrows rose a fraction, and then he chuckled. 'Damn, I've created a fucking monster.'

'What's the matter, Connor, running scared?'

He pinched her chin, angled her head, his gaze roaming over her face. Her breathing caught as she saw the challenge in his eyes. The knife-edge of tension lingered, her heart contracting painfully as his lips hovered so close to hers, and she had a sudden yearning to have him kiss her.

'Sure, why don't you give it your best shot,' he murmured, the words mocking, even as his nostrils flared.

Her breath gushed out, the tension releasing in a rush and pounding into her core as he let go of her chin.

His palm folded around her waist, jerking her closer still, her body as boneless as a rag doll. 'But after that, you're mine for the rest of the night.' His hand cupped her breast, squeezing the tender tip between his fingers. 'Agreed?'

She nodded, her tongue too numb to respond, her heart hammering in her throat.

IT WAS ONLY as she leant over his beautiful body, securing one wrist to the bedpost with the tie of her robe, the outline of his erection already prominent in the boxer briefs, that it occurred to her the desire to challenge him, to provoke him, might not just be about indulging all those dark sexual fantasies she'd never known she had.

What if she didn't just want to pet the tiger, but wanted to tame him, too?

8) Tie Up Any Loose Ends: And be sure to keep your best man on a short leash.

WAY TO GO, McCoy, how the fuck did you get into this position?

Connor tugged on his wrist, his arm anchored above his head, and gulped down the tickle of panic when it didn't give an inch. 'That's pretty damn secure. Were you a marine in a former life?'

Shit, he'd figured she'd do some girly knot, which he could get out of no problem.

'A Girl Scout, actually.' She gave a nervous laugh, straddling him as she leant forward to secure his other wrist. The inside of her thigh brushed his hip and her breasts swayed enticingly in front of his face, where the robe fell open without its belt, the large rosy tips beckoning him.

But then his knuckles bumped against the bedpost as she circled his wrist with the belt, and a thin trickle of sweat slid down his temple. Damn, he would have appreciated the view a lot more if she hadn't been busy trussing him up like a chicken.

She shifted down the bed, pausing for a moment to look at the erection straining against his boxers. The blood in his groin heated and pounded harder, until he could feel his heartbeat in the tip of his cock.

But instead of taking off his shorts, and relieving the pressure, like he'd hoped, she scrambled off the bed.

'What are you doing?' he asked, when she opened his suitcase and began rummaging through his stuff.

She flicked a look over her shoulder. 'Looking for something to tie your ankles.'

He raised his knees.

No fucking way.

His mind screamed, the panic clawing at his chest, his neck muscles straining as he lifted his head to watch her. 'That's gonna be uncomfortable,' he said, trying to keep his voice even and calm.

She turned with a couple of his neckties clutched in her fist, a quizzical little frown bisecting her brow.

'And those are silk—you'll ruin them,' he added, not giving a shit about the neckties. He could buy twenty more tomorrow if he wanted to. He hadn't killed himself turning The Red House into one of Manhattan's most exclusive nightspots so he could be precious about his wardrobe. But he didn't think he could stand to have his ankles tied down, too.

No woman had ever done that… Because it reminded him too much of…

He erased the thought, his erection wilting at the visceral blast of memory.

The biting pain slashing across his buttocks, the salty sweat trickling into the burning welts. His mother's screams and the grunts of her pimp as he wielded the belt. The humiliation as scalding as the pain while he gritted his teeth to stop the whimpers.

'Okay,' she said, worrying her lip again. 'But will you promise to lie still?' Her eyebrows wiggled suggestively and his cock perked up again, the grim memory receding at the eagerness on her face. 'So I can have my wicked way with you?'

'Sure.' He dropped his head back on the bed, the screaming tension in his shoulder blades releasing. 'I'm all yours.'

He didn't know how the hell he'd agreed to this. Or why he'd spilled his guts about his past when she'd asked. Of course, he hadn't told her the whole truth. But he'd told her enough. He guessed hearing her bawling her eyes out in the bathroom, and then seeing her face, all red and puffy from her tears, had rattled him more than he'd thought.

But he was regretting trusting her big time now.

The bed dipped as she crawled back onto it. She knelt at his hip, her teeth catching on that full bottom lip as she studied him.

His flesh rose and lengthened under her inquisitive gaze, stretching the soft cotton of his shorts. He didn't know what the hell she planned to do to him, but at least he wasn't coming out in a cold sweat.

She wrapped her arms around her waist, pulling the lapels of the robe together so he couldn't see those magnificent breasts.

He bit down on the desire to tell her to take it off. He wasn't in charge. Or not yet. Although he had every intention of turning the tables on her. With or without the use of his hands.

Mossy-green eyes met his and she sighed. 'Are you comfortable?' she asked. He heard the tiny hesitation before her gaze darted back to his lap, and realised she was as unsure about this as he was.

This had to be the first time she'd ever tied a guy up. Good to know.

'Not exactly.' He shot a telling glance at his crotch. 'My balls ache like a son-of-a-bitch.'

It wasn't exactly a lie—they did hurt—but it was the sweet, tortuous ache that he'd trained himself over the years to deny—so he could prolong the pleasure.

Problem was, with Sabrina, all his training had been shot to hell already, and the thought of prolonging the pleasure was the furthest thing from his mind. All he was aiming for tonight was to get through this without making an ass of himself.

'Whatever you plan on doing to me, you need to do it soon, or I'm liable to die of the suspense.' He nodded at the robe, trying to put as much conciliation into his tone as possible, given that he was staked out and entirely at her mercy. 'If you want to ensure I die happy, though, you should lose the robe.'

SABRINA HEARD THE edge in his voice, and folded her arms around her midriff. Maybe this hadn't been such a smart idea after all.

She chewed her bottom lip and gazed at his big body, dusted with dark hair, all that mouth-watering muscle and sinew, bulging and flexing as he strained against the restraints. Even with his arms bound, he looked like more than she could handle.

She sucked in a deep breath, blew it out again.

'How about it, Sabrina? I think the robe has to go.'

Her eyes narrowed, hearing the thinly disguised steel behind the request. 'I think you should shut up, actually.' Maybe she was way out of her depth, but she wasn't giving up that easily. 'Or I may have to gag you.'

His dark brows rose up his forehead, and his fingers fisted, but after one quick tug on the ties, he controlled himself. And she congratulated herself on her superlative knot-tying ability. Never doubt the bondage techniques of a member of the Wellesley Park Girl Guide troop.

'You are so gonna pay for this later,' he muttered, the threat thick with innuendo.

'Perhaps.' She swung her leg over his hips to straddle him. The hair on his legs brushed against the sensitive skin of her inner thighs, making her shiver. 'But right now, I'm the one calling the shots.'

She ran her palms up the smooth, tanned skin on his thighs, swirled her fingernails in the fine hair, felt his flanks bunch under the delicate torture.

'So you need to shut up and take this like a man, or I'm going to have to gag you and blindfold you as well as bind you to the bed.'

He swore softly, but didn't say another word, his whole body quivering as she explored him. The planes and angles, so deliciously hard, so potently male. She traced the lean, packed muscles on his abdomen. Counted the clearly defined slabs. Combed her fingers through the tufts of hair that sprouted around the flat brown nipples. Traced the straining sinews on his biceps, the roped sinews above his hip bones, the ripped muscles of his six-pack.

She heard the low, guttural moan as she bent forward at last, letting the robe fall open to reveal her swollen breasts to his gaze, and then cut off his line of sight to press her lips to his collarbone.

His back arched, the solid ridge of his penis—still confined in his boxers—rubbing against her leg.

She lifted up, stopping the contact, even though

her pelvic muscles dissolved, melting at the memory of how good it had felt to impale herself on that enormous shaft.

'That's cheating, Connor. You promised to lie still. Remember.'

'Fuck still,' he growled, his voice gruff with frustration. 'There's a limit to how much teasing I can take.'

She tapped a fingernail to his chest, watched his pectoral muscles tense and met the dark gleam in his eyes, full of the dangerous threat of retribution.

But instead of making her wary, or nervous, that dominant glare only made her feel more bold, more powerful and more determined.

'And you're not even close to being there yet,' she whispered, determined to control her own needs for as long as it took to make him admit his.

'Come on, Sabrina.' His tone became acquiescent. She smiled. It might only be a hairline crack in that indomitable facade, but it was big enough. 'Untie me, damn it. You've had your fun—it's my turn now.'

'Not gonna happen, McCoy,' she shot back, rejoicing when his brows slashed down in an annoyed frown. 'We haven't even gotten to the main event yet.'

'Which is?' he asked, his expression wary.

'You'll see.'

So saying, she dropped her head and swirled her tongue across his flat copper nipple, tugging at it with her teeth.

'Oh, shit.'

She worked her way down his torso—licking and sucking, nipping and biting—to a chorus of swearing, each pained exclamation becoming more husky, more raw than the last.

She ran her nose through the trail of hair below his navel, drew in the delicious scent of him—salt, sweat and the tangy musk of sex. He squirmed under her, and the bulbous purple head of his penis thrust over the waistband of his boxers, the clear liquid at its tip glistening in the dim lighting.

She touched her tongue to the slit, and he lurched off the bed like a wild animal, forcing her to spring back before she got knocked onto the floor.

He stared down at her, his face contorted with something between pleasure and pain, his eyes heavy-lidded with need. Awareness pounded in her sex, the moisture leaking down trembling thighs. The connection she'd sensed arching between them... She was seeing him for the first time, without the shield, without the cocky dominance, the surly charm. This was Connor, raw, animalistic, exposed, vulnerable. The man behind the player's mask.

He'd put himself in her hands, had trusted her when she sensed he trusted very few. And she wanted to show him he hadn't made a mistake. Maybe this was just about sex, but for this one moment in time it felt like more.

'Sorry,' he rasped, the words pained, tortured, as he dropped back onto the bed, the breath gushing out on a sigh of defeat.

'Don't be,' she whispered, then slid her thumbs into the waistband of his boxers and watched his penis leap free.

Even though she'd seen him, admired him once before, the sight of that long column of thrusting flesh— ready for her—had the breath clogging her lungs, squeezing her chest.

'I'm not going to last long.' His voice broke on the words, as if the admission had been wrenched from some deep, dark place inside.

'You don't have to,' she replied, then licked the shaft from base to tip.

The low groan, the staggered pants of his breathing, spurred on the gentle, probing exploration. She circled her fingers round the base, pressed her thumb against the pounding vein, and caressed, while she braced her knees and leant over him, to take as much of the broad head into her mouth as she could, her tongue still lapping at the thick shaft.

His unique aroma, rich, musty, male, filled her senses as his hips lifted off the bed. She opened her throat, to take more, to give more.

'Don't stop,' he murmured, the words part demand, part plea. 'Please. I can't…'

The hoarse cry issued from his lips as his cock swelled even more, and then the hot gush of semen hit the back of her throat. She swallowed, still sucking, loving the taste of him, the thick ropes of his orgasm and the broken cries of his surrender.

'THANKS.' CONNOR'S VOICE sounded raw, different to his own ears, his body still shuddering from the force of his climax.

What had just happened? She'd broken through his biggest taboo. The one thing he never let a woman do to him during sex—mostly because he couldn't maintain an erection thanks to the memories. But this time the memories—of his mother giving her client head, while he'd lain in bed trying not to hear, trying not to look—hadn't come. The sight of Sabrina's lips on his cock hadn't repulsed him—it had seduced him. The feel of her tongue, tentative and untutored, then eager and excited, had heated his blood, made him want to thrust into her mouth.

And then, when he'd come like a fountain, she'd swallowed every drop.

He yanked against the bonds on his wrists.

She lifted her face from his crotch, her eyes full of an emotion he didn't understand—didn't want to understand—but was very much afraid he would remember for the rest of his life.

'Untie me.'

She nodded, moving up the bed to release his wrists. Taking each one in her hand, she rubbed the reddened skin. 'I'm sorry, Connor, I tied you too tight.'

He shook his head. He'd hardly even noticed the bonds once she'd started trailing her tongue, her lips, over every part of him. 'No, you didn't.'

Lifting up on his elbows, he dragged off the robe that was falling off her shoulders, threw it off the bed. Wanting, needing, to feel her naked next to him.

He pulled her back onto the bed until she lay across him, her head tucked into the lee of his shoulder, her hand splayed across his abdomen. He cupped her cheek, lifted her face.

He wanted to thank her again. Wanted more than anything to cover those full lips with his own, to explore her mouth with his tongue and taste himself. The thought was unbearably erotic, but as he dipped his head, he looked into her eyes, saw a yearning that mirrored his own—and forced himself to back off just in time.

'You should have told me you were the queen of

BJs—we could have done that a lot sooner.' He smiled at her, trying to defuse the tension in his chest, and ignore the fist tightening around his heart.

Be cool, man. Don't let her know how much she's gotten to you.

The instant blush lit up her face, making the clenched fist pummel his ribs. 'I'm not usually. You must have inspired me.'

He grinned, trying to ease the ache around his heart. 'Just let me know if you need any more inspiration.'

She smiled, then dipped her head and cuddled against him, her finger twirling in the short hair around his belly button. He bundled her close, tightening his hold as the fist thumping his ribs went nuts.

What the hell was going on, here? He hated cuddling up after sex….

She stretched against him, and he heard the drowsy exhalation as she yawned. Her limbs softened into him.

His cock was already stiffening again, the scent of her hair—clean, fresh and flowery—almost as arousing as the feel of her breasts pillowed on his chest. But instead of jumping her, of staking his claim, he lay there like a dummy, staring blindly at the ceiling, trying to get his heartbeat to quit punching his chest wall.

'Do you mind if I have a nap before the next round?' she asked, her voice thick with sleep.

'Sure,' he heard himself say, stupidly grateful because he needed a time out too, despite the renewed ache in his balls. 'But after that it's payback time.'

She huffed out a little chuckle. But eventually the circling finger stilled on his navel. The soft rise and fall of her breathing brushed the hair on his chest as her lush body relaxed into sleep.

He continued to stare at the ceiling, the fist punching his ribs now like a heavyweight champ, and his cock as hard as an iron spike.

Women didn't generally fall asleep in his arms.

He should wake her up and fuck her again. Play out the bargain they'd made, demand her surrender, the way she'd demanded his. But he couldn't seem to stop his fingers from raking through the fine hair at her nape, or stroking his thumb across the pulse in her neck. Breathing in her scent…

Everything he knew about himself seemed to be floating above him, just out of reach. No longer sure, no longer certain.

This night didn't feel like it was just about the sex anymore. And that couldn't be good.

When she woke up again, he'd get things back on track. He'd fulfil every one of the promises he'd made to her—and fuck her until they both couldn't walk anymore. His rock-hard cock twitched as if in acknowledgement of his plan.

She sighed in her sleep, and his hand stilled on the back of her head.

But for now, it felt okay just to hold her, with the summery scent of her hair filling his senses, and the weight of her head solid on his shoulder.

9) Keep Him Sweet: And your parting won't be sorrowful.

'CAN YOU TAKE me again? Just one more time?'

Sabrina nodded, the husky request almost drowned out by the cascading water as Connor lifted his head from her breast and hoisted her up in his arms.

Her back hit the slick tiles of the shower cubicle as he thrust heavily inside her.

She winced, the soreness a reminder of how many times he'd taken her during the night. But as her tight flesh stretched to accept him again, the ecstasy wasn't far behind. She wrapped her legs round his lean waist, clasped his shoulders in trembling hands, and clung on as he gripped her buttocks and adjusted her hips to take the full force of his thrusts.

She cried out as he drove into her, pounding that place deep inside and angling his pelvis to rub against her aching clitoris. She gave herself up to the harsh swell of orgasm, hanging suspended, then crashing over into the abyss—as white-hot rain poured through her body like a meteor shower.

She must have passed out for a few seconds, only to be dragged back to consciousness when he pulled out, pumping his release against her belly.

His fingers dug into her hips, his breathing harsh and ragged, his head buried in her neck. The splatter of water did nothing to drown out the heavy thud of her heartbeat.

She began to shake, but swallowed down the terrifying wash of emotion, her arms tightening around his neck. Her fingers threaded into the wet hair at his nape. And she held on for a few precious moments. Waiting for her pulse to stop racing, waiting to get the raw pain in her chest under control as she watched the midmorning sunshine sparkle on the droplets of water sliding down the glass wall of the cubicle. Signalling the end of their wild night.

They'd made love so many times, she'd lost count. He'd been a magnificent lover. Broken through all her inhibitions, and shown her how glorious the physical connection could be between two people who had nothing to lose and everything to gain. Unfortunately, the downside was during their long night the emotional connection that she'd been determined to deny had only gotten stronger. To the point where she'd stopped trying to guard her heart hours ago. Because it had already been a lost cause.

She knew falling in love with Connor—a man who wasn't looking for a relationship and certainly wasn't about to fall in love with her—was the height of stupidity. And what she was feeling was quite probably the physical equivalent of an optical illusion anyway, brought on by the adrenaline overload of their sex marathon. But unfortunately all the justifications in the world didn't make it seem any less real.

Keeping his hand banded under her bottom, he raised his head and sent her a sheepish smile that had her pulse thundering into her throat.

Would he kiss her at last?

'That's what I call one for the road,' he murmured, his lips hovering above hers, so close and yet so far—and the yearning in her chest became unbearable.

She nodded, the stupid emotion clogging her lungs again and making it hard to breathe.

Hold it together. Don't you dare freak out.

'I need to shower alone now.' She forced her lips to curl. 'We have to check out soon.'

'Yeah. Right.' He let her down gently. Raked his hand through his wet hair, the warm water spraying off his shoulders. His gaze dipped to her breasts. 'You sure you don't want any help with that?'

The grin came more naturally now, courtesy of the hopeful look in his eyes. She shook her head. 'Get out of here, Connor.'

'Goddamn it, you are such a ball-buster.'

She gave his shoulder a playful punch, then pointed at the door of the cubicle. 'Out. Now.'

'Yes, ma'am.' He sent her a cheeky salute. And left.

She reached for the soap and turned into the spray, the foolish tears mingling with the water washing over her face.

10) A Stolen Kiss Never Goes Amiss: If you find time for some light flirtation, you never know— the next wedding you attend may be yours.

How Sabrina got through the next half an hour she didn't know. Connor insisted she stay with him while he packed. Which involved dumping everything into his suitcase without folding a single solitary thing.

She watched him, and stopped herself from pointing out that his suits would be irrevocably crushed by the time he got home to New York. Not because she knew he probably had a hundred suits in his closet there, and wouldn't balk at a dry-cleaning bill, but because she didn't think she could keep the stupid tears down indefinitely.

She'd had to put her maid of honour gown back on, with no underwear, and felt more than a little self-conscious as they walked through the corridors to the mansion house's entrance. They made weirdly polite conversation about his flight, her return to work in a week's time for the start of a new run. And then they got to the first-floor landing—and she veered off towards her room.

But strong fingers banded around her wrist, halting her getaway.

'Hey, where are you going?'

'I need to get changed, and pack my own bag.'

He looked at his wristwatch. 'The car's picking me up in ten,' he said.

Which was exactly why she needed to get away from him.

'I know.'

She was fairly sure she couldn't stand a long-drawn-out goodbye. And anyway, wasn't this the correct etiquette for a one-night stand? You parted without ceremony the next morning? And went back to your real lives.

She'd be absolutely fine as soon as he was gone. And this ludicrous idea that she'd fallen in love with her one-night fling would fade quietly away. As would the lump of cement currently pressing against her larynx. Hopefully.

'So I guess this is goodbye,' she added, when he continued to hold on to her wrist, apparently not taking the hint. 'It's been really...' She reached for the right word. What did you say to someone who had changed your outlook on life? Who would always mean more to you than you could ever let them know? 'Really fun.'

'Fun seems like kind of an understatement,' he said, the husky tone making her nipples pinch into tight peaks—and her bare clit throb painfully.

'Yes, well.'

He tugged on her wrist, drawing her close. 'Stay with me.' He cupped her cheek, the look in his eyes shuttered but intense.

Sabrina opened her mouth, her heart suddenly battering her throat. What was he asking?

'Well, now, isn't this touching?'

They both jerked round to see Elizabeth, his stepmother, standing on the landing behind them.

Connor stepped back, but kept his hand around her wrist. 'Hello, Elizabeth. I'm just on my way out. I'll see you around.'

'Not if I have the good fortune to see you first,' she replied, the contempt dripping from her tongue.

Sabrina sucked in a breath, horrified by the venom in her tone. But Connor merely shrugged and said through gritted teeth, 'Nice.' Then he turned to her. 'Come on, let's get out of here.'

Maybe it was the emotion Sabrina had had on lockdown for the last ten hours, maybe it was simply physical and mental exhaustion, or maybe it was the weary resignation she saw on Connor's face, but the hot flare of temper was quick and all-consuming as she pulled her hand out of Connor's hold and faced his stepmother.

'What the hell is wrong with you, you sanctimonious bitch?'

Elizabeth flinched as if she'd been struck. 'How dare you talk to me like that,' she said. 'I don't care if you are my daughter-in-law's friend. I will not stand for that kind of language.'

The snooty, self-righteous indignation only made Sabrina's smouldering temper ignite like a firecracker.

'Well, how bloody dare you talk to Connor like that. What gives you the right to treat him as if he's nothing? Just because he's the son of a barmaid? And he lived in a trailer park,' she shouted, stepping towards the woman, suddenly keen to get in her precious personal space.

'Shit, Sabrina, calm the hell down.' Connor's words barely registered, but then his arms locked around her torso, stopping her dead.

'The son of a barmaid?' A cruel smile curved his stepmother's lips. 'Is that what he told you?'

Sabrina struggled to free her arms. 'Let me go, Connor. She has no right to speak to you like that. The snobby cow.'

'He's not the son of a barmaid,' Elizabeth continued, her glare aimed at Connor now. 'He's the son of a prostitute.'

'What?' Sabrina stilled, shocked not by the information, but by the way Connor stiffened behind her, and the pained emotion in his voice as he said, 'Fuck.'

His arms dropped away.

'You heard me,' Elizabeth continued, warming to her theme. 'His mother was a whore. A woman my husband hired for a night in a moment of youthful indiscretion only to end up saddled with her brat.'

'So what?' Sabrina felt her chest implode, her temper dissolving into horrified realisation. Was this what he'd been so ashamed of? Was this why they'd rejected him?

'So *what?*' Elizabeth looked momentarily nonplussed. 'So why would anyone want the child of a prostitute in their home?'

'Because he was your husband's son, because he was Jamie's brother, because…' Sabrina trailed off, as Elizabeth stared blankly back at her as if she'd lost her marbles.

What the hell was she bothering arguing with this woman for? The only person that mattered here was Connor. She swept her hand at the woman in a dismissive gesture. 'Oh, forget it, you'll never understand.'

She turned to tell Connor she was sorry, that he had

such a stupid cow for a stepmother. Only to find the space on the landing behind her empty.

He'd gone.

Ignoring the thundering of her heartbeat, the callous parting remark from the woman behind her, she hiked up her gown and raced down the mansion's staircase. No way was that bitch going to ruin their last moments together.

Bugger it.

She didn't care if it was completely nuts. She had to tell him he mattered to her. That she cared about him. Even if he threw it back in her face, which he undoubtedly would. She wanted him to know he meant more to her than just a one-night stand.

WHERE THE HELL was the fucking limo?

Connor stared down the gravel driveway that meandered miles through the manor's parkland, willing the damn thing to appear on the horizon and quick. He needed to get the hell out of Dodge and fast. His fingers fisted around the handle of his luggage as humiliation and panic scoured his stomach.

He'd nearly spilled his guts for real on that damn landing. Nearly asked to see Sabrina again. For the first time in his life he was actually grateful to his stepmother. Hell, it would have been nice to have gotten out of here before Sabrina had discovered all the sordid details about his childhood, but the humiliation of that was small potatoes compared to the way he'd come damn close to begging moments before. He'd felt the shock rippling through her body when his stepmother had spilled the beans about his mother's choice of profession. But knowing Sabrina and that bleeding heart of hers, she'd probably have already sugar-coated the truth.

'Connor, wait!'

He whipped round. The churning panic in his belly rammed his throat as he watched her walking towards him in that arse-kissing gown—which had once turned him inside out with lust, but now turned him inside out with something more intense. Her hair fell in wild chestnut waves onto her bare shoulders, and her face looked flushed, her eyes bright with intent as she approached. His fingers gripped the leather strap of his bag and he forced himself to stand his ground.

He couldn't see any pity in her expression, which he guessed was a good thing. But the dumb, pointless yearning that had gripped him all through the night, when he'd been driving into her over and over again to quench the damn thirst that never seemed to end, dried up every drop of moisture in his mouth.

His voice came out on a husky croak. 'Hey there. Car'll be here any minute. No need to hang with me if you've got stuff to do.'

Something flickered in her eyes that looked like hurt. But he steeled himself against it and swallowed down the thirst to have her again. To have more. All she'd wanted from him was a good fuck. And he'd given her a lot of those. He didn't have anything else to give.

He turned away from her to stare down the driveway. Still no sign of the fucking car? If it didn't get here soon, he was totally screwed.

SABRINA STARED AT the rigid muscles of Connor's back as he studied the driveway as if his life depended on it. She knew when she was getting the cold shoulder.

Courage, Bree. You're not that wimpy little vanilla girl anymore. You're a sexy, strident ball-buster. You know what you want. And the only way to get it is to go after it.

She stepped to his side, the pebbles of the driveway cold and round against her bare feet. His free hand hung by his side and she noticed it tensing and releasing as he ignored her. She thought of all the ways those clever fingers had brought her pleasure throughout the night, but realised they'd never once held hands, just like they'd never once kissed on the lips.

The painful ache became a dead weight in her chest. If she could take only those two small intimacies away with her, it would be enough. Reaching out when his fist released, she slid her fingers across his palm and held on.

He looked down at their joined hands, then back at her face, his expression unreadable. His fingers remained loose in hers, his Adam's apple bobbing, but he didn't pull away.

She squeezed the callused flesh. And let the wave of sympathy for the boy he'd once been crest. 'I'm sorry your stepmother is such a narrow-minded bitch.'

He huffed out a strained laugh, but his hand tightened on hers. 'Don't let her get to you. She lives to mess with people's heads—fighting with her only encourages her. Believe me, I know.'

She nodded, letting go of the last of her anger. She didn't want it between them. Not when she had one more hurdle to jump. She followed his gaze, saw the black car cresting the hill in the distance, and knew she didn't have long.

She tugged his hand, bringing his attention back to her. 'Could I ask you a favour, Connor?'

His brows lifted, but his eyes remained steady on hers. 'Sure. You can ask. Can't say I'd be able to oblige, though.'

That was fair enough, she thought. Cagey, but fair.

Letting go of his hand, she glanced down at his suitcase. 'Put your case down.'

'That's it?'

She nodded. 'That's part of it.'

He dropped the case, looking confused and wary... and tense.

Maybe he already suspected what she was going to ask. Was already preparing to refuse.

Too late to back out now, Bree. If he leaves you hanging, so be it.

Rising on tiptoes, she placed her hands on his cheeks, felt the rough stubble abrading her palms, the muscle twitching in his jaw. She pulled his head down slowly, until those sensual lips that had kissed every part of her, bar one, were so close she could study the wide dip in the top lip, the small scar on his chin, the tiny creases of the laughter lines at the side of his mouth. Even though he wasn't laughing now, his mouth a thin line of tension.

'Can I kiss you?'

He stiffened, drew in a sharp breath, but he didn't draw back. His gaze searched her face, and then the tension seemed to release in a rush, his warm breath fluttering over her face. And he gave the tiniest inclination of his head.

But it was enough.

Her tongue darted out and she licked the seam of

his closed mouth, rejoicing in his laboured breathing,
before she pressed her lips to his.

The kiss was unbearably tender, unbearably chaste
at first, his hands hanging limp by his sides as she
held his cheeks. Her heart thumped so hard against
her ribs she was sure he could feel it battering the
front of his shirt, where her breasts pressed against
his chest. But she continued to lick, to coax, to taste,
and waited. Waited.

And then, suddenly his breath sighed out, his mouth
opened and his hands rose to clasp her cheeks and
angle her head. She opened her mouth and his tongue
delved at last. Exploring, tasting, devouring, in long
frantic licks, like a man dying of thirst, who was glug-
ging down his first cold drink of water in a lifetime
of want.

She strained towards him, her tongue tangling with
his, dancing forward and then holding back, boldly
beckoning him forth. His hands strayed down to grip
her shoulders, to wrap around her back and then grasp
her buttocks as he clung to her, forcing the hard ridge
of his erection into her belly.

But while arousal blasted through her system,
where their mouths joined it felt like so much more.
The connection as intense, and painful and desperate
as anything she'd ever experienced. His kiss was devastating, delicious, and yet so needy and new.

Her heart blossomed, giddy with pleasure, and
somehow her dazed mind, giddy with love, knew this
was a first for him. He'd never kissed another woman
like this before.

She dimly registered the car's wheels crunch to a
stop beside them, and then the car door slammed. She

jolted in his arms, and he lifted his head at last. They both gasped for breath, their breathing ragged, as his forehead touched hers, and his hands caressed the soft skin of her spine in slow circles.

'Fuck, you're good at that,' he muttered against her lips, then nipped at her bottom lip.

His fingers threaded into her hair, framing her face, as he lifted his head to gaze down. Her skin felt raw, but not as raw as the emotion rising up her throat when his knuckles skimmed across her chin. 'I've marked your face. Beard burn. I should have shaved.'

Her lips tipped up, her heart swelling to bursting. 'Branded me again, huh?'

His lips quirked in a gorgeous smile, his eyes bright with humour and something even more exhilarating. 'I guess.'

'Excuse me, sir. Shall I put this in the boot for you?'

Connor's head turned at the quiet inquiry from the chauffeur, who was standing at a discreet distance. He gave his head a little shake, as if he'd forgotten where he was for a moment. 'Yeah, great, thanks.'

The man gave a polite nod and set about putting his luggage in the truck. A light breeze brushed over Sabrina, pebbling the skin on her arms and making her painfully aware that she was standing out in the driveway with no shoes on, no knickers and the thin satin of her maid of honour dress moulded by the breeze to her bullet-tipped nipples.

But when his attention returned to her and she opened her mouth to say that final goodbye, the joy at their embrace fading fast, he placed a palm on her cheek.

'I've got a favour to ask you now.'

She closed her mouth, folded her arms across her chest to contain the sudden surge of anticipation. 'Okay.'

She tried to swallow down the joy, the hope, the giddy rush of possibilities. They'd shared one hand grope in a restaurant, one cheeky sexting session, one endless night of hot, dirty, sweaty, mind-blowing sex, and a really spectacular, mind-altering kiss. But that was all they'd shared. And all they probably ever could share.

Because they lived on different continents, led conflicting lives. Because she still needed stability, security, safety—as well as hot, sweaty, dirty, mind-blowing sex—while he never even used the R word in jest. The prospects really didn't look that promising when you considered their situation with any degree of pragmatism or practicality.

But then he said: 'Come to New York with me. We've got a week before you have to go back to work. Let's see where we're going with this? Cos it doesn't feel like it's over to me.'

And then the weirdest thing happened: her mind stalled, completely, and her swelling, beating, frantically happy heart took over.

Fuck practicality and pragmatism. If there was one sure thing the past week had taught her, sometimes you just had to go with the flow.

She laughed, flung her arms round his neck, bounced up on her toes and kissed him hard.

He kissed her back, then held her waist, chuckling down at her. 'I'm gonna take that as a yes.'

She nodded, her heart too full to speak.

'Then put a damn fire under it.' He swatted her bottom, the sharp slap sending the now very familiar sizzles migrating all over her body, and whipped his iPhone out of his pocket. 'You've got ten minutes to pack while I book you a ticket.'

'Oh, shit. I'll never make it.'

But as she shot round, preparing to race back into the hotel and grab as much of her stuff as she could cram into her suitcase in ten minutes, his arm whipped out and he snagged her wrist.

'Just one more thing.' He dragged her back, tucked a knuckle under her chin and kissed her again. Clearly he was becoming a bit addicted to the sensation. She liked it, as well as the naughty glint in his eyes when he murmured into her ear, 'Don't bother to pack your panties. You won't need them.'

She stepped back, fluttering her eyelashes at him, and grinned through the blush lighting up her cheeks. 'Nothing doing, big boy.'

The naughty glint became a wicked twinkle. 'I really hope you're not planning to disobey me, Sabrina,' he said in that deep, husky voice, that he had to know by now made every pulse point in her body throb in unison.

'Well, now,' she said, taking careful steps backwards, out of his reach. 'That's for me to know and you to wet your pants wondering about, isn't it.'

'Goddamn it.' He made a dive for her and missed as she turned to run.

She was still laughing ten minutes and five seconds later as the limo sprayed pebbles across the lawn, speeding off to the airport—and Connor set about finding out the answer.

* * * * *